Shadows in the Sand

by Glynis Cooper

First published in the United Kingdom by Design House Northwest Ltd 2011.
Copyright © Glynis Cooper 2011.

The right of Glynis Cooper to be identified as the author of the work has been asserted
by her in accordance with the Copyright, Designs and Patents Act 1988.

All characters in the contemporary [20th/21st century] section of this novel are fictitious and any
resemblance to real persons, living or dead, is purely coincidental [see Author's Historical Note].
The novel is based on a true story. Those events described as happening in the 18th century and most
of the characters involved are real although all dialogue is entirely imaginary and some of their actions
are also entirely imaginary [see Author's Historical Note].

All rights reserved. British Library Cataloging-in-publication data.
A catalogue record of this book is available from the british Library
ISBN: 978-0-9566819-1-1

Book designed, printed and published by
Design House Northwest Ltd
designhousenw.co.uk

Dedications
Dedicated to my brother, Daryl Cooper, and my sister-in-law, Ermila,
for inviting me to stay in their beautiful Californian home with them while
I wrote this novel; to my husband, Mike, who facilitated the completion
of the book by removing the need for me to have a 'day job'; to Mac Mace
and to CISMAS for all their work on the Colossus and the raising of Oscar;
and to all those, both past and present, who have risked
their lives at sea to help others.

acknowledgements are due to:
Joan Slattery, Penny David and Mike Greenman for proof reading;
Liz Hather for the cover and book design;
Claire Reeve for assistance with fieldwork and research for the novel;
Mac Mace and Terry Hiron for information on diving and the Colossus;
C.A.U. and CISMAS for reports on the Colossus;
and to those too numerous to mention who offered their help,
support and encouragement.

Hamlet: Act 1, Scene 5,
'And therefore as a stranger give it welcome.
There are more things in heaven and earth, Horatio,
Than are dreamt of in your philosophy.'

Historical Notes

Most of the historical story is true and is based on real people and events.

The love affair between Admiral Lord Nelson and Emma, Lady Hamilton, is well documented in the numerous biographies of both individuals. Sir William Hamilton is generally less well known but he is an equally important figure on the stage of 18th century politics. His collections formed the basis of the Greek and Roman Antiquities Departments at the British Museum and he was one of the first true archaeologists. The unrest in Naples and the threat of invasion by the French is a matter of historical fact. Queen Maria Carolina and Emma Hamilton were close friends and confidantes for a number of years although Maria Carolina would later turn her back on Emma after the deaths of Sir William Hamilton and Lord Nelson.

Horatia was the only surviving daughter of Emma Hamilton and Lord Nelson. After Nelson's death the British Government completely ignored Nelson's 'bequest to the nation' of Emma and their daughter, Horatia. Emma eventually fled to Calais where she became an alcoholic and died in poverty aged only 49. After her death Horatia returned to England with members of her family. She married the Rev. Philip Ward when she was twenty one and had ten children by him.

In order to link the historical story to the present the author has taken one or two liberties with the historical record and a little poetic licence. There is no historical record and absolutely nothing to suggest that any bequest was ever made by Sir William Hamilton to Horatia Nelson. There is also no record and absolutely nothing to suggest that Horatia Nelson ever gave birth to an eleventh child. Both these events are purely imaginary.

There was a part time policeman in Scilly named Horatio Nelson who died in 1895. There is no historical record and absolutely nothing to suggest that he was in any way related to either Admiral Lord Nelson or Emma Hamilton. Contemporary records show this Horatio Nelson to have been a likeable and popular character in the Islands and this is how he is portrayed in the book. All the members of his family mentioned in the book are entirely imaginary and any likeness to any person, either living or dead, is entirely coincidental.

The Colossus was a fast and respected warship in the navy of George III. She sank after dragging her anchors off the Isles of Scilly during a winter storm in December 1798. Her captain, George Murray, was exonerated from any blame. There was no loss of life except for the quartermaster, Richard King, who fell to his death while taking soundings as the ship impaled herself on treacherous underwater rocks off the island of Samson. There is no historical record and absolutely nothing whatsoever to suggest that Richard King had any knowledge of the cargo that the ship was carrying nor that he had discovered a cache of seal stones and sent two of them to his wife.

Alice Pender, with whom Captain Murray was billeted on Bryher in the story, is an imaginary character, and any likeness to any person, either living or dead, is entirely coincidental.

All dialogue between the historical characters is of necessity, entirely imaginary, although it is based on factual events.

'Oscar' was brought to the surface in 2002 by Mac Mace and members of the CISMAS team, and he is currently [2011] on exhibition in the Valhalla on Tresco. It is strongly suspected that he has a 'twin' which still lies buried beneath the shifting sands of Southward Well off Samson.

The contemporary story is entirely fictitious, although real locations are used. Contemporary characters in the contemporary story are, without exception, completely imaginary, and any likeness to any person, either living or dead, is entirely coincidental.

Prologue

Southward Well, Samson, Isles of Scilly, 7th June 2002

The old face turned upwards and a pale watery sunlight played upon the clear chiseled eyes and the nose now flattened by age. Slowly the light became brighter and then in an instant of dazzling brilliance the face finally broke the surface of the water. It was a strong face atop a sturdy wooden body clad in the intricately carved folds of what appeared to be some sort of Classical costume. The left hand was clutching a laurel wreath, the symbol of victory. For the first time in over two hundred years it had finally emerged from the darkness of its burial in the shifting sands which lay beneath the waves.

Slowly the wooden figure, strapped carefully into the nylon and aluminium frame built specially to support its lifting from the seabed, was winched clear of the water and lowered gently onto the deck of the recovery boat. There it lay, tiny rivulets of water glistening in the sunshine as they ran back down the face and body. Turning, the boat began to gradually inch its way towards the quay on Tresco. Behind the boat shadows played almost imperceptibly across the water under a clear blue sky.

Samson, Isles of Scilly, 19th May 2008

Meg looked again at the little island as the boat rose and fell in the gentle swell. They were quite close to the shore in a stretch of water somewhat inexplicably named the Southward Well. The lines she had read in the old clergyman's battered journal came into her mind once again.

'As we came past Southward Well we saw the men standing up in the scaffs...' She'd had no idea what 'scaffs' meant but the friendly museum assistant had told her that it was an old word for kelp, a straggly slimy sort of seaweed once much collected from the island shores.

Meg pulled her scarf more tightly around her neck. Although the day was quite warm the sea was cold as it always was now in the Islands. She wore jeans and a denim jacket that were a uniform shade of blue and she had added a nautical touch by wearing a blue and white striped t-shirt. The wind tugged at her hair, which, bleached shades of chestnut by the sun, almost matched the colour of her eyes. As she peered over the side of the boat her face wore a slightly anxious expression. She could see a myriad of seaweeds curving sensuously with the currents of water as if in a parody of some exotic Eastern dance.

'As we came past Southward Well we saw the men standing up in the scaffs...' They would have to have been pretty tall men she reflected wryly since the water here was at least fifteen feet deep. Meg looked up at the south coast of Samson with its rocks tumbling down in scattered profusion to the sea. It would have been virtually impossible for anyone to have stood there and why should they have wanted to do so? What on earth would they have been trying to accomplish? She knew that collecting kelp had once been an industry on the island but the small population had gathered it from rocks off the flatter sandy shores to the north. There had been plenty of it and so no need for anyone to risk their lives trying to stand among slippery rocks and strong currents in water which would have come well over their heads. The writer of the book had been very definite in his description though.

'As we came past Southward Well we saw the men standing up in the scaffs...' But how could anyone have seen someone standing there?

'Seen enough?' John Fisher's deep voice cut across Meg's thoughts. She nodded and as he swung the boat skillfully around it rocked like a baby's cradle as the waves rolled beneath them.

'I've got to pick up some people from the quay and take them up to Bryher' he said as the boat nosed its way back towards St Marys.

'If you want to stay on board I can drop you off on the other side of Samson on the way. It's calm enough for that I think.'

'Please. Would you?' Meg's face lit up. She had been told that her smile was one of her best features and transformed her otherwise unremarkable freckled face. John caught her enthusiasm and grinned.

'I'll pick you up about three when I collect my group from Bryher.'

This was an unexpected bonus. She'd assumed that John would simply drop her back at St Marys after he'd taken her to see the Southward Well. It wasn't easy to land on Samson. There was no longer a quay and everything depended upon the tides and the weather. Sometimes it could be days before conditions were right. Meg desperately wanted to visit the island as soon as possible. She'd been before with Steven but that had been in another time. The memory of Steven still pained her. She had thought that marriage was forever but Steven didn't believe in keeping anything he considered past its sell-by date and that included his wife. Well, thought Meg grimly, that had put an end to any return trips to Samson for him. Janine, his new, younger, prettier wife, never wore heels of less than three inches in height. That would make landing on Samson about as easy as landing on the moon. She almost managed a grin at the thought. Plain boring sensible old Meg she might be but at least she wouldn't end up on a deserted island with both ankles broken.

John eased the boat alongside the quay where a small party was perched expectantly, although somewhat perilously, on a steep flight of slippery stone steps cut into the side of the quay. Robin, the deckhand, tied up the boat and offered his arm to steady those clambering aboard. Meg snuggled back into the wooden bench feeling the sun warm on her back. It was a flawless day with clear skies and a wispy breeze. Perfect for visiting Samson. The boat had rounded the end of the quay once more and she could see the twin hills of Samson floating lazily and serenely on the glittering water. So deceptive, she thought, remembering the last time she had been there, the sinister aspect that the island had taken on and the raw fear which had gripped her. The whispering echoes of something which should have been long dead. Despite the heat Meg shivered.

John grounded the boat gently on the wide sandy beach at the northeastern corner of the island. He swung a pair of metal steps over the side and Meg climbed carefully down onto the sand. The folk going to Bryher watched this little diversion with great interest. It was a bit different to the way things were done back home. 'Pick you up at three!' he yelled, then added, with a wicked glint of mischief in his eyes, 'this time next week!'

It was a well known Scillonian jest, and Meg had heard it before, but the group on the boat sat looking uncertainly at each other, unsure as to whether he'd been joking or not.

As the boat slid gracefully back into the water she trudged through the fine white sand sinking in up to her ankles. It was tiring and she was glad when she reached the top of the beach where much of the sand was anchored by the wiry marram grasses which grew there. She sank down gratefully for a moment and took a bottle of water from her rucksack. Unseen insects hummed close by and a couple of gulls wheeled and screeched above her. The sun beat down and Meg fished out her shabby old hat. She'd once learned the hard way about the strength of the Scillonian sunshine. Today Samson had an aura of peace about it. Meg was relieved. She was completely alone on the island and she didn't want her courage failing her. She had about four hours, so, hoisting her rucksack, she began the slow climb up the North Hill.

She could see the row of ancient burial mounds humped along the ridge of the hill like giant mole hills. Somewhere she'd read that they dated back to at least two thousand years before the birth of Christ. If that was the case they were remarkably well preserved and she vaguely wondered why no-one had ever tried to use the land for any other purpose. As she reached the top of the North Hill, Meg made her way along the ridge to one of the better preserved tombs and flopped down onto the grass. Time for a pit stop she decided, pulling her bottle of water out of her rucksack once more. The small stone lined tomb was about three feet six inches long and just over two feet high. A capstone, which would once have covered it, like the lid of a box, lay across the top and was pushed back at right angles so that it was possible to see inside. On the earthen floor grew a mass of tiny purple violets.

Meg looked down to the narrow channel which separated Samson from Bryher. She could see myriads of sunbeams dancing and chasing each other across the glistening water and below her she could just hear the chugging of an engine. A small boat passed the foot of the North Hill heading towards what the locals termed as 'the back of Samson'. That was the side of Samson which was hidden from the view of the other islands and she guessed this was why it had got its name. Idly she wondered what the boat was doing. It was probably a local fisherman going out to check his lobster pots. As she sat there watching, the North Hill wrapped her in a blanket of peace and tranquility. Feelings of happiness and contentment and a sense of being at one with the world swept over her like a magic spell. It was magic. Samson was magical. All the Scillies were magical. The islands had an indefinable quality that captured hearts and minds quite unlike anywhere else she had ever known. As a child Meg had spent holidays in the Isle of Man and, though similar in some ways to the Scillies, it was, to mis-quote some half forgotten satirist, something completely different. Since then she'd been to many other of the British islands: the Shetlands, the Hebrides, Skye, Mull, Lindisfarne, Lundy, and several others. None of them measured up to the Scillies. She struggled to put it into words for herself. She knew that the Scilly Isles [or island as it had once been] were regarded as special and sacred far back into pre-history. Even after the sea had split the island more than a hundred different ways in the wake of the departing Romans, Scilly was still regarded as sacred; like the Celtic 'otherworld', the 'islands far across and sometimes under the Western Ocean.' Perhaps the lost Avalon to which Morgan le Fay and her sisters had brought the dead King Arthur in his funeral boat.

The sudden harsh cawing of a black-back gull snapped Meg out of her reverie. The bird rose and wheeled about, shrieking in protest. Something had disturbed it. She looked around but could see nothing. She knew that the gulls had nesting grounds among the crags on the north side of Samson but she'd taken care to stay well above them. Black-backs could be aggressive when they were protecting their young. The bird's protests continued for a couple of minutes before slowly subsiding. Meg stood up, brushing bits of dead bracken off her jeans. Samson still lay quietly under the warm morning sun but something had disturbed the peace and the sense of tranquility and contentment was gone.

She walked quickly along the ridge of the North Hill, past the crouched tombs of the long dead kings and queens, who were still awaiting their rebirth from their small burial mounds, and picked her way through the bramble bushes down to the central 'waist' of the island. The general shape of Samson was rather like the hour-glass figure so much admired by the Victorians. There were no fields or little ruined farmsteads at all on the North Hill and there never had been. Meg considered this to be quite amazing given that the whole island was scarcely a mile long and never more than half a mile wide. She'd imagined that such land as there was would have been at a premium. The archaeological record showed clearly, however, that there had only ever been settlement of the South Hill and on the 'waist'. The North Hill had remained untouched.

Scrambling across the rough pebbles which littered the 'waist' she marvelled at the vision of 'lush green meadows' which had been described as being here by an enthusiastic 18th century clergyman who had taken it upon himself to visit the more far flung members of his flock. The only covering now was clumps of the ubiquitous marram grass, a few weeds and the flotsam and jetsam washed up by the sea. It was a relief to reach the foot of the South Hill where a small overgrown path led upwards from the 'waist'. The path wound its way around the lower contours of the hill. Tucked into a small niche in the hillside was the old island well. It had been dry for over a hundred and fifty years and was, Meg knew, a major reason for the depopulation of the island in 1855 by the autocratic landowner of Scilly, the self-styled Lord Protector, Augustus Smith. The islanders of Samson had feared and resented him and one of their number had put a curse on him the day he came to tell them that they must leave their island home. Smith had collapsed immediately, so the story went, and had been unable to walk until one of his boatmen had persuaded the woman to lift her curse. A few years ago the well had suddenly filled with water and the reasons for this became the subject of much local debate. Explanations ranged from the final lifting of the curse of Samson to the timely intervention of a film crew who wanted the well full for the purposes of their storyline. Lost in her thoughts, Meg didn't see the small sharp rock protruding from the gorse roots alongside the path until she stumbled heavily. Instinctively putting her hands out to save herself from falling she connected sharply with the low stone rim of the well. The well was empty again.

Pulling herself up in some surprise, she tentatively dipped her fingers into the well. It was a shallow well and the bottom was damp earth. That meant that it hadn't been empty for long. Meg pulled her camera out of her rucksack and took a couple of photographs. She wondered how long the well had been empty and if they knew about it on St Marys. A few years back she had seen a film about the desertion of Samson. It had begun with reminiscences of an old man on the eve of the Great War. He was telling the story of his leaving Samson as a young boy with his mother. Meg could still hear the resonance of his rich deep voice even now as his words came back to her.

'Mother always swore that she would never leave Samson, but then came the hunger and the disease and the well ran dry. It was the curse.'

The curse had never been properly explained in the film but she knew the story well enough. Now, however, was not the time to be dwelling on it. This would only spook her and she didn't need that right now.

A little further up the path was a tumble-down cottage. Last time she was here it had been overgrown with gorse and brambles but someone had cleared the area around the cottage and also a few other cottages which stood close by. These were the remains of the tiny community which had once existed on Samson. She checked her map. The tumble-down cottage was the so-called Armorel's cottage. Over a century ago the writer, Sir Walter Besant, had immortalised it in his novel 'Armorel of Lyonesse'. But Lyonesse was far too grand a name for Samson and Armorel had led the kind of life that the inhabitants of Samson could only ever have dreamed about. She dressed for dinner and drank tea out of dainty china cups and she had shelves full of exotic treasures from distant lands. Besant had obviously never set foot on Samson or seen the reality of grinding poverty and the unrelenting diet of limpets and potatoes on which the inhabitants of the island's small cottages had had to survive. Instead he had preferred to run with his own imaginative version of Lyonesse, the fabled lost land lying beneath the sea somewhere off the Cornish mainland between Land's End and the Scillies. Victorian ladies had picnicked at Armorel's cottage and one of the Gibson family of photographers from St Marys had recorded their picnics for posterity. The cottage had been better kept in those days and Meg thought it a shame that it had been allowed to decay into a tomb of gorse and bramble which had slowly crushed and strangled the stonework like a giant snake.

There was a sudden commotion from the North Hill. Meg turned round quickly. Several Black-backs were wheeling about, screeching in alarm, both frightened and aggressive at the same time. Someone, or something, had made an unwanted intrusion into their world. She couldn't see the cause but it made her uneasy and she quickened her steps.

At the top of the South Hill stood another ruined cottage but, although roofless, it was in a better state and more accessible than Armorel's cottage. The doorway was low and she had to stoop to enter the cottage. There were neat square windows on either side of the door and another in the back wall of the cottage. The fireplace and the huge slab of stone which had formed the mantel shelf were still intact. To one side of the fireplace was a roughly carved niche where the salt box would have been kept. Salt had been a valuable commodity for both cooking and preserving and it had been important that it should not become damp. From the doorway she could see St Marys and Agnes across the water where the South Hill sloped down towards the Southward Well and to the west she could see the top of White Island which lay off the back of Samson. In the distance the thin needle of the Bishop Rock lighthouse rose perpendicular from the sea. From the back window she could see the North Hill which seemed to be peaceful once more. She took another couple of photographs and then settled down on an old stone seat near the fireplace. Taking a notebook out of her rucksack she made a few careful notes and checked her map again. This had indeed been the cottage belonging to Ann Webber, the woman who had cursed the Lord Protector, and who was the last person to leave Samson, rowing away from the island with her small son sitting in the stern of the boat. The sun was high in the sky now and Meg decided that she would eat her sandwiches in the shelter of the cottage and then she would walk as far down the South Hill on its southern flank as she could. That should give her enough time for a fairly leisurely stroll back along the coast to the northern end of East Porth beach where she would wait for John to pick her up.

She was licking bits of tuna mayonnaise off her fingers when she heard the sound. It was faint at first but as she stood up it seemed to become a roaring noise that encompassed her entire world. Rushing to the door she looked wildly about her. A small helicopter was flying low over the South Hill. Meg ran back into the cottage, and, grabbing her rucksack, instinctively hunched herself against the back wall of the cottage in a corner where there were the remains of an old box bed. She was fairly certain that she couldn't be seen here. The helicopter appeared to circle the South Hill a couple of times before turning away in the direction of St Marys. She waited a good few minutes before peering out of the cottage. Everything was quiet once again and she couldn't see anyone, yet she had the strong sensation that she was no longer alone.

Meg stood in the cottage for a few moments wondering what she should do. She took out her mobile phone but there was no signal, a frequent occurrence in the Scillies. She would just have to decide for herself what was best to do. There didn't seem any point in staying where she was. If there was someone else around she would be a sitting target. Samson wasn't that large an island. Anyone searching would find her soon enough through a matter of elimination. She had the temporary advantage that whoever it was didn't know where she was right at that moment. She peered cautiously through the open doorway. There was no one about and if she was quick she could drop rapidly out of sight walking down the south side of Samson where she would only be visible to someone out on the sea. Meg chided herself that she was probably just being fanciful and over-dramatising things but that didn't explain the strange letters and the anonymous phone calls she'd been receiving or the constant feeling that she seemed to have of being watched. Steven would have scoffed at her fears. She could hear him now.

'Watched? What do you mean you think you're being watched? Can you see anyone out there? You're becoming paranoid! Get a grip!'

His logic could be infuriatingly simple. He didn't believe in vibes or instincts. Meg did. After all, she told herself, people do sense danger. It's kind of a survival thing. Cavemen knew when wolves or tigers were stalking them in the same way that wildebeest and antelope knew when the local lions were out looking for lunch. Usually they never saw them, but they knew that they were there and it was this knowledge that gave them a head start and a chance at life.

Anyway Steven wasn't with her now and she was going to rely on her instincts. They didn't usually let her down. She slung her camera around her and hoisted her rucksack onto her back once more. Slipping out of the cottage she walked rapidly down the path that led from the front door towards the southern cliffs of Samson. In a few moments she was lost to view from the rest of the island. The path was steep and rocky but not too difficult to follow. It led over a small outcrop and around the southern tip of the island always keeping well above sea-level. The area marked on the map as Southward Well lay off-shore. Meg paused and took several photographs. She could see the path descending as it made its way north along the eastern coast of the island towards East Porth beach. It was the route she would follow back to her pick-up point by John's boat. The shoreline was rocky and treacherous here and there was no access. The best way around the foot of the island at this point was in fact by boat. Finally she turned northwards and began the trek back to the other end of the island. She had seen and heard nothing further but she remained alert and watchful, still with the sensation of not being alone. The South Hill was not as steep on this side. She could see the ruins of a few more cottages and the map showed that there had been another well somewhere near the cottages but it was lost to view under the bracken and gorse which still covered much of the island. A stone enclosure encircled the tiny village nestling against the side of the South Hill. It had not been built by the villagers but by the Lord Protector. After he had depopulated the island he had conceived the notion of a deer farm on Samson and ordered the wall to be built. The deer were taken across by boat from Tresco to graze there. The hapless animals, however, had not liked the island. Perhaps it was because there were no trees on Samson or perhaps the deer were simply following some deeper instinct of their own. They had scrambled over the wall and tried to swim back to Tresco. Every single one of them had drowned. The Lord Protector had lost heart after that and Samson had been left to itself with only a few black rabbits for company.

Meg reached the East Porth beach and debated whether to retrace her steps over the North Hill or whether to walk along the beach. The afternoon had become hot and sultry and she decided in favour of the beach. Sitting down on the sand she took off her walking boots and tied them to her rucksack by their laces. Tiny waves were breaking in desultory fashion and the wet sand was soothing under her feet as trickles of water squeezed between her toes. It was blissful wandering along the shoreline in a reflective mood and for a while she forgot her fears. When she arrived at the pick-up point she sat down on the warm sand to wait for John.

She remembered sitting here with Steven, talking and planning for their future. Their love had been new then and they were full of ideas for things to do and places to see. Most of it had just been wishful thinking though. Meg thought how it was that she always seemed to come second to Steven's job, but he had dismissed her notion scornfully.

'You don't realise that I do it all for us,' he had said. 'You're just paranoid.'

Paranoid. That word appeared to have been a favourite with Steven. According to him Meg was always getting paranoid about something and when she wasn't being paranoid she was simply demonstrating her insecurities and her lack of faith.

'Of course with the childhood you had I suppose it's not surprising,' he would say with the martyred air of one who has been given a great burden to bear, 'but I know what I'm doing and I do wish you would learn to control your feelings and just trust me to do what is necessary.'

She had trusted him and he had repaid that trust by abandoning her for Janine.

Just then a movement caught the corner of Meg's eye. She looked up at the North Hill thinking it was a gull returning to its nesting place. The figure was standing on the top of the North Hill watching her. At that distance it was hard to tell whether it was male or female but from its stance it appeared to be a man. As she stood there the figure seemed to move towards her. Her first thought was to get away but there was nowhere to go. Instinctively she stepped backwards. She had never felt so alone in her life. Even if she called out for help there was no one to hear her. The figure began to advance slowly down the hill towards her. Paranoia or not, Meg was scared. The back of her neck prickled with fear and her knees felt weak. Droplets of sweat ran down her spine and her arms. She stood there, heart pounding, wondering whether fight or flight was best. Not that she had much choice, she thought, but at that moment she heard a sound and, looking up, she saw John's boat rounding Samson Hill on Bryher and heading straight for her. Her relief was overwhelming. The figure on the North Hill hesitated and stopped as John grounded his boat on the beach and dropped the ladder over the side for her. Meg snatched up her rucksack and scrambled on board with indecent haste, dropping thankfully onto one of the wooden bench seats. John looked at her closely as the boat slid back into the water again. She looked pale and upset.

John Fisher had taken a liking to Meg. He'd seen her before several times but she'd been with her patronising fool of a husband. Ex-husband now he understood. Steven Hamilton had come back last year flashing a new woman on his arm. Daft thing she'd been with skirts so tight she could hardly move and tottering around on heels that high it was a wonder she'd been able to walk at all. John had refused to take her on his boat much to Steven's intense annoyance. Not suitably dressed he'd told Steven. Steven had started on in his usual way but John was having none of it. He might bully Meg but he certainly wasn't going to bully John. Health and Safety regulations were Health and Safety regulations he'd told Steven and that was the end of it. John hadn't seen Steven much since that day but it was no big loss.

Now Meg was here sitting on his boat with huge frightened eyes. He wondered what had happened to upset her so much.

'You OK?' he said gruffly.

She tried hard to pull herself together.

'Yes. Bit hot.' She hesitated. 'It's just that I...' She turned to look back at the North Hill but the figure had gone. John followed her gaze and then turned back to face her. Meg was wearing a puzzled frown.

'You see something up there?' he asked.

'No,' she said, 'but I thought I saw someone standing on top of the North Hill just before you picked me up.'

'Well there wasn't anybody else landed on Samson today by the boats. You were on your own as far as I knew. Of course someone could have landed from their own boat but I haven't seen anyone this side of the island.'

Meg remembered the little fishing boat. At least she'd thought it was a fishing boat. Maybe the fisherman had landed and decided to stretch his legs for a bit but such an explanation sounded feeble and far-fetched even to her own ears. John was looking at her, an expression of guarded concern on his weather-beaten features.

As if reading her thoughts he said slowly 'Sometimes these days you can't tell who's about. Perhaps if you go to Samson again you're best to take a friend with you. It can be a lonely place.'

Meg looked up at him. It was as near as he would come to giving her a warning. Behind the boat shadows swirled briefly through the sand.

Naples, Italy, 22nd September 1798

Emma, Lady Hamilton, was a beauty and she knew it. Enough people had told her so. She had blue eyes and long chestnut brown hair and she also had an instinctive sense of style. Artists vied with each other to paint her. Although of humble birth Emma had charmed her way into society and she was known throughout Europe for both her looks and her graceful 'Attitudes', the poses in full period costume which she adopted to portray both real and mythological characters from history. These performances could also include acting, singing and dancing. She'd learned a lot from her early days as maid to a series of well known actresses and singers at Covent Garden.

One of them she remembered with particular affection. Ann Brown had been a pretty and vivacious young London girl with a sweet melodic voice and a decided talent for acting. They'd been about the same age but Ann had already made a name for herself. Together they'd chatted and giggled and shared girlish confidences. Ann had taught her a lot, especially about timing and holding herself properly, and she had also been responsible for introducing Emma to Sir Harry Featherstonehaugh. Sir Harry had been bewitched by Emma's beauty and had whisked her off to his country seat on the South Downs to act as his hostess. Through him she had met Charles Greville, the nephew of Sir William Hamilton, and it was Charles who introduced her to Sir William. Emma had lost touch with Ann after that but she read the newspapers. Ann had married and taken her new husband's name of Cargill. The marriage had not been happy, however, and Ann had finally eloped to India with a dashing sea captain. So romantic, Emma had thought, but Ann's story had not had a happy ending. She had drowned in a shipwreck off the Isles of Scilly at the age of only twenty four.

Emma was now no stranger in aristocratic circles or to distinguished people. Her husband, Sir William Hamilton, was the British Ambassador to Naples, while her close friend and confidante was Queen Maria Carolina of Naples whose sister, Marie Antoinette, had fallen victim to the guillotine of the French Revolution some five years before. Today the home of Emma and Sir William had been made ready for a grand reception to be followed by dinner and some sparkling entertainment. No expense had been spared for the visitor whom Emma and her husband were to receive was no ordinary person. The French had been in aggressive mode since that upstart Bonaparte had begun making a dangerous nuisance of himself and Sir William had declared it a very great honour to be welcoming the man who had finally routed the French at the Battle of the Nile, Horatio Nelson himself. Emma had met Nelson once some five years before and she was in awe of his reputation as a living legend in his own lifetime. She wondered what he would be like now for she knew that the fighting had taken its toll on him and that he had lost an arm. She was both elated and nervous. Nelson's name was on everyone's lips but it was her house to which he had chosen to come.

Emma stood beside Sir William in eager anticipation, her heart beating fast, watching Nelson walking slowly towards them, his right sleeve pinned carefully across his naval uniform. He had lost his right arm during the Battle of Santa Cruz the year before. Nelson was small in stature but his sheer presence more than made up for what he lacked in height. He had finally also lost the sight of his right eye. It had been damaged by flying sand and gravel from a sandbag which had exploded after being hit by shot. Sometimes he wore a patch to cover his bad eye. Today he was suffering from battle fatigue and a weakness brought on by the recurring bouts of malaria he endured. This made his steps less firm than they might have been and Emma's heart went out to him. He looked completely drained. Yet this was the man who had saved them all from the French. Emma remembered what the French had done to pretty little Marie Antoinette and shuddered at the memory. The whole country was talking about the horrors of the French Revolution. As Nelson reached Sir William and Emma, he bowed low to Emma in greeting. Emma was completely overcome. Here before her stood this diminutive man, who was Europe's saviour, bowing to her as a mark of respect and admiration when she should be the one honouring him. Overwhelmed by it all, Emma ran to him and impulsively flung her arms around him in genuine admiration and welcome.

'Oh God!' she cried, looking up into his tired strained face and giving him her most dazzling smile. 'Is it possible?' Then she fainted, falling in a graceful heap at his feet as she did so.

St Marys, Isles of Scilly, 20th May 2008

Rain pelted against the window panes of the small library and Meg snuggled further into her thick knit fisherman's jersey. Not that it was really cold but the rain always made her think it was. Unbidden, Steven's voice came into her mind.

'Cold! Of course it's not cold! You think it's cold just because of a bit of rain. Rain doesn't have to be cold. You're just paranoid about it.'

She'd tried pointing out to him that the advent of rain always lowered the temperature but Steven, as usual, hadn't been listening. To him his own logic was impeccable and therefore any notion which went against it was flawed by definition. He always had to be right and Meg had learned eventually the total futility of trying to have any sort of a discussion with him. He simply dismissed whatever she said as either paranoia or idiocy.

Annoyed with herself she turned back to her reading. She didn't want to think about Steven at all. He was history as he'd made clear to her on numerous occasions. It was just that Scilly brought back memories and it didn't help either that she was staying where she'd once stayed with Steven. Not from choice, although the place was decent enough, but because she'd left it late to book and she couldn't find anywhere else to take her for a month at such short notice.

Meg had arrived late the previous Saturday and had spent much of Sunday stretched out in brilliant sunshine on Peninnis Head overlooking Porthcressa planning how she would spend her time. Afterwards she'd walked down past the pretty little twelfth century parish church of St Marys into Old Town and had eaten a late lunch at the Tolman café overlooking the sparkling waters of Old Town Bay before strolling back to Hugh Town. Early on Monday morning she'd gone to the quay to try and find someone who would take her out to see Samson. She'd been in luck. John Fisher had done an early morning run to take visitors who had arrived on the first helicopter over to Agnes and she'd found him drinking coffee from a thermos and reading his newspaper on his boat, waiting until it was time to do his eleven o'clock Bryher run. She'd always liked John, although Steven had never had much time for him, but she was free to make her own decisions now and she was glad it was John whom she'd asked.

The glorious weather, which had held for the first three days of her holiday, had broken this morning and the rain had set in for the day. Meg had needed to do some reading on local history and she was spending a very comfortable and cosy morning in the small library at the back of Porthcressa Beach. However her brain was beginning to develop an obsession with finding some coffee and she decided that a short break might be in order. Dibble and Grub, an unusually named bright and cheerful little café with views out over Porthcressa Bay, was close by and she could take a book with her. Meg gathered her belongings and made for the door, opening her umbrella just as she reached the small porch so that she wouldn't get a soaking. There was a thump and a muttered curse as someone cannoned into her, knocking her sideways. Meg lowered her umbrella to find a man standing in front of her rubbing his right eye.

'Hey! You want to watch where you put that thing!' he said nodding at the umbrella.

Meg stuttered apologies but he didn't seem to be very annoyed.

'It's OK' he said gamely. 'I haven't lost my sight or anything so drastic. You just caught my eyebrow actually. I think I'll live!'

Meg grinned in spite of herself. He had a nice face with floppy brown hair falling across his forehead. He smiled back and the smile seemed to reach right up to his eyes.

'I was just going out for a coffee to clear my head' she said by way of explanation 'and I didn't want to get soaked before I'd got out of the door,'

'Coffee,' he said, still smiling, 'is the best suggestion I've heard all morning. Would you mind if I joined you?' he asked.

Meg found herself returning his smile. 'Not at all,' she said without giving herself time to think. I'm going to Dibble and Grub' she said. 'Do you know it?'

'Know it? I love the place!' he said. 'By the way,' he added, 'I don't drink with strangers so I'd better introduce myself. I'm Kevin Brownlow.'

'Pleased to meet you,' said Meg with mock formality. 'Meg Nelson.' She had reverted to her maiden name since the divorce, partly out of pride and partly because she didn't need the constant reminder that someone else, not herself, was now entitled to be called Mrs Hamilton.

They almost ran the hundred yards to the little cafe on the seafront. The few tables and chairs set outside looked forlorn in the rain but inside it was bright and welcoming although the windows were a little misted up. Meg found a table by the window while Kevin ordered their coffee. They settled themselves and the coffee seemed to arrive almost at once. It was served in gaily painted thick earthenware mugs. Meg cupped her hands around her mug and took an appreciative sip. 'This is so good,' she murmured. 'I really need lots of strong coffee when I'm reading stuff and I want to concentrate.'

'What were you reading that needed so much concentration?' asked Kevin. 'I thought you'd just been in the library to choose your weekly novel or something.'

Meg hesitated. 'Oh no,' she said. 'I don't live here. I was reading up on some of the local history and folklore.'

'On holiday like me then,' said Kevin. 'How long are you here for?'

'Four weeks,' said Meg 'or at least four weeks less three days now.'

If you could call what she had come to do a holiday she thought wryly.

'That's a coincidence,' said Kevin. 'So am I.'

Meg was taken aback. It didn't appear to be a corny chat-up line. He seemed too genuine for that. Nevertheless she was still wary of people she didn't really know properly. She heard Steven's voice yet again. 'Oh come on! Loosen up! Who's going to hurt you? You're just being paranoid.' Blast Steven and his constant put-downs with his insistence on her paranoia. She was beginning to think that he was the one who'd been obsessed with paranoia. It was time for new beginnings and here she was having coffee with a man who seemed very pleasant and genuine. If she couldn't respond to him in a naturally friendly manner she really would begin to think that Steven had been right after all and she was truly paranoid.

'Are you here with your family?' Meg thought this seemed a nice safe question. To her surprise a look of pain crossed Kevin's face.

'No.' he said. 'I'm on my own. I don't have a family now.'

'I'm sorry. I didn't mean to upset you.' Meg was flustered again.

Kevin managed a rueful smile.

It's alright' he said. 'It's me. You're not to know. My divorce came through last month and I just had to get away for a bit. It still hurts.' His voice shook a little.

'I know the feeling,' said Meg, surprising herself. 'My divorce came through just over a year ago. He married someone else the week after it was finalised.'

Now it was Kevin's turn to look shocked.

'Oh God!' he said. 'I'd have gone mad if Heather had done that. I mean I think she has someone else but she's being very discreet about it.'

They stared at each other for a few moments. Intimate strangers. Only half an hour ago they had not even known of each other's existence and now they were united by a shared sense of pain and betrayal. Meg drained her coffee mug.

'I ought to get back' she said. 'The library closes at two today and I'd really like to finish what I'm doing.'

Kevin stood up.

'Of course,' he said, 'and the coffee is on me.' He held up a hand to silence her protest. 'Look,' he went on, 'I have some things I need to do in town. What do you say that we meet back here for lunch later?'

Meg smiled. 'That would be lovely,' she said without hesitation. It would be good to take her mind off her problems. Steven, after all, was not the only cloud on her horizon.

Kevin stood watching Meg run back across the street towards the library. She seemed really nice. He had thought he'd caught a glimpse of her on John's boat yesterday going out towards Samson and he'd wondered why she'd wanted to go out to that island. It was a strange place by all accounts. He paid for the coffee and turned up his coat collar before heading into Hugh Town. Town was perhaps too grand a name for a place with a population of scarcely a thousand but perspectives were different out here. The islands were tiny by comparison to the mainland. St Mary's was the largest island and that was only around three miles long and about a mile wide. Kevin smiled to himself. He loved the Scillies and he always had. No matter how small they were they had everything he'd ever wanted or needed. He'd thought Heather had felt the same way but now he would never really know for sure.

Meg arrived about five minutes early for their lunch date only to find Kevin already seated. He smiled in welcome.

'Hi! Did you manage to finish what you were reading?'

Meg nodded as she took off her jacket and shook the raindrops from it before draping it gingerly over the back of her chair.

'Yes. The librarian was very kind and let me photocopy some of it so I didn't have to keep stopping and taking notes. That helped a lot.'

Kevin handed her the menu. Dibble and Grub had taken their inspiration for the food they offered from the Mediterranean but the day didn't seem quite right for a Greek salad or the pasta with lashings of Italian sundried tomato sauce. In the end they both settled on the homemade minestrone soup with hot ciabatta.

'Rain always seems to bring out a need in people for hot soup,' said Kevin. 'Like a nice warm comforter I guess if you haven't got a handy teddy bear around.'

Meg grinned at him in spite of herself. At least Kevin didn't appear to think it was paranoid to feel cold in bad weather.

'What were you reading about?' he asked casually as steaming bowls of soup were placed in front of them.

'Shipwrecks around the Scillies' Meg replied.

'Any particular one?' Kevin broke off a large piece of his ciabatta and dunked it in his soup.

Meg suppressed a smile. If she wasn't careful she'd hear Steven's lecture about table manners go round in her head again. Steven had once told her that he always took new girlfriends to a restaurant on their first date. He wanted to make sure that they knew their manners and their table etiquette, and he abhorred the practice of dunking bread in soup. The man really had been a perfect prig at times. She turned her attention back to Kevin.

'Yes, actually. H.M.S. Colossus. It sank off Samson in 1798.'

Kevin looked at her in surprise. 'What an amazing coincidence. I'm writing an article about the Colossus.'

Now it was Meg's turn to look surprised.

''There's been quite a lot about the Colossus in the newspapers and historical journals during the last few years,' he went on. 'You probably know that a lot of Greek and Etruscan antiquities went down with her. Many of them have been recovered recently and the British Museum wants to stage an exhibition featuring these finds. I'm a freelance journalist and I was offered a commission to write up an article on Colossus for the Sunday supplements. So I used it as an excuse to escape down here.'

He smiled ruefully at her as he wiped his soup bowl clean with the remains of his ciabatta. That would have sent Steven into horrified and disbelieving shock Meg thought wryly. Kevin sat back in his chair and dabbed at his mouth with his serviette. Well at least Steven would have approved of that.

'So what about you?' he asked.

'Long story,' said Meg. 'Part curiosity, part family history, part...' she stopped, unsure if she wanted to tell him the whole story just yet.

'Family history?' said Kevin. 'Did one of your ancestors serve on board Colossus?' As she was about to reply a flash of enlightenment swept over his face.

'Of course! You're Meg Nelson!'

Meg stared at him in nervous bewilderment. He couldn't possibly know the story of her family.

'Nelson,' said Kevin, seeing the expression on her face. 'Colossus was commissioned by Admiral Lord Nelson to bring back the collection of antiquities belonging to his dear friend, Sir William Hamilton, whose lovely wife, Emma, just happened to be Lord Nelson's mistress.'

Meg hadn't expected that but at least he didn't seem to know about her personal reasons for wanting to find out all she could about the Colossus.

'You must have heard of Emma, Lady Hamilton?' Kevin said, mistaking her silence for possible ignorance.

'Of course I have!' said Meg quickly, trying to collect her scattered wits. 'Sir William Hamilton as well. In fact....' she broke off for a moment, then exclaimed 'Good Heavens! Talking of coincidences... I am not only a Nelson but I was married to a Hamilton!'

Kevin burst out laughing.

'You know someone once told me that there was no such thing as coincidence, only fate. That is amazing.'

'There's more,' said Meg, warming now to her subject. 'You are not going to believe this but my great grandfather was called Horatio Nelson.'

'You're too young for him to have been the Horatio Nelson,' said Kevin gallantly, 'but after all his victories Nelson was a great hero to the British people. Quite a few named their sons in his honour.'

'Yes, I know. But there's one more thing.' Meg was suddenly serious. 'This Horatio Nelson lived in Scilly. Right here on St Marys.'

She didn't elaborate but Kevin was puzzled by the significance she seemed to attach to her statement. He sensed, however, that now was not the time to probe further. She would tell him when she was ready.

Below them shadows briefly intertwined as they glided silently across the sands.

Naples, Italy, 29th September 1798

Emma was in a whirl of excitement. Today was Nelson's fortieth birthday. She and Sir William were throwing a party for him. It was to be a grand affair with almost two thousand guests of whom at least eight hundred would sit down to dinner first. Afterwards there would be dancing and champagne and fireworks. Emma had no idea how much all this was going to cost and, as usual, she didn't care. All she cared about was the look on Nelson's face when she had told him what was planned for him. It was a mixture of excitement, pride and affection. Since the night he had arrived, when she had fainted at his feet, she had known that he was attracted to her and she basked in his attention.

Nelson had been unwell when he had first arrived. He was suffering from a combination of battle fatigue, lack of proper sleep and another one of his recurring bouts of malaria. Emma, still overwhelmed by the adulation that Nelson commanded, and immensely flattered that he seemed to be interested in her, had tucked him up in the softest of beds and nursed him tenderly. She even managed to procure asses milk for him with which he could wash himself. Queen Cleopatra of Ancient Egypt was one of Emma's heroines and Emma knew that Cleopatra had bathed regularly in asses milk to preserve her youth and her beauty and her health. She reckoned that if had worked for Cleopatra then it would be good enough for Nelson, and he was certainly looking much better. She took his meals up to him herself, uncaring of the gossip which this caused in the servants quarters, and they would sit for hours just talking. Before long they were exchanging the most intimate of confidences. Sir William was often out and about on his diplomatic duties and scarcely noticed. Emma always took care to dine with him if he was at home but just now this was an infrequent occurrence.

Tonight Nelson was wearing his full naval uniform which Emma had ordered to be cleaned and pressed for him. Despite his prematurely white hair and the loss of his arm, and the black eye patch he wore over one eye, he looked very handsome and distinguished. Emma felt a surge of pride as he offered her his good arm and led her out onto the dance floor. She had taken a great deal of care with her appearance for this evening. She was wearing her best white muslin dress through which silver threads ran and criss-crossed, reflecting the candlelight which glowed from the huge chandeliers. Her long chestnut hair was bound with white and silver ribbons and she knew that she looked her best. Emma was well versed in the arts of flattery and flirting and tonight she simply couldn't help herself. She knew that people were talking about them but it really was none of their business. Nelson's stepson, Josiah, was also making a particular nuisance of himself. He had fought alongside Nelson and he reckoned he was due a good share of Nelson's attention, but he wasn't getting it. Emma considered that her relationship with Nelson was the business of only two people. One was Nelson's wife, Lady Fanny, but she wasn't there. She was hundreds of miles away in England. The other was Emma's husband, Sir William, but Nelson was his hero and he surely wouldn't mind. Even if he had Emma might have sought to remind him that he held such high diplomatic office largely because of her influence with Maria Carolina, the

Queen of Naples. Tonight Nelson was hers, and hers alone, and she wanted the whole world to know it.

Samson, Isles of Scilly, 22nd May 2008

Kevin stood on the sand of East Porth and watched Meg getting the map out of her rucksack. It had been her idea to come to Samson today. The rain had completely cleared away and it promised to be one of those fine idyllic spring days that people always seemed to remember from their childhood. They had spent the previous day researching everything they could find out about the Colossus; he in the Museum, she in the local studies library; and then they had shared and discussed their findings, at his suggestion, over dinner.

HMS Colossus had been a 74-gun ship of the Courageaux Class; one of only four ships built within this class, in similar style to a French ship captured by the English in 1761. The Colossus was built by William Cleverley in Gravesend, where work had begun in October 1782, and the ship was finally launched on 4th April 1787, the year of the mutiny led by Fletcher Christian aboard the Bounty. Coincidentally the first captain of the Colossus had been named Hugh Christian but he did not appear to have been any relation of Fletcher Christian.

Until 1793 Colossus had served mainly around the south coast of Britain, but in the spring of that year she sailed to the Mediterranean for the first time. In August 1793 she had joined in the Siege of Toulon under Lord Hood who commanded HMS Victory, later Nelson's flagship. Colossus had first seen serious action during the Battle of the Groix on 22nd June 1795. Her Scottish captain, John Monkton, had ordered a piper in a kilt to play his bagpipes from the maintop mast during the battle. Three of the crew of Colossus had been killed in the fighting and another thirty had been wounded. The ship returned to England in January 1796 and had been badly damaged in a severe storm off The Lizard.

After a complete re-fit in Plymouth, Colossus sailed once more for the Mediterranean in December 1796 under the command of the man who was to be her last Captain, George Murray. In February 1797 Colossus had again seen action, this time at the Battle of Cape St Vincent, during which she suffered the loss of almost all her sails when the Spanish warships had shot at her masts. Colossus had spent the summer in Cadiz undergoing repairs before joining Nelson the following May on convoy duty in the Mediterranean. The ship had arrived in Naples with Nelson but just two weeks later she had been sent to blockade Malta and she had freed the tiny island of Gozo off the Maltese coast from the French. A week afterwards Nelson had sailed from Naples to support the Colossus in her blockade of Malta.

The evening had been dry and warm after the dampness of the day and after dinner Meg and Kevin sat outside with their coffee and admired the full moon as it rose over Porthcressa Bay, the moonlight painting a shining path across the water. Although Meg had been very forthcoming with what she had found out about the ship Kevin sensed that she was holding something back. She hadn't explained the significance of her great grandfather living on St Marys and sharing a name with Admiral Lord Nelson. It was obviously of great importance to her but she either couldn't or wouldn't confide in him. Be fair, Kevin told himself, she hardly knows you. After all few people confided their intimate family secrets to virtual strangers. Yet she'd trusted him enough to ask him if he'd go to Samson with her. It was a deserted island and they'd be completely alone for over four hours but she'd seemed happy enough with that. Perhaps she did want to confide in him but whatever it was she had to tell was better told where no-one could possibly overhear them.

As the boat slid slowly back into the water from the East Porth John watched Kevin standing on the beach beside Meg while she fiddled with her map. He was pleased that she had heeded his advice and brought a companion with her this time but he was especially pleased that she had chosen Kevin. John had known him for years since Kevin started coming to the Islands with his parents. Nice couple they had been but they were both dead now and Kevin was on his own, more so since the break-up of his marriage. John couldn't understand that. Kevin and Heather had seemed so well suited but then you never could tell what went on behind closed doors. He liked Kevin very much, always had, and whenever Kevin was on the Islands they usually went for a regular pint together in the Mermaid.

Meg straightened up and folded the map carefully. She wanted to retrace the exact steps of her previous visit. She had told Kevin that she had come to Samson three days before to do some field-walking but that she hadn't liked it very much on her own. She wanted to make another trip and she would prefer some company. Would he like to go with her. Kevin had jumped at the chance. He was particularly interested to see the South Hill and the area of Southward Well where the Colossus had sunk. She hadn't told him of her fears or about the unknown watcher on the hill. Time enough for that if it became necessary.

They walked together in companionable silence up to the top of the North Hill. Then they followed the line of tombs along the ridge.

'These guys certainly knew how to pick their eternal resting place,' said Kevin, gazing admiringly at the view. 'You can see for miles on a clear day.'

'Probably not a lot of help if you're dead!' said Meg, her face deadpan.

'True'. Kevin grinned. 'But then didn't they believe they were going into an after-life and that's why their personal things and their pottery and their weapons were buried with them. Maybe they thought that they'd need a good all round view of things as well.'

Meg laughed. She liked Kevin's dry sense of humour. They both heard the engine noise at the same time.

'Sounds like a boat somewhere,' said Kevin, looking around. 'Yes there it is. Just going through the channel between Bryher and Samson. Little fishing boat I think.

Can you see it?'

Meg turned her head in the direction of the sound. It looked exactly like the small boat she had seen three days previously as far as she could tell. It was almost exactly at the same time that she'd seen it as well.

'Probably going out to check his lobster pots,' she said as casually as she could, 'I saw the same boat, at least I think it was the same boat, when I was here three days ago.'

Kevin nodded thoughtfully. He wasn't going to tell her this but he didn't think there were any lobster pots set at the back of Samson. He would have a word about it with John later. Besides there was more to it than that. She'd sounded too casual when she'd mentioned it to him. They scrambled through the brambles and down the side of the North Hill to the 'waist'. Picking their way across the pebbles Meg said 'There used to be green meadows here and a little chapel stood somewhere over there.' She pointed to a heap of seaweed lying by the side of a ruined stone cottage which had been built against the shallow cliff face. 'I think a couple of monks lived the hermit's life here and cared for the chapel. It must have been a lonely existence.'

Kevin nodded. 'Is this the place where they would have brought those they rescued from Colossus and any of the cargo they managed to salvage?' he asked.

'I should think so.' replied Meg. 'I've field-walked the island and the East Porth is the nearest decent beach. The South Hill coast is rather rocky and inhospitable so the gigs probably rowed round to here.'

'This whole island is inhospitable,' said Kevin. 'Not a place I should care to have lived.'

'It would have been different when the cottages had families living in them and the land was farmed,' Meg replied.

They had crossed the 'waist' now and were starting to climb the South Hill.

'Watch the path for rocks and gorse roots,' Meg warned him. 'I took a tumble the other day.'

They had reached the well, which was still empty, and they both stopped for a moment.

'It gets really hot on this island on a sunny day and there aren't many places to shelter from the sun,' Meg said. 'I absolutely plastered factor 30 sun cream on this morning and I'm still turning red already.'

She turned to Kevin but he wasn't listening, his attention distracted by something on the East Porth.

'We've got company,' he said, pointing to a small dinghy which had been pulled up on the beach. 'They've probably come for the sun-bathing as well.'

He turned to Meg and was shocked by how pale she had gone in spite of the heat. Her hands seemed to be trembling slightly.

'Hey, what's wrong?' he asked. 'You look as if you'd seen a ghost.'

'I'm sorry.' She tried to smile. It was time to tell him the truth. 'It's just that when I came a few days ago someone seemed to be following me. First there was the boat, like that one we saw today, and then a helicopter flew over, and when I went to wait for John to pick me up someone was watching me from the top of the North Hill.' Meg stopped, aware that she was babbling. 'I'm sorry, you probably think I'm just being paranoid and stupid.'

There. Even she thought she was paranoid now. Perhaps Steven had been right all along.

Kevin stared at her with concern. Someone had badly dented her confidence at some point. Probably the ex-husband. What kind of a creep divorced his wife and then got remarried to someone else a couple of days later. He'd thought that sort of practice had gone out of fashion with Henry VIII.

'Look,' he said, as gently as he could. 'I believe you. You told me that you thought you were here alone the other day and then suddenly you see someone on the island and you don't know how they got here and there's no other boat around. I'd have been concerned too if it had been me.'

Meg looked at him gratefully and realised just how much she had expected him to tell her that she was simply being paranoid. He didn't seem to dismiss her fears as groundless at all.

Kevin picked up his rucksack and patted her arm reassuringly.

'Come on,' he said. 'It's different today. Whoever it is has left their boat in full view so they're not trying to hide anything and, anyway, you've got me with you. It will be fine.'

Meg nodded and managed a smile. Hoisting her own rucksack onto her shoulders they set off together up the South Hill.

She showed him Armorel's cottage and he laughed out loud at Besant's description of life on Samson.

'If you ask me,' said Kevin, 'Besant never set foot in these islands. I know there's such a thing as poetic licence but that's just plain ridiculous. Golden rule number one: write about what you know and if you're going to write about a specific place at least have some idea of what it really is like.'

By the time they reached Ann Webber's cottage they were both hot and tired and glad of the shade from the sun which the small cottage offered. Meg had brought a packed lunch of bread, cheese and tomatoes, while Kevin produced a large bottle of mineral water and a couple of apples.

They ate their picnic sitting on the rough stone seat by the old fireplace. After they had finished Kevin wandered around and took some pictures of the cottage while Meg packed away the remains of their lunch. She felt much better now that she had told Kevin the truth about her visit to Samson a few days ago and it was very reassuring to have his company. It was also, if she were honest, very pleasant as well.

Then together they followed the path she had taken before which led to the terminal rocky summit of the South Hill. She pointed out the area of the Southward Well to Kevin.

'Just over there beyond those rocks where you can see a patch of seaweed floating on the surface. That's where the Colossus went down.'

Kevin took several photographs then surveyed the treacherous coastline of that part of the island. His eye followed it along until gradually, towards, East Porth, the ground began to level out. The dinghy had gone. He turned towards Meg. 'You're right,' he said. 'They couldn't have landed anyone or anything along this stretch. It looks forbidding enough on a calm day like this and it was a stormy winter's night when the Colossus sank. I suppose, in view of what I said about Besant earlier on, I should come and take my pictures on a dark stormy night to give my readers some idea of what conditions the Colossus endured before she was lost.'

He bent to tie up one of his bootlaces before going on.

'They court-martialled the captain, you know, for losing his ship. No thanks for all the lives he helped to save or all the cargo he helped to salvage. No idea of the problems he faced. Even Nelson supported him, saying that Murray had given him one of Colossus's anchors because Nelson's own ship didn't have sufficient of its own. Murray cleared his name eventually of course but things were never quite the same for him after that.'

Meg listened to him with interest. She'd not known that the captain had been court-martialled for the loss of the ship. How unfair when it had been for something he could not have prevented despite his best efforts. Full of righteous indignation on behalf of the unknown captain Meg stared out across the ruined cottages of the

South Hill to the North Hill beyond. The figure was there again, just watching them. Something about its stance suggested that it was the same person who had been watching Meg on the island a few days before. She gasped and clutched Kevin's arm. Look!' she said urgently. 'Over there. I'm sure it's the same person who was watching me the other day.'

Kevin turned and followed the direction in which her arm was pointing. It could just be another walker, he told himself, but they were the only ones who had got off John's boat and, since the dinghy had left, he had not seen any other boats around. There was something curiously still about the figure. He didn't like it.

'Come on,' he said to Meg in as cheerful a tone as he could manage. 'Time we were getting back to meet John. Don't worry. There are two of us and he's probably just some harmless walker.' He tried to sound far more certain than he felt. They turned to make their way down to the sandy shores of the East Porth and as they did so faint shadows flitted across the sand under the bright sky.

St Marys, Isles of Scilly, 22nd May 2008

Kevin and Meg had been silent during most of the boat trip back to St Marys, each lost in their own thoughts. Meg, however, had agreed to meet him for dinner again. There were things they needed to talk about. Kevin could understand now why she had seemed so apprehensive about Samson. It was neither imagination nor paranoia on her part. Although the figure they had seen had made no move towards them its presence had been somehow threatening and its stillness had been definitely unnerving. John must have noticed that something was amiss because he asked Kevin if everything was alright as they got off the boat. Meg was ahead of him, already making her way up the steps, so he lowered his voice and said to John that there was something strange going on with Samson and could they meet up for a pint later. They arranged to meet in the Mermaid at five thirty before John went home for his tea.

When she got back to her room in Mrs Woodcock's house Meg lay down on the bed. Her head was beginning to ache and she took a couple of paracetamol and closed her eyes. Although she was tired, sleep wouldn't come. Someone was watching her, following her, checking her every move. Her relief that Kevin had been with her and had seen the figure was overwhelming. Steven's hatchet job on her self confidence had been such that she had even begun to doubt the evidence of her own eyes. She was also frightened. Who would want to follow her? She remembered the letters and phone calls she'd received over the past twelve months or so, each with its hint of menace and thinly disguised threats. She knew that someone was interested in something that they thought she had but she had no idea what that could be or why anyone would be interested in her. After all she'd been told for long enough just how uninteresting she was.

Meg thought about Kevin as she walked down Church Street to meet him for dinner. She wore a pretty cotton dress patterned in a myriad of rainbow colours and sandals on her feet. It would be a nice relaxed evening where she didn't have to worry about her cutlery etiquette, make sure her napkin was placed just so, and remember how to hold her wine glass. Kevin seemed to be a kind and decent man, although Steven had appeared like that in the beginning. Meg chided herself crossly. She had to stop comparing every other man to Steven. Besides Kevin had already done something that Steven had never done in all the years of their courtship and their marriage. He had listened to her and he had believed in her. She owed him something for that surely. If she was ever to move on she had to learn to trust again and Kevin had demonstrated that maybe he deserved her trust. That being the case she should at least be honest with him. Tonight, she thought, she would try to do that and tell him everything. If nothing else it would actually be a relief to share the burden of her secret.

They met at Dibble and Grub once more. It was still very warm and so they sat at a table outside looking across Porthcressa.

'They'll think we've moved in here and start offering us bed and breakfast rates', joked Kevin as they settled themselves and gave their order. Kevin had asked Meg what sort of wine she preferred. This was something Steven had never done. He prided himself on being a wine connoisseur and anyone who drank a wine chosen by him should have simply been grateful for his knowledge and his exquisite taste. Meg didn't usually mind whether she drank white or red wine but tonight she decided that she was in a 'red mood'. Kevin smiled and ordered a bottle of rich fruity Burgundy. The waitress brought the bottle with a couple of glasses and a small plate of tapas. Kevin poured them each a glass of wine and they toasted each other and the Islands.

The first course arrived. Both of them had ordered spare ribs in a bar-b-q sauce and neither of them had realised how hungry they were. They set to with relish, dipping the ribs into the sauce with their fingers and then chewing the bones like starving dogs. The waitress brought out a bowl of water with a slice of lemon in it and several serviettes so that they could clean their fingers when they became too covered in sauce. How Steven would have hated this thought Meg with some vicarious pleasure. He had always refused to order dishes which might make any kind of a mess.

'It's like being a child again,' she said happily to Kevin. 'I've not been allowed to make a mess like this for a long time.'

'Allowed!' thought Kevin. Meg was a grown woman capable of making her own choices so why hadn't she been 'allowed' to make a mess if she wished. He was about to ask when a booming voice broke over their heads.

'Well hello!' the voice said in some sardonic surprise. 'What an unexpected pleasure this is!'

Meg almost choked and looked up. She would think of the devil and now here he was, standing before her. He was ridiculously overdressed for the Islands. The pinstripe suit was more in keeping with a London boardroom than a sandy beach on St Mary's. His black shoes were beautifully polished to a high shine. Although it was warm he still wore a shirt and a neatly knotted club tie and he looked hot and uncomfortable. There were beads of sweat on his forehead as he regarded them. Kevin was wearing chinos and an open necked short sleeved shirt and he seemed cool and relaxed in painful contrast to Steven.

'I see you're enjoying yourself', said Steven, looking with some distaste at both Kevin and the spare ribs. Behind him Janine tottered and smirked on impossibly high heels.

'Hi Steven,' Meg said as casually as she could manage. 'What are you doing here?'

'Same as you I should imagine,' said Steven. 'On holiday. After all I brought you here often enough and I don't see why Janine should be denied the pleasure of these beautiful Islands. Aren't you going to introduce me to your friend?'

'Of course.' Meg stood up flustered; angry that Steven had somehow wrong footed her yet again.

'Kevin Brownlow. Steven Hamilton and, um, his wife, Janine.'

Steven shook Kevin's hand almost crushing his fingers to pieces in the process. 'Pleased to meet you,' said Steven in the sort of tone which clearly implied that he was anything but pleased.

'How do you do?' said Kevin, trying hard to suppress the instant and instinctive dislike he felt for the man.

'And this is my lovely wife, Janine,' said Steven with a smug glance at Meg.

'Pleased to meet you I'm sure,' simpered Janine.

'We were just having a little walk before dinner,' Steven went on. 'We're eating at Tregarthen's tonight. Do marvellous food there. Not cheap, but only the best for my darling.'

Kevin was having difficulty resisting the urge to be extremely rude to Steven. So this was the ex-husband. Pompous pratt! No wonder Meg had hang-ups. Who wouldn't, married to a guy like that. What on earth had made her choose him in the first place?

'Don't let us keep you,' he said politely, quietly wrestling control of the situation back from Steven.

Steven glared at him contemptuously.

'Yes, well, I can see we interrupted your supper.' Steven managed to inject a great deal of disdain into the word 'supper' as he glanced at the remains of the ribs and the dirty serviettes on the table, wrinkling his nose in disgust.

'Do enjoy your holiday, my dear,' he said to Meg with the sort of expression that a cat reserves for its prey. 'I'm sure we'll meet up again.'

Turning, he took Janine's arm, and they sauntered off towards Hugh Town, Janine's hips wiggling alarmingly in her over tight red skirt.

Meg sat down again blushing fiercely.

'I'm so sorry about that,' she said. 'I had no idea he was out here in the Islands.'

'You have nothing to apologise for, absolutely nothing!' said Kevin, surprising himself by his own vehemence.

'I know he was your husband but he's a patronising ill mannered idiot!'

Meg gaped at him and then unexpectedly laughed. Kevin had a wonderful knack of putting things into perspective and it had been good to see Steven discomfited for a change.

'He's always been like that,' she said. 'He thinks he's perfect so anything or anyone that doesn't meet his standards is, by very definition, imperfect.'

'Forgive me for asking,' said Kevin, 'and it's probably none of my business, but why on earth did you marry him?'

Meg looked up at him and smiled.

'I fell in love,' she said simply.

The waitress cleared away the remains of their bar-b-q ribs. She put a large plate of home-made moussaka in front of Meg and a bubbling dish of lasagne in front of Kevin, and gave each of them a small bowl of mixed green salad as a side dish. Kevin poured them more wine and they both tucked into their dinners.
'This is really good,' said he appreciatively.

'It is,' agreed Meg. She stopped eating for a moment.

'Don't let Steven ruin our evening,' she said almost pleadingly, then went on in a more spirited fashion, 'I'm sure we're having a better meal than he is.'

'I'll drink to that!' said Kevin, raising his glass and clinking it against Meg's glass.

'To absent friends!' They both laughed.

They ate companionably together, chatting about the Islands, their history and their incredible beauty. Neither noticed the time passing. A dessert of Panna Cotta and fresh fruit had followed the main course and both their appetites had been completely satiated. Mellowed by the wine and sipping appreciatively at her coffee Meg decided the time had come to tell Kevin what she knew. He deserved that much now, especially after Steven's little episode. Where to start was the problem but Kevin solved that for her.

'The other day, Meg,' he began tentatively, 'you told me that your great grandfather lived on St Marys? It seemed to be especially significant that he was called Horatio Nelson but you didn't elaborate on that. I know that during the 19th century a number of boys with the surname Nelson were named Horatio. Why was his name so important to you?'

'It's a long story,' she said, 'and you may not believe all of it, but it is the truth so far as I know.'

Kevin nodded his encouragement and Meg took a deep breath.

'Emma, Lady Hamilton, had one child, one surviving child that is, with Nelson. A daughter named Horatia. Horatia had a difficult childhood, as you might imagine, but she seems to have grown up into a nice young woman. She married a vicar, the Rev. Philip Ward, and she had ten children by him. Several of their Christian names were a play on the words 'Horatio' or 'Nelson' or both; although she never actually publicly acknowledged that Nelson was her father.'

Meg paused to take a sip of her coffee and continued,
'There is a record of a Horatio Nelson living on Scilly in the 19th century. His father was Jim Nelson, a stone mason, and his mother was Sarah Legg.' Meg smiled. 'Legg is an old Scillonian surname. It was said, however, that Horatio was not their blood son and that he had been adopted from the mainland. He was also said to have been Horatia Nelson's eleventh child. Horatia's husband was, at that time, not receiving a large stipend, and apparently they simply couldn't afford to keep him. Jim Nelson had been doing some work on the mainland at the time near Horatia's home. She'd got to know him slightly and the fact that he was a Nelson appealed to her. When she found out where he lived she thought it would be far enough away for the plan she and her husband had been forming to work. She told Jim that sadly they just couldn't afford to keep their new baby and they were looking for someone to adopt him. Jim Nelson caught her drift. He knew who she was, and he considered it would be an honour for him to bring up the legendary Nelson's grandson. So he agreed to the adoption.'

'That was a big hearted thing for him to do,' said Kevin, his voice full of admiration. 'Did the Islanders know whose child it was that he had brought home?'

'Horatia didn't want it publicly known that she had been forced to give up her baby so she asked Jim to be very discreet about his adopted son and said that she would tell anyone who asked that her baby had died. Infant mortality rates then were very high and nobody would think to question her story. I'm not sure how much Jim Nelson actually told people in the Islands but there were lots of rumours that this child really was a descendant of Nelson.'

Meg paused again to drink some more of her coffee then she continued with her story. 'Satisfied that she had done her best for her son, Horatia said that she would never forget Jim's kindness and she asked him to promise that he would tell Horatio who he really was when the boy was grown up. It was said that Jim kept his promise and that, in her later years, Horatia wrote regularly to her son. Horatio went to sea for a time but he eventually returned to the Islands and became a fisherman. He was a real Island personality and he was well liked by everyone.'

She took another sip of her coffee and went on. 'Horatio married an Island girl named Rosie Pender and they had a son named Joseph. He was my grandfather. Joseph married Mary Hicks in the autumn of 1894 but my father wasn't born until 1920. He was an only child and born quite late in life to my grandmother. My father left Scilly to join the Navy in 1940. After the War was over he worked on the mainland where he met and married my mother. I was born when he was in his forties and we used to come to the Scillies regularly when I was a small child. Both my parents died several years ago now so I'm on my own. Then about ten years ago the remains of the Colossus were discovered on the sea-bed off Samson. There were the usual stories of unique discoveries and untold riches, but apparently some of the items they had expected to find were missing. One of the journalists writing up a piece about the treasures from Colossus somehow found out about my great grandfather and hey presto!'

Meg swallowed the remains of her coffee and then took a deep breath.
'About a year ago I started getting these letters. They seemed to suggest that our family knew where these missing items were. That they had been hidden and the secret of their location was being passed down from generation to generation. I'd never heard anything about that from either of my parents or from anyone else. So I just ignored the letters at first. I thought it was some crank.'

She smiled ruefully.

'Then the phone calls started. Always a man's voice and always late at night. Insisting that I knew where the real Colossus treasure was hidden. I'd no idea what he was talking about but he didn't believe me and the calls started to become threatening. I changed my number and went ex-directory but somehow he found out my new number and the calls resumed. I went to the police but there doesn't seem to be much they can do unless he actually contacts me or threatens me in person. So I decided to come out here and see what I could find out and maybe try to discover why this man thinks I have something to hide.'

Meg's voice trembled. 'That is why I was so scared on Samson. Whoever it is seems to know my every move and I think they are intent on making personal contact. But I don't even know what it is that they want from me.'

Instinctively Kevin reached for her hand and held it and Meg didn't attempt to pull it away.

'It's OK,' he said soothingly. 'So that makes you the great great granddaughter of Admiral Lord Nelson and Emma, Lady Hamilton! Wow! That is quite something!' He paused for a few moments, thinking hard about what he had just been told, and considering what his next words would mean to her.
'If you'll let me, we'll work on this together. I've done quite a lot of research on the Colossus and I read those stories too. I was intrigued and I think you're right. The answer does lie somewhere in these Islands. I'm certain of it.'

He paused and Meg nodded in grateful agreement. Then he continued. 'Now I've got something to tell you. I had a drink with John before I met you tonight and he thinks that there is something very odd going on in the Islands. There are lots of little incidents that just don't add up. He also told me that there are no lobster pots set round the back of Samson so the boat you saw probably belonged to whoever thinks you know something. I think you should tell John everything you've told me tonight and then we'll take it from there. Is that OK with you?'

Meg nodded slowly. It felt good to have someone on her side.

'Now,' said Kevin as he stood up, 'if you'll let me be very old fashioned I'll see you home.'

Behind them the night wind whispered gently through the small waves rippling against the shore and shadows played almost imperceptibly across the sand.

Naples, Italy, 15th October 1798

Tears rolled down Emma's cheeks as Nelson sat beside her, stroking her hand. 'Why?' she cried. 'Why do you have to go now?' She twisted her handkerchief tightly into a ball.

'I have already explained to you, my dearest,' he said gently. 'You know that the Maltese have rebelled against the French. Last week, one of my ships, the Colossus, managed to blockade Malta and free Gozo. Gozo is such a beautiful little island, so close to Malta, and it has a fine cathedral. But now I am needed to help the Colossus continue to enforce the blockade around Malta so that the wretched French cannot have their way.'

'I know,' she sobbed. 'I know, but it seems so unfair just when we have found each other in this way.'

'That is true, my love,' Nelson soothed her, 'but I will be back soon.'

He put his good arm around her and held her close.

The truth of the matter was, he thought grimly, that he needed to get away from Naples for a bit. He was being dragged in too deep with the local politics as Queen Maria Carolina capitalized on her friendship with Emma to get to him. She was desperate to enlist his aid in attacking the French but Nelson did not want to get involved. Besides he was not really in a position to do so. It was land troops she needed, not sea power. Privately he did not much care for Naples and had written to a close friend in England that it was 'a country of fiddlers and poets, whores and scoundrels'; but it was also the home, if only the adopted home, of his beloved Emma.

Nelson could not believe that just over three weeks ago Emma Hamilton had been little more than a name to him. He'd met her once, about five years ago, but the meeting had been brief and he'd thought little more about it. Now he knew, beyond all shadow of a doubt, that she would be the love of his life. He thought of his loyal wife, Fanny, waiting for him back home in England. He respected her and loved her as a friend, but it had never been like it was with Emma. In truth his continued absences had turned him and Fanny into almost total strangers to each other. With Emma it was completely different. He needed her so much. He would give her anything she wanted except that he could not stay with her at this time. He owed it to the Colossus and her crew to give them the back-up support they so badly lacked at the moment. Colossus was one of his best and fastest ships and he did not want her in danger a moment longer than was necessary.

Nelson reluctantly disentangled himself from Emma and stood to take his leave. She was trying hard to control her tears although she was still crying.

'But what if the French were to attack us?' she asked tremulously. 'You know how anxious Maria Carolina is for Ferdinand to attack them. She counts on you.'

Nelson knew this already. It was one of the reasons he wanted to leave Naples. Privately however he thought that there was not much chance. Ferdinand, Maria Carolina's husband, had not been known to attack much other than the deer and other hapless animals which he hunted daily.

'There is little danger,' he assured Emma 'and, in any case, I will be back very soon to take care of you.'

Emma gave him a watery little smile and kissed him on the lips.

'Arrivederci my love,' she murmured. 'Go and see to Colossus but come back safely to me.'

Nelson bowed low and, turning, strode from the room. He would go to the assistance of the Colossus with all possible speed and return as soon as he could. He knew that was a contradiction since it was not a good idea in political terms for him to return soon; but at the same time the idea of being away from Emma was as unbearable for him as it was for her. Besides, his stepson was making a thorough nuisance of himself. Josiah Nisbet was the son of Fanny Nisbet who had been a widow when Nelson married her on Nevis in 1787. Nelson had looked after the boy and, when he was old enough, took him into the Navy. Josiah became a captain and held command of a ship in Nelson's fleet. However he had a difficult personality and a number of complaints had been made against him. After his ship, HMS Thalia, was paid off Josiah had never held another command or even any place on a ship. He had also recently quarreled with Nelson over the amount of time Nelson was spending with Emma. Nelson had told him sharply that it was none of his business and Josiah had stormed off, muttering that he would like to break Nelson's neck. As he made his way to the quay Nelson reflected that most of his ships had had a re-fit while he had been in Naples, but not the Colossus for she had sailed almost immediately from Naples to Malta. Maybe he should think soon about ordering the Colossus back to England. He wished he could send Josiah with her but knew that he could not. The captain of Colossus was George Murray. He was a good steady man. It would not be fair to him to inflict Josiah on him even if he could. That did not alter the fact however that Colossus was badly in need of a refit and he really should give this some serious consideration and soon. He stepped smartly aboard his ship, Vanguard, and gave the order to sail.

St Marys, Isles of Scilly, 23rd May 2008

The day was warm and fine again but quite a breeze had sprung up. Kevin had phoned John Fisher to arrange a meeting. John had said he would be at home that afternoon because he had no trips due to the low tides. Kevin knew that the waters around the Islands were very shallow and that on the low tides there would be scarcely a foot of water. On the lowest tides of all it was still possible to walk between some of the islands. Kevin himself had once walked dry-shod, from Tresco to Samson, from Samson to Bryher and then from Bryher back again to Tresco. The three island walk as it was known. He'd heard that it was also possible to walk from Tresco to St Martins, although not dry-shod. You had to take off your socks and shoes and paddle some of the way.

Kevin, still fascinated by Meg's revelations the previous evening, had suggested to her that it might be nice, and appropriate, to spend the morning walking on The Garrison. Star Castle was an interesting Tudor fort turned luxury hotel, and he knew that some of the guns from the Colossus had been mounted on a small green in front of the Duchy offices. The Duchy of Cornwall had owned the Scillies since the days of the Black Prince in the fourteenth century. Kevin didn't know whether the Black Prince, who was also the Prince of Wales, had ever come to the Islands, but he knew that the present Prince of Wales was extremely fond of them and often visited, staying in discreet luxury at a house near the Duchy offices. He would have a grand view of Samson and the Southward Well where the Colossus had sunk, as well as of the mounted canon in front of his offices. He wondered idly if the Prince knew the story of the Colossus. If he didn't know it now, one day soon he would.

Meg strolled up to Sally Port where she had arranged to meet Kevin for a walk. This afternoon they were due to see John Fisher and she would tell him all that she told Kevin last night. It was a relief to have finally shared her secret with him. He took her seriously and he seemed to believe everything she had said. Now that her parents were dead almost no-one knew about the story. She had told Steven of course but he had been highly sceptical about the whole thing.

'You?' he had said in that deprecating tone of voice that she had come to dislike so much. 'You a descendant of the great Admiral Lord Nelson? I don't think so,' and he had smiled patronisingly at her.

'I know you're paranoid and insecure about your childhood, Meg, but there's really no need to come out with stories like that.'

Meg wished for the hundredth time that she had never confided in Steven about her childhood. Her parents had been childless for a long time and her arrival was both untimely and unexpected. They had been happy with just each other for company and the intrusion of a child had been a rude shock to both of them. She was sure they had tried to do their best at first but the strain had proved to be too much for them. When she was twelve they had finally separated with great acrimony and bitterness on both sides. They blamed each other, and, unfortunately for Meg, saw the other's worst traits in their daughter. Meg had stayed with her mother although her father had visited her at first. As he became more critical of what he saw as her mother in her, the visits had tailed off. Meg, hurt and uncomprehending, had railed against both of them. Her mother had told her that she was becoming just like her father and had shut herself off from Meg as she grew from a teenager into a young woman. Meg had felt insecure and excluded from her family, still feeling that somehow the whole thing really had been all her fault. Steven's accusations of paranoia had only served to fuel that belief. Although she didn't believe that Kevin would react in the same way as Steven, she had held back from telling him everything last night because she felt that she didn't yet know him well enough. She hoped that perhaps one day she would.

The Sally Port was a small upwardly curving tunnel through the thick Garrison walls. It had once been used by the soldiers returning from an evening's entertainment at one of the local hostelries. Neither Meg nor Kevin could stand upright in the Sally Port and both of them had to walk through it practically bent double.

'This isn't easy!' said Kevin, who was taller than Meg, and consequently more bent double. 'Why on earth didn't they build it so that you could at least stand up?'

Meg didn't really know. 'Maybe security,' she said, 'or maybe they were just pygmies!'

They both laughed. It was a short steep walk before they came to the Duchy offices. The building was a large 18th century Georgian mansion bearing the Prince of Wales's coat of arms over the front door. A road passed in front of it and on the other side of the road there was a small green. Four polished black cannon stood on the green facing out towards Town Bay and the Eastern Isles. A small information board told people that the guns had come from the Colossus. Meg took some photographs and then tentatively stroked one of the cannon.

'Funny to think that these lay on the sea-bed for over a hundred and fifty years before they were brought up here,' she said thoughtfully. 'I wonder where the rest are.'

'All over the place,' said Kevin. 'A few more are just up the road; others in a museum in Penzance. Several have been lost and there are still some on the sea-bed.'

'What do you mean? Lost?' asked Meg.

'Well,' Kevin shrugged. 'People bring these things up and take them home. They're either sold or distributed, maybe to various military museums or the like, and no-one really keeps a record.'

Meg looked shocked. 'That shouldn't be allowed to happen,' she said.

'Well, officially, it isn't,' said Kevin, 'but out here there's not always anyone to keep an eye on these things. The wreck site is licensed but people dive on it anyway and they get tempted to take a souvenir or two.'

'How do you know all this? asked Meg suspiciously.

Kevin grinned. 'Not much you can't find out over a pint in the Mermaid!'

They walked down the narrow tarmac road to the second site of the cannon which had come from the Colossus and Meg took some more photographs. Below they could see Hugh Town and Porthcressa shimmering in the morning sunlight. Then they continued their walk around the foot of the Garrison. It was very pleasant wandering along the path that ran alongside the old walls. Beneath, spirited little waves, whipped up by the breeze, crashed onto the rocky shore. Opposite, across a channel of deep water, lay the small pretty island of Agnes with its offshore islet of the Gugh. Linked to Agnes only by a sandbar, the Gugh was an island at high tide. Two houses with distinctive Dutch style roofs stood just above the shore facing Agnes. The Gugh had been the last place in Scilly to be connected to the national grid when electricity came to the Scillies in 1987 and its few inhabitants had held a big party to celebrate.

As they rounded the corner of the headland to return to Hugh Town the wind strengthened, whipping the water which lay between the Garrison and the small twin hilled island of Samson into white horses. To the south-east of Samson a three masted sailing ship was anchored. Meg had seen it before and she knew that it was a French ship which offered activity holidays for young people. The ship rocked rhythmically as the waves rolled under her. Just as the Colossus would have done when she had anchored to shelter from the strong winds of the winter storm. Only the seas would have been much rougher and the Colossus would have been much more heavily laden. Somewhere out there beneath the waves lay the Colossus, thought Meg, her back broken and her treasures scattered, and in that moment she felt a genuine grief for the tragic fate of the ship.

'Fancy lunch in the dungeons?' Kevin's voice broke across her thoughts.

Meg dragged her thoughts back to the present.

'Well there's an offer that's hard to refuse,' she said, laughing.

Meg knew that the owners of the Star Castle Hotel ran a small bar in the former dungeons of the old Tudor fortress where it was possible to get excellent lunches. The low stone walls were just as they had been when prisoners had been incarcerated there although they had not had the benefit of the comfortable bench seating with its gaily striped cushions nor the two muskets hung on the walls with which they would have doubtless shot their way to freedom. There were also pictures of sailing ships and old maps. A ship's bell hung over the bar for customers to summon attention.

It was just after midday and Kevin and Meg had the bar to themselves. They each ordered a ploughman's lunch and a pint of real Scilly ale which they carried across to one of the polished wooden tables.

'I think rations must have improved since this place was used for prisoners,' said Meg, examining the variety of cheeses and pickles on her plate. 'Not to mention the beer.'

'Yes. They were probably lucky to get bread and water most of the time,' said Kevin. 'Not like today when you have canteens and a choice of food and special diet menus in prisons.'

'Do you think they brought the sailors they rescued from Colossus up to Star Castle?' said Meg, still thinking of the ship in her watery grave.

'I mean there were nearly six hundred people aboard, some of them wounded. They couldn't just leave them all on Samson and where else would be large enough to take them until another ship could be found for them?'

'Good point,' said Kevin, buttering his second wedge of whole-meal bread. 'I hadn't really thought about that before.'

'Do you think they also brought up the salvaged cargo? For security?' asked Meg.

'Almost certainly,' said Kevin, 'unless they locked it up in the Custom House.'

'It seems strange,' said Meg pensively, 'that after all this time so much is being found from the Colossus and brought to the surface. I mean they were diving on her just five years after she sank and then again in the 1830's, and then everything seemed to stop for well over a century. Curious.'

Kevin looked at her. 'Who dived on her in the 1800s?'

Meg piled cheese and pickle on to her last piece of bread.

'Well there was a commercial salvage operation carried out by two guys named John Braithwaite and Ralph Tonkin. I think they worked on the Colossus from 1803 to 1806...'

'So they started soon after she sank?' interrupted Kevin.

'Yes,' Meg agreed. 'A few years afterwards two brothers, John and Charles Deane, designed a breathing apparatus which could be used under water. In 1833 John and another man, William Edwards, got a contract from the Admiralty to carry out salvage work on Colossus. They brought up a number of guns and some of the copper sheathing.'

It was Kevin's turn now to be suspicious. 'How do you know all this?' he asked.

'I found some very interesting books in the local studies library. Remember?' Meg asked with a mischievous smile. 'In fact,' she went on, 'a few weeks after Deane and Edwards brought up the guns there was a strange accident. The guns had been left lying near the quay and someone struck one of them with a hammer. I've no idea why. Anyway the gun exploded and a guy named Master-Gunner Ross, who was on Rat Island at the time, received severe leg injuries.'

'Where's Rat Island?' said Kevin. He knew the name but couldn't place it.

'It's all joined to St Marys now under the extended quay but the original Rat Island is where that little workshop stood which sold canvas bags. You know Ratbags? They took their name from Rat Island. I think they've moved now,' she added.

'Yes I know it. I guess it just goes to show you shouldn't play with guns,' said Kevin, standing up. 'Time we were making a move. John's expecting us.'

They walked down the steep little path from Star Castle which led to Hugh Town, passing Tregarthen's on their way. The present hotel was a lot larger and more luxurious than the original whitewashed cottage, which was still incorporated within the hotel building. There Captain Tregarthen and his six daughters had once offered hospitality to people like Lord Tennyson and Francis Palgrave. Palgrave's 'Golden Treasury', a book of poetry, had been published as a memorial to their magical days spent in the Islands. The wind was getting up all the time and by the time they were walking along The Strand it was whipping Meg's hair around her face and making her eyes water. It was a relief to pass the secondary school at the top of the hill and descend to a little more shelter. Rosehill, where John and his wife, Sara, lived, was about a quarter of an hour's walk from the school.

As they passed the small building which housed Radio Scilly, the Islands' own radio station, Kevin turned to Meg and said 'Thinking about it perhaps we should appeal for information about the Colossus through Radio Scilly. A lot of people in these Islands must have their own little titbits of information about the wreck which won't have appeared in any of the journals. Radio is kind of anonymous in a way. They can ring in, disguise their voice a little if they want to, no name, no pack-drill... you know the sort of thing, and tell us what they know. I'd guess though that most of them would just want to speak to us privately rather than on air; but you never know what might come out of the woodwork.'

Meg considered this for a moment then she said 'I think that's a good idea. Maybe if we speak to individuals in that way we might get some sort of a clue as to what is supposed to be missing from the Colossus treasure trove.'

They turned a corner and arrived at John Fisher's cottage. It was set back from the road and partly hidden by a feathery tamarisk tree. Hottentot fig sprawled over a garden wall and pretty pale blue agapanthus grew on either side of the front door.

A sleepy black and white cat stretched out on the small lawn opened one eye and regarded them quizzically. John himself answered their knock. His dark hair, now greying at the edges, gave him rather a distinguished look and his blue eyes twinkled in a face that was deeply tanned from years of exposure to bright sunshine and the strong winds which buffeted the Islands.

'Come in! Come in!' he said standing aside for them to enter. Inside the cottage it was cool and quiet. A series of carefully framed small paintings of the Islands hung on the white washed walls.

'Sara did those.' John nodded at the paintings as he led them into a comfortably furnished lounge which had a deep red sofa on one side of the stone fireplace and wooden bookshelves along the length of two walls. A television set skulked in a corner. He paused for a moment then said 'Sara's in the garden. Come on through.'

The kitchen had a large scrubbed pine table and old pine cupboards lined the walls. A jug of wild flowers stood on the kitchen windowsill. The back door was ajar and led to a sheltered kitchen garden. Roses trailed along a trellis on the back of the house and there were two small neatly dug beds where lettuce, beans, potatoes and carrots were growing. It was warm and unseen insects hummed quietly. Meg thought she could smell jasmine and honeysuckle and she could see lavender bushes further down the garden. A woman was sitting at a wooden table threading onions.

'Sara, this is Kevin Brownlow and Meg Nelson. They've come to talk about the Colossus.'

Sara Fisher stood up. She was not quite as tall as her husband, a slim woman whose straw coloured hair was bleached by the sun. She wore a long skirt of multi colour design and a sort of white smock top that made her look as though she were some kind of fashion advertisement from the 1960s. She held out her hands in welcome. Her face, when she smiled, was beautiful, and her brown eyes had a warm expression in them.

'Meg. Kevin. How lovely to meet you at last. John has told me so much about you both.' She turned to Meg. 'What is Meg short for? Megan? Margaret?'

'Megan,' said Meg, 'but I don't use my full name very often.'

'I don't blame you,' said Sara. 'Meg is a nice name anyway.' She smiled again. 'Come and sit down and I'll make some tea and then we can talk.'

She picked up her onions and disappeared into the kitchen while Meg and Kevin sat down at the table with John. They avoided mention of the Colossus and talked about the garden until Sara returned with a tea tray. She had buttered some scones and spread them thickly with strawberry jam. She put the plate of scones on the table along with the teapot and milk jug and handed out cups and saucers to everyone. Then she settled herself next to John and smiled at Meg.

'Kevin told John that you had an unusual story to tell about your family. I'm full of curiosity.'

Meg cradled her tea-cup in her hands. It would be impossible not to like Sara Fisher and she trusted her instinctively. Slowly she told John and Sara everything that she knew about her family and about the Colossus. They listened carefully and with growing interest, Sara abstractedly re-filling the tea-cups occasionally. When she'd finished there was a moment's silence; then Sara said, 'That's quite a story. My mother was a Legg, which probably means we're second cousins twice removed whatever that means,' she smiled, ' but I remember my grandmother telling me her grandmother's sister had brought up a child said to be directly related to Admiral Lord Nelson. I didn't take it too seriously. You know what family stories are like and my grandmother had quite an imagination anyway; although it looks as if she might have been right on this occasion.'

John seemed to consider the implications of what he had heard then he spoke. 'There's quite a few things been happening of late that don't make sense. I can explain the helicopter you heard. It belonged to Trinity House who maintain the Bishop Rock light. They'd been out to the lighthouse, but on the way back they circled Samson a couple of times because they'd been told that there was a boat in difficulties somewhere around the back of the island. They didn't find anything though.'

He paused to take his third cup of tea from Sara.
'But there's been a great deal of interest in the site of the Colossus recently and there have been a few boats around recently that no-one recognises. Their occupants don't seem to come ashore unless it's under cover of darkness. They don't seem to need food or fuel. They don't show any interest in the Scillies. Most genuine visitors generally spend at least two or three days exploring the Islands. These guys also seem to sail in waters most of the locals won't go near. Either they're extremely experienced sailors or they're ignorant fools.'

'Do you think that the small fishing boat I saw from Samson belonged to one of them?' asked Meg.

''Well it certainly wasn't a local boat,' said John. 'Probably came from one of the bigger boats that seem to spend their time moored offshore. No one goes round the back of Samson when the tides are low. If he didn't want to draw attention to himself he should have done his homework better.'

'What is it that they are after do you think?' asked Kevin.

'Search me.' said John. 'One of the local divers told me that they'd got lists of most of the things that were supposed to have gone down with the Colossus and that Sir William Hamilton had drawings done of a number of items that were in his lost collection. Well apparently they found all the crates that had contained his stuff but four of them had already been broken open. Things were missing and there was no trace of them on the sea-bed around the ship. I knew that some of the guns were lost. Guy who used dive on the wreck about forty years ago brought them up to the surface but no one is quite sure where they all are now.'

'You know,' said Sara thoughtfully, 'they brought up a strange wooden carving from the ship about five or six years ago. I think it's in the Valhalla on Tresco now but there was a lot of interest in that at the time. The next year some people started camping out on Samson. The Duchy doesn't allow that so they were told to leave. They did leave but they kept coming back and in the end they were threatened with court action. I don't know what their fascination with the island was. I certainly wouldn't want to camp out on Samson. The island is said to be cursed you know.' She smiled as she said this to suggest that she was simply making a lighthearted remark but Meg felt instinctively that underneath Sara was much more serious about what she had just said than she was prepared to admit.

'That could explain the seeming disinterest of the people on the boats,' said Kevin suddenly. 'John said that they don't seem to land anywhere unless they do it under cover of darkness. Well perhaps they do just that. Perhaps they land on Samson under cover of darkness.'

'Could be,' agreed John.

Meg looked at them all. The letters and phone calls that she had received suddenly took on a more threatening aspect. This wasn't just one person on a mission. This was a whole group, even an organization perhaps, intent on getting whatever it was they wanted and whatever they thought she was hiding. She'd no idea what that was, but it had to be linked to the fact that they believed that she was a descendant, albeit a distant one, of Admiral Lord Nelson and Emma, Lady Hamilton. Of course, she thought in a flash, Nelson probably had little to do with it. Why should he? He was hardly in England anyway after 1798. Emma was an entirely different proposition altogether. It was her husband whose treasures they were seeking.

Unseen, shadows played around the distant shore.

Tresco, Isles of Scilly, 24th May 2008

John had suggested that Meg and Kevin should take a trip to the Valhalla on Tresco to see the carving that had been brought up from the Colossus. Saturday morning had dawned fair and dry so they decided to go across on the day-tripper boat from St Marys. John had a special booking from a group wanting to see the seals and puffins out on the Western Rocks so he was unable to take them himself. The wind had dropped and the twenty minute crossing was calm and uneventful. The boat landed its passengers at Carn Near on the island's southern coast because the tides were still low. A few grumbled about how far it was to walk to Old Grimsby but for Meg and Kevin it had been, in fact, extremely convenient. They walked up the small jetty and around Oliver's Battery, a small earthen gun emplacement used during the Civil War by Admiral Blake to fire on St Marys and force the Islands into submission under Oliver Cromwell's rule. From there it was a short diagonal distance across to the small heliport and Tresco Abbey Gardens where the Valhalla was housed. Kevin and Meg tramped across the sandy heath-land taking in the beauty of Appletree Bay just to the left of their chosen path.

''There's a good chance that King Arthur lies buried somewhere here,' said Meg unexpectedly. 'This area was full of apple trees. Once.' she added wistfully.

'I thought he was buried on the Isle of Avalon,' said Kevin.

'He was,' replied Meg. 'Avalon means apples.' Seeing Kevin's look she added, 'After Steven left I was free to pursue my own interests. I joined a local history group and then I started researching and reading up on the Scillies because I knew that my family had originally come from the Islands.'

'Would Steven have objected to you doing that when you were together?' Kevin asked.

'Probably,' said Meg. 'Steven always wanted me to be just a good little cook and bottle washer, there whenever he needed me. That's why I didn't go out to work or do anything else outside the home.'

'That must have been boring for you,' said Kevin before he could stop himself.

'I got used to it.' she said. 'I actually enjoy cooking and I read quite a lot. Steven didn't mind that as long as I was at his beck and call.'

'It must have been hard for you when he left,' said Kevin gently.

Meg smiled sadly. 'It was hard in lots of ways but in some ways it was liberating. I got a job in the local library and I was free to go out in the evenings. It gave me independence'

They had reached the little wooden hut which acted as an airport terminal for the helicopter. A small wooden tram was drawn up outside. Meg looked at her watch. 'I think the morning helicopter is due,' she said. 'There are only usually two helicopters a day to Tresco; one around eleven fifteen and the other about a quarter to four.'

Right on cue there was an all encompassing rumble from above which made them both look up. A red, blue and white Sikorsky helicopter was hovering unsteadily as it descended slowly towards the ground. They watched it land, rocking slightly on its wheels as it did so. The hatch door was opened and people scurried down the steps trying to hold onto hats and hairstyles against the gale whipped up by the rotating blades. Meg and Kevin could feel the wind against their faces from where they stood. Within five minutes all incoming passengers and cargo had been unloaded and all outgoing passengers and their luggage re-loaded, then the helicopter turned its big black nose into the wind and rose gracefully back into the air, heading once more for Penzance on the mainland some thirty miles distant.

There was a wooden gate behind the airport hut beyond which lay a path to the Abbey Gardens. There had been an abbey on Tresco from the tenth century to the sixteenth century but the present building dated only from the 1840s when Augustus Smith, the Lord Proprietor, had built a large and comfortable house for himself. Not without ideas of grandeur he had also included state rooms within his home in case royalty came to stay. Meg and Kevin walked along the path and came out close to the entrance to the Abbey Gardens. They paid their entrance fee and decided on a quick cup of coffee in the small café before beginning their visit. They took their coffee to one of the wooden tables outside and sat down. The waitress had put a small almond biscuit in a wrapper on each saucer for them to have with their coffee. As they unwrapped the biscuits two sparrows came and sat expectantly on the edge of their table.

'They're very tame,' said Kevin, feeding one of the birds a few crumbs. The other sparrow looked beseechingly at Meg. She gave in to the blackmail of the appeal in its small dark eyes and gave the bird a tiny piece of her biscuit. The sparrow pecked at it appreciatively.

'Spoiled might be a better word, she said, 'but most of the visitors who come here love the birdlife in the Islands and can't resist giving them the odd titbits. These birds aren't stupid. They soon suss out how to make a cushy living.'

Kevin grinned. 'Something I've never quite mastered. Maybe I should study their methods.' He drank some of his coffee. 'I used to come here quite a lot with my parents and then later I brought Heather. She was quite knowledgeable about botany and she loved the Gardens. She said that originally it would just have been a kitchen garden for the Abbey where they grew fruit and vegetables and also herbs for their potions. It was Augustus Smith who expanded the Gardens and made collecting rare and exotic plants something of a lifetime hobby. He used to beg seeds and cuttings from friends and visitors and at one time made a thorough nuisance of himself at Kew Gardens asking for cuttings of the more unusual plants.'

Meg nodded agreement. 'Yes I know he did; but it's a wonderful collection here now so I hope Kew have forgiven him for being such a pest.' She paused and sipped at her coffee, trying to pluck up the courage to ask her next question.

'It's the first time you've talked about Heather,' she said tentatively. 'Was the break-up very awful for you? She could see the pain in Kevin's eyes and cursed herself for her insensitivity. 'Sorry. Maybe I shouldn't ask' she added.

Kevin tried to smile.

'No, it's OK,' he said. 'Time I did talk about it. It was awful but it wasn't like you and Steven. We were very close at first. I thought we were like twin souls. Friends used to call us Hev and Kev. Made us sound like a couple of Cockneys on a day trip to Blackpool.' He laughed ruefully. 'I think we just simply grew apart. We wanted different things. She was very keen to have children but I wasn't ready for them. I wanted to travel. Places to go, people to see. Then one day I came home from work and she wasn't there. She'd left a note saying that she needed some time alone to think. She never came back,' he finished sadly.

'I'm so sorry.' Meg's eyes were full of sympathy. 'I think it's always harder if you're the one that's been left.'

'I think you're right,' said Kevin. He drained his coffee and stood up. 'Come on. Let's not brood. Let's go and do what we came to do.'

They wandered the sunlit avenues of the Gardens admiring the array of trees, bushes, shrubs, ferns, flowers and cacti, and picked their way down the steep flight of steps to the lower levels. At the top of the steps stood a bust of what looked like Neptune, but which some marine experts believed to be the figurehead of 'old Father Thames' taken from a local 19th century wreck. Finally they came to the Valhalla. It was a wooden shed and lean-to tucked away in a corner of the Gardens; a far cry from the legendary hall of the same name in which the Norwegian god, Odin, had received the souls of those who had died heroically in battle. Its purpose was pretty much the same though Meg reflected. There were a number of ship's figureheads and stern boards on display, all relics from ships which had foundered in the Islands. They wandered around looking at them and reading the little information notices besides each exhibit. Suddenly Kevin gave a cry.

'Over here! Look! I've found the stern board from Colossus!'
Meg hurried over. A wooden board some fifteen or sixteen feet long was mounted on the wall. Carved leafy scrolls flanked a central regal crown.

'The only thing is,' said Kevin thoughtfully, 'it doesn't look big enough really to have come from a ship like the Colossus.'

'No,' Meg agreed absently, reading the notice by the side of it.

'In fact it says it only might be the stern board of Colossus. It could have come from another ship.

'They must have found it close enough to the Colossus for them to think it had belonged to the ship.' Kevin was studying it closely.

'The crown looks rather like St Edward's crown. You know, that crown is actually too heavy to wear comfortably apparently; but the Queen ordered that a stylized version of it be used in the Royal Coat of Arms for the UK.' Kevin said, as though he was reading from a guide book.

Meg stared at him in astonishment.

'Are you an authority on the Crown Jewels?' she asked.

He looked at her sheepishly.

'I had to write an article about the Crown Jewels in 2004. It was the 800th anniversary of bad King John losing the original Anglo-Saxon crown jewels in The Wash. My then editor thought it would be a fun thing to do. Once the Yeoman Warders of the Tower realised I was genuine, and not out to steal the Crown Jewels, they proved to be mines of information.'

'Doesn't help really with identifying whether or not the stern board came from Colossus though,' said Meg.

'No,' Kevin agreed, 'but you have to admit it's interesting.'

'I wonder where the figure is?' Meg was looking around. 'It doesn't appear to be here.

'No. Oscar isn't outdoors,' said a voice.

They both turned round. A tall man with dark curly hair and a weather-beaten face stood in front of them. He was wearing dark blue overalls and a pair of green wellington boots which had seen better days.

'Mike Tomkins,' he said holding out his hand to them. 'I'm a gardener for Tresco Estate. I was working round the back and I heard you wondering about the figure. We call him Oscar. He's not kept outside with the others.'

'Why is that?' asked Meg.

'Conservation,' said Mike. 'The other things here were all found on dry land, but Oscar has been under water for two hundred years and they say he will crumble if he's exposed to the elements.'

'Is there any way can we get to see him?' Kevin looked disappointed.

'Oh, simple.' Mike grinned. 'I've got a key. I'll let you into the back room.'

He walked to a door at the rear of the Valhalla and fished a key out of his pocket. The carved figure stood in a glass case in the centre of the room.

'Not ideal', said Mike standing back to let them have a look. 'We're trying to decide how best to house Oscar and display him but for now this is the best we can do.'

The label on the case read:
'The 3.3m high elm carving of a man in neo-classical dress was recovered from HMS Colossus, one of Nelson's Mediterranean Fleet, which ran aground on the Islands in 1798. It has been described as one of the most important historic carvings in a British naval context. The figure would have originally been on the port side of the stern on a round headed window opening.'

[CISMAS]

Oscar was a strange and intricately carved figure with a rather wild looking face. His figure was not quite complete.

'Like Nelson himself,' said Meg with a nervous laugh. 'Right eye and right arm missing'. In spite of the warmth of the day she shivered.

They thanked Mike Tomkins for having shown them Oscar and headed off across the small lawn in front of the Valhalla towards the end of the Gardens. Another wooden gate led down a tarmac road which seemed to have attracted a large number of cyclists. The road wound its way through an avenue of tall Monterey pines and finally emerged onto the coastal track. Meg was enjoying the scenery and the feel of the island but Kevin was unusually quiet. As they walked along the path only a few feet above the sparkling sea Meg asked him what was wrong.

'Nothing really,' said Kevin, 'but it's a bit odd that there was only one.'

'Sorry?' Meg did not immediately follow his drift.

'There was just one carved figure. That carving represented only one side of the window. What about the other side? There must have been another carving on the other side for the sake of symmetry if nothing else.'

Meg looked at him. He was right of course. It would hardly have been a one sided window, especially on a ship as splendid as Colossus had been. So why hadn't another figure been found.

'Perhaps it just didn't survive,' she said. 'The ship was lying on her port side so maybe the other side remained exposed and was destroyed.'

'Possibly,' said Kevin, 'but I think she broke her back when she sank so it may have sheared off and be still lying down there buried somewhere.

Behind them faint shadows drifted in the white sand beneath a brilliant blue sky.

Naples, Italy, 5th November 1798

Nelson stood on the deck of the Vanguard and watched Naples slowly come into view through the sea fret. The late autumn sun gave the city an ethereal quality as it shimmered through the mist. He'd been away from Emma for just three weeks and yet it felt like three years. Part of him could not wait to return to Emma's charms. Part of him chaffed against the implications of being in the city once more. He knew that Maria Carolina was becoming increasingly anxious for Naples to declare war on the French so that the death of her sister, Marie Antoinette, five years before, might be avenged. He was reasonably certain that little would have happened in his absence since Maria Carolina's husband, Ferdinand, was considered to be generally quite ineffectual. However, once the Queen knew that Nelson was back in town she would step up her demands. He doubted that Naples could raise enough troops to confront the French army and he himself would not be able to give adequate support with sea power. Nelson knew that this battle would be essentially a land battle but the Queen either couldn't or wouldn't recognize this fact.

As Vanguard swept around to berth at the quay Nelson caught sight of Colossus moored and swaying gently on the incoming tide. She had made good time in returning from Gibraltar where he had sent her after relieving her siege of Malta. She was by now very badly in need of a re-fit but Nelson didn't want the ship to undergo repairs at Naples because he didn't trust either the French or Maria Carolina's rashness in her eagerness to do battle with the French army. He felt jaded and he was too tired to make any firm decisions now. He would go ashore, clean himself up after his time at sea, and then he would visit Emma. After a good night's sleep he would feel refreshed and able to think coherently. The Vanguard docked and the gang-plank was lowered. Giving a smart salute, Nelson marched off the ship and down into the city.

St Marys, Isles of Scilly, 26th May 2008

A loud knocking at the door interrupted Kevin just as he was switching on his laptop after breakfast. He was renting a self catering cottage in Old Town which had been the main settlement on St Marys until the emphasis had shifted to Hugh Town in the eighteenth century. The cottage faced the pretty twelfth century parish church of St Marys across the bay. This view was one of the things Kevin liked most about the cottage and was the main reason he always tried to rent it whenever he came to Scilly. It also had the advantage of being close to the Old Town Inn who were members of CAMRA and served really good beer. The walls of the cottage lay thick and snug under a low slate roof. It had two bedrooms and a small shower room with a toilet upstairs while downstairs there was a comfortable lounge and a homely kitchen with a well scrubbed old wooden table. A bit early for social calls thought Kevin and wondered who was knocking so frantically. He opened the door to find Meg standing on the doorstep looking pale and flustered.

'Sorry to bother you so early but I've received a letter and I don't know what to do about it,' she said without preamble.

Kevin stood aside to let her enter. He noticed that her hands were shaking as she took off her jacket. She looked so different to the calm happy person she had been the previous day when they had spent the whole day at the cottage, checking and collating all the information they had gathered together about the Colossus. They had gone for a Sunday lunch at the Old Town Inn where they had both tucked into roast beef and Yorkshire pudding and had then spent hours talking over their drinks and coffee. She had been relaxed and natural with him and he had enjoyed their time together very much. Now, as she sat down, he was horrified to see that she had been crying.

'Meg! Whatever's happened?' he asked with concern.

Meg fished the letter out of her bag.

'Look at this. Mrs Woodcock brought it to me when I was eating my breakfast. It was delivered by hand so whoever wrote it must be here on the Islands.'

Kevin took it from her. It was typed on plain white paper and there was no address or signature.

'Dear Meg Nelson,

Hope you enjoyed your trips to Samson. Beautiful island isn't it? Did your friend think so too?

Patience is beginning to run out now and it's time you stopped this ridiculous pretence that you don't know anything.

You will be contacted again soon and it would be in your own interests to start being honest. Otherwise who knows what may happen.'

Meg sat twisting a handkerchief in her hands.

'It's in pretty much the same vein as the others I've received but they're starting to become insistent and that last sentence is definitely some sort of threat. I hope you don't think I'm being paranoid but I'm frightened. Whoever wrote it is here on the Islands and that's not a nice thought.'

Kevin was inclined to agree with her. This was pretty nasty stuff and it was obvious now that the mysterious figure they had seen on Samson had been spying on them. He took hold of her hands to try and comfort her. Her fingers felt ice cold.

'Of course I don't think you're being paranoid. Why should I? I agree with you that whoever wrote this is here in Scilly and must be spying on both of us. It's not a pleasant thought. Do you happen to have any of the other letters with you?'

Meg shook her head. 'They're in a drawer at home. It never occurred to me to bring them with me.'

'No reason it should have done,' said Kevin. 'You weren't to know you'd be followed here.'

He stood up. 'Look. I'll make us a pot of tea. You look as though you could do with some. Then we'll have a brainstorm and try to work out who could be doing this and why.'

Meg nodded gratefully. Kevin switched on the electric fire in the lounge to warm her and went to put the kettle on. She had gone over and over all the possibilities in her mind so often she felt she could no longer think straight. Then she remembered the meeting with John and Sara Fisher and what she had suddenly realised as they were leaving. Kevin came back into the room with two mugs of tea, which he placed on the low coffee table, and sat down opposite her.

Meg picked up her mug and cradled it in her hands. She took a couple of sips of the hot liquid and drew a deep breath.

'I've been thinking,' she said. 'We've done a lot of research on Colossus and we've seen the unusual carving and her stern board. We went to Samson and we saw where the Colossus sank. We've read some of the diving records. But so far it's all been about the ship and Nelson and his fleet; plus of course the fact it seems that I may be distantly related to Nelson.'

'What are you getting at?' asked Kevin, feeling that he was missing something somewhere but couldn't quite see what it was.

'Nelson only had the one child so if I am related to Nelson through his daughter then I am also related to Emma Hamilton and it was her husband whose Greek and Etruscan treasures were lost when the Colossus sank.'

'Ah,' said Kevin, the light beginning to dawn in his mind. 'So you think it maybe has more to do with Sir William Hamilton's losses than with the ship itself.'

'Yes,' said Meg. 'His collections were very important and they formed the basis of the Greek and Roman Antiquities departments at the British Museum.'

'Collections?' asked Kevin. 'I didn't know he had more than one.'

'Oh yes.' Meg was warming to her subject now. 'I read a biography of him just before I came out to the Scillies. It was fascinating. He was the first real modern archaeologist; a good hundred years or so before Schliemann discovered the city of Troy. He didn't favour just digging on ancient sites, taking what you could find and then simply filling the holes in again. He made careful notes and he drew remains and relics in situ and he believed in keeping groups of objects found together in one place for the purposes of provenance and display.'

She paused and then asked 'You've heard of the Portland Vase, haven't you?'

Kevin nodded.

'It was made in Rome a few years before the birth of Christ and it was part of Sir William's first collection which he sold to the British Museum in 1772,' she continued. 'The vase was later loaned to Josiah Wedgewood. He made a number of successful copies of it during the 1790s and it's been popular ever since. The rest of the first collection included Greek and Italian vases, red and black Athenian figure ware, terra-cottas, and bronzes; and there were also gems and coins, some Etruscan and Egyptian scarabs and seal stones, and a number of everyday items used for sacred, farming or domestic purposes.'

Kevin was impressed by her knowledge and said so. Meg found herself blushing. 'It was all in the biography,' she said.

'What was in the second collection then?' asked Kevin.

'Mostly Etruscan items, replied Meg. 'Rhytons, jugs, vases, that sort of thing. The Etruscans were responsible for the founding of Rome so their relics were considered to be very important. There was also quite a lot of Greek stuff, I think, and there may have been some jewellery as well. There was enough to fill eight large wooden boxes and that was only half the collection.'

'Oh,' said Kevin, surprised. 'So not all his collection was lost.'

'No,' said Meg. 'Apparently at first Hamilton was relieved because he believed that the eight boxes lost contained less important items; then he discovered that in fact the eight boxes he'd kept contained the more unimportant stuff and the best of his collection had gone down with the Colossus.'

'That must have been hard for him, 'said Kevin. 'All those years spent collecting and all his hard work aimed at recording and preserving them. Then he discovers that they've ended up at the bottom of the sea.'

'I know,' Meg agreed. 'It's said that he went a little bit crazy after that; but I think Nelson and Emma's love affair was also getting to him. Discretion was the thing in those times and he'd been made a very public cuckold by those two.'

'A what?' asked Kevin.

'Cuckold,' said Meg. It's an old fashioned term for a man whose wife was having an affair.'

'Right!' Kevin grinned. 'Only for a man?'

'Oh yes,' Meg said. 'The women didn't count back then. Still don't in some cases,' she added almost to herself.

Kevin looked at her, an expression of sympathy in his eyes. Her treatment by her ex-husband really had got to her. Blast Hamilton, he thought, then sat bolt upright in his chair.

'Meg!' he almost shouted her name. She looked at him startled.

'You know it really is the most fantastic coincidence that your ex-husband's name is Hamilton. You don't suppose that he, well that he..........'

'Is related in some way to Sir William?' Meg finished slowly for him. 'I honestly don't know. I'd never really thought about it. I mean, Hamilton is quite a common name; but now you mention it...' her voice trailed off as she realised that she'd never really known much about Steven's family at all. She hadn't thought to ask him because, to be honest, it hadn't seemed very important at the time. It wasn't possible, was it? It surely wasn't possible.

Down on the beach swirling shadows linked in lacy patterns and then parted again.

Naples, Italy, 6th November 1798

Nelson awoke refreshed from a deep sleep. It was strange that his surroundings were still and not swaying from side to side as they usually did when he was in his cabin on the ship. Sometimes it was impossible to get much sleep at all on board, especially if the weather was rough. He rang for the maid and ordered his breakfast tray as he let his thoughts roam back to the previous evening. Emma had been ecstatic to see him.

'Darling, darling,' she'd murmured as she clung to him, burying her face in his naval uniform jacket. 'I've missed you sorely. I thought this day would never come.'

The sentiments were a bit dramatic after just three weeks absence, Nelson thought, but he was flattered. Fanny had never been that pleased to see him, even after months of separation. Of course Fanny was more reserved and more refined than Emma but the occasional show of enthusiasm from her would not have come amiss. Nelson had dined with both Sir William and Emma and then Sir William said he had some business to which he must attend and left them alone together in the withdrawing room. Nelson loved the Hamilton's villa. It was elegant and luxurious but, at the same time, also extremely cosy and welcoming. The marble floors and wide marble staircases and expensive hangings made him imagine that he could be living in a villa in ancient Rome; and the bathrooms had every convenience, even a ready supply of asses milk for him to bathe in. It was positively decadent. They had nothing like this in England. Emma had hung a painting of the Battle at Cape St Vincent over the marble fireplace in his honour and he was touched by that simple gesture.

She'd snuggled up to him affectionately, chattering away about inconsequential matters but he couldn't help having the feeling that something was on her mind. He hoped it wasn't bad news and at last he could stand it no longer.

'Dearest Emma,' he began hesitantly, 'it is so good to see you and to be with you again, but you seem a little pre-occupied somehow. Is there something that you want to tell me?'

There had been a moment's silence during which Nelson's heart had constricted painfully at the thought of what she might have to say. Then Emma spoke.

'It is William,' she said. 'He is so dreadfully worried.'

Hiding his relief that it was nothing worse, Nelson had asked her what the problem was.

'He feels that the Queen will not wait much longer to declare war against the French, said Emma hesitantly, 'and he thinks that we may have to leave Naples.' She paused. 'You know that he collects all manner of things from famous historical places and he does not want his prize collections to fall into the hands of the French because he values them highly. About twenty years ago he sent a huge collection of ancient pottery and statues and coins from Greece, and here in Italy, back to England and he sold them all to the British Museum. Now he wants to do the same thing with the remainder of his collections but he is worried that he will not have the chance to do so before Maria Carolina mobilises her troops. He knows that she cannot win against the French.'

Nelson nodded his agreement gravely. Emma had looked up at him, her blue eyes large and beseeching.

'He wondered if perhaps one of your ships could take his precious collection back to England. Oh, he would not expect a ship to make a special journey just for him, but if there is a ship returning home soon perhaps she could take his collection as cargo. He does not want anyone to know, you see. It would be disturbing if people knew that he might be planning to leave so the situation is a little delicate.'

Nelson could well imagine the news that the British Envoy to Naples might be leaving the country would upset a fragile political situation. He also knew that ships sailing for England usually had a full complement of cargo and crew. Besides which the winter season was almost upon them when it was not wise for ships to risk the journey north through treacherous waters in appalling conditions. He patted Emma's hand reassuringly.

'I will see what can be done,' he said. 'Do not worry yourself further about it.'

Emma had shown her gratitude and he could still feel the taste of her kisses sweet upon his lips. He lay in the soft bed, thinking for a few minutes and then the answer came to him. He would send the Colossus. She needed to return to Portsmouth as soon as possible for a re-fit. Colossus was a fast ship and if she left soon then she should reach the safety of the English coast before the winter storms struck. Why hadn't he thought of that before. He would see Captain Murray about it as soon as possible.

There was a lot of noise and bustle down on the quay. Men shouting orders; provision carts arriving for the ships; cargoes being stacked ready for loading; hammering; decks being washed down with pails of water. Nelson slipped quietly aboard Colossus and made his way to Murray's cabin. He knew that he should find him there and he was right. George Murray was sitting at a large wooden desk busily engaged in painstakingly writing up the ship's log. He looked up in surprise as someone came into his cabin without knocking. When he saw it was Nelson he stood up smartly and the two men saluted each other.

'Morning, Murray,' said Nelson casually. 'Good to see you safely back. You did a fine job at Malta.'

'Thank you, Sir,' said Murray. 'We made good time and we've been back several days now. Just arrived yourself, Sir?'

'Last night,' said Nelson. 'Look, Murray, I think that Colossus badly needs a re-fit and you're low on fire-power since you gave me the cannon. I don't want the ship to have a refit here. The whole situation is so unstable it could blow at any moment. I don't want Colossus caught in the middle of that. She's a valuable ship. So I think the refit should be done in England.'

'Aye, Sir.' said Murray.

Captain Murray had willingly given three of the ship's cannon to Nelson before Colossus had sailed for Malta because Nelson's ship, Vanguard, had sustained some damage when both ships had been on convoy duty in the Mediterranean together earlier that year.

'Right!' said Nelson smartly. 'I think you should leave for England as soon as possible.'

Murray had looked at him, surprised, but pleased. He knew that what Nelson had said about the Colossus was true but it was a bit late in the year for setting sail on such a voyage. Still the Colossus was a fast enough ship and they should be back in England before the worst of the winter storms. Besides it would be good to be home for Christmas again. He had not seen his family for longer than he cared to remember.

Aye, Sir.' he said again.

'So do you think you could be ready to leave within a couple of days?' Nelson continued. 'Take some of the war wounded back with you. Oh, and there's a couple of boxes of freight I'd like carried on board as well.'

Murray thought for a moment. He could provision the ship immediately then it would be just a question of loading the cargo and passengers. He nodded. Giving a smile of satisfaction, Nelson bid him farewell and Murray went up on deck to give orders for making ready to sail.

St Marys, Isles of Scilly, 27th May 2008

Meg and Kevin were back at Dibble and Grub for lunch.

'Thought you'd deserted us!' the young waitress joked as she put two plates of Greek salad and a basket of freshly baked bread on the table.

'No chance of that,' said Kevin cheerfully, pouring another glass of cool white wine for Meg.

The day was still and hot and the sun beat down. They sat outside at a blue wooden table shaded by a large umbrella and glowed with the effects of both wine and sunshine. Tucking into their feta cheese and olives it was easy to imagine that they were hundreds of miles from Scilly on the warm shores of exotic Mediterranean countries.

'The only give-away is the temperature of the sea-water,' said Kevin. 'The Med is warm. Here in Scilly the sea is always cold.'

They had spent the morning continuing the work they had begun the previous afternoon. Meg was reading everything she could lay her hands on about Emma Hamilton. Most of what she found seemed to be centered on Emma's romance with Admiral Lord Nelson. Although Emma had lived with Sir William for twenty years, and was married to him for twelve of those years, it was Nelson on whom most writers dwelt. As they ate their lunch she told Kevin what she had discovered and how fascinating she had found Emma's story.

Emma Hamilton had been born Amy Lyon in 1761. Her father had died when she was just two months old and she had been brought up by her mother. In her teens she had worked as a maid in private houses and at Drury Lane Theatre in Covent Garden before being employed as a 'hostess' by Sir Harry Featherstonehaugh at his Uppark estate on the South Downs. She had become his mistress and they'd had an illegitimate daughter. The child was born when Emma was twenty; a girl who was also named Emma. Little Emma was adopted; although she continued to see her real mother fairly frequently while she was still a child. Emma had then formed a relationship with the Honourable Charles Francis Greville. By now her beauty was legendary and during this time she had sat for the painter, George Romney, on several occasions. When Greville wished to marry a wealthy heiress he had sent Emma to stay with his uncle, Sir William Hamilton, in Naples. It was here that Emma had first begun to develop her 'Attitudes'; based on George Romney's idea of combining classical poses with dancing and acting in a silently mimed performance. She had learned enough in her time at Covent Garden about style and timing and costume to ensure that her 'Attitudes' had become wildly successful. In 1791 she and Sir William had married which had given her respectability and the title of Lady Hamilton. Sir William was much older and they had no children. Her second illegitimate child had been Nelson's daughter, Horatia.

'She sounds to have been quite a girl!' said Kevin, half jokingly, half admiringly.

'Bit racy,' laughed Meg. 'I think she might have been disappointed in me as a descendant.'

'Oh I don't know about that,' said Kevin.

Meg blushed at his words and to cover her embarrassment said quickly 'How about you? How's your work gone?'

Kevin had been working on his commission to write an article about the Colossus and Sir William's collections. He had begun with the ship leaving Naples with its precious cargo and followed the journey that had ended with her sinking in the Southward Well off Samson.

'It's amazing you know,' he said, finishing his glass of wine, 'that they actually managed to get everyone off that ship as well as the amount of cargo that was saved. Apparently they couldn't land on Samson because of the sea conditions so the gigs had to row right round to Bryher. I mean imagine doing that with six hundred people, two hundred of whom were wounded, plus some of the cargo and a dead admiral to boot!'

'Did they take everyone down to St Mary's afterwards then, when the weather was calmer?' asked Meg.

'No,' replied Kevin. 'Some went to Tresco; but the rest stayed on Bryher. It took the Biblical forty days before everyone could be got off the Islands and taken back to the mainland.'

'So none of them went to St Marys?' said Meg wonderingly.

'Only Admiral Shuldham and he was dead anyway. I think they took his coffin down to the church to sort of lie in state.'

'What about the cargo?' asked Meg.

'I think that was probably locked up either in Star Castle or the Custom House. The Scillonian boatmen spent some time assisting the Admiralty in salvage work on Colossus after the storm had blown itself out; so there would be quite a bit more than what had originally been saved. St Marys was nearer as well.'

Meg nodded. The waitress brought them coffee and they lingered over it, each unwilling to go back to their work on such a glorious afternoon. When Kevin suggested a walk before they returned to their respective tasks she quickly agreed. They climbed up Buzza Hill and then walked along to Peninnis Head. There was a slight welcome breeze up on the headland which ruffled the grasses and their hair in much the same manner. Gulls soared and swooped and called to each other in that mournful voice said to be like those of lost souls. The sun glittered on the water and there was a peace to the afternoon that both of them knew could not be found anywhere else.

They were passing the grinding stone of an old corn mill when Kevin said, 'Time for tiffin. Let's sit on Harold Wilson's seat.'

A small plaque on a wooden bench announced that this had been one of the former Labour Prime Minister's favourite spots in Scilly.

'He had taste. I'll say that for him,' said Meg, flopping down gratefully.

'He loved the Islands,' said Kevin. 'In fact he's buried in Old Town churchyard. Did you know he held a press conference on Samson once?'

'No! Why?' asked Meg, surprised.

'Some world crisis had arisen while he was on holiday and everyone wanted to know his thoughts,' said Kevin. 'He didn't want to leave the Islands at that point so he thought it would be nice and different if he called a press conference here. It was a beautiful summer's day and he insisted they all went out to Samson. There's a photograph of him, just dressed in shorts and a t-shirt and sandals, standing on the East Porth with the world's press around him.'

Meg giggled. 'That must have been an education for some of them. I wonder what they made of Samson.'

They sat in reflective silence for a few moments until Meg said, 'It's almost unbelievable that no one was lost when the Colossus sank. I know a lot of valuable stuff was lost that night but in human terms the rescue operation was a complete and probably unexpected success.'

'There was one fatality,' said Kevin, 'but he didn't drown.'

'Who was that?' asked Meg. 'What happened?' she added.

'It was the quartermaster, Richard King. Captain Murray had ordered him to take soundings when the Colossus was held fast on the rocks. King went up the main mast but he lost his footing and fell when Colossus lurched unexpectedly on the incoming tide. He hit his head on the deck and was killed instantly.'

'Richard King,' said Meg thoughtfully. 'Now there's another strange coincidence. The girl Steven married after our divorce was called Janine King.'

'Did Steven ever show any interest in the Colossus?' asked Kevin abruptly.

'Not really, 'said Meg. 'At least, not to me. He knew about it of course.

We were over in Scilly the year they were bringing up a lot of the stuff.
It was the talk of the Islands at the time but he never said much.'

'He could have listened though,' said Kevin. 'He knew about your family history.'

'Well, yes, he did,' said Meg, 'but surely I'd have known if he was interested in
the Colossus.'

'Maybe.' Kevin shrugged. 'Just that all these same surnames are a bit too much of
a coincidence. I could accept one coincidence, but three?' He thought for a
moment. 'Pushing the odds a little isn't it?'

They stood up and walked the short remaining distance to the squat lighthouse.
The whitewashed building stood close to the cliff edge among some tortured
geological specimens at whose origins they could only wonder. Kevin stood looking
out to sea with a faraway look in his eyes. Meg watched him, wondering if he was
thinking of Heather, but when he turned and spoke it was evident that his mind
had been a million miles from thoughts of Heather.

'I know this might be uncomfortable for you, Meg, and I'm sorry, but presumably
you know the exact date of Steven's second marriage.'

'Yes I do.' Meg's eyes clouded at the memory. 'I couldn't forget it. Our divorce
became absolute on the 22nd October last year and he married her on the 24th
October.' She looked shrewdly at Kevin. 'Why do you want to know?'

'Just for interest I'd like to try and trace Janine's family history. If I know the date
of their wedding I can get a copy of the wedding certificate and that will give the
name of Janine's father and her age. From that I can try and get hold of a copy
of her birth certificate which will give her mother's name and where she was born.
Then hopefully I can trace back her origins.'

'You don't seriously think that she really was related to Richard King?' asked Meg
in disbelief. 'King is also quite a common surname. Lots of people have it.'

'Yes,' said Kevin, 'but lots of people don't marry a Nelson, who was actually related
to Lord Nelson himself, and then just happen to re-marry to someone else who
might just happen to be a descendant of the quartermaster on one of Nelson's
ships, which just happened to go down off the island from which his first wife's
family came, taking a lot of valuable stuff down with her which just happened to
belong to a namesake of his.'

Meg stared at him doubtfully. 'It could just all be coincidence,' she said.

'Possibly,' conceded Kevin, 'but why was Steven in such indecent haste to
re-marry? Was she pregnant?'

Meg shook her head. That was what she had thought as well but time had proved her wrong. Maybe Kevin did have a point. Why had Steven been so anxious to marry Janine King? Was her family also linked to the Colossus? Were they too supposed to know something or have something in their possession that might be valuable? If Kevin did establish a link between Janine King and Richard King then what did that mean? The answer, when it came, was unwelcome. It meant that Steven might be involved in the attempts to intimidate her. Unbidden, tears came to her eyes and she turned away. Kevin, now contrite at having upset her, put his arm around her shoulders to comfort her. Meg turned again and, burying her face against his chest, sobbed her heart out.

Far below on the tumbled rocky shore shadows wove patterns through the shifting sands.

Naples, Italy, 7th November 1798

Emma had received Nelson's news with great pleasure and had rushed to tell her husband as soon as Nelson had left the previous evening.

'William!' she had cried. 'William! There will be a ship sailing to England in two days. Nelson has said that it will transport your collections. You must have them packed and ready as soon as possible.'

Sir William had looked at her and smiled sadly. To tell the truth he was becoming just a little weary of the time that Emma was spending with Nelson. Of course the man was a hero and deserved every consideration but Sir William would have liked to see a bit more of his own wife. He'd secretly rather enjoyed the three weeks which Nelson had spent at sea. Without the constant distraction of Nelson's presence Emma had been sweetly attentive to him and Sir William had the pleasure of her company all to himself. The political situation was also of great concern to him. He was tired of life in Naples and Maria Carolina's constant demands. He'd been there for over thirty years and he'd done his duty, God knew. In 1796 he had written to London asking to be relieved of his duties but so far he had not heard if his wish was to be granted. Somehow he must soldier on until the orders relieving him of his post arrived.

Still there was the compensation that it seemed as though his treasured collections would be saved. He knew that the Queen was on the brink of declaring war on the French and now that Nelson had returned it would give her every incentive to go ahead with her crazy scheme. Sir William had realised, if she had not, that if the French marched on Naples, they might all have to leave at a moment's notice; probably with little more than they could carry. He supposed he should be grateful to Emma that she had wheedled Nelson into agreeing to help with his dilemma and to Nelson for finding a ship to transport his collections at such short notice; but he was also just a little resentful.

Sir William had called two of his most trusted servants, Giorgio and Lucas, to him early on the morning of the 7th and had given them very precise instructions. They were to obtain a number of wooden crates and plenty of linen sheeting and they were to do this discreetly. Then they were to join him in the library. He would require their services exclusively for two days and they would, of course, not discuss with anyone what they would be helping their master to do. Giving orders that he was not to be disturbed, Sir William took a key from the drawer of his desk and unlocked the door of the room where he kept most of his valuable collection.
It was a handsomely proportioned room with tall windows which lit the displays well. He could see Emma through one of the windows. She was sitting by one of the ornamental fountains prattling away to Nelson. Nelson sat to her left, gazing at her with rapt attention. As Sir William watched, Nelson plucked a flower and gave it to Emma. She smiled at him and lightly kissed his cheek. Sir William turned away. Once all this business was sorted out he really would have to do something about the situation.

Bryher, Isles of Scilly, 28th May 2008

Kevin had worked late into the night trying to establish Janine King's origins. Now he was waiting for return emails. Thank God for modern technology he thought, otherwise he would have been making frequent and expensive trips to the mainland. This morning he had rung John Fisher and had suggested that the four of them should meet up again. John had suggested that they all went out for a pub meal, but Kevin had declined the invitation. He wanted more privacy. Instead he had invited John and Sara to the cottage for supper. Kevin wasn't a bad cook but he felt sure that Meg would help him with the meal. She'd gone home early the previous evening, saying that she wanted to be by herself for a while, but they'd agreed to meet up this morning to decide what to do next. Kevin felt tired and irritable. He'd had little sleep and if he saw Hamilton now he'd want to punch him for all the trouble he seemed to be causing. He looked out of the window. The sun was shining and tiny fleecy clouds raced across the sky. It was a beautiful morning. To hell with Hamilton and the Colossus and all the mystery and aggravation, he thought. He and Meg were going to have a day off. Grabbing his jacket he hurried out to meet her.

Meg bought some more sun cream from Douglas' chemists and then went to the Mermaid. She and Kevin had agreed to meet by the front door which led directly onto the street. It was far too early for the pub to be open. The side doors were open and barrels of beer were being humped noisily from the back of a trailer down the steps to the cellars. Meg leaned against the harbour wall and looked across the water to Bryher and Samson. It was a perfect day and the islands looked very inviting in the sunshine.

'Hi!' Kevin's voice sang in her ear.

She turned round and smiled.

'Hi. Sorry about yesterday. I just felt I needed to be alone after I realised that Steven might be involved in all of this.' She gestured vaguely round at the islands.

'Not a problem,' said Kevin. 'I invited John and Sara to supper at the cottage tonight. Perhaps you would give me a hand with the meal. That is if you've got no other plans for tonight.'

'As if I'd refuse an invitation like that,' laughed Meg. 'Do we need to go shopping?'

'Maybe later,' said Kevin. 'I think we deserve a bit of a break. Do you fancy going up to Bryher for the day? Have a walk, get some lunch, blow away the cobwebs.'

'Love to,' said Meg enthusiastically. Like Kevin she too felt the need to get away from all the problems for a while.

As the boat made its way up the Channel past Samson both Kevin and Meg, by common consent, turned their backs and watched instead the coast of Tresco glide by; past Appletree Bay and the former World War One flying boat base where the old bakehouse had stood, and which now sported several expensive holiday chalets, to New Grimsby and the tower keep of Cromwell's Castle beyond. They landed at the Bar on Bryher, a large sandy beach which had a sturdy wooden quay built twenty years ago as part of one of Anneka Rice's 'challenges'. Climbing off the boat Kevin and Meg trudged through deep sand to reach a stony pathway which led towards Kitchen Porth and the coastal path. An old red telephone box stood in a nearby field and an inquisitive black dog was trying to open the door with one of its front paws. At the top of Kitchen Porth was a long low white-washed Scillonian cottage. Next to the cottage an old barn had been converted into a bar, restaurant and coffee shop. A large sign proclaimed that the place was called Fraggle Rock. Outside the barn were a number of wooden bench tables, some of which had couples and families sitting at them. By tacit agreement they both flopped down onto a spare seat. A young barefoot girl in jeans brought out two cups of freshly brewed coffee and placed them on the table. A tabby cat had followed her and now sat looking up at them hopefully. Meg sipped her coffee appreciatively.

'Doesn't get much better than this,' she said happily, looking all around her and at the sunlight shimmering on the sea.

Kevin agreed. He'd always been fond of Bryher and sometimes on the island he felt as though he'd somehow stepped back in time. Thoughts of the Colossus came unbidden into his mind and he wondered vaguely how on earth Bryher had managed to accommodate the whole complement of the Colossus crew and passengers. The whole island was only a mile long by half a mile wide. Today there was just a handful of families living there although he knew that there had been a larger population in times past.

They left Fraggle Rock and walked up the cliffs on the other side of Kitchen Porth. The bracken was high, sometimes coming above their waists and they had to hold their arms up to avoid any friction. As they reached the summit the bracken grew less and they came out by a large rock on which a couple of gulls were sitting, staring unblinkingly at them. Kevin shooed the gulls away.

'This is known locally as the Thinking Rock,' he said. 'Not because it thinks itself,' he added with a grin, 'but because lots of people like to sit here and think.'

He clambered up and pulled Meg up after him. Behind them the expanse of Shipman Head Down sloped away. Cromwell's Castle lay just yards away, separated from Bryher by a narrow channel of water across which sunbeams danced merrily like hundreds of tiny glow worms. They looked down onto the keep and could see people moving around as though they were busy little ants. Meg sat on the rock, cross-legged, and Kevin joined her.

'I saw the eclipse up here,' she said. 'You know, in August 1999? The Scillies were the only place where the eclipse was total. The complete silence was unnerving as the darkness spread across the land and it was quite eerie. There were a number of us and even the children were quiet. We knew that it should only last a matter of minutes and yet all of us had a moment of doubt that the sun would return. When it did the relief was palpable. Bottles of champagne were cracked open and total strangers hugged one another. It was an incredible experience.'

'I know, said Kevin, 'I was here too. Yet another amazing coincidence!'

Both of them sat for a few minutes lost in their own thoughts, savouring moments taken from time. A wet nose licking Meg's foot broke the spell. Looking down she saw a black and white border collie with big brown eyes looking up at her and wagging its tail furiously.

'We'd better go,' she said. 'I think it's trying to tell us that we've had our turn up here.'

Slithering down off the Thinking Rock they made their way across Shipman Head Down with its myriad patterns of cairns and low stone walls; the remnants of an ancient sacred landscape which belonged to a time before history. Below the waves crashed and pounded the angry rocks of the aptly named Hell Bay that had struck terror into the hearts of seafaring men in the days of sailing ships. They descended from Shipman Head Down onto Great Porth, a lonely stretch of sand and seaweed where, both Meg and Kevin knew, small whales were washed up from time to time. Behind Great Porth was a shallow lake with a couple of ducks swimming around in desultory fashion and beyond the lake lay the Hell Bay Hotel.

'Come on!' said Kevin. 'Lunch!'

The hotel was long, low, luxurious, and seemed to be mostly decorated in shades of blue. They sat outside on a wooden terrace, which had good views of Gweal Head and a fearsome looking rock named Castle Bryher, and shared a platter of locally caught fish served with lots of lemon wedges, fresh brown bread, and a small basket of French fries. The sun beat down until even the ducks left the lake and went off in search of a cooler place. There was a sunshade umbrella at their table and, after a struggle, Kevin put it up.

'I wonder where on earth all those people from the Colossus could have been accommodated', Meg said. 'Even this place was just a small fisherman's cottage back then. You can still see the old part if you go into the bar.'

'I was thinking the same thing this morning,' said Kevin. 'I don't know. Barns perhaps. The church. There might have been a little room in the cottages. It must all have been very cramped and uncomfortable.'

'They were alive,' said Meg simply. 'I don't suppose a bit of discomfort bothered them. They were used to it anyway.'

'There's the reading room and the village hall, of course,' said Kevin, 'but those buildings are twentieth century. There might have been an older village hall I suppose, or a church hall.'

'There were also a few more cottages in 1798, I think,' said Meg. 'It was before the days of Augustus Smith. He cleared a lot of people off the land to give those who were left a better standard of living. Only the eldest sons could inherit the farms and smallholdings. Younger sons had to leave and go to the mainland and make their own way in life.'

'Rather harsh, 'said Kevin.

'I know,' said Meg, 'but the practice of dividing and sub-dividing and then sub-dividing again all the fields was becoming ridiculous. Tiny portions of land were being farmed which couldn't sustain a single person, let alone a whole family. I'm not really a fan of Augustus Smith but something had to be done.'

After lunch they decided to walk around Droppy Nose Point and Rushy Bay before heading up Samson Hill and making their way back round to the quay where the boat would collect them. The sun was still hot and the Norrard Rocks floated dark and serene on the flat shining surface of a calm sea. A couple of seals stretched out lazily on the rocks. The Old School House lay at the top of a bay rather unattractively known as Stinking Porth. There seemed to have been two or three cottages which had been turned into one.

'This place was probably here in 1798,' said Meg, 'as well as the original fisherman's cottage buried in the Hell Bay Hotel complex.'

They turned inland towards a small restored boathouse where a local artist had made a studio with views that would have satisfied even Leonardo da Vinci.

'That too,' she added, pointing to the boathouse, 'and the film cottage.'

'The what?' asked Kevin.

'Don't you remember?' Meg asked with a twinkle in her eye. 'They made a full length feature film on the island at the end of the 1980s. Starred Helen Mirren and Paul Scofield. It was Bryher's fifteen minutes of fame. Helen Mirren is hot Hollywood property today.'

Kevin grinned. 'Of course I remember, but I didn't know that was the cottage they used. Something about whales, wasn't it?'

'When the Whales Came.' Meg supplied the title for him. 'I watched them filming a scene with David Suchet in front of Castle View. He's the definitive Poirot now.'

'Wasn't Castle View the cottage where the last inhabitant to leave Samson ended her days?' Kevin asked, dredging his memory for something he had read about it. 'I'm sure it was. She went there in 1855 and the place wasn't new then so it would probably have been standing in 1798 as well.'

They had turned from Rushy Bay and were beginning to climb a wide path which led up to Samson Hill.

'They built a cottage up here for the film, you know,' Meg said. 'It was burned to the ground for almost the last scene. Shame because it had looked so authentic. I've got some photographs of it somewhere.' She paused reflectively. 'I'm sure there would have been cottages on this hill at some time anyway.'

'Bit exposed,' said Kevin. 'Especially when it's windy.'

'Maybe,' Meg agreed, 'but they could have been built just in the lea of the hill. Stunning views and plenty of grazing land. Someone on the island still tethers their goats up here.'

Right on cue they heard a bleating and looked up to see a nanny goat and her kid regarding them with open curiosity. Someone had cleared the gorse from an area the size of a small field which the goats were grazing with relish. Just beyond the animals was a rectangle of assorted stones enclosing a flattish surface.

'Look! You can still see the remains of the cottage,' said Meg, pointing to the stones. 'I came up here again the year after filming had finished. They'd made a pretty good job of clearing up all the debris but they couldn't be bothered to dig up the foundations.'

Kevin looked around him. Meg had been right when she had said that there must have been cottages up here once. The spot was reasonably sheltered from the prevailing winds and the enthusiasm with which the goats were feeding meant that the grazing should have been good for the little black Dexter cattle for which the Islands had once been famous. The views were certainly stunning. He let his gaze sweep round in a one hundred and eighty degree arc and froze. Someone was standing on the North Hill of Samson watching them. The channel of water between Bryher and Samson was quite narrow. It was the sort of distance which should have been easy to swim but no-one did because of the strong currents. He rummaged in his knapsack for his binoculars which he'd finally remembered to bring with him and trained them onto the North Hill. Any doubts Kevin might have had were dispelled when the figure at once turned and began to run. An innocent person would have been unconcerned about the use of binoculars in such an environment. Kevin didn't get the chance to get a clear look at the figure but he was fairly certain that it was a man and quite a tall man.

Meg had stopped taking photographs and was staring at him in some alarm. 'What is it?' she asked in little more than a whisper.

There was no point in lying to her. 'I think our friendly neighbourhood watch is back again,' he said.

Far below them shadows kaleidoscoped together into the sand.

Naples, Italy, 8th November 1798

Sir William paced restlessly up and down in his library. His precious treasures had been carefully sorted and packed up and loaded onto the cart. He had catalogued all the items with painstaking care. Giorgio and Lucas had taken them to the quay and were doubtless unloading them at this very moment. Sir William had longed to go with them but knew that he did not dare to do so. The utmost discretion was needed and it was essential that the wooden crates should be seen as just a part of the cargo, provisions and supplies which were being loaded onto the ship. They must not be distinguished in any way as belonging to him. Down on the quay Captain Murray was anxious. He had expected the ship to be carrying about four hundred people but nearly another 200 sick and wounded were to travel as well. This meant loading extra supplies, provisions, barrels of fresh water and casks of ale. On top of all this it had been intimated to him that he was to take the body of Admiral Shuldham back to England for burial. The Admiral's body had been preserved and was encased in a lead coffin disguised as a packing case, but Murray knew how superstitious sailors were and most would refuse to sail in a ship which had a corpse on board since they believed this to be extremely unlucky. It would be whispered that the ship was doomed. Murray wasn't too happy about it himself but the order had come from high places.

He was therefore a little dismayed when Giorgio and Lucas arrived with a cart stacked high with the wooden packing cases. He knew of course who the men were. Nelson had come aboard the previous evening and explained that he was doing a discreet favour for a friend and that there would be a few extra crates to load. Murray, thinking in terms of maybe a half dozen boxes, was alarmed to find that there were sixteen wooden crates, each the size of the Admiral's coffin. He knew that the hold was almost full and he couldn't risk stacking anything in the passenger's accommodation area. In any case that would be full to bursting. He took Giorgio and Lucas to one side for a murmured consultation. In the end they managed to load eight of the crates. As dusk was falling Giorgio and Lucas unobtrusively took the rest back to the Hamilton villa, the beautiful Palazzo Sessa, pink and white in the late afternoon sunshine.

Sir William's initial reaction was one of dismay and he cast a glance over the remaining crates with resignation. However, he supposed, it was fortunate that he had got so much away. He couldn't really object to the reasons that Giorgio and Lucas had given him for the ship not being able to take all of the consignment. One could hardly deny wounded men, who had fought well and bravely for their country, the chance to return to England to recover from their often appalling injuries. Sir William gave Giorgio and Lucas strict instructions on where they were to hide the last eight packing cases and then slipped each of them a gold coin which, he knew, would ensure their continued silence. When the men had gone he returned to the library and poured himself a glass of port from the exquisite cut glass decanter standing on a polished side table. Standing by the library window, looking out across the teeming city, he savoured the taste of the vintage port. Down in the harbour the Colossus had already cast off and was sailing west into the late autumn sunset.

St Marys, Isles of Scilly, 28th May 2008

On their return to St Marys Meg and Kevin nipped into the Mermaid for a quick restorative drink. They sat in a darkened corner at the back of the pub and each took a long satisfying mouthful of ice cold beer.

Kevin was pleased to see that Meg was not upset or shaking as she had been the other morning but was considering the matter of the watcher on Samson with some detachment. They had seen no boat drawn up on the shores of Samson on their return trip to St Marys but there was no real reason why they should have done. Whoever had been watching them had had plenty of time to get away.

'Well isn't this just too cosy,' a voice drawled close by. Looking around Meg saw Steven lolling against a wooden pillar. 'Trying to be discreet, are we?' he went on sarcastically. He put his arm around Janine who seemed to have appeared from nowhere, tottering precariously on the uneven floor. 'Of course, some of us have no need to hide ourselves away in corners but I understand why you do it, Meg. You always were a bit paranoid about the way you look and...'

He got no further as Kevin stood up, scraping his chair sharply against the wooden floor.

'Mister Hamilton!' he said, heavily emphasising the word 'mister', as he turned to face Steven. 'I have had just about enough of your ridiculous posturing. If I wish to enjoy a drink with a friend it is no business of yours how she looks or where we choose to sit. If you insist on maintaining this constant harassment I shall have to take further action.' He fixed his eyes firmly onto Steven's face. 'If you understand my meaning.'

Steven, who, like all bullies, knew when to back off in the face of possible retaliation, smiled deprecatingly.

'No offence meant I'm sure,' he said silkily. 'Just trying to be friendly.'

'Goodbye Mister Hamilton!' said Kevin turning his back on Steven as he sat down again.

Steven shot Meg a brief poisonous look then turned on his heel and strode out of the pub with Janine half falling over as she tried to keep up with him. To Kevin's amazement Meg was smiling broadly.

'Well! That certainly told him!' she said, 'and, I have to say, it was very satisfying.'

Soon afterwards they left The Mermaid to go shopping. Kevin bought fresh pate and local strawberries and a bottle of red wine for dinner while Meg contributed minted lamb chops and some new potatoes. Steven was nowhere to be seen although Meg kept an eye open for him. She knew that he would be seeking a chance to get his own back.

Over dinner, they laughed about the incident with Sara and John. 'The expression on his face was priceless,' said Meg, licking her fingers after chewing the bones of her chop. 'Steven doesn't like to be bested.'

'Bullies never do,' said John drily. Meg stared at him in some surprise. Had Steven's treatment of her been so obvious.

'Always too cocky by half,' John went on. 'Always thinks he's in the right and considers the rest of the world stupid by comparison.'

'He's not that bad, John,' said Sara somewhat halfheartedly.

'Oh yes he is,' John said firmly to her. 'Treated you like a halfwit when you asked him why he wanted to go out to Samson.'

He turned to face the others and said by way of explanation, 'He knocked on the door one day and wanted me to take him over to Samson. The weather was bad and I refused. He got a bit insistent so Sara asked him why he had to go that day. Why couldn't he just wait for a better day. He looked at her like she was dirt and said it really wasn't any of her business and in any case she wouldn't understand if he did tell her why. That did it. No one talks to Sara like that. So I told him he could find someone else to take him whenever he went.' John paused and took a long sip of his wine.

'When was this?' asked Meg. 'When did he ask to go to Samson?'

'Couple of weeks ago,' said John. 'Soon after he arrived in the Islands. He came out a few days before you did.'

Meg and Kevin exchanged looks then Kevin said, 'There's something we want to talk to you about. Sound you out on a theory if you like.'

Both John and Sara listened attentively until Kevin had finished telling them about being watched on Samson; of the anonymous letter Meg had received; of the coincidence of the surnames; and of Steven's belligerent attitude.

'Well,' said Sara when he had finished speaking,' Personally, I'd say you'd got something there.' She looked at John. 'Don't you think so? There was all that business with the Colossus a year or so back, then Meg's tale, and now this.' Before John could reply there was a blip and the computer screen in the corner lit up.

'A message has come in,' said Kevin. 'I'll just check it out.'

He went across to the machine and opened his message. As he read it a look of incredulity spread over his face. Coming back to the table he said slowly,

'There's another coincidence too. Janine King is a direct descendant of Richard King. The same Richard King who was killed on the Colossus.'

Outside in the night shadows played across the sands.

Naples, Italy, 23rd November 1798

Sir William was worried. Nelson was furious. Ferdinand, King of Naples, had left the city that morning with an army of 32,000 men and was marching north to protect Rome from the French. Ferdinand, however, was still pretending friendship with the French, which infuriated Nelson. He felt that the least Ferdinand could do was to be honest about his intentions. Ferdinand, however, excused his duplicity on the grounds that he was trying to gain himself time. Sir William knew that the whole exercise was less of a chivalrous gesture towards Rome than a cover for Maria Carolina's determination to attack the French in revenge for the death of her sister. Emma was concerned for them both but she had little time to worry since she was almost constantly at the beck and call of the Queen. Maria Carolina was in a state of high excitement and expectation. She had waited for this moment for five long years, she said, and now those French upstarts were going to be taught a lesson. Her sister would be avenged and Maria Carolina would be a power to be reckoned with. Unlike Sir William and Nelson she did not foresee that the expedition was doomed to end in failure.

Sir William was now glad that Nelson was still with them. It was becoming highly probable that they might have to flee the country. He would have to suffer a lack of attention from his wife again but it was worth it for the security which Nelson represented. He had ships and they could leave at very short notice if it became necessary. At least, he thought, it is some consolation that the most valuable parts of my collection are safe. Soon they will reach England.

Lisbon, Portugal, 23rd November 1798

Captain Murray sat in his cabin writing to Admiral St Vincent. He was reporting the safe arrival of Colossus in the River Tagus after calling at Gibraltar to pick up more wounded troops as per instructions. The ship was now loading spices and preserved foodstuffs from Lisbon. Murray had become concerned that the diversions to Gibraltar and Lisbon had cost him so much valuable time. He should have been well on his way home to England if he was to avoid the onset of the winter storms. Accordingly, he wrote to St Vincent, he was intending to sail at the earliest opportunity, whatever the conditions. The Colossus had sailed from Gibraltar with a small convoy of ships bound for Ireland and the more northern ports of England. Two of the ships had already been lost on the voyage to Lisbon. That was more than enough for Captain Murray. The remainder of the convoy would be leaving Lisbon with Murray and Colossus as soon as possible. A system of signals had been established which would be used by all members of the convoy both day and night. Captain Murray wrote that the convoy would be leaving Lisbon the next day, 24th November, and they hoped to reach England in just under two weeks time. He felt far less optimistic and cheerful than he sounded. Murray thought he must have been mad to agree to this but then he had not realised at the time how much of a delay there would be. He said a quick prayer and hoped against hope that Colossus would make it safely home.

St Marys, Isles of Scilly, 29th May 2008

Meg and Kevin were back once more at Dibble and Grub.

'People will start thinking they're paying us to provide good publicity,' said Meg, depressing the plunger of the cafétierre, 'but it's so perfect here. Food, weather, view, everything.'

'Well they're just fortunate with the weather and the view,' said Kevin, 'but then so are other places on the island. We ought to try some of them really. Not,' he added hastily, seeing Meg's expression, 'that I don't love it here. I do. Just that variety and all that...'

Meg poured out the coffee and leaned back in her chair. She looked out across Porthcressa Bay nestling between the Garrison Hill and Peninnis Head. The sun was rising high in the sky towards its midday zenith. Sunlight twinkled on the surface of the water like a myriad of tiny flashing diamonds and the white sand of the broad beach dazzled her eyes, even through sunglasses. Meg stretched her legs out and sighed with contentment; lost for a moment in the happy memories of childhood summers long ago.

The sound of Kevin's voice brought her back to the present.

'If it turns out that Steven is a descendant of Sir William Hamilton then we'll know for certain that we really are on to something.'

After the revelation about Janine, the implications of which they had all discussed late into the night, John and Sara had agreed that Steven seemed to be the common factor and that it was imperative that they should find out as much about him as they could. Meg had given Kevin all of Steven's family details that she knew which, she had to admit, wasn't much, but she had his date of birth and the names of his parents and she also knew their birthdays, if only because Steven could never be bothered to remember and it was Meg who had had to buy cards and presents for them.

'But Sir William had no children,' protested Meg, still unwilling to believe in the enormity of what Kevin was thinking.

'No,' said Kevin, 'but he had three brothers. If Steven really is a descendant I think it will be from one of the brothers.'

Kevin had found a biography of Sir William Hamilton on the web and discovered that he had been the youngest of four brothers. One brother had drowned in his teens but the other two had married and at least one had had children. Ironically, like Horatia's husband, he too had been a vicar.

'Did Steven ever ask about your family on Scilly?' said Kevin after a pause.

'Not at first,' she said. 'He knew they were mostly all dead anyway. We came out to the Scillies every year though and later on he sometimes mentioned them, usually in a casual context whenever we were in the Islands. At the time I didn't really think much of it.'

No,' said Kevin, 'and I suspect that you weren't meant to either. He needed information about them for some reason but he didn't want you to know that.'

Meg thought for a moment. 'Now you come to mention it,' she said, 'He did keep asking if I knew where they had lived. I don't remember my grandparents. They died soon after I was born and Dad sold the cottage. Said he had no use for it and he couldn't afford the upkeep. Shame that.' She smiled wryly. 'I could have had my very own Scillonian cottage.'

'Did you ever go to the cottage with your parents?' Kevin asked.

'I think so,' said Meg. 'When I was very young, but I don't have any memories of it.'

'We could try asking the locals if they remember where your folks had a cottage. Someone might know. After all, unlike Steven, we don't need to be surreptitious about it.'

Kevin got to his feet. 'I'm just going to nip back home and see if any replies about Steven's family have come in. Meet for lunch later?'

Meg had decided that she was going to the Museum to ask if they had any records she could check to see where her family's cottage might have been located. Hopefully she might discover that from the census returns. That would be so simple. She could not imagine why she had not thought of it before nor why Steven had not thought of it either. It struck her like a slap in the face. Perhaps he had thought of it and if he already knew the answer then what was he doing about it. Meg shivered. How little she had really known him.

The museum was located in a clean, light, modern building that apparently stood on the site of the former Rechabite Hall. The Rechabites had been an obscure temperance group and their name was preserved in a slipway for boats near The Strand. The small museum library was tucked away in a room behind the displays. An assistant took her bag, gave her some paper and a pencil, and briefly explained the archive system to her. Then she closed the door quietly and left Meg to her research. The census returns were filed neatly in bound volumes. She began with the earliest one dated 1801. Neither that nor 1811 yielded any results but she struck gold with 1821. Then her jaw dropped. Kevin was never ever going to believe this latest coincidence. She could hardly believe it herself. Quickly she checked the rest of the volumes. The name, Nelson, appeared for that same address in every census until 1961, but by 1971 there was a stranger's name shown. That would be about right because as far as she could recall the cottage had been sold sometime during the early 1960s. The museum assistant put her head round the door and said the Museum was closing for lunch. Meg gathered her papers together and tucked them into her bag. Excited by her discovery, she couldn't wait to see Kevin's face when she told him.

They had agreed to 'ring the changes' for once and meet in Juliet's Garden for lunch. Kevin was going to walk across country from Old Town to join her after he had finished attending to his emails. Juliet's Garden was situated on a small plateau on the far side of Porthloo. It had stunning views right across to Hugh Town and the Garrison and to most of the off-islands. Meg took the little path along the seashore past Harry's Walls, the foundation remains of a Tudor fortification which was never completed and which boasted a large standing stone right in the middle of what would have been the keep. The short climb up to Juliet's Garden was well worth it. Despite its name there was an indoor restaurant as well, but Meg preferred to sit in the garden on such a day as this. She settled herself at a table in the lower reaches of the terraced garden where she had an uninterrupted view of Star Castle, Samson, Bryher and Tresco. Scillonian III had arrived and was moored at the quay, wearing her smart new coat of fresh white paint. Meg could just make out the people unloading cargo onto the waiting boats. The arrival of the steamer was a major event in the daily life of the Scillies and boats came down from each of the inhabited islands to meet the ship. Meg knew she was a few minutes early and ordered a fresh orange juice while she waited for Kevin and mulled over what she had discovered that morning.

Kevin was late. It was unlike him and after a quarter of an hour or so and the constant checking of her mobile phone Meg was just beginning to wonder if she had misunderstood him when he arrived, apologetic and out of breath. He flopped down on the seat opposite to her. Beads of sweat stood out on his forehead and he tried to wipe them away with the sleeve of his t-shirt. He was as white as a sheet. Meg was shocked. She had never seen him like this before. He was usually so calm and laid back. She hoped fervently that Steven hadn't done something to him. The waitress came for their order but Kevin was oblivious to her and she looked at him curiously.

'He's just a bit hot and bothered, that's all,' said Meg with far more assurance than she felt. 'Two pints of beer please and we'll order the food in a few minutes.' The waitress nodded and cast another doubtful look at Kevin as she went to get the drinks. Meg waited until the waitress had brought their beer. It was ice cold. Kevin rubbed his face gratefully against the glass before taking a sip of the amber liquid.

Meg looked at him with concern.
'Kevin,' she almost whispered. 'Whatever is wrong? You look as if you've seen a ghost.'

'I think I have,' he said hoarsely. 'I just couldn't believe my eyes but it was her. It really was her.'

'Who?' asked Meg softly.

'Heather,' said Kevin. 'It was Heather. She's here on the Islands.'

Meg couldn't quite understand why this should have upset him so much. After all he had told her when they were on Tresco that Heather loved the Islands. Why would he be so surprised that she might have come on holiday to a place that she loved.

'It's OK,' she said. 'It's not a problem, is it?' Meg tried to inject a touch of humour. 'After all she can't be worse than Steven, can she?'

'No, you don't understand,' he said distractedly. 'She was pushing a baby in a pram!'

Meg stared at him puzzled. Lots of people pushed babies in prams all the time. 'Well maybe she's here with friends or family and she's just helping out,' Meg said soothingly. What on earth was the matter with him?

'No!' Kevin almost shouted. 'That's just it! It wasn't just any baby. It was HER baby!' He took a great gulp of his beer.

'Oh!' Meg couldn't think of anything else to say. The look of anguish in his eyes was almost unbearable.

'It was her baby,' he repeated, more calmly. 'A little girl. She's called Bryher.' He almost managed a watery smile. 'I just stared and stared at her. It could have been my baby. It should have been my baby.' Kevin took another swig of beer. 'Then I asked Heather how old the baby was and she told me three months. That set me thinking. Maths was never my strong point but she must have been conceived about a year ago and our divorce only came through last month.' He took yet another large mouthful of beer and tried to steady his voice. 'She could see me working it all out and the pity in her eyes was unbearable. She put her hand on my arm and said she was sorry. His name is Paul and they're getting married in September. I just stood there looking at her. She said she had to go and I said something about wishing her well and then she was gone.'

Kevin stared at her numbly and Meg could see unshed tears in his eyes. She took hold of his hands and he gripped her fingers so tightly she thought he would crush them into pieces. Seeing her wince he relaxed his grip a little.

Sorry,' he said. 'I've no right to burden you with all this.'

'It's not a burden,' said Meg, 'I'm glad to help and anyway I owe you for Steven.'

Kevin almost managed a smile then he leant across the table and gently brushed her lips with his own.

'Thanks, Meg,' he said. 'You're a pal.'

The waitress reappeared at their table.

'You ready to order now?' she asked.

Meg had been going to tell him over lunch what she had discovered but she had not bargained on the running battle which ensued with the local robins and sparrows who seemed to be totally convinced that the plates of sandwiches which arrived were intended for them and not for the folk seated at the table. Their courage and daring helped to restore some of Kevin's equilibrium as he fought with them for his lunch. It was only over coffee afterwards that he managed to remember what Meg had said she would do that morning.

'Sorry,' he said yet again. 'Got a bit distracted this morning. Did you find anything out from the census returns?'

Meg nodded. Her moment had finally arrived.

'Well don't keep me in suspense,' said Kevin. 'Did you find out where your folks used to live?'

Meg took a deep breath. 'Yes. I did,' she said, 'and you're not going to believe this latest coincidence at all. The cottage my family used to own is the cottage where you're staying right now.'

As the tide receded on the beach below shadows danced in the sand.

Naples, Italy, 8th December 1798

What Sir William and Nelson had most feared had happened. Ferdinand had taken Rome and declared it under his protection amid great pomp and ceremony. Then the French had marched on Rome in turn and had retaken the city from Ferdinand three days ago. They had also taken 10,000 Neapolitan troops prisoner. The rest had fled. Ferdinand had returned home hastily, thoroughly humiliated, and had slunk around liked a dog that has been whipped. Maria Carolina was both devastated and horrified. Emma was comforting her as best she could. More importantly, Ferdinand's actions had left Naples wide open to attack and at this moment the French were marching south intent on extracting revenge. Nelson and Sir William, thoroughly exasperated and worried, knew that something had to be done and done soon. Both themselves and the royal family of Naples were in great danger for the French would take no prisoners here.

St Mary's Roads, Isles of Scilly, 8th December 1798

Captain Murray was at his desk in his cabin penning yet another report to Admiral St Vincent. It wasn't easy trying to write properly the way the ship was tossing and pitching about. As he had feared they had been too late to avoid the onset of the fierce winter storms. The first had struck soon after they had left Lisbon. The weather had continued to worsen steadily. By the time they reached the English Channel it was blowing a gale. Colossus had become separated from the rest of the convoy and had found herself heading for the Western Rocks of Scilly. This was one of Murray's worst nightmares. He had managed to signal for one of the local pilots to come on board. Together he and Murray had somehow got the ship through to the relatively calmer waters of St Marys Roads. Murray wondered how on earth the man had managed to reach them at all in the mountainous seas when all he had had was a small six oared gig. Still the Scillonians were noted for their seafaring abilities and any captain who had Scillonian sailors serving under him was considered fortunate indeed.

It was Murray's intention that Colossus should now ride out the storm within the lea of St Marys before completing her voyage. He sealed his letter with melted red wax and his personal stamp. Then he went up on deck to give orders for the anchors to be dropped. There was a slight problem in that Colossus was short of an anchor because he had given one to Nelson for Vanguard which had lost an anchor in battle. Murray was not expecting to engage in battle on the voyage home and had felt he could make do with one less anchor. Shouldn't be too much of a problem he told himself. The seas were a little calmer here and the lee of the Islands should shelter Colossus from the worst of the storm. With luck and a fair wind he thought, smiling wryly to himself. That was just what he did need. Luck and a fair wind.

St Marys, Isles of Scilly, 30th May 2008

Meg was eating her breakfast in thoughtful mood, staring out across the view of the harbour that the small dining room offered. Mrs Woodcock was obviously intent on fattening her up judging by the bacon, egg, tomatoes and sausages which she heaped onto Meg's plate each morning. Although they had stayed there together, Mrs Woodcock had never mentioned Steven once to her but Meg had sensed that she understood how Meg must feel and she always did her best to be kind and tactful. Meg was reflecting on everything that had happened the previous day when she heard a banging at the door and voices in the hall. The next minute Kevin was sitting at her table with her and Mrs Woodcock was fussing around bringing him tea and toast.

'Sorry,' he said sheepishly as she put her knife and fork down. 'First I abandon you to your fate for an afternoon and evening because I want to be alone then the next thing is I'm ruining your breakfast,'

Meg smiled. 'It's OK,' she said. 'I understood how you felt because I felt that way about Steven.'

Kevin shook his head.

'I shut you out, Meg, and I shouldn't have done that. It was selfish of me. Guess my male pride had taken a blow. You know, discovering that Heather had given birth to someone else's baby. I know we weren't together but it still hurt. Anyway she's obviously moved on and so should I, and it was wrong of me to shut a good friend out. I'm sorry.'

Meg nodded. 'It's OK,' she said again, 'but I assume you didn't come battering Mrs Woodcock's door down just to apologise.'

'Actually no,' he said. 'There was something else rather important that I thought you would want to know.'

Mrs Woodcock reappeared with a fresh pot of tea for Meg and cleared away the dirty plates. Meg poured herself some more tea and looked at Kevin.

'OK,' she said, 'I'm all ears.'

'This morning I finally got the confirmation on Steven's background. He's not a direct descendant of Sir William Hamilton, who we know was childless anyway, but he is a descendant of Frederic Hamilton, Sir William's elder brother, who got married in 1757. Frederic was a 'Reverend Gentleman' and probably a little more sober living than Sir William. He certainly wouldn't have approved of Emma Hamilton.'

Meg thought for a moment.

'It's all just a bit too cosy, isn't it?' she said. 'But I can't think what Steven is hoping to achieve and why all the secrecy? I don't imagine for one moment that Janine knows from whom she's descended or that she would even care. There's something missing here and I can't put a finger on it.'

'I'm inclined to agree with you,' said Kevin. 'It has to have something to do with the Colossus. That's the only thing which links all three of you. Richard King wouldn't have known the Hamiltons and he probably didn't know Nelson personally either. I don't believe he ever served directly under him.'

'So it's the Colossus, or maybe the Hamilton treasure, which links him in,' said Meg, 'He would have had access to it on board, wouldn't he?'

'No, maybe not,' said Kevin, 'although when the ship began to founder he might have done.'

'Did Captain Murray know what he was carrying for Nelson?' asked Meg.

'Probably,' said Kevin. 'He might have known better than to ask but he wasn't a stupid man and, given all the circumstances at the time, he could have made an intelligent guess.'

'Are there lists of what Hamilton actually sent aboard the Colossus?'

'There must have been,' said Kevin, 'I'm sure Sir William with his painstaking ways would have listed and catalogued everything; but he had to flee in a hurry and his villa was taken over by the French and badly damaged. Unless he took his lists with him they were probably destroyed.'

'Shame,' said Meg. 'Unless he sent them to someone, maybe a member of the family. Something would be needed to check off the items when they arrived in England and it would be a sort of insurance policy as well since he would know then if anything had gone missing.'

They sat looking at each other for a moment in silence then Meg said, 'There must be divers' lists of items they brought to the surface.'

'There are,' admitted Kevin, 'but, like I said the other day, not everything brought up was recorded.'

'I thought that was just the guns,' said Meg.

'No way of telling, really,' said Kevin. 'It might be hard to bring up vases and jugs and other such items to the surface without being noticed; but smaller things like gems or seals or coins would present no problem. Although,' he added, 'I can't imagine what could be so valuable that anyone would go to all this trouble like Steven is doing.'

'It would also help if we knew what Sir William didn't send over,' said Meg, 'but I'm not sure that he even knew that himself.'

Breakfast over, Meg announced her intention of spending the day in the Museum library reading contemporary accounts of the sinking of the Colossus while Kevin said that he needed to work on his article about the recent discoveries made in the wreck of the Colossus, and also to follow up on some further research. They agreed to meet at Kevin's cottage for dinner.

'Time for you to return to the ancestral home,' said Kevin, 'besides, John is bringing me up some fish today and I'll need someone to help me eat it.'

Meg laughed and left him talking to Mrs Woodcock when she left for the Museum. The weather had changed completely as it so often did in the Islands. Yesterday had been beautifully warm and sunny but today the sky was heavily overcast and a strong south westerly wind was blowing, rattling everything in its path. Meg was relieved to reach the shelter of the Museum. Settled in the library once more she began by reading one of the 'bibles' of the Islands' past history, the journal written by the SPCK minister, John Troutbeck. He had copied the work of his predecessor, Dr William Borlase, for his facts about the Islands, but Meg didn't suppose that much would have changed in the forty years since Dr Borlase had held office. Troutbeck loved gossip, however, and faithfully recorded the many tales he was told. He joined in all the Island's social activities with enthusiasm and described many of the ancient customs, like the harvest feast of Nicla Tise and Tar Barrel Night on Midsummer's Eve, involving quantities of burning pitch and foolhardy young lads, which had now disappeared from the Islands. Troutbeck had resigned his post in 1796, two years before the Colossus had been wrecked, amid speculation that he had been involved in smuggling activities and accusations of 'erratic behaviour'. Meg wondered exactly what form his 'erratic behaviour' had taken.

Unfortunately, Troutbeck's successor had not been quite such a fluent gossip and recorder of events. Not until George Woodley in the 1820s did she again glimpse the cosy community side of life in the Islands. There was hardly a mention of the Colossus, but, Meg reminded herself, there was no real reason why there should have been. To contemporary eyes the Colossus had not been a great tragedy. Apart from the death of the unfortunate quarter-master, there had been no loss of life, unlike the terrible wreck of the Association and her three sister ships in 1707, when over two thousand men had drowned in a single night; more souls lost even than in the sinking of the fabled Titanic two hundred years later. Many effects had been saved from the Colossus and, although salvage crews had later worked on her, the nature and value of the cargo which had gone down with the ship was not known at the time. There was therefore not much reason why the sinking of the Colossus should have merited much more than a paragraph or two at the most. There had been so many wrecks around the Islands with far more tragic consequences.

When the Museum closed for lunch Meg struggled into her waterproofs and decided to brave the elements and go for a walk. She needed to clear her head. The sky was grey and leaden now and the wind had increased, bringing with it the first drops of rain. She made her way through an almost deserted Hugh Town and took the path around the foot of the Garrison to where she would have an uninterrupted view of Samson and the Southward Well. The wind and rain stung her face and she kept her head well down until she had reached a point just before the battery curtain wall turned sharply to the south east as it followed the contours of the headland. Meg turned then and stood looking out across the grey churning waters to the misty outline of the South Hill on Samson. It was not a good day for any boat to be out there and she thought of Colossus, being dragged helplessly towards the Southward Well with its vicious reefs, the depleted number of anchors being unable to hold the ship within the sheltered safety of St Marys Roads. It must have been terrifying for those aboard. Rain trickled down her face and she began to feel chilled right through. Time to go back and find herself a nice hot drink somewhere. As she turned, Meg caught sight of a movement to her right. The figure of a man stood a few yards away watching her. Meg gasped and began to walk quickly back towards the town. She thought she could hear footsteps behind her and, looking over her shoulder, she could see him following her and gaining on her slightly. Panic set in now and she began to run, half slipping over the rough stone path and almost losing her balance. She felt him rather than saw him behind her. He was running too now. She knew it. She could sense it. Steven would have called it paranoia. Meg called it survival instinct. The path had evened out a little and she increased her speed, panting with the effort. She feared he would catch her up and she risked a look behind her. He seemed to have slowed down and the next moment she cannoned heavily into someone. It was John.

'Meg!' he said, his face full of concern. 'Whatever's wrong?'

Meg practically fell into his arms. She was gasping for air so much that at first she couldn't speak. Relieved to have actually reached safety at last, she took her time before finally stammering 'I went for a walk on the Garrison but someone followed me. When I began to run he began to run and I was so frightened. Thank God you were there!' She paused to draw breath before asking him 'Did you see anyone?'

'There was someone on the path a little way behind you,' said John. 'I didn't take much notice to be honest because you were running as though all the demons in Hell were after you.'

'I thought they were!' said Meg, trying to make an attempt at humour. She had almost got her breath back now but she was still shaken.

'You look as though you could do with a stiff drink,' said John. 'Come on. I'll stand you one.'

He took her arm and steered her into the Mermaid. A number of people were in the pub, sheltering from the weather, talking, drinking, eating lunch, doing the usual normal everyday sort of things that people did. Meg envied them. They weren't being chased by someone they didn't know for something they didn't even know about.

'Two brandies, love!' John called to the barmaid as he helped Meg to a seat. 'Make them large ones!'

In deference to the grimness of the weather a small fire had been lit in the grate of the Mermaid and Meg drew up her chair to warm her hands. She knew though that the coldness she felt came from somewhere deep inside her and not from the wind and rain.

A red-haired girl brought the drinks over and smiled at John. 'We'd just begun to wonder where you were,' she said. 'You can usually set your watch by the time you come in here.'

'Cheeky!' said John but he was not offended by it. It was all part of the pub banter that he enjoyed.

He gave Meg one of the brandies.

'Get that down you,' he said gruffly. 'Do you good.

Meg took a large sip and felt the fiery liquid burn her throat. Its warmth seemed to spread through her body instantly. She took another large sip and began to feel a little better. John watched with approval.

'That's better,' he said. 'You were looking like death warmed up. Going to tell me about it?'

'There really isn't a lot to tell,' said Meg. Her voice was quite steady now. 'I was in the library at the Museum all morning. When they closed for lunch I wanted to clear my head so I went for a walk. I'd been reading up on the Colossus, contemporary stuff from the late 1790s when she went down, so I thought I'd walk along the Garrison path and see what the Southward Well looked like on a really rough day. I just wanted to try and get some picture in my head of the sort of conditions Colossus endured before she sank.'

Meg drained her brandy glass. 'Bit morbid, I know, but I wanted to try and get the feel of it. Do you know what I mean?'

John nodded. 'Another?' he asked, indicating her empty glass.

Meg didn't usually drink much at lunchtime but today she felt she needed it. John went over to the bar and brought two fresh glasses of brandy back to their table. As he sat down again he looked at her thoughtfully.

'Any idea who it could have been following you?' he asked.

Meg shook her head. 'No idea at all,' she said. Then an idea struck her. 'How did he know that I would be there? He came from the opposite direction so he couldn't have followed me.'

'He probably didn't,' said John. 'It was most likely just coincidence that he happened to be walking the headland at the same time and then, when he saw you on your own, he tried to...'

John hesitated, unsure how to continue and wanting to choose his words carefully.

'Frighten the living daylights out of me,' Meg finished for him.

'Well, that too.' John laughed. 'This man obviously wants to talk to you pretty badly and he wants to talk to you on your own. He doesn't want other people around. He also seems to be sure that you wouldn't meet him alone even if he asked you or he would have done so already. So he follows you when you go somewhere quiet or lonely, like Samson, where he knows he won't be disturbed in the hope that he can say whatever it is he has to say without interruption. I would think the meeting on the headland this lunchtime really was pure chance and he just seized the opportunity.'

'There's an awful lot of chance and coincidence about this whole affair,' said Meg drily. 'Do you think he might be the same person who has been sending me these letters?'

'I think there's every chance, if you'll pardon that expression,' said John with the hint of a smile.

Meg smiled back at him. She felt quite restored after the brandy and the warmth had returned to her. She looked at her watch.

'I should be getting back to the Museum, but thanks for the brandy and thanks for listening,' she said gratefully. 'I owe you one.'

John shook his head. 'My pleasure,' he said, then as an afterthought, he added, 'Go up and see Sara one afternoon. She'd like to talk to you.'

Back in the Museum library Meg found it hard to concentrate. The brandy had made her feel a little sleepy but her mind was also full of possibilities and conjectures. She was almost glad when it was four thirty and the Museum closed for the day. Back in her room at Mrs Woodcock's modest, although very comfortable, bed and breakfast establishment she took a shower and then lay down on her bed, still wrapped in her towel, staring at the ceiling and going over everything that had happened during the past few days.

She must have fallen asleep for when she next looked at her watch it was a quarter past six. Hastily she got off the bed, pulled on jeans and a red jumper, grabbed her coat and set off for Kevin's cottage. Or rather, her family's old home. The rain had stopped and the sky was beginning to clear. It promised to be a fine evening. It seemed strange to be going to the place where her grandparents had lived and where her father had grown up. She must have stayed there herself as a very young child but she had absolutely no memory of it at all. She tried to imagine her father as a child, riding his bicycle around the lanes of St Marys, playing on the beaches, perhaps going fishing with his father. She knew that her grandfather had been one of the local fishermen; and that her great grandfather had supplemented his income as a part time policeman with selling freshly caught fish to local businesses. Meg suppressed a rueful smile. She supposed that there had obviously been a major crime wave in the Islands since her great grandfather's time because one policeman was now employed full time and two part timers were drafted in from Cornwall for the summer months.

Kevin was waiting for her. He opened the door as soon as she knocked and stood aside with a grand sweeping gesture.

'Welcome to your ancestral seat, madam,' he said with a mock bow.

She pushed at his arm playfully as she entered the small living room. This had been her father's home. This was where he had grown up and yet she could establish no sense of connection. Was that because he had severed that connection when he had finally left her to her teenage tantrums over his parting from her mother and stayed away. They had not met again until she was grown up and by then he had changed. She'd no longer recognized him as the father she had remembered from her childhood. They were strangers to one another.

Kevin put a glass of chilled wine into her hands.

'Cheers!' he said. 'Have you recovered now?'

Before she could answer he went on. 'John called in earlier. Told me what happened at lunch time. You must have been pretty scared.'

'I was,' said Meg. She could still feel the pounding sensation in her heart when she had run headlong in panic from the stranger who had followed her. 'I was just so pleased to see John. I don't know what might have happened if he hadn't been there.'

'Thank goodness he was,' said Kevin. 'He's pretty worried about it all. He's going to have a word with various folk and see what he can find out. This guy must be staying on the Island somewhere.'

'I thought John said he might be a visitor from one of the boats that anchor offshore,' said Meg.

'Yes, he did,' admitted Kevin, 'but he couldn't have come ashore today. It was too rough. The only boat that came into the quay today was the Scillonian. She was the only one big enough to ride out the heavy seas.'

The same thought struck them both at the same time. It was Kevin who got in first. 'What time did this happen?' he asked.

Meg thought hard. 'I left the Museum just after twelve so it must have been about ten to one.'

'It would fit,' said Kevin. 'The Scillonian docked at twelve fifteen. In spite of the rough weather she was on time. John was down on the quay helping to unload her before he met you.'

'So that would have given someone on board the ship time enough to disembark and walk round the Garrison,' said Meg slowly. 'Especially if he was a day tripper or he didn't have much luggage.'

'If he was a day tripper,' said Kevin 'why on earth didn't he fly? Why put himself through that sort of rough crossing twice in one day?'

'If he'd arranged to come over at short notice he might not have been able to get a seat. In weather like today a lot of people would have been trying to switch from the boat to flying across.' She paused. 'Besides the weather out here is so changeable. It's a lovely fine evening now. There should be no problems on the homeward voyage to Penzance.'

'So John could be on a wild goose chase,' said Kevin pensively, 'because you're saying that the man who frightened you so much today may well no longer be in the Islands.'

Meg nodded.

'Oh well,' Kevin said philosophically, 'nothing we can do about it now. Come into the kitchen and give me a hand. I've been trying to take culinary science to the cutting edge. John brought me some sea bass today and I found a recipe for cooking it in a salt crust. Whoever said that if you can read a recipe book you can cook is a liar. I've got this wretched fish all wrapped up in its crust, trussed up neatly as a Christmas turkey, and I've no idea how you can tell when it's ready to eat.'

Meg stifled a giggle. 'Nor have I!'

They went into the kitchen and Kevin took a baking tin out of the oven which contained a large foil wrapped parcel.

'How long has it been in the oven?' asked Meg.

'Well over an hour,' said Kevin.

'I think the fish kind of cooks in its own steam,' said Meg. 'Fish doesn't usually take much cooking so it's probably done.'

Kevin removed the parcel from the tin and laid it on a wooden chopping board. There he proceeded to unwrap it with as much care, Meg thought, as the Egyptology specialists must have taken when they were first unwrapping the mummy of Tut'ank'amun. He cut the crust with all the skill of a top plastic surgeon and revealed the gently steaming fish lying beneath.

'Done to a turn,' said Kevin with satisfaction.

He cut slices from the fish which he put carefully on two plates, whipped a couple of small baked potatoes from the oven, adding a sprig of fresh parsley and a slice of lemon as garnish.

'Voila!' he announced proudly. 'Best French cuisine at your service!'

They ate at the big kitchen table in what had once been her grandmother's kitchen and Meg tried again to picture her father as a small boy playing out on the beach and then running into this same kitchen for his tea. She finally abandoned the effort, deciding that it would be a whole lot easier to imagine life on Mars.

'You're a bit quiet,' said Kevin as he refilled her glass with wine. The cool Chardonnay had complemented the fish perfectly. 'You OK?'

Meg pulled herself out of her reverie.

'Yes,' she said. 'I was just trying to imagine this as my grandmother's kitchen and Dad, when he was a small boy, running in for his tea, but', she added sadly, 'it's not really working.'

She looked up at Kevin. His eyes were full of sympathy and an emotion she couldn't read.

'It must be kind of disorientating for you, seeing it now, with me here and everything,' he said.

'Oh, it's not you,' she said quickly. 'It's just I was trying to recapture something, but I think it died a long time ago.' She looked at him and smiled wanly.

'Let's not talk about it anymore. Tell me about what you were doing today?'

'Well for the most part I was just writing up this article about the recovery work that's been done on the Colossus. I described the carved figure in detail and also the stern board. Quite interesting really. I mentioned that I thought that there should have been two figures but that one might well have been destroyed. Then I got to wondering exactly what Sir William had lost when the Colossus went down. There are exhaustive tomes on his collections of course but they can't really tell us exactly what he kept in Naples and what was lost with the Colossus. I kept thinking about what you had said. That he might have sent the lists to someone for safe keeping. I'd assumed that when Sir William died, which was only about five years after the Colossus sank, he'd have left everything to Emma and that the lists might have ended up among her possessions. I know that she sold almost everything she had after Nelson's death, but the lists wouldn't have been particularly valuable in themselves and there was a fair chance they might have survived.' Kevin paused to drink some more of his wine. 'No such luck,' he said ruefully. 'At least not among Emma's papers,' he added, 'but I did discover something else that is rather strange. When Sir William Hamilton died he didn't leave his estate to Emma, as might have been expected. He left it all to a nephew.'

Meg stared at him, puzzled. 'Why would he have done that? ' she asked.

'Not sure,' said Kevin, 'unless he thought that she would become Nelson's responsibility after he died. He did leave her a small annuity and a London town house but that was only a fraction of the value of his estate. Personally, I think he was making a statement. Nelson and Emma were very indiscreet during the last few years of Sir William's life and they were very inconsiderate of him sometimes. They all lived together and it was a badly kept secret that it was Emma and Nelson who lived together as man and wife while poor Hamilton was treated as an outsider in his own home. It was during this time too that Horatia was born. That must have been hard for him to accept.' Kevin spoke this last sentence with some feeling. 'Anyway,' he went on, 'when Sir William died he gave instructions that he was to be buried with his first wife, Katherine. That was a very public snub to Emma.'

'Which nephew did he leave everything to?' Meg was curious.

'That's the strange thing,' said Kevin. 'You know what it was like. All male line and eldest son and all that. Well, his brother, Charles, was dead by then but Frederic was still alive. He was passed over, so were his children, and I guessed that caused some ill feeling. Especially when the nephew he did leave the bulk of his estate to was only the second son of his elder sister, Elizabeth.'

'What was this nephew called?' asked Meg.

'The Right Honourable Charles Francis Greville to give him his full title,' said Kevin, 'and he was the one who actually introduced Sir William to Emma.'

Meg's head was spinning. She'd thought her own family had been complicated but they'd had nothing on the Hamilton family.

'Why him?' she asked. 'Was it just because he'd been responsible for introducing Emma to his uncle?'

'Probably a bit more to it than that,' replied Kevin.

'But why didn't he just leave it to Emma?' Meg frowned. 'He was supposed to have adored her.'

'He did adore her' said Kevin, 'but I think he knew Emma. She was a spendthrift. She liked to drink and she liked to gamble; and she had hurt him, too, pretty badly, over Nelson. Sir William was a realist. He was much older than Emma and he knew that she would take a lover eventually. He could have lived with that. What he couldn't take was the very public humiliation caused by her total lack of discretion over her affair with Nelson.'

Meg was silent. She was thinking how she had felt when she had first learned of Steven's affair with Janine. Two hundred years later and the wheel had turned full circle when a Hamilton had rubbed a Nelson's nose in it. If Steven knew that he was descended from Frederic Hamilton, and he almost certainly did, it would have given him even greater pleasure to have made a fool of Meg. She felt a stab of the old familiar pain

As if he knew what she was thinking, Kevin put his hand over hers.

'Let bygones be bygones, Meg,' he said softly. He stroked her hair with his other hand and pulling her towards him he kissed her, gently at first, and then with an increasing passion.

Outside in the darkness invisible shadows stirred gently in the sands.

Naples, Italy, 12th December 1798

Frantic negotiations had been taking place and Sir William was pleased to hear that a fresh coalition had been hastily drawn up against the French. Naples and her English allies could now count on support from Russia, Austria, Portugal and Turkey. The French had temporarily ceased their offensive while they considered the implications of this new move but both Nelson and Sir William knew that they would now have to leave Naples, at least for the present, and soon. The problem would be in persuading the royal family that they should also leave. Ferdinand was easily bribed by the promise of fresh hunting grounds, but Maria Carolina was a different matter. She had taken the Neapolitan defeat in Rome badly and she was still determined to wreak her revenge on the French. Emma spent her days pleading with the Queen but at first she could not shake Maria Carolina's resolve to stand her ground and fight.

There was also the threat from within Naples itself to consider. Some members of the nobility were considering switching allegiance to the French in return for retaining the privileges they now enjoyed. The poor of the city were also tempted by the fact the new slogan of the French Republic, 'Liberty, Equality, Fraternity', seemed to promise a better quality of life than that which they had at present. At last Emma managed to persuade the Queen that it would be better for Naples if she and her family remained alive to fight their corner, albeit initially in exile. After all, Emma said, what point would there be in Maria Carolina and her children meeting the same fate as the Queen's sister, Marie Antoinette. Maria Carolina could see the logic of this argument and finally she agreed to start making plans for the royal family to flee to Sicily together with Sir William and Lady Hamilton and Admiral Lord Nelson.

St Mary's Roads, Isles of Scilly, 12th December 1798

Captain Murray was by now becoming seriously concerned. Instead of abating, the storm had gathered strength and strong gale force winds were whipping up the sea into an angry froth. All the anchors been dropped but Murray had loaned Nelson one of the bower anchors for Vanguard as he'd said he would do. Colossus was an anchor short. Normally this should not have mattered but the ship was heavily laden and the strong sea currents were causing her anchors to drag along the sandy sea-bed. Murray decided that soundings would have to be taken and ordered the quarter-master, Richard King, to do this. King, used to rough conditions at sea, did not protest, but climbed the main mast and prepared to take the soundings. The wind howled round the masts, tearing at the sails, as the rain lashed down. Murray watched him anxiously. Suddenly, and without warning, Colossus struck herself against one of the hundreds of treacherous rocks that lurked just beneath the waters in the Islands. The ship lurched violently and King, thrown temporarily off balance, lost his footing and crashed to the deck below, landing at the feet of his horrified captain. He lay there, bizarrely spread eagled with his head and one leg at an unnatural angle. Shocked, Murray dropped to his knees beside him but King had hit his head hard and his neck was broken. He was already dead. At that moment there was a sickening crunching sound of tearing timbers as Colossus impaled herself firmly upon the rocky reef of Southward Well.

St Marys, Isles of Scilly, 31st May 2008

Meg woke early and lay in bed watching the sunbeams dance on the ceiling and thinking about the previous night. After an evening spent curled up on the sofa listening to Mozart, Kevin had walked Meg home under a brilliant starlit sky which evoked the magic of islands everywhere. She had responded to Kevin's kisses in a way that she had never responded to Steven. She had felt guilty about that and then reminded herself sharply that she had nothing to feel guilty about, given Steven's behaviour towards her. He had always been the one in control, the one with the master plan. Within days of them meeting he had announced that she was the girl he was going to marry. He hadn't actually asked her; he'd told her that they were getting married. She'd been younger then and flattered, grateful for his attentions and unable to quite believe that someone actually wanted her. Far too naïve in fact. An older, more worldly wise and confident Meg would have been a little more cautious. But she'd been swept up in the romance of it all and she had loved him, at first. His constant patronising and undermining of her had worn down her love along with her spirit. She suspected now that Steven had never loved her for herself but for who she was. The descendant of Admiral Lord Nelson and Emma Hamilton.

Steven had planned this long ago, she felt sure. He had discovered, either by accident or design, his Hamilton lineage, and had felt cheated that Sir William had not left his fortune to his surviving brother. That would be so like Steven. Afterwards he would have made it his business to put matters right, as he saw it. He would have read the histories and the biographies. He would have learned about Horatia and her children. He would have visited the Scillies to find out as much as he could about the Colossus and, somewhere along the way, he might well have heard about the rumours surrounding Horatio Nelson, the Island's late 19th century one-man police force, and a possible legacy. As Kevin had said, there wasn't much you couldn't find out over a pint in the Mermaid. Then it was just a matter of tracking her down. It wouldn't have been difficult for a man like Steven. It must have been the most terrible disappointment, after going to all that trouble, that she didn't seem to know anything or to have anything that could possibly be of interest to him.

The puzzle now was why Steven had married Janine King. It could just be that he had finally fallen in love but Meg didn't think so. Steven was far too calculating for that and besides it was too much of a coincidence that he had just happened to marry a descendant of the quarter-master on the Colossus. He would have tracked her down in the same way that he had tracked down Meg. Why Janine? Why had he not tried to track down the descendants of the Right Honourable Charles Francis Greville. It was he, after all, who had received the bulk of Sir William's estate. Then Meg remembered. There would be no direct descendants. Charles had been a younger son of a large family and his private means were limited. After conducting a passionate affair with Emma, he had dumped her on his Uncle William without telling her what he was doing in order to marry a wealthy heiress. The heiress, however, had known of the Right Honourable Charles's reputation with women and had graciously declined his kind offer of marriage. Wise girl, thought

Meg. So did all the other wealthy heiresses whom he approached. These eighteenth century heiresses had obviously been a lot more discerning than history gave them credit for and the Right Honourable Charles had remained unmarried. Feeling a bit more buoyed and cheerful than she had been of late, Meg went downstairs in good spirits and found herself quite looking forward to Mrs Woodcock's body building breakfast. Propped against her plate was a buff coloured envelope. It bore a Scillonian postmark. Inside was a single sheet of typed notepaper.

`*Dear Meg Nelson*

So sorry we didn't get to have our little chat yesterday.

The whole matter is becoming very tiresome and my patience with you is exhausted. In fact this whole charade is quite ridiculous.

Next time we meet you will talk to me. Do you understand. One way or another you will talk to me.

Till we meet again'

Like the last time the letter wasn't signed. Unlike last time Meg's first reaction was anger, not fear. Who did the letter writer think they were to be treating her this way? Interesting, she thought, as she buttered her toast, that it had been posted instead of delivered by hand. That could mean that whoever had written it might have left the Islands. They would have had plenty of time to write it and post it before leaving on the Scillonian or even before flying out the previous day. She would discuss it with Kevin when they met up later on but in the meantime she wasn't going to let it ruin her day.

It was warm and sunny once more and Meg strolled though Hugh Town enjoying the bustle of a busy Saturday morning. Saturday was change-over day for most of the self catering places and guest houses. People seemed to be dragging loads of cases down to the quay or standing on every street corner awaiting collection by the heliport bus. All the shops were open and doing a roaring trade in last minute souvenirs. Meg bought some postcards for friends she had so far neglected and decided in a moment of bravado to go to Tregarthen's Hotel where she could have coffee and write her postcards in peace. She climbed a row of steep little steps which led up to the hotel from the heliport bus stop by the chemists. The view from Tregarthen's was breath-taking. A broad panorama sweeping around from Samson and Bryher to Tresco and St Martins in the distance while Hugh Town and St Mary's Harbour lay spread out below. A dark, good looking, young waiter of Latin origin brought her a tray of coffee which he set before her with a broad smile. Meg smiled back. He wasn't really looking for a tip, she decided, it was probably just his way. She poured herself a cup of coffee and began writing her cards. She was on her second cup of coffee and her last postcard when she became aware of a presence at her side. Somehow she just knew it was going to be Steven.

'Good to see you've decided to stop slumming it at last,' Steven said casually. 'Decent coffee and I don't suppose they'd let your friend in here anyway,' he added nastily.

Meg looked up, 'Steven,' she said wearily, 'if you can't say anything pleasant then don't say anything at all.'

Steven gaped at her. He wasn't used to being answered back in such fashion, especially not by Meg.

'I can see your friend has been teaching you bad manners,' he managed finally.

Meg ignored him. She could see the young Latin waiter watching them.

'I'm talking to you,' said Steven, more loudly this time.

'And I'm not talking to you,' she said.

Steven put his hand on her shoulder. 'I said I'm talking to you,' he said insistently.

Meg tried to ignore him but he was twisting her round to face him and she tried to resist him.

The waiter came over to her. 'Is everything alright, Madam?' he asked, eyeing Steven warily.

'Oh, yes thank you,' she said, smiling at the waiter. 'This gentleman was just leaving.'

Steven gave her a venomous stare and hissed 'Bitch!' at her under his breath as he swept out of the coffee lounge with as much dignity as he could muster.

'More coffee, Madam?' the waiter asked her solicitously.

'No thanks,' Meg smiled. She paid her bill and gave the young man a handsome tip anyway. He had more than earned it.

She posted her cards, bought a couple of freshly baked Cornish pasties, and went to meet Kevin at the cottage. They had decided to go for a walk round the coast in the afternoon. Kevin was waiting for her.

'Sorry I'm a bit late,' said Meg. 'I just had a close encounter of the third kind with Steven.'

Kevin's initial look of concern was replaced by a broad smile as Meg related the incident to him.

'He's just jealous,' said Kevin with an air of complacency. 'Doesn't want you himself but he can't bear the thought of anyone else wanting you. It's a man thing.'

Meg laughed and blushed. Kevin was good for her ego if nothing else.

They left the cottage and walked around the coastal path, climbing the hill past the Tolman to walk along the cliffs towards the airport. Kevin laughed at the signs on the cliff path warning ramblers to beware of low flying aircraft and then threw both himself and Meg to the ground as a Skybus Islander aircraft zoomed in just above their heads. This reduced them both to fits of giggles and Meg wondered what the passengers on the plane must have thought if indeed they had seen them at all. A hundred yards or so beyond the runway was the Giant's Castle, a rocky outcrop that was said to have been a pre-historic fortification from the Iron Age. At its foot lay a well cut turf maze which had nine concentric circles.

'Good lunch stop?' said Kevin as he climbed across the rocks and sat on the summit of the ancient fort. 'I must say they had a great view from up here.'

Meg agreed as she flopped down beside him. They ate their Cornish pasties and drank the beer Kevin had brought with him, admiring the beauty of the view around them. A number of gulls had suspected that there might also be a spot of lunch for them if they just hung around long enough and in this they were proved correct when Meg crumbled up the remains of the crust from her pasty and laid it out for them like a small feast on the rocks of the headland. Their desire for the food overcame the natural wariness of the birds and they perched almost close enough for Meg to reach out and touch them. Kevin watched her as she flicked stray crumbs towards the rest of the birds' meal. She was a carer, he thought, a natural born carer.

When Meg had at last finished feeding the birds he said casually,

'I really enjoyed last night.'

'Me too,' she said quietly.

'Would you come out for dinner with me tonight?' he asked diffidently.

She nodded. 'Love to,' she said in barely more than a whisper. How long was it since someone had asked if she would like to go out on a date. Steven had never asked her anything.

'We're going out to dinner tonight,' he would announce. It had never occurred to him that she might have had other plans, other preferences.

'Thought we might have a sizzler at the Atlantic,' said Kevin. 'If that's OK with you?'

Meg agreed enthusiastically. The Atlantic Inn had great views and they served their steaks on red hot stones which grilled the meat to perfection.

'I found out something quite interesting this morning,' he went on. 'Thank God for the internet. It cuts out so much of the hard slog in researching stuff.'

He reached into his knapsack and pulled out a sheet of paper.

'I printed this off for interest because it explains why Sir William didn't leave his estate to Emma.'

Meg took the paper and read it carefully, then she exclaimed,

'His estate was the port of Milford Haven!"

'Yes,' said Kevin. 'He could hardly leave Emma a dockyard, could he?'

Meg read the information again. Steven could have found this out as well but even he would have seen the impracticalities of trying to claim that the docks at Milford Haven should have belonged to him. Besides he would hardly have needed to marry Emma Hamilton's descendant if he had been foolish enough to follow that path. Then there was the question of Janine. It had to be linked to the Colossus. Kevin agreed with her that even someone with Steven's patronising and inflated ego would realise that trying to claim ownership of one of the country's largest dockyards could only lead to grief. Besides, Kevin thought cattily, a dockyard would be far too common for the likes of Steven Hamilton.

'But why Greville?' Meg was saying. 'Why not the brother?'

'Greville was an MP and it was he who applied for, and got passed, the Act of Parliament that allowed Sir William to build the docks, quays, roads and markets in the port of Milford Haven' said Kevin. 'So when Sir William died I guess he thought Greville the ideal person to take over the dockyards. Besides, he'd earned it, hadn't he?'

'So if Emma got Sir William's town house and an annuity, and Charles Greville got Milford Haven, what's left?' said Meg. 'His personal effects and that includes his collections.'

'Well we know that one collection went to the British Museum,' said Kevin, 'and that half of the second collection sank with the Colossus. What we don't seem to know is what happened to the remaining part of the second collection. We also don't appear to know exactly what was in the crates that were lost with the Colossus. That collection has to hold the key to what this is all about.'

'I almost forgot,' said Meg. 'This came this morning.'

She handed the letter to Kevin. He took it, thinking how different her reaction was to this one than it had been to the previous letter she'd received. Then she'd been banging on his door in tears and shaking like a leaf. Now it was barely an afterthought. That didn't alter the fact that something unpleasant was going on and that Meg was definitely being threatened. He had to admit though that she'd be much better equipped to deal with whatever it was if she could keep up this new-found persona. He also liked the way she'd stood up to Hamilton this morning. Not before time either.

They had spent so long at the Giant's Castle that they decided to postpone the rest of the coastal walk to another time when they could take the whole day over it. Going as far as Porth Hellick Bay with its 'loaded camel' rock, where the body of the unfortunate Sir Cloudesley Shovell had been washed ashore after the wrecking of the Association, they cut inland through Higher Moors to Carn Friars Lane and crossed over the road into Holy Vale. Holy Vale, once the fruit growing centre of St Marys, was now a nature reserve. It always reminded Meg of a hobbit's forest from the film *Lord of the Rings* with its silent pools and misty creepers and sense of other-worldness. It was more suited to the South Island of New Zealand, where the film had been made and where, she remembered, stifling a smile at yet another coincidence, an island had been named in honour of Charles Greville's memory.

Meg and Kevin met up just before eight in the bar of the Atlantic Inn. It was busy as might be expected since it was a Saturday night and they had to push their way through a crush of talking, laughing, drinking humanity. Kevin had booked a table by the window. Here the floor of the Atlantic Inn was supported on wooden stilts anchored into the seabed and at high tide it almost felt as if the place was a boat at sea. They ordered their 'stone meals', as the waitress had termed them, and a bottle of red wine. Meg had asked why they were called 'stone' meals and the waitress had shrugged and told them that it was a Maori way of cooking meat by placing it on red hot stones. Both Meg and Kevin had ordered steak and the waitress placed sizzling stones of meat, onions and tomatoes in front of them with a warning not to touch the stones under any circumstances. She brought baskets of French fries and a dish of sautéed mushrooms and then left them to enjoy it. Clouds of steam and smoke issued from the heat of the stones under the food as their steaks grilled themselves to perfection and neighbouring diners stopped eating to share in the experience. Laughing and thoroughly enjoying the whole thing Meg didn't notice the tall figure lumbering over from the bar. It was Steven and he was clearly drunk.

'Bloody pollutionists!' he roared at a level of decibels which silenced most of those in the Atlantic Inn. 'Can't even enjoy a drink in peace and quiet without some toe rag messing up. Why the hell can't you just have a meal without any fuss like everyone else?'

He glared at Meg. 'I told you your friend was common and had no manners and this is proof of it. Still I suppose he was all you could find to take on a silly little idiot like you.' Steven belched loudly.

Two days before Meg would have run in shame from the pub and hidden herself away somewhere but now she said quietly, 'Steven! Go home! You're making an exhibition of yourself!'

'Me!' he yelled, by now thoroughly enraged. 'You stupid bitch! You're paranoid!' He nodded to his audience. 'She's paranoid!' he went on in the sort of tone that he would have used to tell them that she was a murderess. 'I'm not the one breathing fire and brimstone and making an exhibition of themselves!'

The incongruousness of this last remark drew nervous laughter. Steven opened his mouth for a fresh onslaught but before he could utter a word two burly fishermen had grabbed him by the arms and frog-marched him out of the pub.

'OK! Show's over folks!' said a man from behind the bar who was busy polishing the glasses until they shone like diamonds and placing them in neat rows on the shelves.

People turned back to their own tables and started talking quietly to their companions, no doubt discussing the events which had just taken place.
The steaks were still sizzling furiously on their stones.

Kevin and Meg looked at each other.

'I wonder what that was all about?' said Kevin.

'You said something earlier about its being jealousy and a man thing,' Meg smiled.

'I did, but it's gone far beyond that.' Kevin was thoughtful. 'What happened this morning perhaps merited a couple of sarcastic remarks the next time he saw you. Nothing to get blind drunk over. The way he has to keep attacking you is well out of order but it's as if he's driven. He's like a man on the edge.'

Attacking. Driven. On the edge. Wouldn't that include impatience and threats as well?

'Do you think he's behind the letters I've been getting. The phone calls even when I changed my number?' Meg asked slowly. She had of course given Steven her new number.

Kevin thought of the two letters she had shown him. Insistent. Controlling. Threatening. That was a description he could apply to Steven Hamilton.
'I rather think he could be,' he said gently. 'I'm sorry, but it does all fit.'

Meg nodded. When she had started getting the phone calls on her new number she had wondered briefly if it could be Steven and had immediately dismissed the notion as paranoid. How well he had trained her. Now she had to admit the unthinkable.

'It's better to know,' she said sadly, 'it's easier to fight the enemy you know.'

The stones had cooled a little and the steaks, looking succulent and well browned, were now sizzling less enthusiastically. They both regarded the feast laid before them.

'Shame to waste a good meal,' said Kevin with a twinkle in his eye.

'It is,' agreed Meg. 'Let's eat, shall we.'

They raised their glasses of wine in a toast to each other while outside the pub the waters swirled and eddied over the shadows in the shifting sands.

Southward Well, Samson, Isles of Scilly, 12th December 1798

Captain Murray was completely exhausted. The wind was still howling and Colossus was listing at an alarming angle. He had given the order to abandon ship some hours before. Islanders had known that Colossus was in serious trouble the minute her anchors had begun to drag and they had been on stand-by in case evacuation became necessary. As soon as Murray had given the signal the gigs had started taking off crew and wounded men, six at a time. It had been a long slow business and almost every gig in the Islands had been press-ganged into helping. The situation was made worse by the fact that the wind had strengthened and, because of sea conditions, they could not make a landing on Samson but had had to row on round to Bryher. Some of the men could hardly walk and it had sometimes required superhuman endurance on the part of both rescuers and rescued. By late afternoon, however, everyone was safe, if not very comfortable, on dry land. Island women were doing their best to give the cold, hungry and frightened men something hot to eat and drink. Protesting animals were being turned out of their sheds and barns so that shelter could be provided for the shipwrecked sailors; especially those who were wounded. The worst cases had been accommodated in the small church near the quay and given what blankets could be spared.

Back on board Colossus the Islanders and Captain Murray were busy salvaging what they could and the gigs had continued to row back and forth to Bryher so many times that folk had lost count. They carried supplies and goods and personal effects and packing cases until the limits of the rowers' endurance had been tested a dozen times or more. Everyone was cold, wet and exhausted now but somehow they had all kept going. Sometime after three in the afternoon, as the December dusk was beginning to fall, there was an ominous creaking and tearing of timbers. Billy Jenkins, who had been working on the gigs and shipwrecks all his life, knew what that meant. He turned to Captain Murray.

'Aye, Captain,' he said in his soft Scillonian burr, 'if we're leaving at all we had best be leaving now.'

The Captain acknowledged him with a nod of his head. He understood. Taking a last regretful look round he felt pangs of genuine distress for the fate of Colossus. She had been a good ship and she didn't deserve to end like this. He didn't quite understand why the anchors should have dragged as quickly as they had. There was still stuff in the galley and the cabins, and some of the cargo had been left in the hold, but at least everyone had been got away safe, except for the unfortunate King, and even his body had been taken to Bryher. They had all done their best. No-one could have asked for, or expected, more. Captain Murray was amazed that they had managed to save so much. What was left would just have to go down with the ship. Grabbing the old leather pouch in which he kept his own valuables he hurried after Billy Jenkins, clambering over the side of Colossus and lowering himself, non too gracefully in the heavy seas, down into the gig. They had barely begun to pull away when, with a noise like thunder and the splintering of a thousand wooden planks, Colossus turned over on her side and began to sink rapidly into the water. As she disappeared beneath the waves Captain Murray gave her a final farewell salute. It was the least he could do.

St Marys, Isles of Scilly, 1st June 2008

Meg had slept late and was woken by a tap at the door.

'Come in!' she called sleepily, looking at her watch. It was nine o'clock.

Mrs Woodcock came in with a breakfast tray which she placed on the small chest of drawers beside the bed. She drew back the curtains to reveal a clear and sunny morning.

'Mr Brownlow has rung,' she said. 'I told him you was still a-bed. He laughed. Said he thought you might be tired after last night. Asked if I'd be very kind and give you breakfast in bed for a treat. Says he'll meet you later at the quay as you arranged.' Meg struggled to sit up in bed, rubbing the sleep from her eyes.

'Thank you,' she said gratefully. 'That is really good of you.'

'No trouble,' said Mrs Woodcock, arranging the tray on Meg's knees.

'In fact it means I can get the dining room cleared away early. I'm off to Church this morning. When you've finished, just leave the tray outside your door. I'll collect it when I get back from Church.'

Mrs Woodcock bustled out of the room and closed the door, leaving Meg to enjoy her unexpected treat. She looked out of the window where she could see the quay across Town Bay. It was peaceful today. Sunday was still regarded as a day of rest in the Islands. Shops were closed. The Scillonian didn't sail. She remained at her berth in Penzance. No aircraft flew in or out. For the most part there were no day-tripper boats to the other islands unless there was a special event being held. The only concession to visitors was that, after lunch, if the weather was calm enough, there would be a trip around the Eastern Isles or out to the Western Rocks. Last night she and Kevin had studied the boards advertising boat trips and had discovered that there was to be one to the Western Rocks this afternoon. They both wanted to go and had arranged to meet at the quay after lunch.

Meg thought about the previous evening as she ate her breakfast. After Steven's involuntary departure she and Kevin had thoroughly enjoyed themselves. Their 'stone meal' had been excellent and afterwards they had sat out on the wooden balcony of the Atlantic with their brandies and admired the starlit magic of the Scillonian night. Steven had not been mentioned again. Nor had the business of the Colossus. Instead they had talked of other things like Kevin's ambition to travel and explore new horizons and Meg's dream of being able to visit some of the famous historical sites she had read so much about. When Kevin had kissed her goodnight outside Mrs Woodcock's house she had felt as though they were wrapped up in their own world where nothing else existed, a world which was completely separate from the ordinary everyday world in which they lived. She wondered if he had felt the same.

After she had showered and dressed, Meg took her book and went for a morning's sunbathing on Porthcressa beach. She might even go for a swim. A number of others had also had the same idea and several excited children were on the beach, running around, paddling, building sand-castles. Meg watched them for a while then decided that she would test the water herself. She had put on her swimming costume underneath her clothes so she stripped off and left everything in a neat pile on her towel. The sand was warm under feet but the sea was unexpectedly cold. Taking a deep breath she plunged in. It was like being thrown into a tank of ice. After the initial shock however, the effort of her strokes warmed her a little as she swam up and down close to the shore. No-one was staying in for long though and she came out herself after a few minutes, shivering and trying to shake the drops of water off herself. The warmth of her towel as she collapsed onto it was like manna from Heaven. She turned over to lie on her back and let the sun dry her when the old familiar voice she had come to dread said from somewhere above her, 'Trying to show off what we haven't got, are we?'

Wearily she opened her eyes and sat up.

Steven was wearing blue trunks that were a size too small for his increasing waistline and had adopted a pose more suited to Matt Damon in the Bourne Files than to a middle-aged man beginning to run to seed. Beside him stood Janine, wearing a bikini which was so brief that it beggared belief and almost contravened the laws of public decency.

'See if you had a figure like Janine's,' he went on, patting the cellulite of Janine's ample thighs, 'then you could really show it off. But you...'

'Steven!' said Meg irritably. 'Why don't you just get off my case. I'm fed up with your constant disparaging put-downs. In fact, after last night, you've got a nerve.'

Janine looked up at him. 'What happened last night?' she asked sharply.

He hasn't told her! thought Meg, amazed.

She tried to suppress a grin as Steven blustered. 'Oh nothing, nothing. It was nothing.'

'If it was nothing, then why didn't you tell me?' came Janine's crisp retort.

'Well, there wasn't really anything to tell, sweetie,' said Steven in a conciliatory tone. 'We just bumped into each other at the bar.'

'Which bar? You didn't tell me you were going out to a bar! ' Janine was suspicious and she had the bit between her teeth now. Meg decided to put her out of her misery.

'He was in the bar of the Atlantic Inn, Janine,' she said, 'and he was drunk.'

Meg smiled sweetly at Steven. 'I'm sure you don't want me to go into details here,' she said, 'I'll leave you to tell Janine later.'

She picked up her things and headed off down the beach, leaving Steven trying to placate Janine. How things change she thought. If he'd thought that Janine would be an easy push-over he'd obviously got it badly wrong. In that relationship, she guessed, it might be Janine who did at least some of the controlling.

Dibble and Grub were busy but Meg managed to find a small table which was partly shaded by its neighbour's sun umbrella. She ordered a large cappuccino and leaned back in her chair, enjoying the sun on her face. She could see Steven and Janine still arguing further up the beach. Why, she asked herself again, had he ever married her. Whatever he had hoped to gain obviously came at a high price. It was also very unlike Steven to play the role of peacemaker. He'd had no hesitation in treating Meg badly once he had got what he wanted, except, of course, that he hadn't got what he had wanted, which was why he was following her and writing threatening letters. He clearly thought that both she and Janine had something that would be to his advantage and the key to what this was lay with their late eighteenth century ancestors: Sir William Hamilton, British envoy to Naples, and his wife, Emma Hamilton; Admiral Lord Nelson; and Richard King, quarter-master on the ill-fated Colossus. Sir William had the valuable collections. Emma had persuaded Nelson to procure the ship for transporting those collections. King had worked on that ship. He would have been the helmsman responsible for steering the ship but, like the army quarter-masters, he might also have been responsible for supplies which meant that he would have had cause to go into the hold where the collections had been stored in transit. That was the connection. Richard King could have had access to Hamilton's collections during the voyage and possibly his curiosity had got the better of him. Then he would have known of the treasure the ship was carrying. He might also have discovered that the ship was carrying a dead man, the embalmed body of Admiral Shuldham and if he was a superstitious man, which was most likely the case, what would his reaction have been?

Meg finished her coffee and paid her bill. She needed to change before she met Kevin to go on the boat trip and she wanted to check on something in her notes. She had been keeping a careful record of all the information she had researched and something was niggling at the back of her mind. It was hot now and she needed to shower again to remove all the salt from the sea water on her skin and to apply lashings of sun cream to her arms, legs and face, which she could feel were beginning to burn. She knew how strong the Scillonian sunshine could be and she didn't want to end up looking like a freshly broiled lobster.

Kevin was waiting for her at the quay when she arrived. He was looking pleased with himself.

'Enjoyed your morning?' he greeted her.

'Yes,' she said, 'and thanks for the breakfast in bed.'

'Thought you might like that.' Kevin grinned. 'See, I know what you like,' he went on complacently.

'Not to mention the beach entertainment afterwards,' she said and experienced the pleasure of seeing him momentarily lost for words.

She told him of the encounter between herself and Steven and Janine. By the time she had finished Kevin was laughing.

'The biter bit,' he said, 'and serves him right!'

Meg had to agree. It had been extraordinarily satisfying to see Steven getting the sharp end himself for a change. It also took a little of the sinister sting out of the fact that she now believed it was he who had been responsible for the anonymous and threatening letters she had received.

The boat which was to take them out to the Western Rocks was moored against the steps at the end of the quay. They paid for their tickets at a small wooden kiosk and then went on board. They chose seats on the port side, so that they could view Samson better as they passed it on the way out. The afternoon was hot and little white clouds were scudding across the sky giving it a speckled appearance. Meg settled back in her seat and prepared to enjoy her afternoon. Kevin, looking relaxed, casually held her hand. Its propeller churning up the waters, the boat did an about turn in reverse and then headed out towards the open sea.

There was a slight haze over Samson, probably a heat haze thought Meg. She watched the gulls wheeling and calling to each over the South Hill. So different to the stormy dusk in which the Colossus had sunk. She became aware of a commotion at the front of the boat. The girl acting as the deckhand was running up and down the boat looking at Samson and yelling to the skipper who was on a two way radio.

'Yes,' they heard him say into the radio, 'some fool's got a fire lit on Samson. Get the coastguard on to it, will you. Probably on the East Porth or maybe at the foot of South Hill. Time this report as 2.23pm Sunday 1st June. See you later.' Kevin and Meg looked at each other. It could just be unwary holidaymakers deciding to have a weekend bar-b-q on Samson but somehow they didn't think so. That was a coincidence too far.

'I'll find out about it tomorrow,' Kevin whispered in her ear. 'I'm going to see one of the divers who worked on the wreck of the Colossus. Says he's got some interesting stuff to tell me.'

Meg resisted the temptation to shout 'Brilliant!' at him and whispered instead, 'That's great. How did you get to know who dived on the wreck and what they found?'

'Not much you can't find out over a pint in the Mermaid,' said Kevin, echoing what he'd told her before about how he sourced his stories.

The boat had passed St Agnes and the bird sanctuary of Annet and was heading past Hellweathers, the aptly named fingers of rock reaching desperately for the sky like those of a drowning person. In the distance, back towards St Marys, they saw the black and white coastguard launch making its way up to Samson. In front of them loomed the Bishop Rock lighthouse, lancing the horizon like a giant needle, a helipad girding its summit it as though it were a crown of thorns. The wind had freshened as the boat left the lea of the larger islands and headed towards the open sea. Small 'white horses' crowned the waves and flecks of foam hovered among the shoreline rocks of the smaller islets.

Swinging round to the left the boat entered what the skipper told them via his microphone was Brow of Ponds. It was a little calmer here and the boat cruised alongside a tiny island where rows of puffins stood to attention along the rocks, their orange beaks gleaming in the sun. The commentary went on to tell them that puffins were now quite rare, although in medieval times the rent of the Islands had been paid to the King with puffins, and as recently as the mid 19th century a local clergyman had described his inter-island journey as 'sailing through a sea of puffins'. On a neighbouring island was a small colony of seals and some of the pups, full of the curiosity of the young, slipped into the water and swam out to take a look at the intruders who had entered their haven. The children on the boat leaned over the side and crowed their encouragement. Meg took photograph after photograph and even Kevin felt himself caught up in the delight of a world where the animal and birdlife did not have cause to fear their human companions.

Heading out of Brow of Ponds the boat passed close to a collection of craggy sea-washed rocks which they were informed was Rosevean, and that opposite was the small island of Rosevear where the builders of the Bishop Rock lighthouse had lived for ten summers during the late 19th century. Shags and kittiwakes sat silently on the upper reaches of Rosevear, watching the boat and its passengers intently. There had been countless shipwrecks in this area, notably that of the Association in 1707, and legend said that the rocks and islets were haunted by the sound of sweet singing voices. Some said they belonged to mermaids; others that it was the souls of the dead lamenting their fate.

They then headed out across the two miles of open water to the Bishop Lighthouse. The swell was much more noticeable here and the boat pitched and tossed about as it rode the waves. Meg and Kevin held on to the slatted wooden seats to steady themselves. A few of the children had begun to look worried and were being reassured by parents who looked non too certain themselves. The swirls of white water around the foot of the Bishop Lighthouse were awesome and Meg could only imagine the horrendous difficulties of trying to attempt a landing. The light was fully automated now. Trinity House helicopters only visited to do maintenance work and they landed safely on the helipad on the top of the lighthouse.

Circumnavigation of the Bishop complete, the boat turned and headed once more towards St Marys. The clouds had increased and it was beginning to turn cooler. Meg took a blue jumper from her bag and pulled it over her head. She turned to Kevin. 'That was absolutely fantastic,' she said, 'I could murder a pot of tea just now.' Kevin agreed but said that he would rather murder a pint.

'I was going to suggest dinner out again,' he said, 'but it's Sunday evening and not much will be open. Would you like to come up to the cottage?'

Meg nodded enthusiastically.

'Good!' he said. 'I am a real genius at making Spaghetti Bolognese!'

They chatted together companionably about the merits of Italian cooking and the knack of choosing just the right wine and whether Chianti was dry or fruity and didn't notice the passing of time until they were abreast of Samson once again. The island looked starkly clear in the late afternoon light.

'I wonder what that guy meant who wrote that they could see the men standing up in a row near Southward Well?' Meg wondered out loud.

Kevin shrugged. 'Don't know.' He said. 'I've heard guns referred to as men. Maybe he meant the cannon.'

'Which cannon?' asked Meg.

'When Colossus sank she had almost a complete battery of cannon on board.' said Kevin. 'If she landed on one side, the guns on the other side would be standing upright.'

Meg hadn't thought of that. It was a possibility.

'I'll ask Phil Jenkins when I see him tomorrow. You know, the diver I'm going to see. He might be able to tell me more.'

The squall came from nowhere. It even seemed to take the skipper by surprise. Suddenly the wind rose and the sea became a grey heaving mass of water. Raindrops stung their faces as the boat rocked alarmingly. Children started to cry. Kevin and Meg clung onto each other as well as the boat. They were right over the Southward Well and seemingly at the complete mercy of the sea.

'Everyone hold tight!' yelled the skipper. 'I'm cutting the engine!'

People were afraid now. The waves seemed to be getting bigger. Suddenly a sheet of grey water loomed above them. A child screamed. The skipper wrenched the wheel around so that the boat rode parallel to the waves. The grey water smashed into the side of the boat and then rolled underneath it. Spray soaked the clothes of those on board. Meg burrowed her head into Kevin's shoulder. She thought of Colossus and the winter storm and shuddered. Just as suddenly it was all over. The boat had stopped rocking and the skipper had restarted the engine. Meg opened her eyes. The sun was shining again. The wet frightened group on board began to relax and tried to shake the water off their clothes.

'Sorry about that,' said the skipper. 'Happens that way sometimes and when it does you just have to go with it.'

They were pulling alongside the quay and the girl deck-hand threw a rope to a young man standing on the quay steps. He caught it and helped to haul the boat into her mooring. The relief was now evident on the passengers' faces and most gave a hefty tip as they disembarked and felt the security of dry land beneath their feet once more.

'Well!' said Kevin, helping Meg up the steps, 'that was an adventure!'

'It certainly was,' agreed Meg ruefully, 'and right over the Southward Well. Yet another coincidence too far.'

They stopped off at Mrs Woodcock's house so that Meg could change into some dry clothes and then they set off for the cottage. Back on terra firma, it was more sheltered and it felt warmer.

'When we get to the cottage we'll have a glass of wine first, if you like, and sit on the bench outside the front door like Darby and Joan so we can chill,' Kevin said.

'Thought we were chilled enough on the boat!' said Meg ironically.

Kevin laughed. 'That was then and this is now.'

They had reached the cottage and stopped short in front of it. The door was wide open and inside Kevin's papers lay strewn around his desk. His laptop was still on the table but it was on and the screen was lit up. Kevin stared at it.

'It's not even gone to screen saver yet,' he said, 'so not only has someone broken in and gone through my work but we must have disturbed whoever it was. They can't have been long gone.'

He went through to the kitchen. Nothing had been disturbed there but the back door stood wide open and a bewildered looking cat was sitting on the doorstep, where it had obviously been disturbed from sleep, furiously cleaning its paws.

Kevin went back into the lounge. Meg was sitting in front of the laptop studying the screen intently. On it was a list of items recovered from the Colossus.

'Shall I call the police?' she asked Kevin.

He shook his head and started checking round the room.

'I don't think anything will have been taken. It was information they wanted,' he said. 'The police won't really be interested. Anyway this is Scilly,' he went on. 'There's only usually one policeman out here. It's not like on the mainland. We stand a much better chance of finding out who did this through the locals. They've always sorted their own problems. Besides I don't think the severity of this crime really warrants the attention of Her Majesty's Constabulary. Do you?' He smiled at Meg.

Meg had to admit he had a point but she was still worried.

'Don't you have to 'log' a crime?' she asked. 'For insurance purposes.'

'Normally you would, yes,' said Kevin, 'but no damage has been done and I'm pretty certain nothing has been taken. The only casualty, if you like to call it that, is one pretty startled cat which probably got the fright of its life when they rushed out of the back door and practically trod on it!'

The cat in question seemed to have recovered its dignity and had stopped washing its paws, but it had retreated to a safer place in a corner of the small back garden.

'Do you think Steven is behind this?' Meg asked, despite her reluctance to want an answer to her question.

To her surprise Kevin didn't immediately agree. 'Maybe,' he said thoughtfully,' but he might not be the only one who is interested in what was on the Colossus.'

Meg was alarmed. 'Why do you say that?' she asked.

'Lot of pretty important stuff in Sir William's collections. There are people who would pay a great deal to get their hands on some of it. Besides, if Steven was going to break in here to see what information I had, he'd have done it a while ago instead of wasting his time writing you silly notes.'

Meg had to agree with his logic. She had also realised that the man who had chased her on the Garrison wasn't Steven. Then there was the matter of Richard King.

'Kevin,' she said slowly, 'I meant to tell you this earlier but we got a bit distracted this afternoon.'

He turned towards her.

'I got to thinking about Richard King's involvement after the scene with Steven and Janine,' she went on. 'When I went back to change I checked my notes. Captain Murray had made a note in his journal that he must return King's possessions to his wife and a reminder to himself that he had put the special little package for Cathryn in his safe. Cathryn must have been the name of King's wife. Out of respect for Cathryn he hadn't opened it to see what was in it but he thought it might be valuable because King had kept it with him at all times. That's a bit odd, isn't it? If he'd bought her a present wouldn't he just have kept it in his locker?'

'You're probably right,' said Kevin. 'I mean, if he was the quarter-master, it meant he was the helmsman. He'd have been up on deck in all weathers.'

'This whole business is becoming so involved,' said Meg. 'I don't really know what to think anymore.'

'Then let's think supper,' said Kevin, 'and I don't know about you, but I could do with a drink.'

They sat outside the cottage with their wine, watching the rays of the evening sun lengthen over Old Town Bay, wondering just what it was that everyone was searching for from the Colossus.

Down on the beach the shadows of dusk swirled softly across the sands.

Bryher, Isles of Scilly, 15th December 1798

Captain Murray sat in the wooden chair and stretched out his feet towards the small turf fire burning in the grate. The little cottage was sparsely furnished but Alice Pender had made it cosy enough. He had been billeted with her after his arrival on Bryher. As captain of the ill-fated ship it was deemed that he should be treated with some deference. The storm had raged for four days but it was abating now. Tomorrow he and a few of his senior officers would be able leave Bryher for the Star Castle garrison on St Marys. The cottage to which he had been assigned was over on the north east side of Bryher. He could see the round tower of Cromwell's Castle from his bedroom window. It was this which had given the cottage its name of Castle View. Alice Pender was a widow and she had honoured him by allowing him to sit in her dead husband's chair. She had treated him kindly and she had shared her meagre supplies of fish and potatoes with him. Alice had even washed his personal linen. They had spent the long dark evenings sitting companionably together in front of the fire and he, in return, had shared with her the jug of ale which was brought for him every afternoon.

Murray had told her about his family and his life as a sailor; about Colossus and the battles he had fought alongside Nelson. Alice had been entranced by his stories. She had tales to tell, too, and she had told him a lot about life in the Islands. Farming and fishing were the main occupations but it was the piloting work which really brought in the rewards. The men of each island took it in turns to keep watch for incoming ships and as soon as a sail was sighted the cry went up and it was a race as to who could launch the gigs first and thereby secure the work of guiding the ship through the maze of rocks and reefs which infested the shallow waters around the Scillies. Murray had listened with fascination. He knew that she had a son who was at sea and a daughter who had married one of the Webbers on Samson. She had told him how hard conditions were on Samson but that her daughter seemed happy enough; especially since the birth of her twins. He was curious about Samson. Alice had hinted darkly that the island might be cursed. It was on one of the reefs just off the coast of Samson on which his ship had foundered and he was determined to learn more about what she had meant by saying that the island was cursed. He might never have another chance to ask her after tonight. Alice was wary at first.

'I never said it was cursed exactly,' she said, pensively. 'Just there's something not right with that island. Sometimes it has a curious feel to the place and the wells dry up. Then they have to come and get their water from Bryher.'

'How is it not right?' Murray pressed her. 'You said your daughter seemed happy enough there.'

'Oh, Chesen, she's alright. She's happy enough with her Richard. They've got a cottage up top of South Hill. Overlooks South'ard Well where your ship went down. She won't go near North Hill though. Not for anything. She won't go near the North Hill. That's quite deserted. No-one ever made their home there.'

Alice looked at him a little suspiciously.

'Why do you be wanting to know these things anyway?' she asked.

'I lost my ship there,' said Murray, 'and my quarter-master, he was killed there too. Colossus shouldn't have sunk the way she did. She shouldn't have drifted like that. Something about it all bothers me.'

Alice's expression softened a little.

'Aye,' she said slowly,' I can understand that. Maybe it's just that your ship's guardian, it weren't working properly.'

Murray stared at her.

'Guardian?' he said. 'What do you mean?'

Alice looked at him steadily.

'You're a man of the sea,' she said. 'You know that all ships have guardians. Often the figurehead, but not always; sometimes there's something else'.

Murray had heard his men talking about 'guardians' but he was not a particularly superstitious man and he had tended to dismiss it as just shipboard talk. He looked at Alice and said cautiously, 'I have heard such gossip, yes.'

Alice looked shocked. 'T'is not just shipboard gossip,' she said firmly. 'Every ship has a 'guardian' but sometimes it can't work properly. Not if there's a bad omen. Like something on board that the ship should not be carrying.'

Murray's head jerked up. Guiltily he remembered Admiral Shuldham. He'd not wanted to carry the Admiral's dead body as cargo but orders were orders. Superstitious or not, he had to admit that he had felt uneasy about that. Then there was the business of the 'favour to a friend' that Nelson had asked of him. He'd not known what was in those crates and he hadn't felt at ease about that either; but Nelson was not a man you could refuse. He saw Alice watching him.

'I won't ask,' she said, 'but I can see you know that something weren't right on board. That's why your ship sank; and it don't surprise me that she should have sank the way she did. Your guardian weren't working properly.'

Captain Murray stared at the glowing turf fire for a long time then finally he turned to look at Alice.

'Aye, Alice,' he said at length. 'You might be right. I too think there's something strange in what happened but we may never know exactly what it was.'

St Marys, Isles of Scilly, 2nd June 2008

After breakfast the next morning Meg rang Sara Fisher to ask if she would be free at all that day. Sara sounded pleased to hear from her.

'Lovely to hear from you,' she said. 'I asked John to tell you to come up one afternoon. Thing is, I've got a meeting this afternoon, but you can come up for some coffee this morning if you're free.'

'Yes that would be lovely,' said Meg. It suited her very well. Kevin was seeing Phil Jenkins, the diver, first thing, before Phil had to take a group out on a training dive. It was a lovely morning with no sign of any sudden squalls. Meg walked along the Strand and up past the school. She could see children in some of the classrooms and thought that they were probably resenting having to be in school on such a lovely day. Opposite the school stood the former junior school which was now a gym and a Sure Start Centre. She must be standing on approximately the spot where the Strangers Cemetery, in which shipwreck victims had been buried, had once stood. Maybe somewhere beneath her feet lay the remains of Richard King. The road to Rosehill wound down between banks of sweet scented wild flowers and to one side lay a duck pond on which a mother duck was busy trying to teach her ducklings to hunt for food in the water. Meg smiled at them. One of the ducklings was clearly an individualist and intent on doing things his way in his time to the obvious exasperation of his mother. At least she hadn't shut herself off from the errant duckling. As she walked up the path to Rosehill, taking care to latch the rickety wooden gate behind her, Meg could smell fresh coffee brewing. She had barely put up her hand to knock on the door when it opened and Sara stood there, her face wreathed in smiles.

'Come in!' she said, planting a kiss on Meg's cheek. 'John's out on the boats this morning so we shan't be disturbed.'

She led the way through into the garden.

'Make yourself comfortable,' she said. 'I'll just fetch the coffee.'

Meg sat at the wooden garden table where she had sat with Kevin a few days ago. Was it only a few days ago? It seemed like half a lifetime.

Sara brought out a tray which she placed on the table. On it was a cafétierre full of rich dark coffee, a small jug of milk, two cups and saucers, and a plate of chocolate digestives.

'Hear you had a bit of bother in the Atlantic on Saturday night,' she said as she poured out the coffee.

Meg grimaced. 'My ex-husband got drunk and made a fool of himself.'

'It was two of John's friends who helped him leave,' said Sara. 'Said he gave them the sort of mouthful that would have shocked a seasoned trooper. So they put his head under a water tap for him. That sobered him up quickly enough.'

Meg tried, and failed, to stifle a grin. It would have been the blow to his personal pride and dignity that would have sobered him up after the shame of being doused in cold water like a common drunk.

'Can't say he didn't ask for it,' she said to Sara, and they both laughed.

'John and I are pleased that you and Kevin seem to be an item,' Sara said. 'He's a nice guy and the break-up of his marriage hit him hard.'

'His ex-wife is on the Islands,' said Meg. 'He saw her with her new baby and he took it badly.'

'I know,' said Sara. 'That was unfortunate. I liked Heather, too, but she should have told him about the baby before. She was always going to bump into him at some point and it would have been better if he'd had a chance to get used to the idea.'

Meg looked at her. Was there nothing one could keep secret in these Islands. 'Did you know Kevin had a break-in yesterday afternoon?' she asked.

'Oh yes,' said Sara, and went on, oblivious to the irony. 'News travels fast in these Islands.'

'Kevin said there was no point in calling the police,' said Meg. 'He thinks the locals stand a much better chance of solving this crime.'

'Quite right,' said Sara. 'In fact, John said he thinks he may know who it was.'

Well that was probably a faster result than any police force could have produced thought Meg drily. Out loud she asked if he'd mentioned a name.

'No. He wants to be sure first,' said Sara.

'What is it that they're all after?' asked Meg, a little desperately.

Sara re-filled their coffee cups.

'Well, she said slowly. 'I think there's more than one thing, but in your case...' she paused. 'Did your parents never tell you the story?'

'They never told me much of anything,' said Meg. 'I know that my great grandfather was supposed to have been Admiral Lord Nelson's grandson who was adopted because his parents couldn't afford any more children. But after my father sold the cottage I never really heard anything more about it.'

'Oh I don't think there's much doubt that your great grandfather was Lord Nelson's grandson,' said Sara. 'Jim Nelson kept his promise when Horatio had grown up and told him that his real mother was Horatia Nelson, daughter of Admiral Lord Nelson. It had always been Horatio's ambition to go to sea and he did. Sailed the seven seas as they say. Saw the world. Even got involved in the American Civil War taking supplies over for the, the...' she hesitated, 'the Union supporters I think it was, anyway the ones who were fighting against slavery. Horatia was said to be very proud of him and it's believed that the two of them corresponded fairly frequently. She wasn't rich, as you know, despite the fact that she was Nelson's daughter, but when she died in 1881 she wanted to leave Horatio something special. No-one knows quite what it was but it was said to have a connection with both Lord Nelson and Lady Hamilton, They, of course, were Horatia's parents and Horatio's grandparents. When Horatio died he left whatever it was to his son, Joseph, who, in his turn, left it to his son who was your father.'

Meg stared at her. 'I didn't know any of this. My father certainly never left anything like that to me. In fact,' she added, 'he didn't leave me much of anything at all.'

Sara looked sympathetically at her.

'Your father was different to the others,' she said slowly. 'He never really settled in the Islands, even though he was born here. Saw his chance to leave, took it and never came back, except for holidays, and I think that was at your mother's instigation. Don't get me wrong. Your father was a decent enough guy; he just felt that he didn't really belong here.'

'But why wouldn't he pass on whatever it was to me?' Meg was hurt. 'Was it because I was a girl and because there was no son for him to pass it on to?'

'I don't think so,' Sara said slowly. 'He had his faults but I don't think he'd have discriminated against you just because you were a girl.' She thought for a moment.'Knowing him, it was more likely because he felt that it would burden you in some way.'

'It's certainly done that,' said Meg bitterly, 'and I don't even know what it was.'

Kevin had left his cottage straight after breakfast and walked the short distance to Phil Jenkins's cottage. The break-in the previous evening had more angered than disturbed him although he knew that Meg had been genuinely upset. Kevin was certain that whoever it was had just been snooping to try and find out how much he knew or how much he had discovered. He didn't think it would have been Hamilton himself who had done it; that would have been too much beneath him; but he was fairly certain that Hamilton was involved. He'd acted reassuring and unworried to Meg because he felt that she had had enough grief from her idiot of an ex-husband but after he had walked her back to Mrs Woodcock's house he'd rung John. John had been concerned but not surprised. He'd said he'd ask around on Monday morning but he had a feeling he knew who had done it. Kevin had arranged to meet John in the Mermaid for a quick lunch. He knew that Meg was going to see Sara Fisher and he hoped that between them all they could maybe start to make some sense out of this whole thing.

The outside of the cottage had recently been whitewashed and fresh blue paint gleamed on the wooden window frames and doorway. Phil Jenkins answered his door on the first knock which made Kevin wonder if he'd been hiding behind it just waiting for the summons.

'Come in,' Phil said, leading the way into a small, cluttered, but clean and pretty, living room.

'Excuse the mess,' he said, pushing a pile of wetsuits off one of the chairs.

'I'm just getting things together for my eleven o'clock group.'

A door to the kitchen stood open at the far end of the living room and Phil hovered in the doorway.

'Want a brew?' he asked Kevin.

Kevin smiled. 'Please,' he said. 'Milk but no sugar.'

Phil nodded and went off into the kitchen. Kevin could hear him filling the kettle and switching it on, getting mugs from a cupboard, taking milk from the fridge. He looked around the room. Hung on the walls were lots of prints and old photographs of sailing ships. The blue sofa and its two matching armchairs were of the squashy and comfortable sort. A television stood in the far corner. There was an old stone fireplace and in the recesses on either side of the fireplace wooden bookshelves had been built. Kevin loved nosing into other people's books. Phil Jenkins's taste ranged from books on diving and naval history to shipwrecks and tales of the sea. He saw one which had the word 'Colossus' printed on the spine and took it carefully down from the shelf for further examination. Phil came back into the room with two mugs of tea which he placed on a low coffee table in front of the sofa.

'That's the real definitive work on Colossus,' he said, nodding at the book which Kevin had taken from the shelf. 'Borrow it if you like. There's some good stuff in it.'

'Thanks.' Kevin sat down on the squashy chair which had been cleared for him. He took the mug of tea Phil offered and tried to decide how best to begin, but Phil spoke first.

'Colossus is a big thing in the Islands at the moment,' Phil began. 'She's believed to be the only surviving warship of her class and there's been all the fuss about the lost collection of Sir William Hamilton.' He took a sip of his tea and continued.

'Of course we're not the first to be interested in her. There was a pair called Braithwaite and Tonkin who dived on her as early as 1805/1806. Claimed they were working for the Admiralty. But it was the Dean Brothers in the 1830s who I regard as the first serious divers. They'd invented a kind of breathing apparatus which meant that they could stay under water for longer. Strangely they didn't seem to find that much. Then of course there was Roland Morris in the 1960s and 1970s. He brought up a lot of the cannon and about 30,000 fragments from Hamilton's collection. Everyone thought the site was exhausted after that but in the 1990s local divers started to find more stuff down there and brought it up to the surface.' Phil paused to take another mouthful of his cooling tea and went on, 'Then in 2001 came the big one. They found the stern board and Oscar.'

He grinned at Kevin. 'You know who Oscar is?'

'Oh yes,' said Kevin, 'we've been to Tresco to see him.'

'Good,' said Phil. 'You've already made his acquaintance. What did you think of him?'

Kevin thought for a moment. 'I don't know really. He seemed a strange thing to have on a battleship. Apparently he's quite unique in British naval history. I thought maybe he should have had a partner to hold up the other side of the window frame he was curved around.'

'Good point,' said Phil. 'I wondered that too.'

'Meg was with me as well,' said Kevin, not bothering to explain who Meg was and how she fitted in to all this. He knew that Phil would already know that.

'She seemed to find him rather strange and wild. In fact,' he went on, 'it was Meg who noticed that he was missing his right eye and his right arm, just like Lord Nelson.'

Kevin had half expected Phil to laugh at this but Phil's face wore a grave expression. 'I know,' he said. 'I was on that dive when they found Oscar. He was unusual and it occurred to me that he might have been the ship's guardian.'

'Ship's guardian?' asked Kevin, bemused.

'Yes. All ships were supposed to have guardians. Mostly they were the figureheads, but sometimes it might be something else.' There was a short pause. 'Supposed to protect or guard the ships while they were at sea,' Phil went on. 'If a ship was wrecked it was said that for some reason the guardian wasn't working properly. Might have been an unlucky omen or something on board that shouldn't have been there.'

He laughed at Kevin's expression.

'My grandmother knew all the folklore of these Islands,' he said. 'I loved the stories she told me when I was a kid. I'd sit and listen to her for hours. A lot of it actually made perfect sense.'

Phil drained the remainder of his tea.

'Strange thing is,' he said slowly, 'they weren't going to bring Oscar up to the surface. They were just going to leave him where he was found. He was carefully re-buried in the sand to protect him from erosion in the water.'

'But he was found in the water,' Kevin interrupted.

'No,' said Phil firmly. 'He'd been buried in the sand by the angle at which Colossus settled on the seabed after she sank. The ship was lying on her port side. Her starboard side was uppermost and it suffered a lot of water damage from tides and currents and storm surges. Oscar may well have had a partner but he or she might have long since disintegrated.'

'Why leave Oscar down there though?' asked Kevin. 'Surely he was a really important, not to say unique, find.'

'Yes he was,' agreed Phil, 'but then almost certainly it was Oscar who was the ship's guardian and it was felt that he should stay with the remains of the ship he was made to guard.'

Kevin stared at him, trying hard to remind himself that this was the twenty first century and surely such stories were no longer really believed. Phil himself though seemed to see nothing unusual about it.

'So why did they eventually bring him up?' Kevin finally managed to ask.

Phil gave a resigned shrug.

'The powers that be insisted. Unique find. Valuable contribution to history. Preservation for posterity. The usual kind of reasons. So the next year we went down to bring Oscar back up to daylight but everything that could go wrong did go wrong. Bad weather. Equipment failed. High tides at inconvenient times. We started at Easter in 2002 but it was early September that year before we got him to the surface.'

Both men were quiet for a moment, reflecting on Oscar's forced and unwilling ascent back to the world of the living, then Phil continued.

'Strange thing was that much of the Colossus had been buried in the shifting sands for over two hundred years; then Oscar is brought to the surface and the sands start shifting in earnest exposing wood and metal and artifacts which had previously been protected. After that it was a race against time. We've dived on the wreck every spring and summer up to and including this year and we're just about coming to the end of it at last.'

'Why did the sands start shifting again after such a long time?' asked Kevin.

Phil smiled. 'No-one knows. Officially that is. There's little doubt in my mind.' He looked at Kevin, his expression sombre. 'You get my drift?'

Kevin did get his drift. How he would ever translate that into a serious article for the up-market Sunday colour supplements he didn't know, but he felt sure, in spite of himself, that there could be much truth in what Phil Jenkins was suggesting.

Phil looked at his watch. 'I have to go,' he said apologetically. 'I'll be late for my group otherwise. Borrow any books you like.'

He started gathering all his things together as Kevin stood up.

'Tell you what,' Phil said as Kevin picked up the book on Colossus that he'd been looking at and prepared to leave, 'There's quite a bit more we should talk over. Been some weird things happening in the Islands recently. How about meeting later for a pint in the Mermaid. Six suit you?'

'Fine by me,' said Kevin cheerfully, 'and thanks for the tea and chat.'

'My pleasure,' Phil grinned. 'See you later then. Bring Meg with you if you like.'

With that he was gone. Kevin walked back to the cottage lost in thought. He wasn't the type to believe in old wives tales and guardians of ships with seemingly supernatural powers but when something fitted together so well he had to ask himself if perhaps there might be just a grain of truth in there somewhere.

Meg had walked back into town after seeing Sara. She needed to think carefully about everything that Sara had told her. It was hot and she bought herself a long cool drink and sat staring out to sea, watching the sunbeams shimmering across Porthcressa Bay, and trying desperately to remember anything her father might have said or done that would have been a clue. It was in vain. She'd had little communication with him in his later years and when he'd died prematurely of some kind of liver disease she wasn't as grief stricken as she thought she should have been. In truth she'd done her grieving a long time before. Then, as she finished her drink, it came to her. If anything at all had been left for her then surely the family solicitors, Brown, Ormesher and Ockenthwaite, should know. They'd handled things for her when her mother had died. Her mother had still been alive when Meg had lost her father and she had dealt with all the legal matters at that time. It was just possible that there had been something and perhaps it had been overlooked.

Meg almost ran down the street to the post office. There was a phone box situated inside the post office which would be quieter and more private than the ones in

Hugh Town. It took rather longer than she had anticipated to get their number from what now passed for Directory Enquiries but at last she was through to Brown, Ormesher and Ockenthwaite. Who did she want to speak to, a young and polite voice asked her. Meg had no idea so she asked for Mr Brown, the first named partner. Miss young and polite voice informed her in tones of suitable gravity that they were terribly sorry but Mr Brown had passed on. Would she care to speak to Mr Ormesher instead. By this time Meg couldn't have cared less if she spoke to the cat but she controlled her impatience. It wasn't Miss young and polite voice's fault that Directory Enquiries were less than efficient and that Mr Brown had been inconsiderate enough to 'pass on'. Yes, she said, it would be fine for her to speak to Mr Ormesher, Another interminable length of time passed then a man's voice came on the line that sounded both ancient and wheezy. Dear God! Didn't they have young solicitors any more. She hoped fervently that Mr Ormesher would live long enough to finish the call.

Despite how awful he sounded Mr Ormesher was, in fact, quite efficient.

'Miss Nelson,' he said, 'how lovely to hear from you again. Of course it's some years since your poor mother died but I remember you. I'd heard you'd married and, er,' he coughed delicately, 'sadly it didn't work out. Anyway, enough of that. How can I help you?'

Meg explained to him briefly that she was trying to sort out some family affairs and wondered if he had still had any of the family papers.

His tone suddenly changed.

'I wonder if you would specify for what exactly you are searching Miss Nelson, and why,' he said formally.

He knows, thought Meg suddenly. He knows what I'm looking for but he wants to make sure. He wants to hear me say it.

She took a deep breath and launched into a brief account of events to date.

'Ah yes, Miss Nelson,' he said when she had finished. His earlier more friendly tone of voice was evident once more. 'I had to be sure, you see. Your father instructed me that I was not to voluntarily give you any information or, indeed, what he has left for you; but if you were ever to come asking for it then I should give you every assistance that I can.'

Meg stared at the telephone receiver in her hand. So there was something. Her father had left her something.

Are you still there, Miss Nelson?' Mr Ormesher asked in a hesitant tone.

'What? Oh yes. I'm still here.' Meg was initially too bewildered to even think of asking what had been left for her. Before she could marshal her thoughts, Mr Ormesher continued as though she had spoken.

'I am reluctant to discuss this matter on the telephone,' he said. 'All modern devices of communication seem to have ears; and of course I am not prepared to send what was left for you through the post. It has become too unreliable these days and besides I will need a signature from you.' Mr Ormesher paused. 'However,' he went on, 'I am prepared to write to you explaining your father's actions and to tell you what it is that he has left for you. If you will let me have your address I will do that this afternoon.'

Meg gave him Mrs Woodcock's address and remembered to thank him before replacing the telephone receiver in a daze. She walked out into the bright sunshine feeling as though she was on another plane somewhere, a parallel plane to her real life. Had Steven known about that or did he just suspect it? If he had known, how had he found out? On the other hand if he had known, surely he would have pushed and bullied her into claiming her father's bequest. He might well have suspected and when he finally realised that she genuinely didn't know anything about it he simply dumped her. If, however, as she believed, he was responsible for the letters and phone calls then he must have known something, but what. Meg was so pre-occupied that she didn't notice Kevin at all until she walked straight into him outside Lloyds bank in Hugh Town.

'Hey!' he said laughing. 'You're beginning to make a habit of walking into strange men!'

Meg smiled absently. Kevin looked at her.

'What is it, Meg?' he asked. 'Are you OK?'

'Me?' she said vaguely. 'Yes. I think so.'

It was blindingly obvious that her mind was elsewhere.

'Meg!' Kevin almost shouted at her. 'This is me! Kevin! What's happened? It's like you're out on Planet Zog.'

Meg dragged her attention back to him. 'Sorry.' She smiled at him. 'I've just had the most incredible news. My father did leave me something. Our family solicitor has just confirmed it. He wouldn't say what it was over the phone but he's writing to me so we should know either tomorrow or the next day.'

'Good heavens!' Kevin was taken aback. So there really was something.

'No wonder you're in a daze,' he said. 'and in a couple of days we might know what all this is about. I saw Phil this morning and he told me a lot of interesting stuff that

I'll tell you about later. I said we'd meet him in the Mermaid at six because he's got more to tell us and he'd like to see you as well. That OK?'

Meg nodded. That might be interesting.

'I just had lunch with John in the Mermaid,' Kevin continued. 'He knows who broke into my cottage.'

Meg's head jerked up. 'Who was it?'

'You'll never believe this because I didn't at first.' Kevin paused for effect. 'It was Janine King.'

Shadows flickered across the sands of the Town Bay beach.

Naples, Italy, 23rd December 1798

Emma was in a complete whirl of activity. This evening there was to be a grand reception held in Nelson's honour by the Sultan of Turkey who was to present Nelson with the coveted Plume of Triumph as a reward for defeating the French. Unusually, however, it was not the social niceties or the manner of her ball gown that was occupying her. She knew that tonight they were going to try and make their escape. After Maria Carolina had finally agreed to leave, Nelson and Sir William had worked out a plan for spiriting the royal family away from under the noses of those treacherous Neapolitans who were siding with the French. The mood on the streets was ugly and even the slightest hint that the royal family were plotting an escape would cause the mobs to riot. Everything had to be conducted with the utmost secrecy.

Sir William had told Nelson that a series of tunnels ran beneath the embassy and the palace down towards the shore and the quay. The plan was for people to slip unobtrusively away from the reception and make their way to where Nelson's ship, Vanguard, would be waiting and go quietly aboard. When everyone had arrived Vanguard would set sail for Palermo in Sicily where the royal family could stay until it was safe for them to return to Naples. Nelson had urged that they should only take such valuables with them as they could carry. Prudence was not a word that the royal family appeared to understand however. Linen, silver, cash, jewellery, servants, nursemaids, clothes, personal effects, all had to be taken, and it was Emma's job to ensure that everything arrived on board.

Alone in his library Sir William wondered what he should do about his precious collection. Taking and loading eight large crates was quite out of the question. They were well hidden but if the French should find them...Sir William did not care to speculate on that eventuality. He had, however, some rather good pieces of gold jewellery and a bag of precious stones which he had kept out of the packing crates on account of their small size. He would take those with him. Quickly wrapping the items in a nightshirt, he opened his valise and packed them in. Everything else would just have to take a chance.

Nelson had wanted to leave by 7pm. Emma and Sir William came aboard in good time, having, like Nelson, slipped quietly away from the reception without either fuss or fanfare. However, the various members of the royal family dithered and prevaricated, and Nelson grew ever more impatient. Emma tried to calm him but without much success. Notes flew backwards and forwards. The royal family would not be hurried. They found every excuse to delay and Nelson had begun to fear that they would not get away in time. It was nearly midnight before they were ready to cast off. In the meantime a bad storm had blown up. It was a wild dark wet night and a heavy sea was running. Nelson was used to winter storms but he told Emma and Sir William that this was the worst he had seen in thirty years. He would have preferred to ride out the storm at anchor but in the end he had little choice except to put out to sea. Sir William went to his cabin looking grim. He loaded his pistols and told Emma that if they sank he would shoot himself rather than drown. Emma was worried too but Nelson had assured her that, although it might be a bad voyage, they would not sink. As Vanguard lurched out of Naples into the open waters she prayed desperately that he was right.

St Marys, Isles of Scilly, 2nd June 2008

Kevin and Meg were on their third mug of tea at Dibble and Grub when the waitress came over to ask them if everything was alright.

'Only you both look like you might have seen ghosts and Emmie says that you can just sit here if you like and you don't have to keep on ordering mugs of tea,' she finished nervously, looking back over her shoulder to a dark haired girl working in the kitchen behind the counter who was obviously Emmie.

Meg and Kevin both smiled at this little speech. Islanders could be very understanding and compassionate to those they believed to be in trouble.

'Tell Emmie that it's very kind of her and thank you. I guess we have both seen ghosts of a kind but we wanted to see them anyway. It's very hot and we've got lots to talk over and we're drinking your tea because we're actually working up a grand thirst while we talk, but it was a very kind thought.'

The girl looked slightly non-plussed and retreated behind the counter where she and Emmie could be seen having a whispered conference.

'That was nice of her,' said Meg. 'Lots of places would just take your money or tell you that they needed the table.'

'Not in these Islands,' said Kevin. 'That's part of what I like so much about them.' They had retraced their steps to Dibble and Grub after their meeting outside Lloyd's bank. Kevin had been a little concerned about Meg's abstracted manner and insisted that she tell him her news first. She had started at the beginning and related her conversation with Sara Fisher which had finally led her to think of ringing the family solicitors and the startling news that she had received as a result.

'So there really is something,' said Kevin pensively, 'but you've no idea what it could be?'

Meg shook her head.

'Do you think Steven knew that?' asked Kevin.

'Don't see how he could have done,' Meg said thoughtfully. 'He didn't meet my father many times and they didn't really get on. It's not exactly the sort of thing you would blurt out to a virtual stranger whom you didn't much like anyway.'

Kevin had to agree with her but he privately thought that where Steven Hamilton was concerned there was more than one way of skinning a bird.

'Your turn now,' said Meg, 'I'm bursting with curiosity.'

Kevin told her everything that Phil had said. She was intrigued, as Kevin had been, by the fact that Oscar had been re-buried after his initial discovery and that the intention had been to leave him where he was on the sea-bed.

'What would be left for him to guard down there now?' she asked with a puzzled frown.

'My thoughts exactly,' said Kevin. 'The remains of the wreck, I suppose, but there's more to it than that. We might have a better idea after we've seen Phil this evening.'

'So how on earth did you discover that Janine King was responsible for the break-in at your cottage?' she asked.

'John said he thought he knew who it might be when I rang him last night,' said Kevin.

'Sara said as much this morning,' Meg put in, 'but he wouldn't name names until he was sure.'

'I met him in the Mermaid for a pie and a pint at lunchtime,' said Kevin. 'He'd seen Janine out shopping this morning and he went and spoke to her. Told her what he suspected and that he was sure that Steven didn't know about it. If she told him honestly what she had done, and why, then that would be the end of the matter. Otherwise he'd have to have a word with Steven.'

Kevin drained his mug of tea and signalled to the bewildered waitress that yes he really would like another one. She brought two more mugs of tea over to their table with a cautious smile and whispered,

'Emmie says this one's on the house.'

'Ah, bless,' said Meg gratefully. 'That's very sweet of them. Anyway how did John suspect that it was Janine?'

'He saw her,' said Kevin simply. 'He'd been out checking his pots in Old Town Bay. As he was rowing back to shore he saw her go into the cottage. It wasn't really a break-in as such; I mean the door wasn't even locked; but John knew we'd gone out on the trip to the Western Rocks and so he reasoned she'd gone there to snoop around. When he explained all this to her Janine burst into tears and said that all she wanted to do was find out more about Richard King. She knew that he'd been the quarter-master on the Colossus and she knew that she was descended from him but she needed to know why this was so important to Steven. They'd had a row on the beach yesterday morning and he'd flung back at her that her relationship to Richard King was the only reason he'd married such a cheap little tart as her in the first place.'

Poor Janine. Meg could almost feel sorry for her. Steven would never change.

Then she remembered. It was she, Meg, who had precipitated that quarrel and had watched it rage from a safe distance. Kevin could read her thoughts in her face.

'Don't waste your sympathy on her, Meg. She got what she asked for but I agree that she's not in a good place right now,' he said. 'She knew that I was writing an article about the Colossus and so I was the best place to start; but she also knew that I was unlikely to be forthcoming to her. She probably saw us go out on the boat and took her chance.'

He grinned suddenly. 'Bad timing of course, but it must have taken forever for her to totter over there in those heels.'

Meg laughed at his ridiculous vision of Janine but almost certainly it wouldn't have occurred to her to dress more sensibly for a walking expedition.

'I wonder how she got away from Steven for long enough,' she said.

'Oh, apparently he stormed off after the quarrel and went to drown his sorrows in the Mermaid. Gave the Atlantic a wide berth this time!'

They sat a little while longer, each ruminating their own thoughts on everything that had happened. For the first time it seemed as if they were actually getting somewhere instead of just waiting for things to happen. Meg was longing to know what her father had left for her but she was realistic enough to understand that she might have to be patient. The mail was brought into the Islands by helicopter and, depending upon what time Mr Ormesher posted his letter to her, it might arrive either the next day or the day after that. To take her mind off it she would listen to what Phil had to say to them that evening and then she would update her notes and try to work out just what was going on in the Islands; why the finds from the Colossus had suddenly become so important, and to try and establish the significance of Oscar.

Phil was waiting for them when they arrived at the Mermaid. He already had a glass of beer in front of him which was now half empty.

'Couldn't wait,' he grinned sheepishly. 'Got a thirst on me.'

Meg sat down while Kevin went to the bar to order three pints of beer. She was relieved that there seemed to be no sign of Steven.

'Hi. I'm Meg.' She introduced herself to Phil.

'Phil Jenkins,' he said, smiling. 'Now we've got the niceties over do you want to update me on what's been happening. We didn't really have enough time this morning.'

Kevin had returned with the drinks which he placed carefully on the table. He sat and listened quietly while Meg recounted almost everything that had happened. She didn't tell him about her phone call to the solicitor. That was private for now. It was personal to her and to her alone. Of course she had told Kevin but she had got to know him quite well and she trusted him. It wasn't that she didn't trust Phil, just that she didn't know him and some of her old reserve had reasserted itself. Kevin picked up on her omission but he did not betray her by either expression or gesture. He smiled at her with what would have been assumed by any on-looker to be general approval at the way she had told the story, but which also implied tacit acknowledgement of their shared secret. Phil had listened carefully and without interruption until she had finished.

'A lot of what you've told me fits in with little odd incidents we've been having here', he said. 'Like yachts anchoring in the Roadsteads but whoever is on board never comes ashore. Day visitors wearing sharply tailored suits. No-one dresses sharp in these Islands!'

They all laughed then Phil continued.

'Your ex-husband has been making a real nuisance of himself and then there's been all the business with Samson. Boats poking around where they shouldn't be poking around. Lines to some of the pots have been cut. People have been sighted on the island at times when they shouldn't be there. Then there was yesterday.'

Phil paused to take a drink of beer from his glass. In all the excitement Kevin had forgotten to ask John about what had happened on Samson the previous day. Setting his glass down Phil went on.

'Some lunatic lit a fire down by the East Porth. The coastguards were alerted and went straight up there in the launch. No sign of anyone but the fire was blazing away merrily enough. Bracken is tinder dry this time of year. Bloody idiots. The coastguards had the devil of a job putting it out. Strange thing was it looked as though it had been set to burn rubbish. We get a few lighting fires there, either stupid campers who want the forbidden thrill of spending a night on the island, or, as is mostly the case, those who simply want to enjoy a bar-b-q on the East Porth. But this one was different. Quite different.'

He took another swig of beer.

'It looked as though someone had been burning papers, and there was a great deal of domestic rubbish. Almost like a binful of the stuff. But where on earth had it all come from? No-one lives on Samson, or is even allowed to camp there, so...'

He was interrupted by a commotion near the door. A young blond haired man raced into the Mermaid and asked someone to phone for the Island ambulance to come down to the quay. Then he asked one of the barmaids to fetch a blanket. Phil was on his feet with Kevin and together they pushed their way through to the door. Meg sat there, uncertain as to what she should do. She was full of curiosity but unsure if she could help and she didn't want to just stand and gawp at someone else's misfortune. The next minute however Kevin was back by her side.

'What is it?' asked Meg. 'Whatever's happened?'

Kevin looked unusually grim.

'It's Janine King,' he said. 'Someone has attacked Janine King.'

Dark shadows swept through the sands.

Vanguard, on the Tyrrhenian Sea off the coast of Italy, Christmas Day 1798

It was the worst Christmas that Emma had ever known and she hoped to God that she would never know another one like it. The storm had raged for three days and it showed no sign of abating. The ship pitched and tossed ceaselessly. She had come to accept the constant rolling and lurching now and accepted Nelson's reassurances that, although the voyage might be very uncomfortable. they would not sink. Uncomfortable! Now there was an understatement if ever there was one she thought. Everyone, it seemed, except Emma, was violently seasick. Sir William lay on his bunk groaning and clutching at his stomach. He had not shot himself as he had threatened to do if things got really bad. Emma didn't think he would have the strength to do so now, no matter how much he might want to try. Maria Carolina was prostrated with the sickness. So too was Ferdinand who, much to his disgust, could not even manage to drink a glass of restorative wine. Most of the royal servants were too ill to move and Ferdinand had suffered the added indignity of having to clean himself up after being sick. Many of the crew had a greenish tinge to their faces and even Nelson himself had lost his customary cheerfulness. Emma thought of all the provisions that Maria Carolina had insisted should be brought on board so that they could have a Christmas Day banquet on the high seas to celebrate their escape. Wild boar and venison, fowls and capons, fruit and small sweet cakes, all would still be lying in the hold going rotten. As far as she knew no-one had eaten much of anything since they left Naples. The sheer force of the storm had slowed them down and Nelson thought it would be about the 27th before they made landfall. Emma sighed. She had to keep faith but two more days of this was a pretty grim prospect.

She was worried too about the royal children. Their nurse was completely incapable of looking after them and so Emma had taken over her duties. The children lay on their bunks, listless, alternating between being sick and drifting into fitful sleep. Emma had soaked clean cloths in some of the drinking water and gently sponged their lips, squeezing the cloth so that drops of water trickled into their mouths, but it was little Carlo who really concerned her. Carlo was just six years old. He had never been a strong child and his physical weakness may have been a reason why he was a favourite with Maria Carolina. Emma had nursed him in her arms for most of the voyage. His small body was wracked with the sickness and after yet another bout he lay pale and gasping against Emma's body. His eyes were sunken and huge and Emma could hardly bear the pleading expression in them. She had tried to tell Maria Carolina that she was worried about him but the Queen was too ill herself to understand much of what Emma was saying. Emma had sponged Carlo's face and tried to squeeze water from the cloth between his lips but without success. Carlo was too weak to even swallow a few drops and the water just trickled down his chin. She looked at the poor sick child cuddled up against her and involuntarily thought of her own daughter, Emma. She had not seen her for several years but she knew that she was alive and well. The child had grown up and was now working as a governess somewhere. She had done well and Emma had a twinge of conscience that she had not been there for her daughter as she was growing up. As Maria Carolina was not there for Carlo.

Carlo was growing weaker and Emma had begun to fear for his life. There was nothing she could do, no-one who could help either her or Carlo. She held him tightly. At least if he did die he would not die alone or unloved. The little boy was heaving yet again. There was nothing left for him to bring up and yet he could not stop the incessant motions of throwing up. When finally he lay back, exhausted and gasping, Emma held him close to her, stroking his forehead and murmuring comforting and loving words. His breathing seemed to grow more and more shallow and then he suddenly gave a convulsive shudder. Emma held him tightly, frightened for him. She looked down, and to her horror, saw that he had stopped breathing. Little Carlo was dead.

Tears streamed down Emma's face and she cried for him as she would have cried for her own child. Maria Carolina would be distraught when she was well enough to be told. Emma winced. How did you tell a mother that her child had died? In someone else's arms when that mother had been so close by. Emma finally dried her tears. She laid Carlo's body reverently on her own bunk. Then she carefully washed him and dressed him and laid him out as she had seen so many other women do in her time. The storm was relentless and Emma was thrown around the cabin as she performed those last pitiful services for Carlo. Then she struggled out of the cabin and made her way to the bridge. Nelson would need to know what had happened and she wanted to be the one to tell him. She knew that Nelson was fond of children, all children, and this would hit him hard. He was staring out at the angry grey seas and the angry grey skies as waves lashed the decks and the helmsman, taking his instructions from Nelson, fought to control the wheel. Emma took a deep breath and whispered the news into his ear. He turned abruptly towards her, both shocked and distressed, as she had known he would be. She could have sworn that a single tear had formed in the corner of his good eye. Desperate to offer him some comfort she leaned into him and whispered again into his ear. When all this was over and the time was right they would make a child of their own together.

St Marys. Isles of Scilly, 3rd June 2008

The sun streaming in through the windows woke Meg early the next morning. She had slept deeply and at first she couldn't think where she was or what she was supposed to be doing. Then it all came flooding back to her. She got up and drew back the curtains before switching the kettle on. She needed to think clearly and she needed some strong tea to revive her brain.

Janine King had been found unconscious on the quay. A young fisherman, returning with his day's catch, had moored his boat at the quay and had taken his fish to store them in the communal refrigerators at the back of the quay on what had once been Rat Island. He had quite literally fallen over Janine's body which had been lying at an angle just around a corner. Janine had been taken to the cottage hospital for assessment and treatment. She had received a blow to the back of her head, which had knocked her unconscious, but it wasn't known if she had suffered any other injuries.

Steven had been told what had happened but hadn't shown overly much concern. The Islands' policeman had been notified of the attack and, much to Steven's disgust, had taken him in for questioning. A lot of people had heard the quarrel between him and Janine on the beach the day before and a number of them had been disgusted by the way he had spoken to her and had said so publicly. That, and the fact that Steven had got himself seriously drunk twice in as many days, had not looked good for him.

Phil had declined their offer to join them for supper, saying that he was diving with a group on Colossus the following morning and he had some preparations to do. He promised to let them know if there were any further developments on the Colossus wreck site. Both Meg and Kevin were tired so they had settled for a quick bar meal with a stiff brandy to follow in the Mermaid. They had sat quietly and reflectively together in the stone flagged dining room of the pub, close to the bar which had been fashioned from one half of a blue and white painted rowing boat. News of the attack on Janine had shocked them both. Meg simply did not believe that Steven was guilty of the attack. It was just not his style. Verbal and emotional abuse, yes; but not physical abuse like this. However, if Steven wasn't guilty, then who was, and why had Janine been attacked so viciously?

Meg took her tea back to bed and sat looking out of the window in silent contemplation, feeling the hot liquid slip satisfyingly down her throat as she sipped her tea slowly. Presently she felt a little better and certainly more alert. She showered and dressed and went down to breakfast. Mrs Woodcock had obviously heard about the events of last night and fussed round Meg like a mother hen.

'Such a dreadful thing to happen,' she said, as she put the usual plateful of bacon, eggs, sausages and tomatoes in front of Meg.

'In these Islands too. We're not used to that sort of thing here. The odd drunken brawl yes, but not a nasty attack like that on a helpless young girl.'

Meg restrained herself from telling Mrs Woodcock that Janine King was not exactly a helpless young girl. She'd obviously been attacked from behind and would not have had the opportunity to defend herself, but if her attacker had come at her from the front he would probably have had a few weals and bruises to show for his pains.

'More tea?' asked Mrs Woodcock before Meg had scarcely drunk her first cup. Meg had declined but Mrs Woodcock had brought her another pot anyway. She knew that Janine King was Steven's second wife and she seemed to think that Meg might be either concerned or frightened by the attack. Meg's main reaction, however, was that of curiosity. Who and why? She didn't tell Mrs Woodcock as much because that would have led to endless questions and explanations and she didn't want that just at the moment.

Mrs Woodcock's attention was finally distracted by a knock at the door and she went to answer it. When she came back she was holding a registered envelope in her hands.

'This just came,' she said. 'I had to sign for it. It's for you.'

She handed the envelope to Meg. Meg looked at it and turned it over. Mr Ormesher's name and his firm's address were clearly printed on the back. She felt her heartbeat quicken.

'Thanks,' she said, and, ignoring Mrs Woodcock's obvious curiosity, escaped up to her room.

Silently she blessed Mr Ormesher. He had known how desperate she would be to learn what had been left for her and he must have written the letter as soon as he had put the phone down and sent it by registered post to ensure that she would have it the next morning. She didn't want to read the letter here in Mrs Woodcock's house. She wanted to be somewhere alone and private. Grabbing her bag and her jacket Meg slipped out of the house and made her way to Porthcressa beach. At the northeast end of the beach lay Buzza Hill. There was a path winding up to a building that had once been a windmill and had been rebuilt as a small tower to commemorate a visit by King Edward VII to the Islands in 1902. Around the base were wooden seats beneath a sheltering canopy and there were stunning views of the Islands. Meg chose a seat facing Porthcressa Bay and settled herself down. She took the registered envelope from her bag. Now at last she would learn the answer to so many unanswered questions.

'*Dear Miss Nelson,*' the letter began.

'*Your late father left a bequest with us to be given to you only on the condition that you came to us and asked about the afore-mentioned bequest. He felt that it might burden you in ways he did not wish and he believed that it was better you remained in ignorance if that were possible.*

If you were to ask us about the bequest your late father felt that you would have already learned of the circumstances which led to this bequest being made and therefore we need not repeat them here.

In our safe we hold a box which contains precious gems, including diamonds, rubies, emeralds and sapphires, and some items of jewellery worked in gold. We understand that this bequest has been handed down through generations of your family and was originally the gift of Sir William Hamilton.

Sir William was the British Ambassador to Naples during the latter part of the eighteenth century. His wife, Emma, Lady Hamilton, became the mistress of Admiral Lord Nelson and bore him a daughter in 1801. Your late father, and therefore yourself, are descended from Lord Nelson's daughter to whom Sir William made the original bequest,

You are free to claim your bequest which will be given to you upon your signing of the release form. We urge you however to consider carefully the value of this bequest and to make appropriate arrangements for its future security. Should you wish to sell the gems we can furnish you with appropriate owner documentation and advise you as to whom you should consult to obtain the best possible return.

We look forward to hearing from you soonest.

Yours faithfully

George Ormesher of Brown, Ormesher and Ockenthwaite.'

Meg sat staring out across the bay. She was stunned. Never had she dreamed it would be anything like this. Now she understood why other people were so interested. Steven, as a descendant of the Hamilton family, must have somehow discovered the bequest made by his great uncle several times removed. By marrying Meg he must have assumed that sooner or later he would get his hands on the gems; though if that were the case, why the sudden switch to Janine King. That didn't make any sense.

The stones and the jewellery must be worth an absolute fortune. Sir William was known to have collected antiquities from Greece and Rome, the Near East and the Etruscans. They must have a unique historical value. Why had he separated these items from his main collections? What reasons could he have had for bequeathing such priceless jewels to Horatia. He must have kept the bequest a secret from his wife, Emma, since in the years following the deaths of Sir William and Lord Nelson she had been forced to sell everything that she owned, or that she could lay her hands upon, and she had been in a debtor's prison more than once. Why had Sir William left such a fortune to Horatia, who was not even a blood relative, and not to his wife? Furthermore, why had Horatia not sold them? Why had she simply passed them on to one member of the family? Or had she come to realise by then that riches do not necessarily buy happiness?

Meg didn't know how long she sat there, just staring at the sunlight glittering across the sea and the Islands shimmering on the water. She needed to share this with someone and Kevin was the only person she felt she could trust not to betray her. Others she might tell could betray her inadvertently but with Kevin it was different. Pulling her mobile phone out of her bag she dialled his number. There was no reply so she left a message asking him to meet her at Dibble and Grub urgently because she had something of the utmost importance she wanted to tell him. That done she spent a few minutes more in her sheltered seclusion under the canopy of the old Tower, then resolutely she stood up and began to make her way down the curving path to the beach.

Kevin arrived at a run as Meg started to sip her first cappuccino. He was hot and out of breath.

'Whatever's happened Meg?' he asked in between gasps for much needed air. Meg looked at him guiltily.

'I didn't mean you to half kill yourself,' she said.

'You said it was urgent and, well, after last night, I didn't know what had happened,' he said, still sounding breathless.

Meg had completely forgotten about Janine.

'Sorry,' she said, sounding even more guilty. 'I'd forgotten about Janine.'

Kevin stared at her, wondering what on earth could have happened this morning to make her forget something like that. The waitress brought another cappuccino for Kevin. They could see her and Emmie watching them from behind the counter, their faces a mixture of concern and curiosity.

'I wasn't completely truthful but I couldn't tell you this on the phone. I just couldn't.' she said.

Kevin took her hand.

'What is it?' he said, his voice full of concern. 'What's happened?'

Meg took the letter from her bag and handed it to him. She looked away while he read it, studying the small waves breaking on the shore with the intentness born of deliberation. She didn't want to read what might be in his face.

'Bloody hell!' said Kevin with feeling as he finished reading the letter. 'What can I say? No wonder people have been chasing you if this is what is at stake.'

Meg turned back to face him.

'I haven't told anyone else,' she said quietly. 'I don't want to tell anyone else. I can't tell anyone else. But I need to share this with someone and you're the only person I feel I can trust completely. I'm not being rude to people like John and Sara and Phil, but this is a small island community and things get said inadvertently and then someone else half hears and, well you know, it gets a bit like Chinese whispers. Steven mustn't know about this at any cost. I don't mean to burden you but I really don't know who else I could share such a thing with. I hope you don't mind,' she finished lamely, well aware that she had been gabbling.

Kevin took both her hands in his.

'Oh Meg!' he said. 'Of course I don't mind. In fact I'm immensely flattered. I won't betray your confidence. Not to anyone. You can be absolutely sure about that.'

He leaned forward and kissed the tip of her nose. Emmie and the waitress were now watching them with open interest from their station behind the counter. 'I think,' he went on, 'if you can bear it, we should have an early lunch. Try and act a bit normal. God knows what those two think is up!' He nodded towards Emmie and her friend.

Meg smiled back. 'I guess so,' she said,' and I am actually quite peckish since you come to mention it.'

They ordered two Greek salads and a glass of chilled white wine each.

'We should at least toast your good fortune,' said Kevin quietly. 'If it is good fortune,' he added sombrely. 'Your father doesn't seem to have reckoned much to it.'

'No,' said Meg pensively. 'If he had any of the hassle that I've had I can actually see his point.'

'Maybe we'll just toast Sir William then,' said Kevin. 'After all it was pretty decent of him to leave something like that to the child his wife had by another man.'

His eyes clouded for a moment as he thought of Heather. He could see the sympathy in Meg's eyes.

'Perhaps Sir William was just more big hearted than me,' he said ruefully.

Meg shook her head.

'You are pretty big hearted yourself,' she told Kevin seriously. 'I don't think that is the case at all. I read in Sir William's biography that he never had children with his first wife and then he never had any with Emma either. He himself believed that there might be something wrong with him. He adored Emma to the end of his life and Horatia was at least half Emma. I think when he saw the baby he was probably just overcome and he wanted to do something for her. He knew that Emma and Nelson wouldn't let him have much say in her upbringing so he made her a little present. Simple as that.'

Kevin smiled gratefully at her. Meg had a definite knack of making him feel better about himself.

'Do you think I should go and see Janine?' she asked, surprising him.

He stared at her thoughtfully for a few moments before he said carefully 'Do you really want to see her? She hasn't exactly been very sociable to you.'

No,' Meg agreed, 'but it must be pretty horrible for her lying alone and injured in hospital.'

'She's got Steven,' said Kevin.

'I don't think so.' Meg looked down at her feet as though she was concentrating on something neutral so that she could explain without having to look him in the eye. 'Steven won't forgive her that public quarrel and he'll simply justify himself in that she got what she deserved.'

Kevin looked horrified. 'But she didn't ask to be attacked and beaten up,' he said hotly, 'and anyway the cause of the quarrel was entirely Steven's own fault. You were not to blame.'

'Yes,' said Meg wearily, 'but he won't see it that way. It was my fault for stirring things and her fault for rising to the bait and showing him up. Whatever happens that is unpleasant is never his responsibility, you see. In this case he'll blame me for telling Janine about him being drunk and he'll blame Janine for her reaction.'

'So he's never responsible for anything anyone else does then,' said Kevin angrily.

'That's about it,' said Meg. 'That way it's always everyone else's fault but his own and he can keep his image of his own perfection intact.'

'How crass and juvenile is that?'

Kevin was having difficulty controlling his temper. Now Steven had even got Meg feeling guilty again She was so kind in lots of ways and she always seemed loathe to think ill of people, even though she'd have been justified enough in the case of that stupid bastard. Nothing at that moment could have pleased him more than to punch Mr Perfect in the teeth.

'I thought I'd take her some flowers,' Meg was saying. 'She must be feeling pretty low, and besides, she might want someone to talk to about what happened. After all we have got Steven in common.' She smiled ruefully.

Kevin nodded sympathetically. He'd have felt sorry for anyone who 'had Steven in common' and it would certainly be useful to get Janine's side of the story. He wondered if she remembered anything about the attack.

'I wish you luck,' he said as cheerfully as he could manage. 'Meet back here later?' he asked.

'That would be good.' Meg looked relieved. 'See you about six then, and with that she was gone.

The shadows swirled across the sands as though following in her wake.

St Marys, Isles of Scilly, 11th January 1799

Tomorrow he would be leaving the Islands. Captain George Murray stared around the room he had been allocated for use as both bedroom and office in Star Castle. A small fire burned in the grate but it did little to counter-act the constant chill he felt from the winds howling around the Castle walls and he thought longingly of Alice's cosy living room in her cottage on Bryher. In a strange way he'd missed her. Of course he ate better quality food in the garrison dining room, in the company of his fellow officers, but nothing seemed to taste as good as the fish and potato soup or the fresh grilled mackerel she had given him with big chunks of her coarse home-baked bread. He also, if the truth be told, missed the chats they had had together in front of the turf fire, sharing his jug of ale set on the table between them. He had seen her just once more after he had left Bryher. It had been taking a damnably long time for the Admiralty to send sufficient ships to take the men off the Islands. Murray had sent some of the men to Tresco to lessen the pressure on Bryher of the necessity of accommodating them and feeding them. He had also sent money to the folk of both Tresco and Bryher to reimburse them for their troubles.

At the same time he'd had to write endless reports for the Admiralty on what had happened to the Colossus and reports on the defects of the ship. The date for his court martial had been set for 19th January. Although Murray knew that a court martial was standard procedure for any officer in charge who lost his ship he couldn't help feeling resentful that he was being called upon to account for something that had not been his fault. There had been no loss of life, except of course for the unfortunate Richard King, and they had even salvaged some of the cargo, so the sinking was not the disaster it could have been. Nelson had sent him a kind letter of condolence and support, and he told Murray that he'd written to the Admiralty in support of Murray's case. Captain Murray was grateful for this gesture since it would almost certainly gain him an honourable discharge from his court martial. Nelson had also hinted that he might ask Murray to become the captain of his fleet and that was a great honour indeed; but he was not at all sure that he would want to accept it.

Captain Murray had packed his few things and considered the pathetic bundle of belongings which was all that remained of Richard King. King had been buried in the Strangers' Cemetery at the top of the little rise that marked the boundary of Hugh Town. Murray had retrieved the fellow's clothing and a few personal effects to send back to his distressed wife. In an inside pocket of King's jacket there had been a small neat sealed package addressed to 'my belov'd wyfe Cathryn.' Murray had wondered about the package; had wondered why King should have carried it around with him; had even considered opening it, but he had decided against that. It was probably some little love token King had picked up in the Mediterranean as a surprise gift for her. King's 'belov'd wyfe' would have little enough left of her husband. Let her have her bit of privacy.

Captain Murray had also gone to Bryher one last time to take his final leave of Alice before he returned to the mainland. He'd told the boatman to wait for him at the quay then he walked round the Town Beach and along the sandy track to Castle View. Alice was tending her small garden. She'd seemed pleased to see him and he had pressed two gold sovereigns into her hand and told her that he would never forget the kindness and the hospitality she had shown him. Alice had gazed at the unimaginable small fortune lying in the palm of her hand and tears had come to her eyes. She had closed her fingers over the gold coins and then she had reached up and kissed his cheek, murmuring as she did so.

'Thank you, Captain, and don't forget, it was not your fault. Your guardian wasn't working properly.'

Murray had smiled uncertainly at her, then turned on his heel and walked back the way he had come, feeling strangely bereft that he would probably never see Alice again. That had been yesterday and tomorrow he would be leaving the Islands bound for London. Back to another world he thought. A world that didn't believe in islands with bad feelings and guardians that didn't work. He knew that the court martial would probably decide that the wrecking of Colossus had simply been the unfortunate result of a winter storm. The ship had dragged her anchors and then struck a submerged reef. There was nothing more to it than that. Such things happened. Secretly, however, although he would never say so, Captain Murray knew that there had been more to it than that. He agreed with Alice. There was much more to it.

St Marys, Isles of Scilly, 3rd June 2008

A path led from Porthcressa beach up Buzza Hill with its small stone tower, where she had sat reading her letter that morning, and then a short way along the cliffs to the cottage hospital. Meg stopped to buy some flowers from a shop next to a small garage on the sandy road which ran alongside the beach. Then she started the climb up the hill. The sun was hot on her back and she hoped that the bunch of sweet-smelling pinks she'd bought wouldn't wilt before she could put them in cold water.

The cottage hospital was a low modern building of modest proportions and the reception area was light and cheerful. The walls were painted cream and the floor was carpeted in a restful shade of forest green. Blue vinyl armchairs stood ranged round the room and there was a large cheese plant by the side of a small children's play desk tucked in a corner. A receptionist sat behind the long neat white desk at one end. She looked up as Meg entered.

'Would it be possible to see Janine King, please?' Meg asked in as firm a voice as she could manage.

The receptionist smiled. 'Of course,' she said getting up from her chair. 'I'll just take you down.'

She led Meg along a narrow tiled corridor to a small ward which held six beds. Janine lay in a bed at the far end. There was no-one else in the ward.

'Shall I get you a vase and some water?' the receptionist asked, seeing the bunch of pinks clutched in Meg's hand.

'Please.' Meg smiled gratefully. Nervously she made her way down to Janine's bed. Janine was awake, staring listlessly at the ceiling. She had a bandage around her head and a plaster on her cheek. Her left arm was in a sling. She turned her head at the sound of Meg's footsteps.

'Hi!' Meg smiled nervously. 'How are you feeling now?'

The apprehension was evident in Janine's eyes as she sized Meg up. 'I feel terrible,' she said. 'Come to gloat, have you?'

'No!' said Meg sharply. 'Whatever Steven may have told you otherwise. I felt genuinely sorry for you; and,' she added in what she hoped what was a conspiratorial tone, 'I know what Steven can be like.'

'Sorry,' Janine mumbled. 'It's just that I hurt all over and he's not even been to see me.' A tear rolled down her cheek and she hastily brushed it away with her good arm.

The receptionist returned holding a vase filled with fresh water. Meg thanked her and began to arrange the flowers she'd bought for Janine. 'I got these to cheer you up,' she said.

'Thank you,' Janine said hesitantly. 'I'm surprised you want to cheer me up. I thought you'd hate me.'

'No. I don't hate you, 'said Meg wearily. 'Why would you think that?'

'Well I did marry your husband and I haven't been very nice to you.' Janine looked down at the white coverlet on her bed and twitched at a thread with the fingers of her good hand.

'Steven wasn't my husband any longer when he married you. He'd made it perfectly clear before he left me that he considered me to be long past my sell-by date and he was moving on. That wasn't your fault,' Meg said generously.

Janine managed the ghost of a smile. 'Actually,' she said in a confidential tone, 'Steven told me all that and he went on so much about how awful it had been that I was expecting some real old battle axe; but then, when we were first introduced, I thought you seemed quite nice and I told him so. He wasn't pleased and he said some really hurtful things like...' She smiled half embarrassed, half coy. 'Well, you know Steven. He didn't want me to like you and he certainly didn't want me to be nice to you.'

Meg smiled back. 'Yes,' she said 'I know Steven and I can imagine that.'

Although on the surface she and Janine were very different people, underneath, the sisterhood bond between two women who had suffered at the hands of the same man was as strong as tradition had always proclaimed that it should be.

The receptionist reappeared carrying a tray with two cups of tea which she placed on the trolley table used for Janine's meals.

'I was making my mid afternoon cuppa and I thought you two might like one as well,' she said, 'it's so hot out there and tea is very refreshing.'

Meg moved the table carefully up towards Janine so that she could take her tea with her good hand. Picking up her own cup, Meg sat down on the edge of the bed and studied Janine's injuries.

'What happened to your arm?' she asked. 'I thought you'd just been knocked unconscious.'

'Broke it when I fell,' said Janine. 'He hit me with some force.'

'He?' said Meg. 'Do you know who attacked you?'

'No,' replied Janine. 'I was attacked from behind but no woman could, or would, have hit me that hard.'

Meg had to admit to herself that Janine probably had a point.

Janine's eyes filled with tears. 'Do you think Steven could have done it?' she whispered. 'He was pretty mad at me after we had that quarrel on the beach and he's not been to see me at all.'

'I'm sorry about your quarrel, Janine,' said Meg. 'In a way I provoked it.'

Janine shook her head. 'No. He'd been acting strangely for a bit. Very secretive. He kept going out for no good reason. He wouldn't let me go with him and he wouldn't tell me where he was going or what he was doing. There was a quarrel brewing anyway. But do you think he could have done this to me?'

She brushed away her tears again but more followed and trickled down her cheeks. Meg shook her head and smiled sympathetically at Janine.

'I don't think so,' she said. 'It's just not his style. He blusters and bullies and he'll use emotional blackmail to get what he wants but he still thinks he's got standards. He worries all the time about what everyone else is thinking of him. He would see hitting a woman, and in public, as low and common behaviour, not 'befitting a person of his station' as he would say.'

Janine gave a rueful smile. 'I think you're right,' she agreed. 'It's just nice to have some confirmation and reassurance. Why doesn't he come to see me though?'

'He's not good with hospitals,' said Meg. 'Besides,' she added, a trifle cattily, 'if it's not about him he's not really interested.'

To her surprise Janine burst out laughing. 'You know,' she said, almost merrily, 'Steven said you didn't know him at all, but I'd say you know him only too well!'

Encouraged by the camaraderie which seemed to have sprung up between them, Meg took a deep breath and plunged in with her question.

'Janine, forgive me for asking you this now, but why did you go into Kevin's cottage when he wasn't there? What did you want?'

Janine blushed bright red and stared hard at her teacup as though she'd just seen something amazing in its depths.

'I'm sorry about that,' she mumbled. 'I didn't take anything. I'm not a thief. I just wanted to try and find out something.'

'What is it you wanted to know?' said Meg softly. 'You could have asked Kevin.'

'I didn't think he'd want to talk to me because Steven was so horrible to him,' Janine said softly.

Meg was in private agreement with her but she said 'I think, if you'd at least asked him, he might have offered to help.'

Janine nodded miserably. 'I know. He seems a decent enough guy; but Steven was so adamant that he was not to be trusted because he was a journalist and the way he was sneaking around with you was just disgusting.'

The emphasis Janine put on 'just disgusting' made them both laugh despite the gravity of the situation. They could both hear Steven saying it.

'But what was it you were so keen to find out about?' Meg was anxious not to lose sight of her focus and Janine sighed.

'Steven went on and on about the Colossus. He was convinced that I was a descendant of the quartermaster on the ship and that my family was holding something very valuable which had been taken from the Colossus.'

Meg nodded knowingly. After all, she'd been down that road as well.

'I hadn't got a clue what he was talking about,' Janine continued. 'I've never been interested in family trees. Knew who my mum and my dad and my nan were and that was about it. But Steven insisted that I was a direct descendant of a guy called Richard King and that I must know something. I didn't know anything but I'm not sure he believed me. I knew that Kevin was researching the Colossus and I thought that he might know something about this Richard King.' Janine paused. 'That's all it was,' she added pleadingly.

'I believe you,' said Meg quietly.

'Anyway,' Janine went on, 'you came back and caught me unawares. I just rushed out of the back door. Fell over the cat as I went. It looked so startled and offended.' She smiled at her memory. 'Then the next day John came up to me while I was shopping in Hugh Town and told me he'd seen me running away from the cottage. He said if I came clean with him and told him the truth it would go no further. Otherwise he'd have to have a word with Steven. I believed him and so I told him what I've just told you. He seemed satisfied with that. No harm had been done, he said, so we'd just forget about it. I was so relieved. Steven would have gone absolutely ballistic if he'd found out.'

The receptionist came back for the tea tray.

'Visiting time is almost over and the doctor is on his way to do his rounds,' she whispered, 'but you can come back tomorrow if you like.'

Meg got up and turned to Janine. 'Would you like me to come again tomorrow?' she asked.

Janine nodded her head as vigorously as she could, given its bandaged state. 'Please,' she said. 'It will give me something to look forward too.'

'OK.' Meg waved her hand in greeting and left the ward.

She emerged into the unrelenting heat of a hot June afternoon. The hospital had air conditioning and she had not realised how heavy and oppressive the heat had become. She took her time walking along the winding path that led down Buzza Hill back to Porthcressa beach, stopping to admire the view a couple of times. In spite of herself she was warming towards Janine. She was quite a likeable girl at heart who had found herself under Steven's controlling thumb and was struggling as Meg had struggled. Meg wondered if he'd told Janine that she was paranoid just as he used to tell her that she was paranoid. She would ask her about that tomorrow. She had almost reached the bottom of the path when a figure blocked her way. She looked up and to her dismay found Steven standing there.

'Hello Meg,' he said in what, for him, passed for a friendly tone. 'I want to talk to you.'

'Well I don't want to talk to you,' said Meg. 'Why don't you go and talk to your wife instead? She'd love to see you, I'm sure.'

'I said I wanted to talk to you.' Steven's tone had become more insistent.

'Steven, we have nothing left to say to each other and I'd be grateful if you'd just leave me alone.'

Meg was annoyed. How dare he still try to order her around. He grabbed her arm with the pincer like grip of a determined crab.

'I said I wanted to talk to you,' he hissed. 'Now come along!'

Meg tried to wrestle her arm free.

'Steven! I said I don't want to talk to you!'

Ignoring her protests he kept his hand clamped on her arm and began to drag her back up the hill as she struggled to free herself.

'Steven!' she shouted. 'Let me go! I have nothing to say to you!'

'Just be quiet, will you.' Steven was beginning to pant with the exertion of dragging her along.

The next minute a hand grabbed his arm.

'The lady says she doesn't want to talk to you.' Kevin's voice was dangerously low.

'Oh push off, jerk!' said Steven contemptuously. 'What the hell has it got to do with you?'

'It's got quite a lot to do with me, actually' said Kevin icily. 'Now let her go.'

'You've no right to come between a man and his wife,' spat Steven.

'Your wife,' said Kevin, heavily emphasising the word 'wife', 'is in the cottage hospital recovering from a savage attack and she would no doubt welcome your company. Meg is not your wife and she does not want to talk to you.'

Steven dropped Meg's arm and glowered menacingly at Kevin.

'It's none of your business who I decide to talk to,' he said, 'and I thought I told you to get lost. Push off you ignorant interfering creep!'

He made as if to turn back to Meg but there was a sharp crack as Kevin's right fist connected sharply with Steven's jaw. The force of the blow sent Steven flying backwards into a clump of bracken where he lay for a moment looking totally bewildered and feeling his jaw tenderly. A small trickle of blood ran down the side of his mouth. Kevin rubbed his knuckles with a grimace.

'I've been wanting to do that for a long time,' he said, 'but it didn't half hurt.'

'Serves you right!' said Meg with mock severity. 'Playing fisticuffs like that!'

'Felt good though,' grinned Kevin. 'I suppose we'd better help him up,' he said, turning towards Steven again but Steven had dragged himself to his feet unaided.

'Are you OK?' Meg asked before she could stop herself.

'Fat lot you care,' muttered Steven sulkily, dabbing at the trickle of blood with a clean white handkerchief. 'That's what comes of mixing with people like him,' he sneered, inclining his head in Kevin's direction, and then, gathering the remaining shreds of his dignity together, he strode off towards the beach, head held high and without a backward glance.

Kevin turned to Meg with concern and said 'Sorry. Did you mind me hitting him? You seem to be worried about him.'

'Not at all,' said Meg. 'He had that coming to him and he did ask for it. It might just teach him a lesson though I very much doubt it. He's not even been to see Janine you know.'

'Doesn't surprise me,' said Kevin. 'Did she have any idea who attacked her?'

'No. She was attacked from behind but she is certain it was a man. She's very contrite about going into your cottage. She says all she wanted to do was to find out if you had any information on Richard King. Steven has been insisting that she and her family are harbouring some valuable secret which is connected with him.'

'He might actually be right in a way,' said Kevin unexpectedly. 'I got my friend in the Record Office to email me copies of the letters written by Captain Murray after the Colossus sank. In one of them Murray describes King's death and says that he's sending King's effects back to his wife, Cathryn. He mentions a mysterious little package which, by rights, he should have opened, but it was addressed in loving terms to Cathryn and he thought she'd had enough grief without him spoiling King's last gift to her. He did say that he was surprised that King had kept it on him rather than down in his quarters. Apparently Murray found it in King's jacket which they removed before he was buried.'

'So,' said Meg slowly, 'that might explain a number of things if Steven had also discovered that fact.'

'It might,' said Kevin, 'but it might also mean that Richard King really did have something in his possession that was immensely valuable. The question is, was it connected in any way with the Colossus?'

Unseen, shadows played quietly across the sands.

Palermo, Sicily, 14th February 1799

It had been a grim few weeks, Nelson thought, as he watched Emma drinking her umpteenth glass of champagne. She was drinking far too much but under the circumstances he could hardly blame her. The French had taken Naples on 23rd January; and both Emma and Sir William had been busy trying to comfort the royal family on the loss of their kingdom. In addition Maria Carolina was still inconsolable over the death of her six year old son, Carlo, during the nightmare voyage from Naples to Palermo just before Christmas. On top of all this Sir William had been told that two and a half thousand French troops had been garrisoned at his three houses in Naples. Sir William had shuddered visibly at the news and had said that he dreaded to think of the looting and the damage which would have been caused. Nelson himself was beginning to chaff at the inaction he was forced to endure and he had become ever more demanding of Emma's company whenever he could get it.

They had also learned that the Colossus had been lost in the Isles of Scilly. She had sunk during a winter storm after dragging her anchors and Captain Murray had been court martialled. Nelson felt both guilty and furious. He knew the risk that Captain Murray had run by giving Vanguard one of the Colossus's anchors and now one of his best ships had been lost. Nelson also knew that a court martial was standard procedure in the case of any ship which was wrecked but, damn it all, Murray was a good and able captain and he had simply been carrying out orders. There had been no loss of life, except for an unfortunate accident in which the quarter-master had been killed, and at least some of the cargo had been salvaged. All in all, Murray had got a raw deal. Nelson had sat down and written an immediate letter of support for Captain Murray, a man he admired, taking full responsibility for the fact that the Colossus did not have all her anchors. It had been time that those fools at the Admiralty learned a few home truths about the realities of military life at sea. This ruse appeared to have worked for Captain Murray had been honourably acquitted on 19th January. It was the only piece of good news that they had received.

Emma had been shocked when he told her what had happened to the Colossus. 'Just like Ann,' she had murmured.

Nelson had stared at her nonplussed and she had told him about the pretty singer who had been a dear friend to her when she was a girl and who had become a well known actress.

'I started working for her as a lady's maid but we quickly became friends and I learned a lot about acting and singing from her. We had some fun together for a while.' Emma smiled fondly at the memory. 'She drowned in a shipwreck out among the Western Rocks of Scilly about fifteen years ago,' she finished.

Enlightenment dawned on Nelson's face.

'Ann Brown,' he said, 'who became Ann Cargill. I saw her act once when I was about twenty. She played the role of MacHeath in The Beggar's Opera. T'was strange to see a woman dressed up as a man like that.'

Emma laughed. 'She enjoyed shocking people.'

Nelson grinned ruefully. 'I know,' he said. 'I read the papers too.'

Sir William had been very distressed as well to learn of the loss of Colossus. No details had been given of what cargo had been salvaged so Nelson was unable to set Sir William's mind at rest as to whether his precious collection had been saved. He knew that Sir William had spent hours pacing in his study, desperately wondering how much he had lost. Sir William had said that he had made careful lists of his collections but in all the excitement of affecting their escape from Naples they had been left with the remaining crates which Captain Murray had been unable to take on board the Colossus. Sir William had racked his brains to remember what had been in the crates sent with the ship. He half hoped that it had been the less valuable pieces but he knew in his heart of hearts that was probably not the case. He would just have to wait and hope that the French would not find the place where the rest of his collection lay hidden. Nelson felt rather sorry for Sir William and he supposed that he should let Emma spend longer with her husband but he couldn't help himself. He needed to have Emma with him all the time.

Samson, Isles of Scilly, 4th June 2008

The phone had rung while Meg was eating her breakfast. She could hear Mrs Woodcock's voice as she answered the call and then her footsteps as she came hurriedly down the passage into the dining room.

'That was Mr Brownlow,' she had said to Meg. 'He says as soon as you've finished breakfast would you meet him on the quay. It's urgent and he says to bring a warm jumper, waterproofs and a torch. He also asked if I'd make you a packed lunch. I'll do that while you finish your breakfast.'

Two other couples, also having breakfast in the dining room, looked up with interest at her words, wondering what island drama was taking place. Meg smiled distantly at them, not wanting to encourage their curiosity. If the truth were known she was as much in the dark as they were. She hadn't lingered over the toast and marmalade as she usually did but went straight to her room. She'd packed the items Kevin had asked her to bring in her rucksack, added her camera and notebook and then gone quickly downstairs. Mrs Woodcock had been waiting by the front door and gave Meg a plastic lunch box.

'I've put a bit extra in just in case Mr Brownlow didn't have time to make his own sandwiches,' she said. 'He did sound pretty excited on the phone.'

Meg thanked her and, taking the lunch box, she had practically run all the way to the quay. Kevin was standing there with John and Phil and a man she didn't know.

'Hi!' she said breathlessly. 'Sorry to keep you waiting. What's all this about?'

Kevin and John exchanged glances then Kevin said slowly 'It's Steven. He's gone missing.'

'Missing?' Meg looked from one to the other. 'I don't understand. You mean he's left the Islands? He doesn't need anyone's permission to do that. He's a grown man.'

'No. It's not as simple as that.' John spoke quietly. 'We don't think he's gone missing of his own accord. We think he's being held somewhere against his will.'

'Kidnapped?' Meg clapped her hand to her mouth. 'Why on earth would anyone want to kidnap Steven?'

If this was true Steven must have upset someone pretty badly. Either that or he had something someone wanted pretty badly. Kevin saw the sudden realisation dawn in her eyes. Someone had spied on Meg and threatened her because they believed that she held something of great value from the Colossus. Janine had been attacked probably because the same people believed that she also held something valuable from the Colossus. Now Steven, who had been husband to them both, and the person responsible for unearthing all that information, had gone missing.

'Shouldn't we call the police?' she whispered.

'They already have.' The man she had not recognised spoke. 'I am the police!' He smiled at her bewilderment. 'Dan Nelson at your service.'

Nelson. Meg looked at him. Dan was wearing yellow oilskins over the dark navy serge of his police uniform. Her great grandfather had been a policeman on the Islands and he had been a Nelson too. Dan seemed to read her thoughts.

'My great grandfather was Jim Nelson's natural son. Your great grandfather was his adopted son. I guess that makes us kind of related but I'm not sure how.' He smiled sheepishly.

Meg smiled back. He was the first Island relative she'd ever met even if he was only a kind of relative.

'We'd better be getting on.' John looked anxiously at them all. 'It's going to be difficult with the tides as they are today.'

They filed down the stone steps set into the quayside wall and clambered aboard John's boat. Kevin sat next to Meg while Phil and Dan stood chatting up front with John as he eased the boat away from her moorings and turned towards the harbour entrance. A black and white border collie sat on top of the life rafts regarding them solemnly from big brown eyes.

'That's Ellie,' said Kevin. 'She's Dan's dog. He won't go anywhere without her.'

'Is she friendly?' asked Meg. She was a little nervous of what she called working dogs since they always seemed to be more aggressive than their non-working colleagues.

'She's OK,' said Kevin. 'Border collies can be a bit tetchy if anyone who isn't their owner strokes them but Dan has trained Ellie to be friendly, especially to children. She can be quite protective of Dan, though. If she senses any hostility towards him she goes into guard dog mode.'

'Where are we going?' asked Meg. 'If Steven really has gone missing, how do we know where to start looking for him?'

'We don't really,' said Kevin, 'but there's a strong chance that he's been taken to Samson.'

'What makes you think that?' she asked.

'Steven was in the Mermaid last night, until about ten o'clock,' said Kevin. 'Apparently he was very quiet and sat in a corner by himself just drinking whisky. He didn't talk to anyone in particular. He wasn't drunk or unsteady when he left, according to witnesses. About ten thirty Dan got a phone call saying that there seemed to be a bit of a scuffle on the quay, people shouting and that sort of thing. By the time Dan got there about ten minutes later everything was quiet. He couldn't see or hear anyone so he just went home again but he logged the time of the phone call and his response to it.'

Ellie wagged her tail at the sound of her master's name and Kevin patted her with his hand.

'Anyway,' he went on, 'John was down on the quay early this morning and they were all talking about the fight that never was. Then one of the boatmen said lights had been seen on Samson last night. He and his wife do bed and breakfast and one of their guests is keen on photography. This guy had stayed up late last night sitting at his bedroom window because he wanted to get a picture of the full moon over Samson. This morning at breakfast he told them he'd seen lights on the South Hill and he wanted to know what they were because he'd thought that Samson was uninhabited.'

It was beginning to make a kind of sense.

'Phil rang me this morning. He'd been talking to one of his diving group in the Scillonian Club last night and the guy was asking about the precious gems from the Colossus and did Phil think that they would ever be found. Phil didn't know what he was talking about. This guy had apparently done his PhD on the collections of Sir William Hamilton. He'd studied the lists Sir William had made of his collections, which are apparently held in some restricted archive at the British Museum, and he'd tried to reconcile every item on those lists. Amazingly he managed to account for most of the stuff except for some Eastern seal stones, a few items of gold jewellery and what Sir William termed 'his box of precious jewels containing gems all colours of the rainbow'. Phil said that he'd never heard of them but that if they had gone down with the Colossus they would probably be scattered to the four winds by now. The guy seemed satisfied with that but later Phil got to thinking that with everything else that was going on it was a strange coincidence that this guy should turn up now talking about a hoard of missing jewels.'

Meg was inclined to agree with Phil. It was another coincidence too far. More importantly it was a lead on how and where Steven had got his information on what was missing from the Colossus's treasure. If Steven had also read Captain Murray's letters and Sir William Hamilton's papers it would explain why he thought she and Janine might be involved. Janine! In all the rush she had forgotten that she had promised to go and see Janine today.

'Kevin!' she tapped his arm and he turned towards her.

'I promised Janine that I'd go and see her today and I left without thinking to leave her any sort of message. She won't know what's happened.'

'I think she will,' said Kevin. 'One of Dan's colleagues, a woman police constable, has gone to the hospital to try and get a statement from her about Steven's recent activities, and also to sit with her. You've been threatened and Janine has been attacked so whoever has taken Steven is also interested in his wives. You're here with us and it was felt that Janine should have someone to look after her as well.'

Meg looked at him, a mixture of apprehension and curiosity on her face.
She couldn't quite believe the last few days and she thought of the letter from Mr Ormesher safely tucked away in her bag. That was what this was all about. Well, most of it anyway.

'What exactly are seal stones?' she asked Kevin. 'Are they what they sound as though they are?'

'I think they were polished stones or gems, sometimes pieces of wood or bone, maybe even ivory or metal, that were carved and used in Antiquity for sealing all sorts of things from clay tablets to tombs,' he said. 'Rather like they used wax to seal letters and someone would push their personal seal into the melted wax to show who the letter was from and that it hadn't been opened. The seals on the clay tablets which held the records of the Mycenean and Minoan civilisations in Greece and Crete were supposed to have been very intricate and exquisite.'

'That's what I thought seal stones might be,' said Meg. 'Like the brass seals with wooden handles that they sell in Past Times and shops specialising in calligraphy.'

She fell silent for a moment, watching John chatting with Phil and Dan.
Then another thought struck her and she turned back to Kevin.

'I thought Phil said he was taking a diving group out today. That's why he wouldn't join us for supper last night.'

'He was,' replied Kevin, 'but he thought this was more important. He rang them up and made some excuse about the tides. Said he'd take them out tomorrow.'

They had drawn level with Samson now and John was heading towards the East Porth. He stopped in mid channel and dropped anchor.

'Can't take her in any further,' he said, 'not with the tides as they are today.
Phil will take you across in the dinghy and I'll stay here with the boat.'

Phil had untied the dinghy, which John had been towing along behind the boat, and pulled it around to the side. He tied its rope to one of the boat's stanchions and then hopped over the side and down into the dinghy. Dan followed him and they both helped Meg down. Kevin was last, untying the mooring rope as he came and almost losing his footing in the process. For a moment the little rubber craft rocked alarmingly. When they were all safely seated Phil tugged at a cord and the outboard motor sprang into life. The dinghy turned and sped away from John's boat and within a couple of minutes they were grounded firmly on the sandy shore of the East Porth. Everyone clambered out and stood on the sand, uncertain for a moment as to what they should do next. Dan took charge.

'I think we should split into two pairs,' he said. Turning to Meg he went on. 'Phil and I will take the South Hill if you and Kevin would like to take the North Hill. Stay in sight of John's boat at all times. He's got field glasses and he's going to keep an eye on us, so if anyone tries anything he can summon help quickly. Don't drop down the back of Samson where you'd be out of John's line of vision. Is that OK with everyone?'

There was general agreement. At that moment there was a commotion in the water and Ellie came splashing ashore. She stood on the warm sand shaking herself vigorously.

'Ellie!' There was a mock sternness in Dan's voice. 'Didn't I tell you to stay on the boat?'

Ellie sat looking up at him out of her big brown eyes and wagged her tail furiously.

'What can you do with her?' Dan spread his big hands helplessly. 'She follows me everywhere.'

'How do we keep in touch?' asked Kevin. 'There's no mobile signal out here.'

'I've got a two way radio,' said Dan. 'Unfortunately only one handset but as we'll be in sight of one another all the time just gesture wildly if you need help. I can let John know and then we'll come to your aid.'

Meg looked a bit uncertain but she could see that was the only way. She wouldn't be alone and it was broad daylight; but then it had been broad daylight the other times. Kevin gave a mock salute and they all set off in their chosen directions. Meg was grateful that the weather seemed to be holding. Samson was tolerable in the sunshine. She didn't want to think about being on the island when it was wild and wet and windy. She knew how quickly the atmosphere could change and become menacing.

'Are you OK?' said Kevin, mistaking her silence for apprehension.

'I'm fine.' She smiled at him reassuringly. 'I was just thinking what a strange island this is. It can be so serene and tranquil and then, in a moment, it can change to, well, to terrifying.'

She expected him to laugh at her but he didn't.

'I know. I used to come here for picnics with mum and dad when I was a kid. It was all I could do sometimes not to cling to my parents like a frightened baby.'

Meg looked at him with sympathy and understanding.

'Yes I've often felt that way too and for no apparent reason. Steven thought I was just paranoid about the place. He didn't seem to pick up any vibes at all.'

'Well he's not the most sensitive of souls, is he?' said Kevin drily.

Meg smiled.

'You could say that,' she said, 'but then some people don't seem to pick up on vibes. Look at Sir Billy Butlin.'

'Sir Billy Butlin?' said Kevin, astonished. 'What on earth has he got to do with it?'

'Dad said Billy Butlin came to the Scillies sometime in the very early 1960s. He wanted to build one of his holiday camps out here and he thought Samson would be ideal.'

'A holiday camp!' Kevin shouted in amazement. 'I don't believe it! What happened?'

'Oh, the Duchy saw him off,' said Meg. 'Told him no way at no time would they ever consent to that. People complain about the Duchy but sometimes they do actually have the interests of the islands at heart.'

She stopped to adjust her rucksack, then went on.

'It was soon after, I think, that they started to forbid people to camp on Samson or to spend the night here. Not that it was hard to enforce that rule. I think that there is something more than the Duchy of Cornwall's by-laws that discourages people from wanting to spend the night here.'

They had reached the ridge of the North Hill now and they turned to look at the South Hill. They could see the two figures of Dan and Phil heading up the hill between Armorel's cottage and Ann Webber's house. As if they had heard someone calling, Dan and Phil turned round and waved cheerfully at them. Meg and Kevin waved back.

'So far so good, or so it seems,' said Kevin. He threw himself down onto the springy grass. 'Time for a tiffin, I think.'

Meg sat down beside him. They could see John's boat anchored off-shore, bobbing gently up and down on the water. She took a Kit-Kat from her rucksack and broke it in half, giving two of the chocolate fingers to Kevin.

'Thanks,' he said absently, as though he were lost in thought.

'If Steven was brought out here last night,' said Meg, munching on her Kit-Kat, 'where on earth would they have hidden him? I mean they could probably have spent the night in one of the cottages without fear of discovery but whoever took him must have realised that during the day there might be visitors on Samson.'

'My thoughts exactly,' said Kevin, finishing the last of his share of the Kit-Kat. 'They could have taken him out to one of the boats, I guess, but then why bring him here in the first place? I think they're probably intelligent enough to work out that if Steven is reported missing a search might be made of vessels in the area. It's my guess that he's here on the island somewhere but there aren't a lot of places to hide someone if you really don't want them to be found.'

Kevin scrambled to his feet and helped Meg up.

'Right, come on then. I don't know what we're looking for but we'll continue looking for it.'

Together they surveyed the North Hill. Most of the lower slopes were covered in bracken and gorse which showed no signs of being recently disturbed. There were no trees, no buildings, no obvious nooks or crannies for anyone to hide anything or anyone. There was nothing for it but to continue along the path which snaked across the summit. Meg wondered if searching the North Hill was simply a formality which was why Dan and Phil had volunteered to take the South Hill. There were more opportunities for hiding there.

'I don't think there is anyone else on the island today,' said Meg. 'Strange, as it's a nice day.'

'Tides,' said Kevin. They're really quite low today, remember. That's why John couldn't bring us right in. The tripper boats won't come here when the tides are low, although people with their own small boats might be able to land.'

Meg nodded, remembering how on the very low tides there might be no water between Samson and Tresco. A thought struck her.

'People can walk across from Tresco,' she said, 'when the water is very low.'

'I know. I've done it myself,' said Kevin, 'but I don't think the tides are quite that low at the moment.'

They had reached a row of small humps where grass covered the small stone cists which had once contained the remains of the Bronze Age nobility who had owned the islands in pre-history. A couple had been carefully excavated and then reconstructed to show what they would have looked like nearly three thousand years ago when they were first used.

'You know,' Meg turned to face Kevin, 'when I came up here on my own the first time one of the cist graves was full of tiny purple violets. They were so pretty. There are a couple of ancient graves like that on Great Arthur out in the Eastern Isles and I think there's one on Bryher too. All full of tiny purple violets. I'll show you.'

She walked on ahead and then came to an abrupt stop. 'The capstone has been moved,' she said in astonishment. 'Look!'

Kevin came to stand beside her and looked at where she was pointing. Just to the side of the path lay a small almost perfect cist grave. The area around it had been neatly cleared of vegetation.

'When I was here before,' said Meg, 'the capstone was pushed across at right angles so that you could see inside. That's where I saw the violets growing.'

There was a sound like a groan and Meg jumped.

'What on earth was that?' she asked fearfully.

The sound came again. Meg looked all around her a bit wildly and then down at her feet.

'I think it's coming from beneath that capstone,' she said in a frightened voice.

They both knelt down and tried to move the capstone. It would not budge. They could hear a faint movement from beneath the stone, a sort of shuffling, and then another groan, fainter this time.

'Oh God!' Meg whispered. 'There's someone in there! Could that be where they've hidden Steven?'

'Probably.' Kevin was on his feet gesticulating wildly towards the South Hill. It took a couple of minutes for the two figures descending the South Hill by the coastal path to see him but when they did they both broke into a run.

Meg knelt down and put her mouth to the capstone.

'Can you hear me in there?' she called. There was no reply. She called again but there was only silence.

Scrambling, slipping, running, climbing as fast as they could, both Phil and Dan were panting hard when they reached Meg and Kevin. Ellie rushed around in circles, her tongue hanging out. She was probably thirsty, poor thing, thought Meg.

'What is it?' gasped Phil. 'What's happened?'

'There's someone in that grave,' Meg pointed to the capstone at her feet, 'and whoever it is seems to be still alive. We heard groans and shuffling but we can't budge the capstone. I tried calling but I didn't get any response.'

'Right!' Phil was on his hands and knees examining the capstone and the grave it covered. Ellie was beside him, sniffing excitedly and barking. 'I think so too,' he said.

'I think she agrees with you, Phil,' said Dan, watching his dog carefully.

'The stone is probably too heavy to lift completely but we should be able to lever it and push it aside. There's plenty of overlap so it's not going to fall into the grave,' Phil said, dusting down his hands.

By common consent the three men took hold of one corner and through their combined strength managed to shift it a little so that it jutted at a slight angle. Then all four of them got down on their knees and pushed with all their might. Ellie sat quietly now, watching them. Inch by painful inch the stone slowly slid aside until it was almost at right angles to the stone box it had covered. Phil took a torch out of his knapsack and shone it into the small space uncovered by pushing aside the stone.

'Oh my God!' he said in a shocked tone.

'What is it?' asked Meg, scared now and her voice rising.

'Is it Steven? Is he alright?'

Phil shone the torch further into the aperture.

'Yes it's Steven,' he said. He put his hand into the grave and felt around.

'He's still got a pulse. Dan has radioed John that you wanted help but we need the air ambulance here as soon as possible and we need to shift this stone further back.'

Dan pulled out his radio and Meg could hear it crackling away as he spoke into it asking for the emergency services. That done they knelt down once more and put their shoulders against the stone, pushing and heaving until they were sweating and exhausted. By now they could see at least half of Steven's body. He lay on his side, his hands tied in front of his face as though he were praying. His ankles were bound together and his knees were drawn up under his chin. There was a gag in his mouth which had been partly pulled aside.

'What on earth have they done to him?' Meg was shocked.

'Contracted inhumation,' said Phil, almost to himself.

'Sorry?' Meg had never heard such a term.

'It's how they used to bury them in the Bronze Age,' said Phil. 'Lying on their side, knees doubled up under their chin and hands clasped together as though in an attitude of supplication.'

'But why the gag?' asked Meg, still staring at Steven's inert form.

'That wasn't a Bronze Age custom,' said Phil, 'but back then people were usually dead before they were buried.'

Meg stared at him in horror and disbelief.

'Are you saying they buried him alive?' she whispered.

'Yes,' said Phil. 'That's just what I'm saying.'

Shadows flitted unseen across the sands on the beach below.

Palermo, Sicily, 13th June 1799

Today the news had been received that Naples had finally been liberated from the French by the army of Cardinal Fabrizio Ruffo. Maria Carolina was jubilant. Sir William was relieved. Emma and Nelson were unsure whether to be pleased at the French defeat or sad that their special time together in Palermo was coming to an end. Nelson knew that it would have ended soon anyway for he had received orders from his superior commander, Lord Keith, to set sail immediately and go to assist in the defence of Minorca. He hadn't told Emma yet. Summer had come and she had been enjoying long lazy days with the Queen and performing her Attitudes at night to much local acclaim. After the horrors of their flight by sea from Naples the previous Christmas, learning of the sinking of the Colossus, and the dreadful news coming out of Naples since then, he reckoned that she had earned some respite. Their jubilation on learning that Naples had been freed was tempered by the fact that Cardinal Ruffo had then granted an armistice to the Neapolitan rebels who had joined the French. The King and Queen were outraged, Maria Carolina in particular. They had both demanded that the rebels should be punished in a proper manner, and had requested that Nelson should return to Naples at once to attend to this matter. The Queen also asked that Emma and Sir William should accompany him as translator and advisor. Nelson was in a quandary. He knew that he should obey Lord Keith's orders but he didn't want to do so. It would not be the first time he had defied a commanding officer and he knew it would not sit well with Lord Keith. He had heard the jokes about Lady Hamilton now being in command of the fleet and while Nelson had felt there was no truth in that, he had become less and less willing to be parted from her and he also had to admit that some of his decisions might have been influenced by his need to be near her.

Nelson sat in his room and stared out across the shimmering blue of the bay. Emma was with the Queen, as was usual in the afternoons, and Sir William was taking a nap after lunch. He would have to make a decision very soon. His orders were to defend Minorca but how could he let Emma and the royal family down? That was it, he thought. The royal family. Surely Lord Keith would not expect him to just abandon the royal family of Naples to its fate. There were other ships which were defending Minorca but there was no-one to defend the King and Queen of Naples. It was his duty to restore the rightful rulers to Naples. Lord Keith would see it this way eventually, he was sure, and he would be proud of Nelson for having the courage to take the decision to support the royal family. The fact that Emma could remain by his side was just the icing on the cake. He had a moral duty not to abandon the royal family just when they needed him so much.

Samson, Isles of Scilly, 4th June 2008

The four of them stared, shocked and disbelieving, at Steven's inert form. Phil pulled a penknife from his pocket.

'I'll cut his bonds. At least we can do that for him.'

'Wait!' Kevin's voice was authoritative. He turned to Meg. 'Did you bring your camera?'

She nodded mutely.

'Take some photographs of him before Phil cuts the bonds. They might be useful as evidence.'

Meg fished her camera out of her rucksack and took half a dozen snaps. It seemed indecent somehow, as though Steven were some freak of nature to be immortalised on film and gawped at by future generations. As soon as she had finished Phil cut the thin tight rope that bound Steven's feet, knees and hands. Then he pulled the gag free.

'Poor sod looks as though he managed to partially tug off the gag with his hands,' he said, 'though he can't have had very much leverage.'

'Can't we get him out of there before the air ambulance comes?' asked Meg.

'Better not to move him until the medics get here,' said Phil. 'We don't know if he's been injured at all and we could do him even more harm by moving him.'

Ellie had been sitting by the grave regarding Steven's body solemnly for some minutes, her eyes large and her nose twitching. Then she started sniffing at the surrounding area before suddenly taking off into the bracken. At that moment there was a noise like that of a busy three lane motorway on a bank holiday and they looked up to see a large green and grey helicopter descending onto the island. The pilot held the aircraft about a foot above ground level and three figures dropped from its open door into the soft bracken. They ran quickly across to where the four of them were clustered around the tomb.

The first of the figures to reach them introduced himself.

'I'm Dr Evans,' he said. 'Can I see the patient please.'

Everyone stood back as Dr Evans dropped to his knees and made a cursory examination of Steven.

'Nothing broken,' he said. 'There may be internal injuries of course but we have to move him anyway.'

A stretcher was fetched from the helicopter and everyone helped to carefully extricate Steven from the constricting stone tomb and lay him gently on the stretcher. Phil and Dan helped to carry the stretcher to the helicopter and load it on to the aircraft. Dr Evans was the last to board after Steven had been safely stowed.

'Sorry,' he said, 'no room for any of you to come with us but he'll be well looked after.'

He fished a card from his pocket and gave it to Meg.

'We're taking him to Truro Hospital. Ring me in a couple of hours or so and I'll update you on his progress.'

He turned to Dan and added 'I'll notify Truro police of course and they will liaise with you.'

With a wave of his hand he slammed shut the door and the helicopter rose once more into the air, turned its nose north eastwards and rapidly became a tiny black dot in the bright blue sky as it headed off back towards Truro.

Dan was on his hands and knees placing the remains of the bindings used to secure Steven into a large plastic bag. Ellie was still nowhere to be seen. Dan's radio crackled and he spoke into the handset, then he turned to the others.

'John's been asked if he'll do a special pick-up from Tresco and take them over to Bryher. Says he'll be about forty five minutes then he'll pick us up on his way back. So I guess we should go back down to the beach now.'

He stood up, his hands brushing down his trousers.

'Where is that wretched dog of mine?'

Right on cue Ellie reappeared. She was carrying something in her mouth which she dropped at Dan's feet, her tail wagging furiously. It was a small booklet. Dan bent and picked it up. The others looked at him expectantly.

'Tide timetables for Scilly,' he said with a shrug. 'Dropped by some visitor I expect.'

He put the booklet into his pocket and they began the descent back to the East Porth to wait for John. No one spoke, each lost in their own thoughts of the morning's events. Within a quarter of an hour they were back down on the East Porth where Phil had left the dinghy and sat down on the warm sand to wait for John's boat.

'All that has given me an appetite,' said Phil.

'Me too,' said Dan. 'Let's hope John isn't too long.'

Meg fished in her rucksack and brought out the lunchbox.

'Mrs Woodcock made me a packed lunch,' she said. 'I'm sure she made enough to feed an army so help yourselves.'

She took the lid off the box which was packed to the brim with sandwiches. Phil and Dan eyed them greedily before they gratefully accepted her offer and set about eating them.

'I made a couple of sandwiches before I left home as well,' said Kevin. 'Bit of a doorstep effort but quite edible all the same.'

He added his own contribution to the impromptu picnic. Meg wasn't hungry and munched half heartedly on a cheese and tomato sandwich thinking how surreal it seemed to be sitting having a picnic on the beach where once an international press conference had been held with the British Prime Minister; and on the same deserted island where they had just rescued her ex-husband from a Bronze Age style burial. Ellie sat politely on the sand at a little distance from them but she eyed the food speculatively. Meg smiled at her and gave her the remains of her sandwich which she'd not really wanted in the first place. Ellie snatched it up and chomped rapidly, then licked her lips appreciatively. She obviously had a liking for cheese and tomato sandwiches. Meg fed her another one.

Dan had taken the tide times from his pocket and was idly studying them. That's odd,' he said, half to himself. 'This tides timetable isn't at all damaged so it can't have been there very long.'

Turning to the others he said 'When Ellie ran off it was almost as if she was following a scent. She sat by that grave for a while sniffing around and suddenly she was gone. Then she comes back and she's found this. I wonder if the person who dropped it was one of those who brought Steven out to Samson?'

He flicked though its pages again.

'Another thing,' he said thoughtfully, 'is that someone has underlined today's tide times in red biro and there's a note on the top of the page which just says 'ring Chris to confirm'. It would be interesting to know exactly who this Chris is.'

'Oh my God!' Phil had gone pale.

'What's the matter Phil?' asked Meg anxiously. 'What is it?'

'This really is a coincidence too far,' said Phil. 'Chris was the name of the diving guy who was asking me if Sir William Hamilton's jewels had been on the Colossus and what might have happened to them.'

Shadows swirled silently and furiously through the sands.

Naples, Italy, 25th June 1799

Sir William and Nelson were both travel weary and unwell. Sir William had been ill with bilious fevers on the voyage while Nelson suffered badly from headaches and had not been sleeping well. Emma was tense but she had fared better than either of the men. She had nursed them both but she had focused most of her attention on Nelson. He was growing ever closer to Emma and that May he had added a codicil to his will that in the event of his death Emma was to receive a small box encrusted with diamonds and Sir William should have fifty guineas for a memorial ring.

Yesterday they had finally arrived back in Naples from Palermo where they had remained in exile with the King and Queen of Naples since that dreadful Christmas of 1798. The home-coming had not been a happy one. The Palazzo Sessa had been thoroughly ransacked and its beautiful furnishings destroyed, while Sir William's two other apartments had been plundered and smashed up beyond redemption. They had taken refuge in one wing of the Palazzo Sessa which had been less severely damaged than its neighbours and the servants had set about making it as comfortable as possible for them. Sir William, made more peevish than usual by his various ailments, had taken it hard. Emma had burst into tears and now she was depressed. Nelson was angry at all the wanton destruction and had stormed out in a rage hell bent on revenge. He had behaved completely ruthlessly towards all the rebels and had rounded up a number of them, ordering that they be summarily put to death in such a manner that it brought protests and condemnation from his own officers. Nelson didn't care. No one was going to make Emma cry like that and get away with it.

Sir William had only one thought in mind which was to discover if his precious collections were still in their hiding place. There was no sign of either Giorgio or Lucas and Sir William knew that it was more than possible that they had not survived. Now that he was back on dry land once more he felt a little better. That morning while Emma was with Nelson, carrying out translation services for him, Sir William slipped quietly out of their lodgings. Unnoticed he made his way through the noisy crowded streets of Naples and approached the Palazzo Sessa from the rear. Glancing around him to see that the street was deserted he took a bunch of keys from under his cloak and unlocked a narrow door in the garden wall. He edged through in an instant and relocked the door behind him. The Palazzo was mostly deserted and though it saddened him to see it neglected like this, its beauty destroyed, it suited his purpose well. Quickly crossing the garden he made for a corner of the Palazzo where a large bougainvillea was growing against the wall. Cautiously he slipped behind the trailing plant. Yes. There was the door. The French, in their haste to despoil the villa, had paid scant regard to the gardens; a fact for which Sir William was immensely grateful. Selecting another key from his bunch he inserted it in the lock of the door and turned. Miraculously it opened at once. Taking a last look round to assure himself that the garden was empty, he slipped through the door and into a hidden sub-terranean chamber of the Palazzo. A few steps led down into darkness and he felt clumsily in the niche by the door for the storm lantern. It was still there. He took a pack of flints from his pocket and within minutes he had the lantern lit. Holding it aloft he made his way carefully down the steep steps. Once at the bottom he looked around him. His packed crates were still lying there untouched and on top of one of them were his precious lists. Sir William grabbed them. As he had thought it was the less important and valuable stuff he had hoarded down here. Hastily he forced open a couple of the crates, hoping against hope that the lists might be wrong, but the contents only served to confirm what he already knew. The most priceless treasures in his collection were lying on the seabed in the wreck of the Colossus, and probably smashed into pieces. A sob escaped Sir William's lips. Quickly he made everything secure once more and pocketed his lists. Then wearily he climbed back up the few steps and snuffed out the lantern which he returned to its niche. He let himself out again, locking the door securely behind him. Back in the street there was still no-one about and Sir William re-traced his steps with a heavy heart. He had encouraged Emma's close friendship with Nelson at first precisely so that he might be able to save his collections. Now he had not only lost his best and most valuable pieces, he knew that he had also lost his wife as well. The whole thing was a complete and utter tragedy.

Southward Well, Samson, Isles of Scilly 4th June 2008

The four of them sat on John's boat trying to decide what to do next. Ellie sat up on her favourite spot on top of the life rafts where she could see what was going on all around but from where she could also keep a surreptitious eye on her master. John had arrived back opposite East Porth just after they had made the discovery that the tide times might have belonged to one of Phil's diving group who was, almost certainly, one of those who had kidnapped Steven. Meg, Kevin, Phil and Dan had grabbed rucksacks, lunch boxes and Ellie and had run to the dinghy. They reached the boat in no time at all and scrambled on board in such haste that both Meg and Ellie fell over.

'Hey!' said John, as Phil made fast the dinghy behind the boat, 'what's the rush?'

Phil wasted no time in bringing John up to speed with the developments.

'Bloody hell!' John was shocked.

He turned the boat around and put the engine in full throttle. Meg could see him talking on his radio but she couldn't hear what he was saying. Within a few minutes they were clear of the lea of Samson and heading across the open stretch of water towards St Marys. Meg was sitting next to Ellie on the life rafts facing the three men who had their backs to the side of the boat. Over their heads she could see the edge of the rocky cliffs on the South Hill and beyond the thin needle of the Bishop Rock lighthouse piercing the distant horizon. A boat lay anchored a short distance from the South Hill about level with the Southward Well. It took a moment for Meg to register the significance of what she was seeing. It was the same spot where Phil had said he dropped anchor when he took his diving group out to explore the area around the Colossus.

'I thought your group were going out with you tomorrow,' she shouted to Phil above the noise of the boat's engine.

'They are!' Phil shouted back.

'No! I think they've decided to go out without you. There's a boat moored out there.'

Phil whipped round to look.

'The hell they did!' he yelled. 'They've got no right to do that and they're contravening the terms of my licence. I can take them out to the wreck on a dive. They've no business going out there on their own!'

Dan and Kevin had also turned round and were watching the boat.

'The tide times,' said Dan, taking them out of his pocket. 'Today's tide times were highlighted for this Chris to confirm.'

'This really is far too much of a coincidence,' said Kevin. 'They have to be the same guys who are causing all this trouble.'

'All the locals know that site is licensed to me' said Phil. 'No one would take them out there or even loan them a boat.'

'So they must be the same people who threatened me and attacked Janine and kidnapped Steven?' said Meg, trembling a little.

The whole thing was fast spiralling out of control into realms that she'd never even known existed before the last few days. Was this why her father had been trying to protect her? Had he too suffered like this? Was that the reason he had left Scilly and sold the family home? How much had her mother known? Or had she even known anything about it at all? Her father had always been an introverted and secretive man. Was this why? Well she would never have the chance to ask either of her parents now and she wished desperately that at least one of them had taken her into their confidence before they died.

'I'm going to radio for reinforcements then we're going in to take a look,' said Dan.

'Reinforcements?' said Meg. The only reinforcements the police had in the Islands were two part-timers and one of them was sitting with Janine. 'From the mainland you mean?' she asked puzzled.

Dan laughed. 'No. They would take too long to get here. But we do have some extra back-up here in the Islands.'

He caught John's eye and the two men smiled in mutual acknowledgement of a shared secret to which the others were not privy.

Dan went to stand beside John and spoke briefly into his radio, then he returned to his seat with the others. John swung the boat round and headed towards the boat anchored off Southward Well. Meg was scared now. She hoped they all knew what they were doing. Kevin, seeing the look of apprehension on her face, came and sat next to her, and took her hand in his, squeezing it reassuringly. Ellie inched a little closer as if to protect her as well.

John's boat was almost level with the anchored boat now and they could see diving gear and two men on the deck. One of them turned at their approach. To their horror he held a rifle in his hands and as they came alongside he raised it to his shoulder.

'Get away if you know what's good for you!' he shouted. 'I mean it!' he yelled ominously.

Meg clutched Kevin's hand so tightly her nails dug into his flesh. She saw him wince but he made no attempt to pull his hand away. She looked wildly around her.

They were sitting ducks. There was nowhere to hide. It might be cowardly but surely John would turn around and do as he said. He wouldn't want their deaths on his conscience. At that moment Dan stood up.

'Come on,' he said in a calm voice. 'Put the gun down. That's no way to solve the problem and you wouldn't get away with shooting us.'

'Shut up!' yelled the man holding the rifle. 'I told you to go away! Now go!'

'I can't do that,' said Dan bravely, 'unless you put that gun down.'

Meg admired his courage. He was unarmed and he was standing up to a man wielding a rifle. She didn't think she could do the same thing in his position. The man seemed to hesitate for a moment then a wave rolled under the boat and Dan temporarily lost his balance and staggered against the side of the boat, moving a little nearer to the man with the rifle. There was a deafening crack as a shot rang out and Dan slumped onto the wooden bench seats blood pouring from a wound to his arm. Meg screamed.

The man quickly re-loaded his rifle and then he raised it to his shoulder and aimed it at them again.

'Now get the hell out of here!' he roared.

He'd reckoned without Ellie. She gave a sudden snarl of rage and, making one clean leap from John's boat to the diving boat, she hurled herself at him. As dog and man crashed to the floor of the boat the rifle was knocked from his hands into the sea. Immediately John swung the boat around to nudge the diving boat while Kevin and Phil scrambled to their feet and then followed Ellie over the side of John's boat and onto the deck of the diving boat. Meg ran to Dan's side. He was losing a lot of blood. Trying desperately hard to remember what she'd seen on hospital television programmes, she pulled off the thin scarf she'd worn as a sunscreen for her neck and shoulders and tied it as tightly as she could around Dan's arm just above the wound. To her relief the blood flow began to lessen. She shrugged off her jumper and, rolling it up, placed it underneath his head. Then she took her waterproof jacket out of her rucksack and covered him with it as best she could. His face was pale and his skin was cold and clammy to the touch. He was probably in shock. She turned to John.

'Dan needs medical help urgently,' she said desperately.

'I know,' John replied. 'It will be here in a minute.'

He gestured towards the back of the boat. She looked behind to see the coastguard and the ambulance launch coming alongside followed by a flotilla of boats of all shapes and sizes. Despite everything she smiled. So this was what Dan had meant by calling for reinforcements. She turned back to Dan. There seemed to be an awful lot of blood everywhere and she had to be careful not to slip in it. She had a brief vision of how it must have been on Colossus when the ship was engaged in battle. The roar of the cannon. The smoke of gun powder and grape shot. Injured men lying everywhere, blood flowing, screams of pain and shouts for help. At least Dan would receive the full benefit of 21st century medical care. He wouldn't have to have his wounds operated on without anaesthetic. He wouldn't be left in pain, staring at the dirty dressings, seeing the onset of gangrene, watching the advancing maggots attracted by the stench of rotting flesh. Meg shuddered.

John waved at the green and yellow ambulance launch, pointing to his own boat to indicate that there was a casualty on board. Moments later a man clutching a doctor's bag climbed on to John's boat. He came straight across to where Meg was sitting, stroking Dan's hand to comfort him. The flow of blood was now reduced to a trickle but Dan's eyes were glazed and he seemed to be lapsing in and out of consciousness.

'Dr Morgan,' said the man to Meg as he knelt down beside Dan, 'I'm from the cottage hospital.'

He took Dan's pulse before opening his bag and taking out a large white bandage which he tied tightly around Dan's arm just above the point where Meg had tied her scarf.

'Good thinking,' he said to Meg. 'He's lost a lot of blood but he'd have lost a really dangerous amount if you hadn't applied that tourniquet.'

He stood up and waved a couple of the boats which had followed the launch and the lifeboat to come alongside John's boat.

'I need help to stretcher Dan into the ambulance!' he yelled.

Two men, whom Meg recognized by sight from the quay, climbed on board and a stretcher was handed up from the ambulance launch. Dan was laid gently down on it and carefully strapped in, then Meg helped the three men hoist the stretcher over the side of the boat and down onto the ambulance launch where waiting arms received it.

'Is he going to be OK?' she asked tremulously.

'Oh yes,' said Dr Morgan in a bluff reassuring tone that he doubtless used with all his patients. 'Once we get him back to the hospital and I sort that arm out for him he'll be as right as rain. Come and visit him later if you like.'

Meg smiled at him wryly. Her hospital visiting list seemed to be getting longer by the minute. First Janine, then Steven, and now Dan.

'Does anyone need medical treatment?' Dr Morgan yelled across to the diving boat where Meg could see Phil and Kevin with three other men.

'No!' Phil yelled back. 'Customs will take this lot back to St Marys and hold them until Devon and Cornwall Police can send someone over.'

As the ambulance turned and headed back towards St Marys, Meg turned her attention to the other boat. A couple of customs officials had come on board and Kevin was obviously explaining events to them while Phil was talking to a man who looked as though he was the skipper. The gunman sat in a corner of the boat and Ellie stood guard over him. She wasn't touching him but if he made the slightest movement she bared her teeth and growled. The third man, who was dressed in diving gear, sat by himself, staring straight ahead. His face was expressionless. Meg saw Phil go over to him and say something but the diver didn't respond at all. One of the customs officials joined Phil and said something to the diver as well but he didn't get a response either. Both men helped the diver to his feet and led him to a seat next to the gunman. The diver's face was completely devoid of expression and his eyes had a vacant stare. Meg wondered what was wrong with him. The gunman made as if to move but Ellie fixed him with a stare and growled again.

'Can't you get this bloody dog away from me?' the gunman said.

'Sorry, mate, no,' said Phil cheerfully. 'She's doing a great job of making sure you stay put.'

He turned towards Meg. 'You OK?' he asked.

Meg nodded mutely.

'I'm going to help Customs take this lot back to St Marys,' Phil went on. 'Kevin will come back with you. He'll fill you in on what's been happening.'

Kevin swung himself back onto John's boat and John, who had been deep in conversation with someone on one of the other boats, started up the engine again as all the boats turned and began to head back to St Marys.

'What's the matter with the guy in diving gear?' asked Meg. 'His face has no expression at all and he just keeps staring, unseeing.'

'I don't know,' said Kevin. 'Nor does anyone else. All we know is that about twenty minutes into his dive there was a violent tugging at the rope and he came up as though all the devils in Hell were after him. Since then he's not spoken a word. Just sat there, mute and staring.'

'Who are the others?' said Meg, full of curiosity now.

'The skipper is from St Ives. Says he was just asked to sail a charter boat out to the Islands. Claims he knows nothing about anything. The other one, who shot Dan, is a nasty piece of work from the East End. He'll do anything if the price is right.'

Meg's eyes were like saucers. What on earth had Steven got himself mixed up in, and with whom, and why.

'They're not the brains behind all of this,' Kevin went on. 'They're just the workers, the drones. Of course they're not saying anything but I think that whoever is behind it isn't very far away.'

Meg shivered. She thought of the way the diver had looked and wondered if he felt as scared as she did.

'Do you think that's why the diver is in that state. Is he as terrified as I am now?' she asked.

'I think he is terrified,' said Kevin, 'but not of his boss. I think something happened down there on that dive. I think he found something, or he saw something, and it quite literally scared the living daylights out of him.'

Behind the boat shadows played almost imperceptibly across the water under the pale blue sky.

Palermo, Sicily, 18th August 1799

Sir William, Emma and Nelson had finally returned from Naples to Palermo on 8th August that year to a heroes' welcome. Emma wore a new dress especially for the occasion which she had had made to honour the Feast of St Rosalio, the patron saint of Palermo. It was a pretty dress and had sported the motif Nelson-Bronte -Nelson. King Ferdinand of Naples had recently created Nelson the Duke of Bronte, a dukedom in Sicily, as grateful thanks for his services. Nelson had been immensely flattered, both by the creation of his new title and Emma's tribute to it. Their welcome was tremendous. Twenty-one gun salutes were fired. Banquets were held in their honour. Firework displays lit up the night skies. They were showered with presents of jewels and money by the grateful royal family. Emma and Nelson revelled in all the attention.

Then there had followed an exhausting round of balls, dinners and official receptions. Nelson and Emma attended them all, thoroughly enjoying being the centre of attention, but Sir William longed for a quieter life. He was after all almost seventy years of age. He was also well aware of the gossip about Emma and Nelson and he knew that their insistence on his attendance at all these events with them was as much for the sake of superficial propriety as for the pleasure of his company. Often in fact he would have preferred to dine quietly at home with Emma but whenever he suggested it she would be scathing about his reluctance to allow her to enjoy herself, and then cajoling and then pleading. It was easier in the end, he decided, to just let her have her way.

Sir William wished with all his heart that his recall papers would arrive. He knew these things took time but it had been over three years now since he had written and asked to be relieved of his duties. After almost thirty years spent in the service of his country he felt that the time had come for him to enjoy the fruits of his labours in peace. Besides, he reflected wryly, if things had moved more quickly he might have been able to leave Naples with all his treasures intact and with his wife by his side since Nelson had not really arrived in their lives until the autumn of 1798. Then there would have been no need for any of his precious collections to have been on the Colossus in the first place and they would not now be lying lost to him on the sea-bed. Besides, he had a sneaking suspicion that the Colossus would never have sailed when she did if it had not been for his insistence that he needed to get his collections out of Naples and then she would never have sunk in the manner that she did. It was something he preferred not to think about too much.

St Marys, Isles of Scilly, 4th June 2008

Even though the evening was warm Meg felt a chill inside her as she replayed the day's events in her mind. Sara Fisher had been on the quay to meet them when all the boats had returned to St Marys along with, it seemed, half the Islands' population. The Scillonian was moored at her usual berth, rocking lazily up and down on the gentle swell. Visitors due to depart with her when she sailed at 16.30 prompt were gathered in twos and threes on the quay waiting to board and watching the drama with great interest. They could see an ambulance carefully negotiating the narrow lane which led to the quay as it drove away taking Dan and Dr Morgan up to the cottage hospital. John moored his boat alongside the diving boat and the customs launch moored up behind.

A policeman was waiting for them on the quay. He was a tall burly man who looked hot with his dark hair plastered against his face and his white uniform shirt sleeves rolled up. He stepped down into the diving boat and began a consultation with Phil and the customs officers.

'Who's that?' whispered Meg.

'Tom Jackson,' said Kevin. 'Dan's other part time colleague.'

Taking a pair of handcuffs from his belt Tom Jackson went over to the gunman and handcuffed him securely. The gunman had begun to protest about his rights but after Ellie moved closer to him and growled ominously he thought better of it and fell silent. The diver was still sitting staring straight ahead.

'Excuse me sir.'

Tom crouched down to bring his face level with the diver's face.

'I need to ask you a few questions and we're going to want a statement from you.'

There was no response and the man continued staring straight ahead as though he'd not heard.

'Can you hear me sir?'

There was still no response and Tom frowned, unsure of what to do next.

'He's in shock and he needs treatment urgently.'

The woman's voice came from above them and everyone looked up.
Sara was standing on the quay looking down into the boat.

'He's in deep shock,' she repeated. 'I think he should go to the hospital.'

'I'll take him,' volunteered Phil. 'I've got the van.'

Tom stood up.

'Not sure if you should,' he said. 'By rights I should take him into custody. No knowing what he might do.

'Look at the state of him, 'said Phil. 'He's not going to do anything. I'll take him up to see Dr Morgan and then I'll bring him down to you. OK?'

Tom nodded reluctantly but he trusted Phil and something needed to be done. The guy looked like a spaced out weirdo.

'What are we going to do with Ellie?' he asked Phil. 'If we can prise her away from him in the corner.' He nodded to where Ellie was still glaring menacingly at the gunman.

'I think she'll come with me, 'said Phil. 'She knows me quite well and I'll look after her while Dan is in hospital.'

Tom went over and yanked the gunman to his feet. Ellie growled but at Phil's whistle she hesitated for a moment then she turned and ran to him. As the gunman was frog-marched off the boat he turned to Phil and said nastily 'If I ever see that bloody dog of yours again, I'll...'

'You'll what?' said Phil, interrupting him. 'Making threats again already are you, and this time in front of dozens of witnesses.'

He nodded up towards the quay where quite a crowd had gathered to watch the proceedings. The gunman scowled at him and lapsed into a sulky silence. Phil helped the diver off the boat and up the steps. As they reached the top the diver turned to face the crowd, as an actor does his audience, although he was completely oblivious to their presence.

'It moved,' he said in a tone of complete disbelief. 'It actually moved.'

Then he crashed to the cobbles at Phil's feet. Kevin, John and Meg raced up the steps to Phil's aid and, with the help of a couple of men from the crowd, they got the diver into the back of Phil's van which was parked by the harbour offices.

'I'll go with Phil to the hospital and give him a hand,' said Kevin, jumping into the van beside Phil. He turned to Meg. 'Sorry. I'm kind of running out on you again,' he said with a rueful smile. 'You go with John and Sara and I'll come straight down to their house as soon as we've got this guy to hospital.'

Meg stood there forlornly as the van sped away. She had had so many shocks herself that she felt lost and bewildered and totally incapable of coherent thought. A comforting arm came around her shoulders and Sara whispered 'You're coming

home with us. You look as though you're in shock yourself and what you need is a good strong cup of tea and a drop of the hard stuff.'

John's van was parked close to where Phil's had been and the three of them piled in. It was only a five minute drive to Rosehill and when they arrived Sara took Meg straight in and sat her down at the big kitchen table. A kettle was humming away to itself on the Aga. Sara fetched a large red teapot down off one of the shelves and spooned in fresh tea leaves onto which she poured the boiling water. John came in and she set three cups and saucers on the table. When she had poured the tea and added milk, Sara took a small bottle from one of the kitchen cupboards and unscrewed the top. She poured a little of its contents into each cup.

'Brandy,' she said. 'For medicinal purposes of course!'

The tea tasted surprisingly good and warmed her stomach. Meg felt her cheeks go hot as the brandy flamed her skin.

'That's better,' said John approvingly. 'You've got some of your colour back. You were that pale I thought we'd have yet another casualty for the hospital.'

'Poor old Morgan must be doing double time and a half,' Sara laughed. 'He's had as many patients taken to that hospital in the last twenty four hours as he normally admits in six months!'

Meg smiled in spite of herself. She had to admit that the tea and brandy had made her feel much better. She turned to Sara.

'What do you think was wrong with the guy in the diving outfit?'

Sara exchanged glances with John 'I think he's had some sort of very bad shock,' she said.

Meg had not missed the look that had passed between them.
'What sort of shock?' she asked. 'I've never seen anyone look like that before. Not even my mother when she learned that my father had died.'

Sara considered for a minute as though trying to choose her words carefully. 'It's difficult to explain,' she began, 'but...'

At that moment there was a knock on the door and Kevin came in. He sat down next to Meg and Sara got up to brew another pot of tea.

'How is he?' she asked Kevin.

'He'll be OK when he wakes up,' said Kevin. 'So Dr Morgan says.'

He accepted his cup of tea gratefully from Sara. She had added brandy to it as well. She poured them all another cup of tea topped up with brandy and then settled down to listen.

'He came round just as we got him into the hospital,' Kevin went on. 'He was very confused and very frightened but at least he was talking. His name is Paul Smith and he's a professional diver. He was asked to do a series of dives on the site of the Colossus ostensibly to take photographs for a new book. Says he was warned about the problem of the shifting sands and that he might have to search carefully for the different parts of the ship. He knew what she was carrying when she went down and he was told that if he found anything, you know, any small object, he should bring it to the surface so that it could be passed on to the site licence holder and recorded.'

What a good plausible story thought Meg, and a perfect foil for the real intentions of those who had hired him.

'Did he know the man with the gun?' she asked.

'Not really,' said Kevin. 'He just knew him as Jamie. Thought he'd simply come along to help with everything.'

'But the rifle? The shooting?' Meg was incredulous.

'Paul said he never saw a gun anywhere and he doesn't remember anything about the shooting. He was in pretty deep trauma by the time he'd got back on board.'

'Why?' Meg was bursting with curiosity now. 'What shocked him so much that he went into a mute trance?' She looked expectantly from Kevin to Sara and back again to Kevin.

'He claims,' said Kevin slowly, 'that while he was down there he saw a dark shadow in the sand. He went over and began to brush the surface sand away and a piece of what he believed to be carved wood began to emerge. It looked like some sort of a figure wearing what he thought might have been a short toga or the sort of pleated dress the Romans favoured. He cleared away a bit more of the sand and started to set up a photograph. He turned his back for a minute to position his equipment properly and when he turned round he swears that the figure was standing up and coming straight towards him!'

Kevin paused and took a swig from his tea which Sara at once topped up. Then he continued his strange story. 'For a split second Paul was so terrified that he couldn't move, then he turned, grabbed his camera and fled. He tugged on the rope from the boat for all he was worth and went straight up to the surface. After that he says he doesn't remember anything until he came round in the hospital.'

Kevin finished his tea and added 'Fortunately, the Colossus is only lying about forty five feet down. It's a good job he was diving in shallow waters. Otherwise the bends might have killed him.'

They all looked at each other.

'Is that what you were trying to tell me when Kevin came in?' Meg asked Sara.

'Something of the sort,' said Sara. 'I didn't know the details of course but I had a pretty good idea why he was in that state. It was just the ship's guardian doing its job.'

'But Oscar was Colossus's guardian!' Meg interrupted. 'At least that's what we believed he was.'

Sara smiled. 'So he may have been,' she said quietly. 'Ships could have more than one guardian.'

'What will happen to Paul now?' asked Meg.

'We managed to get his wet suit off him at last,' said Kevin. 'That was not easy, believe me! Dr Morgan found him a bed and gave him a heavy sedative. Says he wants Paul to stay in until the morning just so that he can check he's OK. Which reminds me. Paul's got his fiancée staying with him on St Marys. He asked if I'd ring her and explain otherwise she'll be out of her mind with worry.'

Kevin pulled out his mobile phone and dialled the number he'd been given. When it was answered he briefly explained the afternoon's events. The person he was talking to said something and Kevin went as white as a sheet.

'Oh God!' he said. 'I didn't realise. I didn't know. I'm so sorry. I should have thought but there was so much happening. I really am sorry!'

He flipped his mobile phone shut and turned to face the others. He looked absolutely crestfallen.

'Kevin! Whatever is it?' Meg spoke softly. 'Who was that?'

'I should have thought,' Kevin said helplessly. 'She did tell me his name. Paul Smith is Heather's fiancé and the father of her baby.

Shadows in the sand flickered softly against the night sky.

Palermo, Sicily, 10th June 1800

Sir William Hamilton stood on the deck of the Foudroyant watching the city recede into the distance. He knew that he would not see it again. His re-call orders had finally come in April after thirty six years faithful service as the British Ambassador to Naples. Nelson had not wanted to leave Palermo either, he said, but then his own re-call orders had come through in May. Neither man had had much choice but to obey and Emma could do little but follow them. They were all returning to the old country but they were going to have to make most of the return journey by land since Lord Keith had forbidden Nelson the use of a ship to sail them back to England. Nelson had disobeyed his commanding officer once too often, it seemed, in his desire to remain close to Emma, and Lord Keith had finally completely lost patience with him. Even now, Nelson was defying his commanding officer in sailing the Foudroyant to Tuscany but he stuck to his excuse was that he was escorting the royal family of Naples on the first leg of its long journey to Austria where they were joining other family members. Sir William shuddered at the thought of the endless travelling which lay ahead before they reached England and wondered if he would survive it.

It had been a busy and eventful year since Nelson had regained control of Naples in the June of 1799. Sir William had heard the tales of Nelson's excesses in punishing the rebels and privately thought that Nelson had gone too far, though of course he had taken care never to voice this opinion. Maria Carolina had been delighted, and so had Ferdinand, but they had very excitable Latin temperaments which demanded and expected satisfaction in that way. They did not realise how such things would be viewed in the calmer more controlled atmosphere of England and their reputations would not have to suffer the aftermath. While they had still been in Naples Sir William had managed to have the remainder of his collection shipped unobtrusively to England. This time he had not bothered either Emma or Nelson with the request but had quietly overseen the arrangements himself. He still had the little bag of jewellery and the precious stones that he had taken when they fled Naples that dreadful Christmas of 1798. He had kept these gems by him but was unsure why he had done so. One thing was certain. He had not told Emma of their existence.

Soon after Easter in 1800 Sir William had noticed a change in Emma. At first he could not pinpoint its cause but as the days and weeks wore on it became obvious what the cause was. Emma was pregnant. The child was Nelson's of course. Sir William felt a twinge of envy. Neither his first wife, Katherine, nor Emma, had given him any children and he had begun to wonder if the fault lay within himself. Now he had his answer. Ironically the child might be officially his child but he knew that he would have no say in its future or its welfare. The thought saddened him a little. He had always wanted children of his own and now he would never have them.

St Marys, Isles of Scilly, 5th June 2008

Meg had woken late. Her eyelids felt heavy and her mind seemed to be struggling through several layers of fog. It was almost ten o'clock. She wasn't used to drinking brandy and they seemed to have spent most of the evening drinking it after the revelations of what had happened to Paul on his dive and Kevin's subsequent discovery that Paul was, in fact, Heather's fiancé. Meg realized that breakfast would have finished but she didn't think she could have faced one of Mrs Woodcock's body building platefuls this morning anyway. Getting slowly out of bed she opened the bedroom curtains. It was another glorious summer's morning. Far too good to spend indoors in a zombie like state. She took a long shower which refreshed her body and cleared her brain. Feeling much better she dressed quickly and went downstairs. To her relief Mrs Woodcock was nowhere to be seen. She could put off explanations until later.

Dibble and Grub were busy. The sunshine had drawn a number of people to the broad white sands of Porthcressa beach and they were sitting outside the cafe enjoying a variety of hot and cold drinks and melting ice creams. Meg sat down at a tiny table in a corner of the patio. The little waitress came hurrying over at once when she saw her.

'One coffee please,' said Meg. 'Large, hot and strong.'

The waitress wrote down her order, then looked up expectantly as though waiting for something else. Meg, guessing she'd thought Kevin would be with her as he usually was, added 'That's all, thanks.'

Kevin had left a text message on her mobile to say that he was going to see Phil and would meet up with her later. Meg had decided on a quick reviving coffee and then she would go up to the cottage hospital and see Janine. The waitress brought her a large cup of strong black coffee and a tiny jug of cream on a tray which she set carefully down on the table in front of Meg. She was obviously dying to ask Meg about Kevin but was too polite to do so. Meg decided to put her out of her misery. 'Thank you,' she said, putting the correct money for the coffee onto the tray. 'I expect we'll both be in for lunch so see you later.'

Meg closed her eyes and drank her coffee slowly. She tried to make her mind a blank but she couldn't erase the image of Paul's face as he said 'It moved. It actually moved,' before he'd collapsed at Phil's feet. To think he was Heather's fiancé as well. It had given Kevin quite a shock and no wonder. After all he and Phil had taken the guy to hospital and Kevin had even helped the doctor undress him and get him into bed. Then to discover that he was, in fact, the father of his ex-wife's new baby, must have shaken him to the core. It was an amazing coincidence and there were already far too many coincidences about this whole thing. She drained her coffee cup and stood up resolutely. Seeing Janine would take her mind off it for a while.

Janine was sitting up in bed looking much brighter. She wasn't alone this time. A policewoman sat in a chair by her side and Dan was sleeping in a bed at the other end of the small ward. The size and resources of the cottage hospital ran to a separate ward of six beds for each sex but she'd been told that the ward for male patients was currently closed for refurbishment when she'd enquired about Dan. There was no sign of Paul.

'Hi!' she said cheerfully as she approached Janine. 'How are you?'

The policewoman stood up as Meg reached the bed. Meg turned to her.

'Meg Nelson,' she said. 'I've come to visit Janine if that's OK.' She laid her bag on Janine's bed and added 'Janine's married to my ex-husband so I guess that makes us sort of family.'

If the policewoman was surprised she didn't show it. She simply smiled and said that she would go and get some coffee while Meg and Janine chatted. Meg sat down on the same chair the policewoman had been using. The seat was warm. 'Do you know everything that's been happening?' she asked.

'Most of the excitement I guess,' said Janine. 'A tall guy in police uniform came in to see my police watchdog yesterday. Actually she's quite good fun. Her name is Polly. Well he was stood there talking to Polly for ages. They'd tried to talk so I couldn't hear but I heard enough to get the gist of it and when he'd gone I gave Polly third degree.'

Janine looked please with herself then her face grew solemn.

'Bit awful about Steven, isn't it?' She looked down at the cover on her bed instead of at Meg. 'I hope he's alright. I know he said some horrible things to me but I wouldn't have wished that on him.'

She paused then said uncertainly 'Do you know how he is?'

Meg shook her head.

'Not really,' she said. In all the excitement of the previous afternoon and evening she had almost forgotten to ring the hospital in Truro. When she finally remembered the doctor had already left and the staff nurse had been reserved and non-committal.

'They just said that he was comfortable when I rang. They wouldn't tell me any more because I'm not family. Not now.' She smiled ruefully.

Janine looked faintly embarrassed.

'Well you are in a sort of way as you said to Polly. One thing is for certain. You've been better 'family' to me than my husband.'

Meg smiled. Janine was trying to pay her a compliment.

'Is there anything you'd like me to do?' she asked. 'Anyone you'd like me to contact?'

Janine shook her head.

'No thanks. It's kind of you to offer but I don't want to worry my own family. They don't like Steven anyway and I don't need the hassle.'

She paused for a moment.

'It's been quite exciting in here really. First they bring him in.' She nodded towards the bed in the far corner where Dan was still sleeping.

'Said he'd been shot. I made Polly tell me the whole story.'

Meg wondered if Dan would have approved of his erstwhile colleague's lack of discretion but he was an islander himself and he would know that it was virtually impossible to keep anything secret in the Islands.

'Then this other guy was brought in,' Janine continued. 'He didn't appear to be hurt but, boy, was he sleeping soundly. He snored all night! Kept me awake.'

Meg suppressed a grin. So Paul snored, did he. She wondered briefly if Kevin snored as well.

'Being treated for shock or something,' Janine was saying. 'I asked what had happened to him but Polly didn't seem to know.'

She shifted her position slightly in the bed and leaned as far she could towards Meg.'Do you know what all this is really about?' she whispered. 'Why do they think I need a police guard. Polly won't tell me that even if she knows. Just says it's common practice when someone has been attacked. I'm not that stupid. People only usually have a police guard when they're in danger. Why am I in danger and who from?'

She looked pleadingly at Meg. Meg wished she knew the answer to that question herself.

'I don't know either,' she said, 'but I'm convinced that it's linked to the Colossus.' A sudden thought struck her.

'Janine. Was anything taken from you after you were attacked?'

'I don't know. I was unconscious,' said Janine. She began to fumble at her locker with her good hand.

'Polly asked me the same thing. I said I didn't think so but I wasn't thinking too clearly at first.'

Janine started suddenly and bit her nail. 'Ouch!' she snapped. Turning towards Meg she said

'Do you think you could get my handbag out of my locker? I don't seem to be able to reach properly.'

Meg opened the locker drawer and took out Janine's handbag. Janine tipped the contents onto the bed. All the usual things seemed to be there. Mobile phone, purse, credit cards, lipstick, a couple of tissues and a room key.

'Polly thought they would have taken the cash and credit cards but they were untouched,' said Janine, 'and she was also surprised that my mobile phone was still there.' She was fumbling with something inside her bag.

'There's a zipped pocket in here and...aaahhh!' she exclaimed. 'It's gone!'

'The zipped pocket?' asked Meg in surprise.

'No. No. There's a zipped pocket in my handbag and I keep my passport in there. That's still there,' she added, throwing a small maroon booklet embossed with gold lettering onto the bed, 'but the envelope has gone.'

'What envelope?' Meg was alert now.

'Steven gave me a sealed envelope which he said he wanted me to keep in the pocket of my handbag. He didn't want it left in the room and he said he wanted it with us at all times. He didn't want to put it in his own pockets because he wanted to make sure it was really secure.'

'What on earth did it contain that made it so important?' Meg asked.

'I don't know, 'said Janine. 'Of course I asked him but he was secretive and evasive and I didn't push it. You know what he could be like.'

Meg did know, only too well. A proper wife would trust her husband without nagging him over every tiny irrelevant detail. She could hear him saying it in that injured tone which indicated that she had wounded him grievously by not agreeing to an innocent little request and then he would sulk for hours. She couldn't blame Janine for not being overly curious.

But who knew that Janine would have the envelope in her possession like that? Only Steven. And if he'd wanted it why didn't he just ask her for it? Because, Meg reminded herself sharply, they'd had that very public quarrel, for which she was at least partly responsible, and Steven would have been in a major sulk over what he saw as Janine showing him up. He would refuse to speak to her for days and then only after trying to make her crawl and beg forgiveness even though most of the fault had been on his side. Meg knew this only too well from her own bitter experience. Was it possible that Steven had actually arranged for his wife to be attacked simply because he was in a huff.

Meg was uncomfortably aware that Janine was watching her closely but she wasn't at all sure that she wanted to share her thoughts with her. Janine had been through enough already; although Meg was fairly certain that she must be harbouring suspicions of her own as well. Janine seemed about to ask her something when Polly came hurrying back into the ward and resumed her seat by Janine's bed. 'Carry on,' she said with a smile. 'Don't mind me. I'd have given you a bit longer myself but I'm under strict orders not to leave Janine's side.'

'Why?' Janine was puzzled. 'Am I in danger or something?'

'I don't know.' Polly was suddenly serious. 'There have been certain developments and it was decided that you should not be left alone.'

'What developments?' asked Janine suspiciously. 'Come on, Polly, give.'

'I can't tell you.' Polly had lowered her voice now. 'I told you far more than I should have done last night and besides my boss is lying in that bed over there.'

Janine and Meg followed Polly's gaze. Dan seemed to be stirring. Meg got up and went across to him. He lay, with his wounded arm heavily bandaged, in that no man's land between conscious and unconscious. His eyelids were flickering but he was not awake. She stood there for a moment watching him, the only known link she now had with her family in the Islands. A nurse came in to check his temperature and blood pressure, briskly noting the results on a chart which hung on the end of his bed.

'He's fine,' she said, seeing Meg's anxious expression, 'but you won't be getting much sense out of him for a while.'

Meg nodded at her and went back to Janine who was still trying to wheedle information out of Polly.

'I'm going now,' she said. 'I promised to meet Kevin, but I'll come and see you again tomorrow.'

Janine was putting her things back into her bag. It was a slow task for her with only the use of one hand.

'OK,' she mumbled. 'Will you tell Kevin what we talked about?'

'Of course.' Meg smiled at her. Polly was looking from one to the other of them. She knew that they were keeping something from her.

'I'm not sure what's going on,' she said at length, 'but both of you need to be very careful. Steven Hamilton walked out of Truro Hospital early this morning and we don't know where he is. He may try to contact one or both of you but he's angry and disorientated after his ordeal and this is making him unpredictable. I shouldn't be telling you all this but we do have reason to fear that he might turn to violence. I am here for you, Janine, but Meg, you make sure that you have someone with you all the time as well.'

Polly stopped, aware that she had said far too much, but she felt she owed them both a duty of care and how else was she going to warn them. Steven was not only in a highly charged state, but he had made threats, and, although Polly had not told them this, not wanting to panic Meg and Janine completely, the police also believed that Steven might be armed.

Meg stared at Polly aghast. The Steven she knew was certainly controlling and an emotional bully, but this? He had never ever laid a finger on her and she found it hard to believe that he would do so now. He could be patronising and dismissive, calculating and insensitive, emotionally distant even, but he had never actually threatened her. Then she remembered the anger in his eyes when he had shouted at her in the Atlantic Inn, and the way he had held her arm in a vice like grip as he had tried to drag her up Buzza Hill to 'talk to her.' What might have happened if Kevin had not been there. Trembling and close to tears she fumbled in her bag for her mobile phone as she said her goodbyes to Polly and Janine. Polly watched her with concern but it was better that she was aware of the danger she could be in rather than blissfully ignorant until it was too late.

Out in the hospital foyer, Meg sat down on one of the blue vinyl chairs provided for friends and relatives waiting for news of those who had been admitted. Her hand was shaking as she called Kevin's number. When he didn't answer she left a voice message for him and then brought up Sara's number. She didn't know who else she could turn to for help. Sara answered on the first ring. She told Meg to stay where she was and that she would come to the hospital for her at once. Meg snapped her phone shut and sat there, staring disbelievingly at the cream walls. The tears she had managed to hold at bay so far started to trickle unbidden down her cheeks. How could it all have come to this? How could it?

Unseen, shadows twirled lightly across the sea like dancers in a ballet.

London, 31st January 1801

Sir William stood staring down at the two day old baby girl lying in her crib. She was beautiful. Her long lashes fluttered lightly as she lay fast asleep, her little hands clenched into tiny fistballs. Her head had dark wispy hair and she looked the spitting image of Emma. Sir William felt an unexpected surge of affection for this scrap of humanity and an overwhelming need to protect her in some way. She might be Nelson's daughter but she was also a part of Emma.

Emma planned to farm her out to a wet nurse and a nanny and to pass her off as the god-child of herself and Nelson. Sir William would have much preferred her to stay with the family but Emma was adamant. They had finally arrived back in England just three months ago, on 6th November 1800. Nelson had unwillingly and briefly returned to his wife, Lady Fanny, to give some semblance of respectability. This had lasted for about a month until Nelson had come knocking on their door one night begging hospitality after a quarrel with his wife. Since then they had been living as a ménage a trois. Sir William didn't really care who knew it. He was now over seventy and in poor health. As long as he was comfortable and well looked after he left Emma and Nelson to do pretty much as they liked.

Sir William put out his finger and gently stroked the baby's cheek. It was so soft to the touch. She had been named Horatia for her father and Sir William thought it a pretty and unusual name. He desperately wanted to do something special for Horatia; perhaps give her something that only he could give her, by which she might think fondly of him in later years when he was no longer on this earth. As he stood there, watching her sleep, little bubbles like tiny pearls playing around her slightly open mouth, it came to him what he would do.

Turning from the cradle, Sir William strode upstairs to his study. He took the small bag of jewellery and precious stones from a locked drawer in his bureau. Then he sat down and wrote a letter to his solicitor, instructing him to give the enclosed gems to Horatia on the occasion of her thirty fifth birthday. That should be late enough to prevent fortune hunters from taking advantage and long enough to stop Emma getting her hands on them after he had gone. Much as he adored Emma he knew that she was a spendthrift and that she loved gambling. No. He would secure this little gift for Horatia's use and for her use alone.

St Marys, Isles of Scilly, 5th June 2008

Sara and Meg sat together in the sunshine outside Dibble and Grub nursing two large cappuccinos. Meg had told Sara that she was supposed to meet Kevin there for lunch, and besides they had both reasoned that if Steven was going to try anything violent he was far less likely to do so in a public place with a ready-made audience who would come to their aid.

'I just can't believe it,' said Sara after Meg had brought her up to date on what had been happening. 'What is it with Steven and all these other folk? Threats. Kidnappings. Shootings. What are they looking for and what could be so important that they are prepared to go to these lengths for it?'

Meg looked at her guiltily. She was very tempted to tell Sara the truth. On the other hand the less people who knew the better; a view her father had obviously shared. Did this mean that she didn't trust Sara? She had told Kevin everything after all. No, it wasn't that she decided. She'd had a need to confide in someone and Kevin's main qualification for being the recipient of her confidences, apart from the fact that she did trust him, was that he was not an Islander. She did trust Sara but this bequest had been kept secret from the Islanders for a reason. As yet she didn't know what that reason was, but her father, and his father before him, must have known, otherwise why had such pains been taken to conceal the bequest. Her whole family could have lived in luxury from such an inheritance and yet they had chosen not to do so. She was saved from further analysis and the need to give Sara an answer by the arrival of Kevin. He threw himself down into a chair with a sigh. 'What a morning!' he said wearily, signaling to the waitress to bring him something cold to drink. 'Apparently Steven has escaped from Truro hospital. They think he's making his way back to the Islands.'

'Escaped!' exclaimed Meg. 'He wasn't being held there against his will, was he?'

'Not exactly,' said Kevin, 'but he was under police guard. When he asked to be discharged early this morning the policeman with him said he wasn't just free to go; that he would need to come down to Truro police station to give a statement and answer some questions first.'

'What happened?' asked Sara.

'He hit the officer over the head with his water jug,' said Kevin. 'It was full and it stunned the guy for a minute. When he got back on to his feet Steven had gone.' He took a long swig of his drink and continued.

'By the time they got the alert out they think he was probably on a train headed for Penzance. There was no sign of him at the heliport or down at Lands End airport but he'd have stood out trying to get a seat on an aircraft and they think he probably bought a ticket for the Scillonian. He could have simply mingled with the crowds to escape notice.'

'Why on earth didn't the police just check the trains arriving at Penzance station?' asked Meg.

'Oh they did,' said Kevin,' but he wasn't on any of them. He may well have got off at St Erth and caught a bus for the last few miles into Penzance. He's a very cunning and calculating man after all.'

Sara looked at her watch.

'The Scillonian must be docked by now? Was he on it?'

'He didn't disembark with the other passengers,' said Kevin, 'that doesn't necessarily mean he wasn't on the boat.'

They all looked at each other.

'Anyway,' Kevin went on, 'Tom spent the morning questioning Jamie, the guy who shot Dan. He refused to say anything of interest but he gave Tom mouthfuls of abuse. He only quietened down when Phil came in with Ellie to see if there had been much progress on the case.'

Meg thought of Ellie and remembered how she had leapt to her master's defence. 'It's a pity Phil can't take Ellie into the hospital to see Dan,' she said. 'He'd love it and it might reassure Ellie.'

'Oh I think Ellie knows he's going to be OK,' said Kevin. 'Animals have a sort of sixth sense. Phil said she'd calmed down a lot by the time he got her home and had rung the hospital to ask how Dan was. That doesn't mean though that she's ever going to forgive the man who shot him.'

Meg explained to Kevin what had happened earlier at the hospital and his expression became grave.

'I think the police know a lot more than they're letting on,' he said, 'and Polly told you more than she should, although she obviously did that for the right reasons. She wanted you to be on your guard.'

He turned to Sara.

'Are you free this afternoon?' he asked. 'I know we haven't really got any right to drag you into all this but Meg needs help. I promised Phil I'd go out with him this afternoon to Southward Well and it would be good if Meg could stay with you.'

'No problem.' Sara smiled. 'Delighted to help.'

Meg looked alarmed.

'Why are you going out there after what happened yesterday?' she asked.

'Phil wants to test out a theory he's got and he needs someone on the boat while he does his dive.'

Kevin had tried hard to make his tone sound normal but Meg was not taken in by it. 'Isn't there anyone else he could ask?' she said fearfully.

'Not without telling them the whole story and we agreed that we wanted to keep as much under wraps as possible,' said Kevin.

'But suppose he sees what Paul saw?' Meg could not forget the look on Paul Smith's face as he sat trance like on the boat.

'He's prepared for that,' said Kevin. 'Phil's an Islander. He's heard the stories. He knows the score. It came as such a shock to Paul because he didn't understand what was happening.'

A fleeting shadow of pain crossed Kevin's face at the mention of Paul's name and Meg thought again how hard this must be for him. Sara had seen it too. 'I'm sure John would go with him if he asked,' she said softly.

'I think he would have done,' said Kevin, 'but Phil needs to go this afternoon because of the tides and because the weather is forecast to change tomorrow. John is taking a group bird watching in the Eastern Isles this afternoon. So it was Hobson's choice really.'

He smiled self deprecatingly then he said, almost in jocular fashion, 'I'm starving and you two must be as well. I suggest we have some lunch and give our inner persons some strength to face what might be coming to us.'

'You sound like a general urging his troops into battle,' said Meg half jokingly.

'I wish I could treat that remark as a jest,' said Kevin seriously, 'but it might be nearer to the truth than we think.'

He called the waitress over and ordered three pints of beer and three large cheese and pickle sandwiches. The waitress was about to say that cheese and pickle sandwiches weren't on the menu but she took one look at the three upturned faces and changed her mind. Kevin watched her walk back towards the kitchen. 'That will give her and Emmie something to talk about for the rest of the day,' he grinned.

Sara looked fazed by this remark so Meg told her what had happened a couple of days back with the endless cups of tea. Sara smiled as understanding dawned. 'They mean well,' she said, 'and which of us doesn't like a good gossip given half the chance.'

The waitress brought out their lunch. She placed three little baskets full of carefully cut cheese and pickle sandwiches attractively garnished with bits of salad in front of them. Emmie had obviously gone to a lot of trouble preparing a meal which wasn't even on the menu. Kevin raised his glass of beer.
'To Emmie, bless her!' he said.

'To Emmie!' Meg and Sara echoed him, raising their glasses and taking a long draught of the deliciously cold beer.

The waitress blushed and giggled and almost ran back to the kitchen. They couldn't resist turning round as they drank another toast to the obliging Emmie and from her small kitchen at the back of the restaurant Emmie raised a hand in half embarrassed acknowledgement of their appreciation.

As soon as they had eaten Kevin went to meet Phil after arranging to see Meg and Sara later in the Mermaid.

'I'm meeting John for a pint,' he'd said to them, 'so we can all meet up there together.'

Sara and Meg stretched out in their chairs savouring the last of their beer.
'Why don't we go and see my mother this afternoon?' Sara said suddenly.
'She's getting on a bit now but her memory is still sharp and she loves talking about family. She's kept all sorts of stuff from the past. She may have one or two mementoes of the Sarah Legg who married Jim Nelson. It will keep us out of harm's way,' she added, making some attempt to lighten the situation in which they'd found themselves.

Meg agreed enthusiastically. It might also give her a chance to check out Dan Nelson's line of descent and to see whether Jim and Sarah Nelson had had any other bloodline children. They finished their beer, then paid for their lunch and set off for the house of Sara's mother.

Shadows curled and uncurled themselves in the sands down by the shore.

Tenterden, Kent, 29th January 1836

Horatia Ward stared at the letter in her hand and then looked up at the man standing in front of her. He was from a firm of London solicitors and he had come specially to see her today, her thirty fifth birthday. She did not remember Sir William Hamilton. He had died when she was only two but she had heard mention of his name often enough from Emma. He would also have known that her real birthday was 29th January 1801 and not three months earlier, on 29th October 1800, a fiction devised by Emma for the sake of appearances. She read his letter through again. It was simple and touching and she wiped a tear from her eye with her lace handkerchief. Gravely the solicitor handed her a small box in which lay Sir William's legacy to her. Slowly she opened it and gasped. There were diamonds, rubies, emeralds, sapphires nestling on a bed of velvet. Tucked beneath the velvet were some gold chains, carefully and individually wrapped.

'For me?' she had asked disbelievingly.

The solicitor had nodded gravely and, assuring her that all was as it should be, had taken his leave.

Horatia sat staring out at the winter landscape. Snow lay on the bare branches of the trees and covered the garden. Inside the rectory however it was warm and snug, not draughty like so many of these places were. She had married the Rev. Philip Ward in 1822 when she was twenty one. It had been a happy marriage and the love and contentment she had experienced had done much to heal the wounds of the unhappy and poverty stricken childhood she had endured with Emma after the death of her father, Admiral Lord Nelson, in 1805. She knew that her father would never have expected her to have suffered the treatment that she had received but she had learned enough now to know that this was just the way of a world steeped in envy and greed and double standards.

She and Philip had had ten children together. No. She checked herself. Eleven. The last child, a boy, had been born at a time of great poverty in their lives, and he had been secretly adopted and taken to live in the Isles of Scilly. She received occasional letters from his adoptive father and she knew that he was well and happy. They had named him Horatio in honour of the great admiral and Horatia had been ridiculously pleased by that simple act. She looked again at the riches in her lap. Her husband had a better living now and they had plenty of riches that money could never buy. She did not want her children to grow up spoilt. Besides she could remember with unwelcome clarity what the acquisition and pursuit of riches had done to Emma.

Emma had been generous to a fault with family and friends. She had spent lavishly on entertaining and she had indulged in drinking and gambling to her heart's content while she still had ready cash. Afterwards there were the debtors' prisons, the flight to France, the long slow decline into poverty. Where had all their friends been then, Horatia wondered. Emma's beauty had gradually faded. She had become bloated and her hair had turned grey. As her spirit finally failed her she became ill and lay on her bed in the squalid little room in a poor part of Calais that had become 'home', lamenting her misfortunes and pleading with Horatia for yet more alcohol to dull her pain. Horatia had watched helplessly as Emma's life had slowly drained away long before her time. When she finally died she was buried hastily in the churchyard of St Pierre in Calais, hundreds of miles away from the grand tomb given to Nelson in the crypt of St Paul's Cathedral.

Horatia shook her head sadly. She would talk to Philip and she would explain and then she would hide this bequest away until the time was right. If Horatio grew into a decent man and proved himself, he would know how to handle the responsibility of such a bequest. In her eyes he was the most deserving of all her children because he was the one who had had to grow up without his own loving family around him. Satisfied, she locked away the precious box in her bureau.

Holy Vale, St Marys, Isles of Scilly, 5th June 2008

Annie Legg lived in a small cottage up in the middle of the island near Holy Vale. Bearing in mind Kevin's repeated warnings, and knowing that the road up to Holy Vale was a lonely road, Sara suggested taking the community bus. The ancient vehicle rattled and shook its way around the island until it eventually arrived at the crossroads above Holy Vale.

'Back every hour on the half hour,' said the driver confusingly in reply to Meg's question about return times. She thanked him and they stepped down off the bus on to the tarmac road. A couple of ducks came waddling up and looked at them curiously as the bus pulled away belching clouds of exhaust.

'There's a duck pond just up the road there,' said Sara, pointing to a narrow lane which turned off the road close to where they had left the bus. 'The local ducks consider this to be their patch and they come to investigate any trespassers.'

Two stone cottages and an old farmstead stood down a short steep lane opposite where the bus had dropped them off. Sara's mother lived in the farthest cottage. They pushed open the gate and it was like stepping straight into a fairy story. Honeysuckle and jasmine grew around the doorway and the garden was full of purple-mauve lupins and the creamy white flowers of meadowsweet, brilliant red fuschia and sweet smelling pink and yellow roses. A blue agapanthus stood in a corner. Meg half remembered an old pop song about 'how many kinds of sweet flowers grow in an English country garden' and thought that it must have been written with this particular garden in mind. All the windows were open and neat little curtains fluttered in the breeze. The front door stood ajar and a delicious smell of baking wafted out onto the small lawn. She stopped for a minute, lost in admiration and briefly losing herself in another world in another time. Sara smiled at her.

'Pretty isn't it?' she said quietly. 'Mum loves her garden.'

She pushed open the door and called a greeting. A small rosy cheeked old lady appeared in the doorway, wiping her hands on a blue and white striped apron. Her grey hair was tied back in a neat ponytail and she wore a white blouse with short sleeves and a pair of grey trousers. She beamed a greeting at Sara and hugged her, then she turned to Meg.

'You must be Meg,' she said with a warm smile. 'Sara told me about you. She thinks you might share a great great grandmother or something with her.'

Meg smiled back. It would be impossible not to like this woman.

'Pleased to meet you Mrs Legg,' she said.

'Oh, call me Annie please,' said the older woman. 'I hate formalities. Now would you like tea or some homemade lemonade?'

They both opted for the lemonade. The afternoon had become very hot and sultry and they could hear bees humming around the flowers as they sat down in a couple of deckchairs beneath the shade of an old apple tree. Annie carried out a tray with three glasses and a jug of lemonade in which pieces of fresh lemon floated. She placed the tray carefully on a rather rickety old table before sitting down in an ancient rocking chair that had obviously seen better days and had been put out to grass.

'Now,' she said, starting to pour out the lemonade, 'do you want to tell me what all this is about?'

Meg looked taken aback for a minute but Sara smiled.

'Mum always knows if I'm troubled about anything,' she said by way of explanation. 'I don't need to tell her.'

Annie looked shrewdly at her daughter.

'It wouldn't be anything to do with all this business of Dan getting shot, would it?'

'Sort of,' Sara agreed, 'but it would be better if I let Meg tell you everything from start to finish.'

Annie Legg was a good listener. She didn't interrupt Meg's narrative once. Meg told her about her family history, about Steven, and about everything that had happened since but she didn't tell about the bequest. When she had finished she sat back in her chair and took a long cool drink of her lemonade. Annie seemed to be considering the story she had been told.

'My grandmother knew Horatio Nelson,' said Annie at length. 'She grew up with his son, Joseph. They were sort of cousins. Horatio's adoptive mother, Sarah Legg, was her great aunt.'

'Told you we would be some sort of relation,' Sara smiled happily. 'Everyone is on this island.'

'There was a rumour that Horatio had received some kind of legacy from his real mother before she died,' said Annie. 'He would never talk about it. My grandmother said Joseph mentioned to her once that there was something but he never said what it was. He and your grandmother had quite given up hope of having children so they were over the moon when your father was born. He was an only child so Joseph probably left all he had to him. No one was ever any the wiser though as to whether there actually was any special legacy.'

Annie paused and looked closely at Meg.

'You're an only child as well,' she said, 'so if there was anything it would most likely have been left to you.'

Meg couldn't meet her eyes and looked down at her hands resting in her lap. She should be able to trust these people. They had only ever shown her kindness and they were the nearest thing she had to a family. What was holding her back? She could hear Steven's voice in her head.

'You're paranoid you are; you're just paranoid.'

Then, unbidden, a much earlier memory came back to her. She must have been about eight or nine years old and she had been sitting with her father in the garden while her mother was making the tea. For some reason that she could no longer recall he had turned to her and said solemnly,
'Never trust anyone but yourself, Meg. Remember that always.'

Why had he said that to her? What had he been trying to achieve? Did she want to go through her life as insular and as unhappy as he had been?

She raised her head slowly to meet Annie's gaze. She knew that Sara was watching her closely too. Annie took Meg's hands in her own.

'People like Sara and me,' Annie said, 'we're not interested in other people's legacies. We have all the riches we could ever want already. You're a part of our family and ...'

Meg opened her mouth to protest but Annie continued firmly.
'Yes you are. You're a part of our family. There may not be a blood line but Jim and Sarah raised Horatio and loved him as their own. They made him the man he became. He was as much a son to them as their natural son, John, was.'

Meg was close to tears. If she was ever going to learn to trust properly she had to do it now but it was hard to formulate the words.
'There is a legacy,' she whispered, 'but... but it's not money. It's precious stones, uncut jewels, from the collections of Sir William Hamilton. I knew nothing about it until a couple of days ago. My father never told me and he instructed his solicitors never to tell me unless I came asking for it.'
Meg pulled out her handkerchief and dabbed at her eyes and nose.
'Steven found out about it somehow; I don't know how; but he married me so that he could get his hands on the legacy. When he discovered that I knew nothing about it he divorced me and married Janine.'
Tears were streaming down Meg's face now. She sniffed loudly and wiped her eyes again.

'He married Janine because she was the descendant of Richard King, the quartermaster on the Colossus, although no-one knows why that was so important to him. Then he started sending me threatening letters and making abusive phone calls, only I didn't know at the time that it was Steven doing that. He just seems driven, as though he'll go to any lengths and do whatever is necessary to get his hands on that legacy.'

Meg put her head in her hands and sobbed brokenly. Both Annie and Sara put their arms around her and held her until her tears had subsided.

'How do you feel about the legacy, Meg?' Annie asked gently.

'I don't know,' said Meg. 'It's worth an awful lot of money but if people want those jewels so badly that they're even willing to kill for them then I'm not sure I want to know. I think my father was perhaps just trying to protect me from all these predators.'

'No,' said Annie softly. 'He was trying to protect you from yourself.'
She stood up and said 'I think we could all do with a nice strong cup of tea.'

Picking up the tray with jug and glasses on it, Annie headed for the cottage door. Meg turned to Sara.
'What did she mean? Protect me from myself.'

'Mum knew your father quite well. She was one of the few people he seemed at ease with and able to talk to without clamming up. When you got engaged he came to see her. He didn't like Steven and he didn't trust him. He knew that you were in love with him but he didn't think it was reciprocated. He also thought that Steven was controlling and he didn't think that you would be able to stand up to him very well. He didn't tell Mum about the legacy but he did say to her that he wanted to make his will and he wanted to ensure that Steven wouldn't get his hands on what was intended for you. She knew that he wasn't telling her everything and it was she who suggested that he talk to his solicitor and devise some plan for safeguarding your inheritance.'

So her father had cared at least a little bit for her. He had cared enough to try and protect her from Steven. Maybe her mother had too. Meg remembered the way her mother had brushed aside her offers of help to sort out her father's affairs after his death. Meg had just taken it as her usual standoffishness but perhaps she, too, in her own way, had been trying to help and protect Meg.

Annie came back into the garden carrying a tea tray on which there also stood a small bottle of brandy. In spite of herself Meg smiled. She was learning that a good strong cup of tea in the Islands meant adding a drop of the hard stuff. Annie poured out the tea and handed the cups round leaving everyone to add their own shot of brandy. The honeysuckle and roses and meadowsweet perfumed the garden with their delicate yet pungent scents. Bees burrowed deep into the petals seeking the nectar with which they would make the honey to feed their Queen and her young. The ducks were quacking over something in the lane. Despite everything that had happened and all the emotional upheaval she had suffered, Meg felt strangely content. She added a little more brandy to her tea, raised her cup and said simply, 'To my family.'

'Just what would you know about family when you couldn't even give your own husband his rightful family inheritance?' said a voice.

All three of them jumped and turned in the direction of the speaker.
Steven stood just inside the gate watching them, his face surly, his manner aggressive. He looked terrible. His face was haggard and unshaved and his hair had not been combed. His clothes looked as though they had spent the night scrunched in a hedge. He strode across the grass, limping slightly, and turned to face the three of them.

'Cackling away here like the bloody witches in MacBeth,' he said rudely, 'while I am left to suffer for the sake of my family honour.'

Annie and Sara stared at him uncomprehendingly.

'Steven,' said Meg, as calmly as she could, and remembering Polly's warning that morning, 'perhaps you'd like to sit down and join us and we can discuss your problems.'

'My problems!' he bawled. 'I'm not the one with problems! You're the one who's paranoid, who goes swanning around, flaunting it with all and sundry, while plotting to keep me from my rightful inheritance.' Steven was working himself up into a state. 'My inheritance! How dare you!' he yelled.

'What inheritance is that?' asked Sara quietly, hoping to calm him down a little.

'What inheritance?' he shouted at her. 'How stupid are you? That silly little bitch must have told you about the jewels. As you are her family,' he sneered.

'Meg has told us about a legacy that she was left by her father,' said Sara. 'As you are divorced I cannot see that it has anything to do with you.'

'You bloody women are all the same. Stick together to do a man out of what is rightfully his,' Steven snarled.

'Steven!' said Meg. 'The jewels were left to me as a bequest from my father after they were handed down through the family to him. The original bequest was made by Sir William Hamilton to Horatia Nelson who was my great great grandmother. I really don't see what that has to do with you either.'

'Oh you don't, don't you?' said Steven unpleasantly. 'Well, I'll tell you. Those jewels should never have been given to Horatia in the first place. She had no right to them. She was not even a member of Sir William's family. He was morally obliged to bequeath them to his own flesh and blood, to the brother he forgot, the brother to whom he left nothing.'

Without asking Steven grabbed the bottle of brandy off the tray, unscrewed the top and took a long drink. Then he screwed the top back on, replaced the bottle on the tray and, bowing slightly to Annie, said sarcastically, 'Why thank you ma'am for your hospitality.'

Annie ignored him and sat looking straight ahead as though he did not exist.

'Perhaps Sir William and his brother were not on good terms,' said Meg icily.

'Well he certainly didn't approve of that silly little tart Sir William married,' said Steven. 'From whom, incidently,' he added nastily, 'you are descended.'

Meg ignored the jibe. 'Really, Steven,' she said, 'it was up to Sir William to whom he left his fortune. Not you.'

'He did our family out of a fortune by leaving most of it to that idiot Greville as thanks or something for introducing him to that silly little tart in the first place,' said Steven. 'He should have left it to Frederic. He had the children. He was keeping the family line going. If Sir William couldn't leave his docks to him he should at least have left a sweetener like the jewels he threw away on somebody who wasn't even a family member and who had no right to them. I tried for years to get my father to see the monumental injustice that had been done and to put it right but he didn't want to know. Told me I was mad. ME!'

He was shouting again.

'So it was left to me to restore the family honour. God knows I've been hampered at every turn by a stupid bloody woman. Those jewels belong to me and I mean to have them. Do you understand?'

'No!' said Meg firmly, surprising herself. 'I don't understand you at all Steven. Sir William Hamilton was free to leave whatever he wanted to whomever he wanted. He died over two hundred years ago. You are just a distant descendant. You have no claim on him at all.'

A sudden thought struck her. 'How did you know where to find us?'

'Simple!' Steven smirked. 'You weren't to be seen around Hugh Town and I thought you might be hiding from me somewhere. Just like you to do that. So I asked the local bus driver if he'd seen anyone answering your description.

Hardly rocket science was it? I might have known you'd be with her.' He jerked his head in Sara's direction.

'So what do you want?' Meg knew the answer to this already but she was playing for time and making him spell it out.

'The jewels of course, you silly cow.' Steven looked at her as though she was a complete and utter fool.

'I don't have them,' said Meg calmly.

'Don't lie!' Steven's voice was rising again. 'Of course you have them. Why else do you think I married you?' He was sneering again. 'It was hardly for your beauty, charm and wit, was it?'

His words were intended to wound and just a few short days ago Meg would have been devastated but now she just felt numb. He had lost the power to hurt her. 'I don't have them,' she said firmly. 'They are held in a safe in an English solicitor's office. I didn't even know of their existence until a couple of days ago so how did you find out about them?'

Steven's face took on the pained expression of someone who is condemned to spend his entire life with ignorant fools.

'Sir William Hamilton left behind lists of what his collections contained. He also kept a journal. They're kept in the Public Record Office where anyone with an ounce of initiative can track them down.'

Meg was playing for time and she knew it. It was important to keep Steven talking. He could never resist showing off how clever he was and that was his big weakness. 'So how did you discover that you were descended from Sir William Hamilton?'

'I'm not descended from him as you well know,' said Steven scornfully. 'He had no children of his own. He left the carrying on of the family name to his brother, Frederic, whom he treated with such total disdain. Frederic's eldest son was my great great grandfather.' He paused for this statement to take effect.
'I found all this out when I was still a child. My parents took me to the British Museum one day and while we were in the Greek and Roman Antiquities section my father showed me the Hamilton Collections and explained the distant connection with our family. I was impressed and soon afterwards I borrowed a biography of Sir William from the library. He had been immensely wealthy and I began to wonder why, if we really were descendants, we weren't better off. Dad worked in an office all his life. It was boring, mundane, repetitive work and there was never much money to spare, so I made it my business to find out why we were not richer. I read Sir William's journals and I found a copy of his will and it was then that I realised that a great injustice had been done. I tried to persuade Dad to go to the courts but he didn't want to know. He couldn't seem to follow my reasoning.'

Like the rest of us thought Meg. Out loud she said 'So you tracked me down and thought that if you married me the inheritance would be yours by right.'

For the first time Steven smiled. 'Yes,' he said, 'inspired wasn't I?'

'But Horatia had eleven children,' said Meg. 'How did you know which one she would have left her legacy to? How did you know that she hadn't shared it among them all?'

'I didn't at first,' said Steven. 'Then I realised that if she'd split the bequest some of her children would have probably sold their share; but there was no trace of any such jewels being sold at all. I thought it would be a long hard slog to track each of her children down but then I had a stroke of luck. I read the story of the Colossus in the newspapers and how there was a rumour that one of Horatia's children had been adopted on Scilly. There was also talk of some sort of bequest made to this child and that narrowed the field considerably.'

He looked at Meg with distaste. 'Only I hadn't struck lucky, had I? You seemed to know nothing about any inheritance and your tight lipped old skinflint of a father wasn't giving anything away. I couldn't get beyond the whispered rumour here on Scilly and I began to wonder if I'd made a dreadful mistake.'

Meg looked at him coldly. 'No,' she said. 'I made the dreadful mistake.'
Steven bristled at this and she said quickly 'Though I can understand why you divorced me, why did you marry Janine?'

He sighed heavily. 'I bought a book about the Colossus and I read Murray's despatches and his description of Richard King's death. There is still a small collection of priceless ancient seal stones missing from the Colossus and I thought it possible that King might be implicated. When I read of the unopened package he left for his wife I became convinced that he was involved. Marrying Janine was a high price to pay for the information,' he said, dismissing Janine as simply another means to an end, 'but I had more luck there. I eventually wheedled the remains of the package out of her stupid mother. King had known about the seal stones. He'd discovered them by accident but he instinctively realised that they might be something important. He took a couple and sent them to his wife telling her that he thought he'd found a way to make their fortune and instructing her to sell them when she received the package.'

In spite of herself; in spite of Steven's strange and disgraceful behaviour, his unpredictable mood and his possible recourse to violence, Meg was fascinated. She also knew that the longer she could keep him talking the more likely it was that some form of help would arrive. She had glanced only briefly at Sara but she knew that Sara had realised what she was doing. Annie was sitting absolutely still, looking at Sara. She did not seem to be frightened but perhaps she was just doing a good job of hiding her fear. Meg knew that animals could scent fear and so too could people, and that this could act as a stimulus for attack. Annie was probably defending herself in the best way that she knew.

'What happened?' asked Meg. 'Did Cathryn sell the seal stones?'

'Oh well done!' Steven mocked. 'We actually know her name, do we?'

Meg smiled a tight little smile and held her peace with difficulty.

'Yes, it seems that she did,' he went on. 'Janine's mother gave me the letter and there was some sort of crumpled receipt with it. Cathryn did well for herself.'

Yes, Meg reflected, but it was probably all she'd had to live on for the rest of her life. Richard King had died long before the days of widows' pensions.

'In the letter King said that he had hidden more of the same in a safe place,' Steven went on. 'That had to be on board the Colossus somewhere. Richard King didn't seem to have realised that Sir William had kept detailed lists of his collections. Probably as stupid as his great great granddaughter,' he said contemptuously. 'Anyway that collection is priceless and so far it's not been re-discovered. That's why we hired a diver to take another look at the wreck. Those stones were most likely hidden in the living quarters. Fat lot of good that was,' he said bitterly. 'What do we get for our pains? Some complete idiot who returns empty handed and wittering on about strange figures walking along the seabed. How ridiculous is that?'

'Who's we?' said Meg before she could stop herself.

'Ha!' said Steven, rubbing the side of his nose with his finger. 'Wouldn't you just like to know?'

'They shot Dan,' she said simply.

'Yes. Well. He should have done as he was told.'

'But, Steven, they kidnapped you as well and left you for dead!' Meg burst out.

'Thanks to you and Janine they thought I was holding out on them,' he said. 'Prize pair of stupid cows you two are.'

'Did you have Janine attacked?' Meg asked, still unable to quite believe that he would have done such a thing.

'I didn't expect him to hit her quite so hard,' said Steven, a defensive note in his voice.

'Why didn't you just ask her to give you the envelope back?' whispered Meg, horrified at what he had done.

'What?' he asked in an outraged tone. 'You expected me to speak to her again after the way she showed me up on that beach? You have to be joking!'

Meg stared at him. The man she thought she had known had completely disappeared and this total stranger had appeared in his place. There was just one more thing she had to ask.

'How did you know that I had finally learned about the legacy?'

'Public phones can be overheard,' he said grimly. 'Someone heard you ask Directory Enquiries for the telephone number of Brown, Ormesher and Ockenthwaite. Who else but solicitors would have names like that? Then about five minutes later you staggered out of the post office looking as though you were on Planet Zog. It was obvious what you'd just been told.'

Meg cursed herself. She'd not used her mobile phone because she'd needed to use Directory Enquiries and she knew that the service was available on public payphones. She remembered her impatience and the state she'd been in afterwards and she desperately tried to recall who else had been in the post office. To be honest though, she'd been so wrapped up in what she had been doing and what she had learned that she'd not noticed anyone else; but someone had clearly noticed her.

Steven smiled at her frustration and said a trifle smugly, 'You really are not very bright sometimes, are you Meg?'

Meg glared at him but she could think of nothing else to say. He knew she had the jewels and he had said that he would stop at nothing to get them. She glanced desperately at Sara. Why didn't somebody come? She sneaked a look at her watch. It was four o'clock. John would be back soon but of course he didn't know where they were. Neither did Kevin nor Phil.

'Hoping someone will come to your rescue, are you?' said Steven who had noticed her gesture. 'Well I'm sorry to disappoint you but by the time anybody figures out where you went you and I will be long gone.'

Sara made a slight movement and Steven turned on her.

'Don't even think it!' he growled. 'Now stand up all of you!'

Meg's knees had turned to jelly. Slowly she stood up and Sara did the same. Annie however seemed transfixed and they watched in horror as he yanked her out of her chair.

'When I say stand!' he blazed at her, 'I expect you to stand, not to sit there liked a stuffed duck. Do you understand me?'

Annie made no response at all and Steven, by now enraged, raised his hand as if to hit her. It was too much for Sara.

'Leave my mother alone!' she said in a tone which could have frozen the blood.

Steven whipped round.

'Leave my mother alone!' he mimicked. 'It is me giving the orders around here you stupid bitch and you will do as I say or it will be the worse for all of you.'

His hand went to his pocket and Meg heard Polly's words in her head 'We have reason to think that he may be violent.' Perhaps he was even armed, but surely he wouldn't harm Sara or her mother. She made as if to go to Annie but Steven pushed her roughly aside. Meg stumbled and landed at Annie's feet.

'Now,' said Steven, as he stood in front of Sara, 'I am going to teach you a lesson you won't forget in a hurry.'

He raised his arm and smacked her hard around the face.

'Right,' he said authoritatively, 'kneel down!'

Meg scrambled to her feet and lunged at Steven but his hand connected unexpectedly with her cheekbone and she fell to the ground again.
Meg dragged herself into a sitting position but she was too dazed to stand upright. Sara hadn't moved.

'I said kneel down!' Steven roared and raised his hand to strike her again.
The next moment Steven seemed to rise slowly and gracefully into the air, turn head over heels, and in an instant he was lying flat on his back on the grass, gasping and completely winded. Sara was rubbing her wrist.

'Wasn't really sure I could still do that,' she said, bending down and deftly removing a handgun from Steven's pocket, 'but it seems to have worked well enough.'
Meg stared in astonishment at her.

'I learned judo when I was younger,' she said, 'but I haven't practiced it for years. They do say though that you never forget how to do it.'

Annie came over and hugged them both.

'Are you OK?' asked Meg anxiously.

'Oh yes, I'm fine.' She smiled at Meg. 'I'd just gone into shut down mode,' she said. 'It's a form of self defence.'

'Have you got some of the string left that you use to tie back the roses?' asked Sara, turning to her mother. Annie nodded.

'I think we should tie his hands behind his back just in case he has any thoughts of retaliation,' said Sara. 'Then we should call Tom.'

Meg helped Sara tie Steven's hands up and then for good measure they tied his feet together. Annie rang Tom and by the time he arrived Steven was sitting against the apple tree like a trussed up chicken. He scowled at Tom as he was hoisted to his feet.

'Right!' said Tom. 'You, sir, have some explaining to do, and then I shall charge you with common assault, unlawful possession of a firearm and conspiracy to defraud. You do not have to say anything, but it may harm your defence if you do not mention when questioned something which you later rely on in court. Anything you do say may be given in evidence.'

Steven's jaw dropped in surprise as he heard the words of the formal caution. 'Are you arresting me?' he asked in amazement.

'In a word, sir, yes,' said Tom.

'But I haven't done anything wrong,' protested Steven. 'She assaulted me!' He nodded towards Sara as he spoke.

'In self defence only,' said Tom. 'Threats, intimidation, intent to defraud, and smacking people around the face hardly constitutes not doing anything wrong.'

'Oh come on!' said Steven. 'You know what women are like. Just need handling with a bit of firmness.'

'Yes, sir.' Tom smiled sardonically. 'I'm sure the judge will understand.'

He walked Steven over to the police car and opened the rear door. Ellie was sitting on the back seat. Steven glared at her.

'I am not getting in there with that thing!' he shouted.

Ellie glared back at him.

'You will do what you are told, sir,' Tom said firmly and pushed him into the back seat. He slammed the door firmly on Steven's continuing protests.

'John's on his way up!' Tom called over his shoulder as he got into the driving seat. 'I radioed him and told him what's been happening. He was just coming in to the quay when I left.'

The engine of the police car started up and with a wave of his hand through the car window Tom was gone.

Tom was hardly out of sight when John's van appeared. He stopped with a jolt in front of the cottage and jumped out.

'Sara!' he shouted, sweeping her into his arms and holding her to him until she was breathless. 'Are you alright?'

'Come on, John,' she laughed, when she could get her breath, pleased but a little embarrassed. 'It wasn't that bad. Meg has to share the credit too. She kept him talking and managed to diffuse some of his anger. It was just when he went to hit Mum. I couldn't have stood that and it wouldn't have stopped there. He had a gun, you know!'

Sara finally struggled free from his crushing embrace and said, a little more calmly, 'He was planning to take Meg and return to the mainland. Once he'd got his hands on Meg's legacy he would have had no further use for her and... and...' she broke off, unwilling to put into words what she had feared Steven would do to Meg. She had realised that, although Meg was safe from Steven at last, there were still others at large who would harm her.

They did not meet in the Mermaid that evening. Instead Phil and Kevin came up to Annie's house. They needed to relax and talk things over without fighting against a multitude of voices in a sea of faces. Sara had offered to cook supper for them all at Rosehill but Annie would not hear of it. She had spent most of the day baking and what had she done that for if they could not now enjoy eating it, she said. Besides, as she confided to Meg, she didn't want to miss out on any of the excitement. The six of them gathered around the big farmhouse table in Annie's kitchen. Annie put a large quiche, still warm, and a dish of hot buttered new potatoes in front of them together with the mixed green salad that Sara had made and gaily decorated with pink and yellow rose petals which, she assured everyone, were perfectly edible if a little bland. A big fresh baked cob loaf sat on the table and there were seemingly endless jugs of beer. The door of the cottage still stood ajar and the heavy evening scent of the roses and honeysuckle teased at their senses.

Everyone seemed to be tired and ravenous, and at first they ate in near silence. The homemade food and drink soon revived spirits however and by the time Annie produced her summer pudding, the dark juice of the berries deeply staining the moist white bread case, there was a lively exchange of conversation going on. John, Phil and Kevin had insisted on hearing about what had happened with Steven before they would relate their own afternoon's experiences. The men were impressed by the way Meg and Sara had handled Steven and said so; and there was considerable amusement at the way in which Sara had floored him.

'No one messes with my Sara!' John had said proudly and there was further laughter.

Then Meg grew suddenly solemn and said 'OK guys. It's your turn now. I am dying of curiosity.'

Kevin and Phil looked at each other and to cover the slightly awkward silence John said cheerfully 'I haven't really got much to tell. Just took my group around the Eastern Isles and they seemed to enjoy themselves. There were also quite a lot of seals out there today and enough photographs were taken to fill several books. Then on the way back I got a call from Tom telling me what had happened and I got here as soon as I could.'

Annie refilled glasses from yet another jug of beer while Meg and Sara looked expectantly at Kevin and Phil. Both of them seemed a little ill at ease.

'Come on!' Meg was impatient. 'Don't keep us in suspense.'

Finally Kevin said hesitantly 'You're really not going to believe this. We didn't at first; but it did actually happen and we've just got to accept it somehow.

Somewhere in the sands below the cottage shadows moved imperceptibly in the gathering darkness.

St Marys, Isles of Scilly, 6th June 2008

Meg lay in bed watching the rain streaming down the windows. As forecast, the weather had indeed broken. It was still early but she had been unable to sleep much, her mind going over and over the fantastic story that Kevin and Phil had told them all the night before.

It was Kevin who had finally spoken first as they had sat around Annie's kitchen table waiting to hear Phil and Kevin's account of their afternoon spent out on the boat off Southward Well. Kevin had cleared his throat self consciously and looked at Phil who nodded.

'We took the boat out just after John left,' Kevin had begun hesitantly. 'Phil wanted to do a dive on the site where Paul had suffered his traumatic experience. He wanted to try and find out exactly what was going on. I've never done any diving but I do know how to handle a boat so I said I'd be the surface guy and look after things up top. Phil didn't want to ask around in case the wrong people got to hear about what he was intending to do.'

He paused and swallowed the remains of his beer.

'So we sailed out and anchored over Southward Well about half past two. Phil changed into his diving gear and slipped over the side saying he'd probably be about forty minutes; maybe an hour, but no longer. I said I'd watch out for any signals from him. I kept looking around nervously for other boats in case Steven's friends showed up and started taking an interest but there was no-one about. It was very peaceful in fact and I started to relax a bit. I kept an eye on my watch though in case Phil might need help. When the hour was up I went to the side of the boat to watch for him coming up. He didn't come and I was trying not to be anxious. He had told me that he had a few minutes leeway in any case. By the time another five minutes had passed and he'd not surfaced I was beginning to get seriously worried and I was on the point of calling the coastguard when a hand appeared on the side of the boat. I rushed over and Phil was just hauling himself up. I helped him into the boat and took the underwater camera from him. That was a heavy beast. Phil took his diving helmet off and pushed back the rubber hood of his wetsuit from his face. He looked very pale and he just flopped down onto the seat. He said he needed a drink badly.'

Phil had grinned sheepishly at this last remark.

'I knew he kept a small bottle of brandy in the cabin for emergency and medicinal purposes' Kevin went on, 'so I poured some into a mug for him. He drank the whole lot straight down in one gulp and asked for another. I got the bottle but it was almost empty and he downed what was left and then just sat shaking his head at me. I asked him if he was alright and he stopped shaking his head just long enough to nod at me, then I told him I couldn't take the suspense any longer and what the hell was going on.'

At this point Kevin turned to Phil who had been listening with rapt attention.

'Over to you, I think,' he said, re-filling his beer glass.

Phil had nodded in assent and taken up the story.

'Like Kevin said it all started off fairly normally. I wanted to go down and see if the site had been disturbed by Paul after he panicked, but I was also interested to see if the shifting sands had revealed anything else. I took the camera so I could photograph any changes or any new stuff which had come to light and might need excavating and bringing to the surface. As soon as I got down there I could tell that there had been some disturbance. I was clicking away with the camera when I noticed what looked like the upturned hull of a boat. Not a sailing ship but a smaller boat, some sort of yacht, or a motor boat maybe. I swam over and that's exactly what it was; the hull of a boat some twenty feet long or so. That was strange in itself because it hadn't been there the last time I went on a dive there a few days ago and there had been no reports of missing boats recently.'

Phil held out his glass for a refill of beer and took a long drink.

'Anyway,' he went on, 'this boat had been split in three as though it had been ripped apart by some kind of explosion. I was frantically clicking away with the camera, like the paparazzi who used to chase after Princess Diana, and then I saw something lying on the sand a few feet away. When I went to investigate I realised it was a body. Well, two bodies to be precise. They were both male and the odd thing was that something seemed to be lying across them. I edged closer and around to get a better look and, unbelievable as this sounds but I swear to God I saw it, it was a wooden figure.'

Meg and Sara had both gasped but Annie had said nothing, just sat quietly, watching Phil carefully. He took a long swig of his beer before continuing.
'I just stood there staring at it. I lost all sense of time and direction. Everything. All I could do was stand there looking at it. Finally some sort of survival instinct kicked in. I knew I'd been down there too long. I stayed just long enough to get a couple of shots and as I did so I realised that I knew one of the dead men. It was Chris who had been asking me all those questions about the Colossus. I was shaken, I can tell you. Somehow I made my way back to the surface but I was all in by the time I got back on the boat. Kevin was worried, I could tell. I drank all the brandy I'd got on board before I could even begin to tell him what had happened. We called the coastguard soon afterwards and told them what I'd found, and they sent a recovery team to bring up the bodies. The strange thing was that by the time their divers reached the bodies there was no wooden figure to be seen anywhere.'

Everyone had sat round the table and looked at Phil. No one said anything. There was, Meg reflected, nothing anyone really could say. Finally Annie had broken the silence.

'There's more things in heaven and earth...,' she said, paraphrasing Shakespeare's immortal quotation. 'I think what we all need is a nice strong cup of tea.'

Meg knew what that phrase meant now and she had smiled wryly as she watched Annie put the kettle on. The plates and dishes were cleared away and Annie set out cups and saucers, milk and sugar, before placing a large teapot and a full half bottle of brandy on the table. No one protested as some brandy was poured into each tea cup. They had all felt in need of a good stiff drink after the tale Phil had just told them. Fortified by the liberal helpings of brandy in their tea they had all speculated for hours about what had happened to Chris and his unfortunate companion and what it all meant. Finally tiredness had got the better of them. John and Sara had decided to stay the night with Annie to make sure she was OK so Phil gave Kevin and Meg a lift back in his van. They had parted with promises to all meet up for lunch the following day.

It seemed to be raining harder than ever. Meg dragged herself out of bed and switched on the small kettle thoughtfully provided by Mrs Woodcock for her guests. Breakfast wouldn't be served for another hour yet so she had plenty of time to savour her early morning tea. She could hardly believe everything that had happened yesterday. Steven's escape; Polly's warning; Steven's abrupt and hostile intrusion into Annie's garden; his attempts to hurt Sara and his arrest; then Phil and Kevin's revelations. In all the excitement she had almost forgotten the cause of it all which was explained by the contents of the neatly typed letter from Mr Ormesher that still lay in her bag. She would have to decide what to do about that soon. Mrs Woodcock was buzzing with all the gossip at breakfast. The other holidaymakers staying in her guest house got far more drama with their bacon and eggs than if they had spent two hours watching a James Bond movie. Meg was quite glad to make her escape from the eight curious pairs of eyes regarding her in the wake of Mrs Woodcock's revelations.

She zipped herself into her waterproofs, took a large umbrella and hurried out to meet Kevin. He and Phil were down in the harbourmaster's office checking out boats that had been in the area recently.

'I think that's the only one unaccounted for now,' the harbourmaster was saying as she walked in. 'Most of them called into St Marys so I've got their details. Emerald anchored out in the Roadstead but so far as I know she never came into port. Customs took a brief interest in her but she seemed clean and she wasn't in contact with any of the other boats while she was here. Then their attention was diverted by all that business with the French yachts over at Tresco and they didn't really pay Emerald any more attention.'

'I think she was in contact with one or two of the other boats,' said Phil, 'but they were clever. They used Samson as a meeting place and a dropping off point. All the boats had small dinghies, or a rowing boat with an outboard motor, for going ashore. No one would think twice about seeing a dinghy on Samson's beaches at this time of year.'

'You could be right,' the harbourmaster said pensively.

'I'm certain I am,' said Phil. 'When Dan and I were there we were intrigued by that huge heap of seaweed on one side of the 'waist' by the old cottage. Ellie spent ages sniffing around it. I think that was used as a cover for any exchanges they wanted to make.'

The whole thing was beginning to make sense to Meg. She too had wondered about the huge mound of seaweed. It would also explain the small boats that she had seen going round the back of Samson. Far less obvious to load or unload a boat on the blind side of the island.

'Who owned Emerald?' asked Meg as she shook the raindrops off her umbrella. Emerald would be an apt name for a boat engaged in a search for precious jewels.

'Emerald was a rental boat,' said the harbourmaster. 'She was out of St Ives and she was chartered for a couple of weeks to sail around the Scillies. Got the name of the guy who hired her here somewhere.'

He rummaged through the papers on his desk.

'Ah yes, that's right. Bloke by the name of Steven Hamilton.'

Meg drew a sharp breath. So Steven had planned this all along. He had plotted for years to rob her of her inheritance and then he had planned the final operation in meticulous detail. He was cold, calculating and ruthless. How he must have hated her. Tears pricked at the back of her eyes but she would not cry. Not any more.

'Who were the two men who died?' she asked in a small voice.

'Chris Hoyles was the diving guy, the one I knew,' said Phil. 'We're awaiting definite confirmation on the other one but we think he was called Reggie Price. Devon and Cornwall Police were tipped off by the Metropolitan Police that a small time gangster from London was on their patch. They tracked him to St Ives and then, nothing. He's not been seen for two or three weeks now and his description matches that of the other dead guy.'

Meg wondered how on earth Steven had got himself mixed up with such people but then greed and desperation could be lethal bedfellows. He had been determined to achieve his goal at any cost. Thinking of Steven reminded her of Janine. She wasn't going to be seeing much of her husband now even if she wanted to do so, which Meg considered to be very unlikely. Then there was Dan. Dr Morgan had said that he would make a full recovery but that his arm would always bear the scars of the shooting. Two of Steven's associates were dead and the other one was in jail. She was fairly certain that there would be no more phone calls or letters; no more fear and harassment, but at what cost. Would she ever really be able to come to terms with all that had happened and accept that Steven had been a completely false husband who really had meant her harm. She smiled sadly. She would have to do so if ever she was to move on.

As if reading her thoughts, Kevin took her arm gently.
'Come on,' he whispered, 'we'll go for a coffee and then we'll go and see Tom to make a statement. After that you can begin to try and forget that Steven Hamilton ever existed.'

They drank their coffee in Kavorna, a small café and bistro, which lay midway between the quay and the police station. There was an impressive display of freshly made cakes and pastries on the shelves of the chiller behind the glass fronted counter but this morning neither of them were tempted. Both of them simply wanted to get the formalities over and then they could start to try and put the whole thing behind them. Except, Meg reflected wryly, that was not going to be so easy for her. She still had to make a decision about the bequest from her father. It was a truly amazing thing that four generations of her family had not wanted the riches and the life of luxury that the contents of that bequest could have brought. Nor was she at all sure that she would either. She had been shocked by the lengths to which people were prepared to go when they were driven by greed and lust. Dan could have died after Jamie had shot him. They all might have died if Ellie, blinded by rage at the attack on her master, had not brought Jamie down. Then there was Steven. Meg could still hardly believe that her own husband had been prepared to threaten and harm, even kill her if necessary. She had loved him but she had been nothing more to him than a means to an end. Then she thought of Janine lying in hospital with her broken arm and her bandaged head. She had not been quite so lucky as Meg. Meg had at least escaped physical harm. She thought of Sara and Annie. Steven had had a gun in his pocket and she did not think that he would have hesitated to use it on any of them if Sara had not floored him as she had. She shook her head. It was as if she had been married to a complete stranger. In spite of herself she shivered.

'Are you OK?' Kevin's hand was resting on her arm and he was looking at her with a concerned expression on his face.

'Yes.' Meg forced herself back to the present. 'I was just thinking how many lives Steven and his friends were prepared to destroy just to get their hands on those jewels; and maybe the seal stones.'

'I know. It's not very pretty, is it?' said Kevin grimly. If Steven had succeeded in harming Meg, he thought, he would happily have killed him with his own bare hands.

'What do you think happened to the seal stones?' asked Meg. 'Do you think that Richard King did hide them and that is why they haven't been found so far?'

'Possibly,' said Kevin. 'Most of them were quite small and wherever they were it's most likely that they were scattered in the aftermath of the sinking of Colossus.

Possibly they might still have been wrapped up in a box in one of the crates and they could have been buried by the impact of the Colossus breaking her back when she hit the sea-bed.'

'Do you think the guardian was trying to protect them?' Meg asked, feeling a little foolish talking about wooden figures that could supposedly move unaided along the sea-bed. Phil had said that he had photographic proof of the figure's existence even though the coastguard divers had found no trace of it.

'Actually, I think it was trying to protect the remains of the ship rather than the seal stones in particular,' said Kevin, looking serious.

Meg looked at him puzzled.
'But there were no such incidents when Oscar and all the subsequent artefacts were brought to the surface,' she protested.

'Those were from the port side of the ship for which Oscar was the guardian. Oscar was damaged and he may not have been able to function properly. Besides, those items weren't taken for personal gain but to preserve them, and thereby the ship, for posterity.'

Understanding began to dawn on Meg's face as Kevin went on.

'This other figure appeared to be undamaged, or so Phil says. The shifting of the sands took place over a period of about ten years and then there was all the disturbance which obviously freed it from its resting place. It must have been the guardian for the starboard side. Remember I said that there should have been another figure after we saw Oscar? If some of Sir William Hamilton's packing cases were stored on the starboard side then they would have been under the other guardian's protection.'

'So,' she said slowly, 'if someone went searching for something and didn't care what they destroyed to get it then the other guardian might have swung into action.'

'Exactly,' said Kevin.

Meg stared at him. Here they were, part of the Age of hi-tech and space travel, having a seemingly quite normal conversation about things happening which should have belonged only to the realms of history and folklore. Shakespeare had been right. There certainly were more things in heaven and earth than she had ever dreamed of.

They finished their coffees and set out for the police station. It wasn't far; just around the corner from Kavorna and up a short steep hill. Both Tom and Polly were there, doubtless doing overtime while Dan was in hospital. Tom greeted them both and took them into the office to give their statements. To save time, and trouble, he said, he would take Kevin's statement while Polly took Meg's statement.

'How is Dan?' asked Meg, 'and Janine?' she added, concerned now that Polly had left her on her own.

'Dan's fine,' said Tom, 'he's sitting up in bed now and wanting to be at home with Ellie.'

'But what about Janine?' persisted Meg. 'Will she be OK on her own?'

'Oh yes!' Tom smiled. 'Now we've got Steven and Jamie behind bars and the other two are dead there's no danger to either of you.'

'She'll be lonely without you, Polly,' Meg said, turning to the policewoman.

Polly laughed. 'I don't think so,' she said. 'She's struck up quite a rapport with Dan. He'll keep her occupied until they're discharged.'

'Who was it that was following me?' asked Meg. 'Did the same person make the anonymous phone calls and write those letters as well? Or was Steven really behind it all?'

Tom looked at her sympathetically. She had a right to know but she wasn't going to like it.

'Steven married you because he thought you would receive the Hamilton legacy on your parents' deaths,' he said as gently as he could.

'I know that,' said Meg a little tremulously.

'Well,' Tom went on, 'when it became obvious that you knew nothing about any legacy, and your father wouldn't tell him anything either, he got impatient and thought he might just have made a mistake. He already knew about the Richard King connection so he divorced you and married Janine instead. Are you OK with hearing this?' he asked in concern as Meg had paled a little.

She nodded. 'It's just unbelievable that he was so cold and calculating about it all,' she said.

'Then he read about all the new finds from Colossus but nothing about any jewels,' Tom continued, 'and he decided that perhaps you did know about them and had just been holding out on him. Not entirely logical but then Steven stopped being entirely logical a while ago. He considered you to be a fairly timid person and he thought he could scare you into revealing their whereabouts. However he couldn't afford to take the chance that you might recognise his voice or his handwriting so he went looking for someone who could put the frighteners on you.'

Meg gasped at this revelation. Steven really hadn't cared what he did in his pursuit of what he saw as rightfully his.

'We don't yet know how he met Reggie Price,' Tom went on, 'but if you go into pubs in certain parts of London and let it be known what you're looking for someone will always oblige in return for ready cash. Reggie Price was good at putting the frighteners on people. He was known for it and he was used to working on the fringes of London's gangland.'

Tom paused to give Polly a broad smile and to ask if she would like to make some tea for them all. Polly got up with a sigh and switched on the kettle.

'However,' Tom continued, 'Steven was thrown when you came out to the Scillies. He hadn't expected that. Then you got friendly with Kevin. He knew who Kevin was and he didn't want you being friendly with him in case you found out things that Steven would really rather you didn't know. He asked Reggie to step up the pressure. It was Reggie who followed you to Samson and it was Reggie you met briefly on the Garrison headland. It was Reggie who attacked Janine and it was also Reggie who overheard you on the telephone in the post office. He knew you were ringing your solicitor and it was then he began to think that Steven had been holding out on him.'

'How did Chris Hoyles fit into it all?' asked Kevin.

'Chris Hoyles was a friend of Steven,' said Tom. 'They talked a lot about the Colossus. Chris had done a little diving before but he was no expert. They both agreed it would be a great cover if he came down and joined one of Phil's diving groups, especially as they knew that he held a licence for the site of the Colossus.'

Polly handed round mugs of tea, giving Tom his mug with an air of long suffering.

'So why involve Paul Smith?' asked Kevin.

'They were all beginning to get the jitters,' Tom said, taking a sip of his tea and smiling sweetly at Polly. 'Things were not going their way at all. Then Reggie got the idea that Steven had been holding out on him about the jewels. He told Chris what had happened and Chris agreed with him. So they attacked Steven and took him over to Samson thinking that by the time anyone found him it would be too late. Paul Smith was Chris's idea. Chris had seen his work in diving magazines and thought it would be a good front. Their idea was to try and locate the seal stones mentioned in the letter Reggie stole from Janine. Chris hired Paul and chartered a boat. Reggie phoned up one his gangland pals in London and asked him to come down and make sure there was no trouble while they were diving on the site of the Colossus. Jamie was introduced to Paul and the charter skipper as just a general helper. They didn't think anything about it.'

'If they had found something down there would they have left me alone?' asked Meg.

'I don't think so,' said Tom. 'Reggie would have waited until all the fuss had died down and then he would have come after you. As it is, you're off the hook completely now since both Reggie and Chris died together.'

Meg shivered. How could Steven have even thought of asking London hit-men to chase after her. Just how desperate had he been to get his hands on those jewels.

As if reading her mind Tom said 'In all fairness I don't think Steven knew quite what he was getting himself into with those guys. He thinks he's so clever and that he knows it all but in some ways he's wet behind the ears when it comes to dealing with people. Maybe he had some time to think while he was lying in that tomb. Whatever. It certainly sent him over the edge. He's singing like a bird now and he's told us that if he had got his hands on your legacy he was going to find Chris and Reggie and kill them himself.'

'Would he have killed me as well?' asked Meg in small voice.

Kevin took her hand and said 'Don't ask that question, Meg.'

'I need to know the answer,' said Meg determinedly. 'It's important.'

'We don't know for certain,' said Tom gently, 'but, in his current state of mind, I think there is a strong probability that he might have done.'

Meg gave a tight little smile. 'Thanks,' she said. 'That's all I needed to know.'

They gave their statements to Tom and Polly who wrote them down neatly and efficiently before handing them back to be carefully re-read and signed.

'You'll want to stay for the Coroner's inquest I expect,' said Tom. 'That will be held next Tuesday in the Town Hall. That will about wrap up our involvement and we'll hand over to the Devon and Cornwall police.'

'What will happen to Steven now?' asked Meg quietly. Tom looked at her pityingly. The man was a nasty piece of work and this poor woman had actually been married to him.

'I think he'll be going down for quite a stretch,' he said. 'He needs psychiatric help as well and he'll get that in prison,' he added. Privately Tom thought that Steven Hamilton could also do with a punch in the teeth as well to knock some of the arrogance out of him and he didn't doubt that a few of those would be coming his way once he was inside.

Meg and Kevin walked back, hand in hand, down the hill and along Hugh Street to the quay with the wind and rain blowing in their faces. They stood just above the harbour wall watching the storm blown waves, the spray whipped up by the high tides rising in a misty cloud above the harbour wall then gracefully falling again like the damp sparks of spent fireworks.

'Have you thought what you will do with your bequest?' asked Kevin softly. 'It's an awesome responsibility you have there.'

'I know,' Meg agreed, 'and it's brought so much misery in its wake. Like my father and grandfather I'm not at all sure that I want to keep it.'

'Why not give it to the British Museum to go with the rest of the Hamilton Collections?' suggested Kevin. 'It would be safe enough with them and that is probably the best option if you really don't want to keep it. Those gems must be beautiful but they've just been hidden away for two hundred years and what is the point of that? No one can see them or enjoy them. All that happens is that they gather dust and they have caused enough grief. I'm sure that would never have been Sir William's intention, even if the child he left them to was not his own child,' he added with a half smile.

Meg had already briefly considered this option but it was not a decision she intended to make in haste. She needed to think long and hard about what she should do and about what she really wanted to do. Her head was too full of recent events for her to be able to think sensibly and logically. There was no rush. Mr Ormesher would keep them in his safe for her until she was ready. John appeared alongside them in his van.

'Want a lift?' he asked. 'It's lunchtime and we're all meeting up at the Bishop.' Kevin and Meg smiled at each other and got into his van.

Somewhere beneath their feet shadows moved imperceptibly across the sands.

St Marys, Isles of Scilly, 21st March 1881

Horatio Nelson sat on the small rough wooden bench he had placed outside his front door to catch the sunshine. It was the beginning of spring today, a season of renewed hope with the hardships of winter finally over for another year. He loved this view and watching the sunbeams winking across the waters of Old Town Bay. A fresh breeze had whipped up lacy white tops to the waves and he could see the fishing boats bobbing up and down by the old quay. He took his favourite clay pipe from his pocket and filled it with a few strands of tobacco from the battered old tin that had once belonged to his father. Not to his real father but to the man he had always thought of as Dad. His real father had been a clergyman who had died when Horatio was still a child. Horatio lit the tobacco and sucked deeply and satisfyingly on his pipe. His real mother had died only three weeks ago. Although he had corresponded with her for near on twenty years before her death he still thought of Sarah Nelson, née Legg, as 'Mother' and he always would.

He reflected briefly on the sharing of his name with one of the greatest admirals in British naval history. It had been an honour bestowed upon quite a few young men of his generation but, Horatio thought, maybe he had more claim to it than most for Horatio, Admiral Lord Nelson, had actually been his grandfather. He could still remember his amazement and disbelief when Mother and Dad had told him that he was adopted. Dad had carefully explained the circumstances to him and he'd understood that it had all been for the best. He was happy in the Islands and he'd never wanted to be anywhere else. Dad had also explained that his real mother had been the daughter of Admiral Lord Nelson. He'd told Horatio how hard it had been for her to give him up and that as he had now become a young man she wanted to write regularly to him, to try and establish some sort of bond. Horatio had found this difficult at first but as time went on it had got easier, especially after they had met for the first time. He'd found Horatia a loving gentle woman who seemed to have been blessed with finding real happiness in her life.

Horatio puffed away on his pipe and smiled at the antics of a small group of children who were playing on the beach. He was middle aged himself now and felt that he had been fortunate to find everything he had wanted for himself in life. As a young man he had gone to sea and he had sailed round the world and back. Along the way he'd seen lots of strange and exotic sights and he'd had some great adventures. When finally he had been ready to settle down, Rosie had still been waiting for him. They had married and they had a son of their own whom they'd named Joseph. Horatio, always very practical with his hands, made his living from fishing and doing odd jobs. More than anything he loved being out in his boat on the open sea, free like the wind, following the shoals of ling. He was a deeply contented man and more than happy with his lot, which was why it had been such a shock when the solicitor had arrived from England to tell him of his real mother's death and to bring the legacy which she had left for him.

He closed his eyes in the sunshine and registered again the astonishment he'd felt when he had read Horatia's last letter to him and then opened the box.

Thunderstruck, he'd stared at the glittering jewels lying on their bed of velvet. He barely remembered the solicitor taking his leave. He'd just sat there, Horatia's letter in his hand, staring out across the deep blue sea and azure sky of Old Town Bay. By the time coherent thought had returned he knew what he was going to do. Horatia had judged her son well. Like his real mother, Horatio knew that many riches could not be bought. His love for Rosie; Joseph, his fine strong son; the peace and joy in the little cottage standing looking across Old Town Bay; nothing could buy what he had now.

He knew well enough the story of Admiral Lord Nelson and Emma, Lady Hamilton. They had both had whole fortunes at their feet and much good it had done them. The Admiral at least had died knowing that he had rendered the ultimate service to his country by freeing England from Napoleon Bonaparte and the threat of a French invasion. Emma was quite a different matter. She had been his grandmother, and he had no wish to disrespect her memory, but she had been reckless, a profligate spendthrift and gambler. No amount of money had ever been sufficient for her and she had ended her days alone, except for Horatia of course, lying embittered and drunk in a cheap Calais boarding house. That road was not one which Horatio either wished or intended to travel. He opened the box again and looked at the sapphires and rubies, diamonds and emeralds. Gently he lifted each one out and held it in his fingers. Beneath the velvet lay a few dull gold chains. He fingered them thoughtfully. Then he covered them up again carefully with the velvet and replaced the jewels. They lay there winking up at him, tiny miracles of nature tarnished by the greed and lust of those who would lie, cheat, steal or even kill to possess them. Horatio shook his head sadly. He decided that he would say nothing about it to anyone. Once folks knew, gossip would always find its way to the wrong ears. He had closed the box and wrapped it in an old cloth. Then he had hidden it carefully beneath the rafters of the small cottage. No-one would ever find it there. He would write a letter to his son, Joseph, explaining what he had done, and why, and he would ensure that Joseph only received the letter after he, Horatio, was already dead. He hoped that Joseph would be wise enough to know what he should do and that someday, maybe, Joseph's son in turn would learn from the wisdom of his father and grandfather. Satisfied, he knocked out his pipe on the little stone wall which surrounded the cottage garden and strolled down to the beach. Tomorrow he would take the young ones out fishing.

St Marys, Isles of Scilly, 10th June 2008

Meg stood by the stone steps outside the Town Hall that led up to the Court House, shivering in the chill winds and a fine drizzle which soaked through everything much more quickly than a heavy downpour. The weather had remained changed for the worse since the day that Kevin and Phil had discovered the boat off Southward Well with its drowned occupants. The Court House doubled as auction rooms and the Registry Office for Island weddings. Today, however, it was in use as a Coroner's Court. She looked at her watch. She was early and if she was quick about it she just had time for a coffee. She chose a small café near the Town Hall. Part of the café had been turned into a delicatessen and the fragrance of mixed spices and a variety of European cooked meats and aromatic cheeses assailed her nostrils. Meg took her coffee over to a small table in the corner by the large window that had fronted the former butcher's shop which had occupied the premises.

She stirred her coffee absently, looking out at the dismal skies and grey drizzle which seemed to be dampening everyone's spirits, going over and over the events in her mind. The story that Kevin and Phil had told was almost too incredible to be believed and she wondered what the Coroner would make of it. She wondered if she would have to admit publicly to her legacy in court and she fervently hoped that she wouldn't have to do so. Part of her just wanted to forget about it, but part of her knew that she would have to think about it soon because she had some decisions to make which could not be put off forever. Returning to the present with something of a start Meg realised that her coffee was going cold. She looked at her watch, quickly drained her coffee cup, and, taking up her umbrella, went out once again into the drab morning. Kevin was waiting for her just inside the doors to the Court House which now stood open.

'You OK?' he whispered as they took their seats on the hard wooden chairs which had been set out for the Court. Meg nodded, although a little uncertainly, and Kevin took her hand and held it tightly in a gesture of solidarity. The Coroner had flown in from Penzance on the helicopter that morning to deal with the required formalities before the bodies were taken back to the mainland where a full inquest would be held at a later date. Phil was sitting across the courtroom, instead of with Kevin and Meg, since the Coroner would call him as a witness because he had discovered the bodies. Just before the proceedings began John and Sara slid into the seats next to them and then Annie hurried in. She was not going to be cheated of the resolution to all the intrigue and mystery.

The Coroner mounted the small wooden platform at one end of the room and took his place in a comfortable chair placed behind the pitted wooden desk. He was a dark haired, serious looking, middle aged man in a neat grey suit. Although his appearance was formal his manner was friendly and courteous. He peered over his glasses to establish that his clerk was in place at a small desk below him to his left, to take notes, then he declared the Court to be convened.

Dr Morgan was the first witness to be called. He had examined the bodies of the dead men when they were brought back to St Marys and announced that he believed that death was due to drowning. There were numerous bruises and abrasions on the bodies of both men but he thought that these could have been caused by being swept against hard objects through water movement and also by the action of crabs. Meg winced at this thought. Being dinner for the crabs was not a good ending to one's life. The Coroner seemed to agree with Dr Morgan's assessment but he expressed curiosity as to how the two men came to be in the water.

Tom took the stand next and was asked if he had established formal identification. He told the Coroner that Phil had positively identified one of the men as Chris Hoyles, a member of his diving group. The other one was known to the Metropolitan Police as Reggie Price, a small time crook who had connections with London's gangland. Formal identification would be made once the body had been returned to the mainland. The Coroner wrote a few notes rapidly in ball point pen on the A4 pad thoughtfully provided for him before telling Tom he could step down.

After Tom, the Coroner heard testimony from the two coastguard divers who had brought the bodies to the surface. He questioned them on how the bodies were lying, the position of their boat, and whether there were any indications of what had caused their craft to break up in the way it had. He frowned a little when one of the divers said that there were no rocks in that particular area of the sea where the casualties had been found but that the boat was in pieces, almost as though it had been blown apart. Dr Morgan was recalled to the stand briefly and asked if the injuries could be consistent with having been received in an explosion but Dr Morgan shook his head. He didn't think that was the case at all.

Finally it was Phil's turn to be called to the stand. The Coroner asked him to recount everything exactly as it had happened. There was a hushed expectancy in the courtroom. Phil repeated his story clearly in a steady voice, just as he had told it to the others a few days before. The Coroner listened intently to every word.

When Phil had finished the Coroner turned to him and said 'Mr Jenkins. You have told us that when you first discovered these two unfortunate individuals there was some sort of a wooden figure lying across them.'

'That's correct,' said Phil.

'Yet when the coastguard divers went down to retrieve the bodies and bring them up to the surface, they reported that there was nothing lying across them.'

'Yes sir.' Phil said without any further embellishment.

'How long was it between you surfacing and the two coastguard divers going down?' asked the Coroner.

'Maybe an hour, an hour and a half,' answered Phil.

'And you, yourself, did not dive again?'

'No.' Phil knew the Coroner was having difficulty with credibility. 'I wasn't in any fit state.'

'You saw no one else in the vicinity?'

Phil shook his head again.

'So how do you account for the disappearance of this wooden figure?'

'I can't,' said Phil simply.

'Well,' ventured the Coroner, 'is it not possible that perhaps you imagined it?'

'No sir!' said Phil firmly. 'I can prove it and I've brought the photographs to show you.'

He handed the Coroner an envelope. The Coroner removed the contents and studied them carefully for a few minutes before turning back to Phil.

'Have you any idea what this figure might be?'

'Yes sir,' said Phil without hesitation. 'The Colossus, a ship in Admiral Lord Nelson's fleet, sank at that same spot in 1798 and I believe it was one of the guardians of that ship. His twin is in the Valhalla on Tresco.'

There were audible gasps of surprise in the Courtroom. The Coroner peered at Phil over the rim of his spectacles.

'Would you care to explain that statement to the Court?'

'Sailors have always been very superstitious,' said Phil. 'Ships were believed to need some sort of a guardian to keep them safe when they were at sea. More often than not this was the figurehead. The Colossus was built as a warship. Perhaps it was considered that she might need extra protection and maybe they thought that just a simple figurehead would be too vulnerable in battle. Whatever the case, the Colossus had a carved wooden figure curved around each side of the window in the stern. The one from the port side was discovered and brought to the surface in 2002 and it's now in the Valhalla on Tresco. He's called Oscar.'

A titter could be heard in the Courtroom and the Coroner seemed to be having some difficulty with his own facial expression but he managed to keep his tone grave.

'Go on,' he said to Phil.

'The figure from the starboard side has never been found,' said Phil. 'When the ship sank she broke her back and her port side was embedded in the sand on the seabed and practically buried. Her starboard side seems to have been scattered. About ten years ago the sands on the sea-bed shifted, as they often do out here, and the remains of the port side together with Oscar were revealed. Excavations were carried out over a number of years and numerous artifacts were brought up to the surface. I have dived on that ship myself countless times but I have never seen any sign of the figure from the starboard side until last Thursday.'

The Coroner scribbled more notes on the pad in front of him then he turned back to Phil and said 'Do you have any idea where this figure might be now?'

Phil shook his head. 'No.'

'Is it possible that you might have moved it yourself? Dislodged it perhaps as you were taking your photographs?'

'No way,' said Phil. 'It took at least three of us to lift Oscar. Those wooden figures were large and heavy. Besides I took care not to touch it. Scene of crime and all that.'

He laughed awkwardly. He had no intention of telling the Coroner that he would not have touched it if he had been offered a fortune to do so. That was what he had told them all when they were sitting round Annie's kitchen table. Every instinct in his body had warned him not to go anywhere near that figure, not to touch it at all costs and to get the hell out of there and back to the surface as quickly as he possibly could. He had stopped just long enough to take two or three shots and then he had hightailed it back to the surface. He'd remembered how Paul had looked after his experience and he could understand only too well his shock and disbelief.

The Coroner was summing up his findings.

'It would appear that a boat sank off Samson in good weather conditions without any reasonable explanation. I am satisfied from evidence given that there are no rocks in the area of the sinking which would have caused the extent of damage that the boat suffered. The remains of the vessel indicate that it seems to have been torn apart as though by some violent explosion. No-one has come forward to say that they heard any such explosion. There were two men on board and their bodies were later recovered by the local Coastguard. When first discovered the bodies appeared to be lying beneath a heavy wooden figure for which I have been given photographic evidence. However the coastguard say that there was no evidence of this figure when they retrieved the bodies of the two men. Cause of death for the casualties has been established as drowning.' He paused and seemed to be thinking intently, then he continued. 'There are certain aspects of this case which remain unexplained and disturbing. However I am satisfied that foul play was not involved and I do not believe that the men took their own lives. Therefore I am recording death by some sort of misadventure, the exact nature of which may never become known.'

The Coroner then thanked those who had given evidence and extended his sympathies to the families of the two dead men, after which he stood up and left the Courtroom.

Meg turned to the others. 'I guess that's a sort of closure, isn't it?' she said.

Phil was making his way over to them. They stood up to greet him as he approached.

'Thank God that's over!' he said with feeling. 'I could do with a drink.' He grinned. 'Several in fact!'

No one had noticed Paul approaching. He must have come in to the Courtroom at the last moment and slipped unseen into a seat to listen to the proceedings. He tapped Phil nervously on the shoulder.

'Don't take this the wrong way,' he said 'but I am so glad you saw that figure. It wasn't just me. I'm not going mad.'

'No.' Phil managed a half smile. 'You're not going mad. It was a pretty awful experience for both of us.'

'You seemed to cope better than I did,' said Paul uncertainly.

'I knew something of the legends,' said Phil kindly, 'so I was a bit more prepared and it wasn't as completely unexpected as it might have been. Even so it's not something I'd ever want to see again. We're just going for a drink. Would you like to join us?'

'Better not actually, thanks,' said Paul. 'I promised Heather I'd be back soon.' He turned to Kevin and said shyly 'Thanks for your help when I was in shock. Heather told me who you were. It can't have been easy for you. Sorry, mate.'

Meg watched Kevin's face with concern but his expression was equable as he said 'It doesn't matter now. Really,' he added, seeing the look on Paul's face. 'It was just one of those things. Didn't Heather come with you today?'

Paul shook his head.

'She thought it might be inappropriate and she didn't want to cause any further upset.'

Kevin looked a bit shamefaced. 'It wasn't her fault. The baby was just a bit of a surprise. That's all.'

He smiled suddenly. 'Tell Heather that I really do wish her all the best and good luck to you as well.' He held out his hand to Paul and the two men shook hands warmly as though they were old friends. Kevin watched as Paul left the Courtroom to return to Heather. To her intense relief Meg could see no trace of regret or envy on his features; just an acceptance that his life had moved on.

Her life was moving on as well in ways that she could never have foreseen. Both Dan and Janine were being discharged that afternoon and both were to spend their convalescence with Annie.

'Dan is family, after all,' said Annie firmly when Meg had looked at her incredulously, 'and Janine, well t'is not her fault that Steven Hamilton is as he is. She's as much his victim as you and Dan and she needs a little kindness in her life right now.'

Her charity and her sense of decency had made Meg feel ashamed. Annie was right. Janine was as much a victim of Steven as she herself had been. She too had been caught up in something that she had not understood. Meg would need to return to the mainland soon and perhaps she should spend the remainder of her time left on the Islands getting to know Annie, Dan and Janine better.

Kevin would be going home as well, if it could be called that since he regarded the Scillies as more his home than anywhere else. Meg understood how he felt. She felt it herself. In some ways they were so alike and Kevin had made it very clear that he wanted her to be a part of his life. For now though she would concentrate on getting to know her 'family' and on deciding what to do about her inheritance. Everything else could wait.

Somewhere close by shadows rippled through the sands and slipped unnoticed into the water.

Tregawethan, Cornwall, 26th June 1998

David Nelson sat in the early morning sunshine cradling his cup of coffee in his hands. The cottage he had rented sat high up on the cliffs and afforded him a magnificent view out across to Lands End and, on a clear day such as today he could see as far as the Isles of Scilly. He thought briefly of his old childhood home on St Marys and wondered exactly why it was that he had never felt that he really belonged there. He had been an only child born late in life to his parents but that hadn't stopped him having his friends his own age and, to be fair, his parents had always welcomed his friends into their home. He smiled nostalgically as he remembered the way they had raced their bikes up to Telegraph and then yelled 'last one home is the rascal!' as they sped down the lanes into Old Town. They had usually ended up in his mother's kitchen and she would give them orange juice and biscuits to keep them fortified until their next meal.

As soon as they had started in secondary school David had known he was destined for different things. He had a sharp brain and enjoyed puzzling out the intricacies of chemical formulae and algebraic equations. While he liked going fishing with his father and helping to tend the small plot of land which kept them supplied with fresh vegetables, he knew he could not face a life-time doing that for a living. He needed fresh stimulae and challenges that would satisfy his active brain. When he reached his teens Dad had told him about the legacy. He hadn't quite fully understood then why Dad had never made use of it but Dad had said that he had all he wanted. What more was there? The young David thought that there was lots more and at first he was full of enthusiasm for what could be done with such a fortune when he grew up, but then came the War.

David had enlisted like many other young men of his generation. He was bright enough to serve in the RAF although, to his frustration, he spent the first two years of the War on desk duties. Finally he was given his wings and allowed to fly. He loved the freedom of the open skies, weaving around as he cruised in his small single seater plane, dodging the heavier clumsier German planes, helping defend his country against the terrible threat of Nazism. Sometimes he almost wished that the War would go on forever. Then his luck ran out and he was shot down somewhere over the Rühr. Somehow he managed to eject from the plane before it crashed into a fireball of flame and he watched it in horrified fascination as he drifted down towards the earth. His parachute had snagged in the branches of a large oak tree and there he hung helplessly until German soldiers had cut him down. To his surprise he was treated fairly well and sent to a labour camp to work out the rest of the War. Some of his colleagues in the camp had told him horrific stories of the atrocities said to have been committed against foreigners in other camps; especially against the Jews. David had no reason to either believe them or disbelieve them until liberation came.

His own camp was liberated by a British task force on its way to Northern Germany and then the Polish border to liberate two of the camps his colleagues had mentioned: Bergen-Belsen and Auschwitz. As he was young, British, and relatively fit, he had offered his services to the task force and they had been gratefully accepted. So it was that he had marched with them to free other victims from the Nazi regime. The shock of his first sighting of Bergen-Belsen was so profound that it changed his whole life. He would never ever forget the sight of the bulldozers edging the piles of bodies into mass graves. The pitiful sight of small children, their limbs like matchsticks, their faces distorted by the suffering they had endured, lying discarded around the place like pieces of litter. Most were dead and those that weren't might just as well have been. The stench of death in the air was overwhelming.

'How could anyone do such a thing?' he had whispered to no one in particular. Auschwitz had been as bad. It was full of barely living skeletons of all ages in blue striped prison clothing clutching the wire surrounding the camp, too weak to even move when someone called out 'You're free!' Many of the task force were in tears. David didn't cry. All he could see was the expression of hopelessness and suffering in their eyes. Many of them were Jewish and he knew that Jewish people had a reputation for good business brains. Some of them must have had money, must have tried to buy a way out for their families, if not for themselves. He thought of the dead children he had seen at Bergen-Belsen. No fortune in the world could bring back those lives snuffed out with such horror and suffering. In that moment David lost all his own ambition, his hopes for the future and his trust.

He became silent and introspective. If this was what human beings were capable of then he didn't want to know. Gone were all the fine plans of his boyhood. What use was money when people would do that to each other. Some of them must have had money once and it hadn't helped them one bit. The world was vicious and greedy and evil. He returned to England and took an office job. He didn't really care any more what became of him. Then he met Cerys, a Welsh girl, who had come to England during the War, and ended up working in the same office as David. Cerys was warm and kind; the first person he had felt able to tell about the atrocities he had witnessed. She seemed to understand completely how he had felt and gradually she had brought him out of himself. They fell in love and married and as time went on he relied on her absolutely to keep his demons at bay. Their relationship was so close that it sometimes felt as if he was smothering her but he clung to her desperately for if she was not there he knew that he would fall back into the black abyss he had inhabited when he met her. They told each other that they didn't need children and, just when they thought there would be none, Megan was born. It was the beginning of the end.

Cerys had loved the Scillies but David did not feel at ease there now. His mother had died during the War; although they had taken the infant Megan out to the Islands to see his father. When his father, Joseph, died he went to St Marys for the funeral and retrieved the precious legacy Joseph had told him about from its hiding place under the rafters. He put the cottage up for sale and vowed that he would not come back to the Islands. They reminded him too much of the carefree time of his boyhood when life had seemed to hold such promise. There was only one person whom he would miss and that was Annie Legg. They had always been close, right from being small children, and he could talk to her in a way that he couldn't talk to anyone else except Cerys. His father had told him that they and the Leggs were related, but fairly distantly. David hadn't thought much of it. He knew that practically everyone was related to everyone else in the Islands; but he did feel a special bond with Annie. He wrote to her from time to time and he always sent her Christmas and birthday cards.

The divorce had come when Megan was twelve. It was horrible, unthinkable, and incredibly bitter. David had retreated into himself again. He saw Megan at first but she seemed to be just like her mother and just as resentful. He gave up the visits. What was the point. He didn't know that Cerys also saw him in Megan and had shut the girl out as a result. As far as he knew she continued to look after Megan, feeding her, sending her to school, making a comfortable home for her. Megan herself had agreed that her physical needs were fulfilled but she had written to him once that emotionally and spiritually she was an orphan. He had dismissed her letter at the time thinking it was just another way for Cerys to get at him. Now he wished that he hadn't.

Then Megan had fallen in love and he didn't like her fiancé, not one little bit. The boy was arrogant and full of himself and he kept asking David if Megan had any expectations of an inheritance. At first David assumed he was just tactlessly ascertaining what Megan stood to gain when both her parents were dead. Calculating little bastard. Then he remembered the legacy. He'd not thought about the jewels since he'd brought them back from St Marys and lodged them safely with his solicitor. He'd not wanted them. He'd already lost the things he really cared about. He knew that his father and grandfather hadn't wanted them either but for the opposite reason. They'd already had everything that they had wanted from life. Now he had to decide what to do about the legacy. He'd never told Megan about it. They were hardly on those sort of terms. It was as well Megan didn't know. She stood no chance of standing up to the demands of that controlling creep she was insisting on marrying. However, like himself, she had no siblings and he had to think what he should do for the best. One thing he was sure of was that whatever he did he would ensure that the controlling creep wasn't going to get his hands on them. He needed to think and he needed to talk to someone. He could no longer talk to Cerys but he could talk to Annie. He took a day trip to St Marys to see her to try and sort it all out in his mind.

Annie had been stunned to find David Nelson standing on the step when she answered the knock on her door.
'Thought you were never coming back to the Islands,' she had said in amazement.

'I wasn't,' said David, looking a little shamefaced, 'but I need someone to talk to and you're the only person I can turn to.'

Annie hadn't been sure whether to be flattered or not.
'What about Cerys?' she had asked, puzzled as to why he should turn to her and not to his wife. She knew how close they had been.

'We're divorced,' mumbled David. 'About six years ago now.'

'Oh!' Annie was taken aback. Something dreadful must have happened. Those two had been inseparable.

'It was pretty awful,' said David, his eyes downcast. 'Very bitter. It was just horrible.'

'What happened?' Annie had whispered, feeling that she had to ask now.

'Oh there wasn't anyone else if that's what you mean.' David blushed. 'It's just, well, we grew apart. I think having Megan, you know, it sort of came between us.'

Annie was shocked. Children were meant to bring folk together not drive them apart. She'd put the kettle on the range to boil then she had said softly, 'But that's not why you came to see me, is it?'

'Well, no.' David was a little taken aback by her directness. 'It's, well, it's just that Megan has got herself engaged.'

'Is that such a bad thing?' Annie had asked.

'Not in itself, no,' David admitted. 'It's her choice of husband. He's so arrogant and controlling.'

Normally Annie would have put this down to the usual paternal jealousy at such times but she knew that David and Megan weren't close and hadn't been for a long time.

'He's probably nervous,' she said, 'and he's anxious to impress and maybe he just comes across like that.'

No.' David was certain. 'It's not nerves. He actually asked me whether Megan had any expectations of an inheritance from us.'

Annie was shocked. That was hardly a question you went round asking your prospective in-laws.

'The thing is that there is something which has been handed down through my family for about a hundred and fifty years now,' he blurted out suddenly. 'I've no idea how he could possibly know about that, if indeed he does. I've never told Megan and Cerys swears that she hasn't done so either, but I don't like the guy and I don't trust him. He should be marrying Megan for love and if he isn't then he's damn well not going to get a penny out of me.'

Annie had got up to make some tea for them both and to give her time to think. There had long been rumours that Horatio Nelson had been left some sort of legacy by his real mother, the daughter of Admiral Lord Nelson. If he had, Horatio had never said anything about it and nor had his son, Joseph, with whom Annie had grown up. Then again, why should they have done so. It was family business and if they chose to keep it to themselves then that was up to them. Joseph had obviously said something to his own son, David, or else how would David have known anything about it. Whatever it was it couldn't have been that valuable since none of their lives had changed much in any noticeable way. On the other hand, if it wasn't something that might be valuable, why all the secrecy. Annie however was not about to ask this question. Every family had a right to keep its own secrets. She poured the tea into two mugs and, placing one in front of David, she sat down again.

'I'm not going to ask what it is that was handed down about which you're so worried,' she said, 'but I will try and give you some general advice.

David smiled gratefully at her. He had known he could rely on her discretion.

'You don't want to tell Megan in case her young man gets to hear about it,' Annie went on. David inclined his head in agreement.

'On the other hand,' said Annie firmly, 'if it is a family legacy it is her birthright and it needs to be held for her in a secure place, perhaps with your solicitor. Explain to him the circumstances and devise some way of safeguarding her inheritance, either for her at some time in the future or for the next generation.'

David looked at her. She made it seem so simple. Why on earth couldn't he think like that.

'You should tell Cerys what you are doing,' Annie was saying, 'so that she knows what you are doing and why. I assume she doesn't like this young man any more than you do?'

David shook his head in answer. It was one of the very few things he and Cerys had agreed on in recent years.

'Then she needs to know,' said Annie, 'in case anything happens to you.'

She gave him a shrewd look and David wondered briefly if she might have guessed the truth. He had been unwell for some time now and he knew it was serious. The doctor had murmured all the usual reassuring things about new treatments and plenty of time but David knew otherwise. Possibly he could recover if he really tried but he wasn't interested. He had simply lost the will to live.

They had parted with vague promises to keep in touch, promises which both knew would not be kept. Now, looking out across the clear early morning sea to the faint misty outlines of the Scillies far away on the horizon, he was pleased that he had gone to see her. It had been a farewell to the only place where he had ever been truly happy and to one of the few people whom he had ever been able to really talk to.

David had gone to see his solicitors and told them the whole story. Mr Ormesher had been very kind, very helpful, and it was he who had suggested that Meg should only ever be told about the legacy if she asked and could give a satisfactory account of its history and why she wanted to know about it. Both men had sat for a few moments, studying the precious stones nestling on their bed of velvet in the box on the desk between them. So much beauty yet so much potential misery lay in that box. They agreed that David's father and grandfather had been wise men and that now, in turn, David was doing the best thing he possibly could do. David simply hoped that if Meg ever learned about her legacy then she too would have enough wisdom to know the right thing to do.

Epilogue

St Marys, Isles of Scilly, 17th September 2010

Meg stood in the cottage doorway, stretching out her arms to the morning sunshine like an ancient goddess calling on her devoted followers. This year they were having a glorious Indian summer and the doors and windows of the cottage had remained constantly open for what seemed like weeks. No one bothered to lock their doors on the Islands anyway. There was still a level of trust which had disappeared completely on the mainland. She could hardly believe the cottage was hers. Well, theirs, actually.

She and Kevin had been married six months ago in the small Courthouse that doubled as a Registry Office. It had been a beautiful spring day and the Courtroom had been filled with sweetly fragranced flowers from both Annie and Sara's gardens. John had been their best man and Phil had been master of ceremonies. She had worn a long cotton dress with short sleeves in very much the same style that Emma Hamilton might have once worn. Afterwards there had been a champagne wedding breakfast on the balcony of the Atlantic Inn. She had even invited Janine who was dressing in much more flattering styles these days and was frequently to be seen in Dan's company enjoying a drink at the Mermaid.

Steven and Jamie had been brought to trial. Steven's defence had been that the whole business was everyone else's fault; that they had all either misunderstood or misread everything that he said and did. The jury were neither convinced by his belief in his own innocence nor by his attempts to portray himself as a victim, and found him guilty. Much to his disbelief, he had received a seven year jail sentence. Jamie, who had shot Dan, got ten years. The nature of the misadventure which had befallen Chris Hoyles and Reggie Grey, resulting in their deaths, had never been fully determined.

A few weeks after leaving the Islands, Meg had gone to see Mr Ormesher. She had finally decided that the jewels should be given to the British Museum, believing that their rightful place was really with the rest of the Hamilton Collections. Like those in her family before her, she too thought that such riches might only bring personal unhappiness. Mr Ormesher had smiled at her and told her that she was making a very wise decision and that her father would have been proud of her. The British Museum, almost unable to believe their good fortune in gaining such an acquisition, had insisted on making a small ex gratia payment as a mark of gratitude which had enabled Meg and Kevin to buy back her old family home overlooking Old Town Bay and the twelfth century Norman church. She and Kevin had received invitations to be guests of honour at the official opening of the new and extended Hamilton Collections which were now the talk of London.

Meg had absolutely no doubts that she had made the right choice. Secretly she liked to think that Sir William would have approved of what she had done as well. He had meant well when he had left his legacy for the infant Horatia but he had not thought through what his generous gift might mean for those who received it and she certainly didn't believe he would have wished upon them the grief which it had brought. She looked out across the sparkling sea and thought of Colossus in her watery grave. The ship would only give up more of her secrets when she was ready to do so.

On the beach below the cottage shadows swirled imperceptibly through the sands at the water's edge and slowly disappeared.

Shadows in the Sand

Other Books on the Isles of Scilly by Glynis Cooper

Bryher...land of the hills [1994]

Tresco...a history of a sacred place of elder trees [1995]

Rosevear...a desert island story [2000]

Mary's Song...a novel [2000]

St Martins...the ancient port of Scilly [2002]

The Curse of Samson...history plus a little poetic licence [2003]

Agnes...the last outpost [2004]

The Real Off Islands of Scilly...Eastern Isles...Norrard Rocks.. Western Rocks [2005]

St Marys...history and legends [2009]

Books on other subjects by Glynis Cooper

Illustrated History of the Manchester Suburbs [Breedon Books, 2002]

Hidden Manchester [Breedon Books, 2004]

Salford – an illustrated history [Breedon Books, 2005]

Wharncliff Companion to Manchester [Wharncliff Press, 2005]

Foul Deeds and Suspicious Deaths in Bolton [Pen & Sword, 2005]

Foul Deeds and Suspicious Deaths in Guernsey [Pen & Sword, 2006]

Foul Deeds and Suspicious Deaths in Jersey [Pen & Sword, 2008]